Saga OF THE Tournament OF Souls

Annie Mars

DEDICATION

For Mum & Dad,
who taught me the love of stories

CONTENTS

ACKNOWLEDGMENTS

There are a lot of fight scenes in this book and hopefully, there will be many more as the series progresses, but I can honestly say that they're only possible because of the people that taught me those very same skills. Now, I may not be as talented as Saga and Navi are but I hopefully have learned the fundamentals of good Aikido in order to use those skills and bring their fights to life, in hand to hand combat, staff fighting and the occasional sword fight (my sword work is mediocre at best!) but I do hope I portray it better than I practice it!

So, my biggest thanks to Michael Nagle Sensei and Mark Matcott Sensei who first taught me the fundamentals of Aikido at Monash University Aikido Club and inspired my love of Aikido. Then to those who took me further than I ever believed myself capable of, Linda Godfrey Sensei and Robert Botterill Shihan, who continued to push me and encouraged me to be the best that I could, even when I didn't believe that I had it in me. You coached me through every grading, even as I panicked, certain that I was going mess it all up. Saga is so much more confident than I will ever be, but that's because she knows what she's doing.

There are too many people to thank by name for training with me, encouraging me and making training memorable and likely inspiring the relationships between Saga and her friends; Diana & Luke (seriously, you two are my rocks! I don't know what I'd do without you!) and everybody at Aiki-Kai GWD. Plus a special mention to James Waller Sensei who, in my opinion, has the best Jo moves, and all the teachers who've taught a class I've been to, not only have you been a part of my Aikido journey, you probably never knew that you've been a part of creating the world, not only here in the Saga of Toserra Sorose series, but also The Kahzer Chronicles and other projects still in the works. It's because of all of you that these characters live to see another day!

WHISPER ON THE WIND

"I can help you bring her back."

The young elf whirled around, the balalaika in his hands held before him like a weapon as he searched the dark night for the speaker. He had stalked out of the bar moments earlier, hoping that the fresh air outside would clear his head. Instead of the crisp night air he had been wanting, he was confronted with the stench of ash, death and ruin. That's all there was here now. All there ever would be, he thought.

"Who's there?" he said, his voice shaky with emotion and drink.

A shadowy figure stepped closer, his silhouette becoming more evident against the backdrop of the illuminated building behind them. He chuckled. "I fear that will do you no good."

The elf lowered his hands again, the instrument falling to his side as he realised just how ridiculous he looked. "Go away," he said and turned back to the remains of Dorbe Manor. He stared at the hulking shadow of the former house. He could still see it lit up with lights glowing in every window. It had been like that only mere weeks ago. He looked up to where her window would have been. All he saw was the night sky, the stars twinkling back at him instead of her silhouette.

"I can help you bring her back," the shadowy figure said again, staying two steps behind where the elf stood, forcing him to look back over his shoulder at him, away from the remains of the house. Behind the silhouette, the bar was alive with life, as though nothing had ever happened.

"You don't know what you're talking about," the elf said, scowling as he thought about the crowd, so oblivious to anything around them except their drinks, of which, they'd had plenty that night.

Standing there on the stage earlier in the night, people had cheered as his fingers moved delicately over the strings of the balalaika, the strings scratching at the tips of his fingers, he'd wanted to scream. How could they be so happy, so carefree? The crowd listening seemed to not notice anything as he played the sad, mournful lament. It had been several weeks already since anything playful, jaunty or happy had emanated from his instrument. They thought he was just an anxious young man, but no one bothered to check on him. No one knew to check on him.

Couldn't they see that the world had ended that fateful night? The remnants of the old school residence were only next door, not yet torn down. Who knew when or if it ever would be. Here they sat, in this building, safe and secure from the fire that had claimed so many lives only a few short weeks ago. He had let his voice carry the words of death and misery to the crowd and yet as the tune came to an end, his heart breaking once more, they cheered, they clapped, someone even wolf whistled at him. How could they be so heartless?

The silhouetted man stepped up beside him, staring out over the ruins of the former residence. "I know a lot more about you than you think, Sidawi Harmeet, Prefect of Yeatwens House."

Sidawi turned to the man. "How do you know my name?"

"Unimportant," the man said, waving his hand as though wiping the question away.

Sidawi scowled and started to step around the man. He didn't have the time or the energy for this mysterious conversation. He thought about going back inside, but the idea made him sick. He'd come here in the hopes that the music and atmosphere would carry him away from himself, but that hadn't happened.

Sidawi stared at the man but couldn't make out any features of his face. "What is it you want?"

"I've already told you that," the man said. "It's up to you now," then he walked away, leaving Sidawi standing there in the dark.

Another day passed. Then, another week. It seemed that the more time that passed, the more the town around him seemed to move on. The names and pictures on the notice board browned and curled in the weather. They went about their classes and tournaments as though nothing had happened.

"I can help you bring her back." The words reverberated in his ears whenever it was quiet, whenever he didn't have anything to concentrate on.

When the holidays came finally and school let out, he returned to his childhood home. They only lived in town, so it was just a case of packing his things and walking a few streets over. He hoped that the comfort and familiarity of home would calm him, that the lack of the hectic schedule of school would allow him some time to rest.

"So sallow, my boy," his mother said as he came downstairs after putting his things away.

Did he say anything? No. She would never understand. "Just tired, ma," he murmured.

She ran her hands over his shoulders and down his arms. "Eat some real food. What they feed you in that boarding house must be pitiful. Look at you, just look at you!"

Food was the last thing he wanted. He didn't remember the last time he'd been hungry. Had it been that night? The night when he'd lost everything. They'd eaten dinner over homework before he'd walked back to his own student residence, leaving her to face the end all on her own. How long had it been between when he'd left, and the bell had rung out? An hour? Two? He couldn't remember. So no, he didn't want food. He wanted to run. He wanted to scream. He wanted to say her name and let the tears fall. He just didn't want to pretend anymore that he was alright when he wasn't.

"There we go, my Prefect of a boy," his father said, clapping him on the back so hard he stumbled forward. "At least now that's a title you can be proud of."

He looked up at his father. "What do you mean?" he asked.

"Well," his father huffed. "I couldn't imagine having to share that title with an ash face."

Sidawi flinched. His father couldn't know what his words did to him, and he'd heard the complaints often enough. The mutterings that they couldn't keep slaves in Nýr Ásgardr, the way they treated the slaves at their country estate. Then from the day they'd discovered her presence at the school, then again when her sister had been accepted. Every year the same thing and then this year, when she had been announced as a prefect. Sidawi cringed at his own behaviour before he'd gotten to know her. He'd been no better than his mother and his father or any other Ljósálfar he knew.

That fateful day in the library, it had sparked the friendship that had become so much more. The only bad thing about them both being named prefects had been the fact that they had been assigned to different houses when they'd been considering applying to Farnphrey Cottage or Shcacku Cottage, both fourth year restricted houses. Maybe then they would have been able to spend more time together. In the end though, the decision had been made for them and they'd stayed in their respective houses.

"Too bad the others didn't go with her," his mother added. It was like a slap in the face. Her sisters and her brother. He was fond of them too, perhaps fondest of her youngest sister, Navi, one of the only people to ever check on him, the real him, not the fake him he put on the outside world. He didn't know what to say.

"I... I have a lot of homework and studying to do. Exams will be here before we know it," he said, backing away from them both before he exploded and said something he would regret. There was no point in blowing up his life now. She wasn't there to spend it with him.

He backed out of the room, darted by his sister, who shot him an inquisitive look and as soon as he reached his room, he slammed the door shut. In the solitude of the room, he sunk into his bed and wept as silently as he could. He reached out to the stack of papers he'd left by his bed, rifled through them and found the one he was after, hidden away amongst music notes, magic runes and other schoolwork.

"One more semester," he whispered to the sketch. "That was all we needed... six months and we could have been free." Ziva's smiling face stared back at him. "What am I going to do?"

"I can help you bring her back." He flopped back onto the bed, the voice echoing in his ears.

Seeing her sister daily at the restaurant didn't help. As fond as he was of her, Navi looked so much like Ziva that he often found himself about to call out to her. Then she would move or speak or Saga, Navi's best friend, would appear and the spell would be broken.

"I can bring her back," that's what the shadowy figure had said. Was it true? Did it matter if it was true. That kind of magic, the kind of debt would be unimaginable. He tried to imagine going on with his life without her. A delicate blond-haired elf at his side, matching children whom his parents would adore. He would likely wind up running the restaurant and living his entire life in Nýr Ásgardr.

"It could have all been different." he said to the picture. "Everything could have been so different."

"I can help you bring her back." The words echoed in his mind. Who had the man been and how had he known? They had kept their relationship as secret as possible. Only a few select friends knew, friends who could or would cover for them.

So, who was he?

Sid sat up in bed, the picture in one hand. Maybe he could have the life he'd been dreaming of back. So where did he find the man? He'd been at The Witch's Brew that night, but here at home with his parents, he had less freedom than he did when living at Yeatwens. He was expected at the restaurant. He was expected at formal dinners and to be at their beck and call. He fell back to the soft mattress with a groan.

"I should have said yes."

~ * ~

"Get that down yourself," the bartender said, slamming a mug of dark, frothy ale down before Sidawi.

Sidawi looked up at the man in surprise. The last time he'd been there, he'd stormed out in aggravation after a waitress in a provocatively low-cut blouse had passed by, leaving a mug overflowing with frothy ale before him. He'd already been infuriated with the crowd's overly joyous and raucous reaction to his music. That was the night he'd met the man.

"I can help you bring her back." The words echoed in his head day and night. Why had he walked away that night?

Was it that obvious to everyone else except his own parents that he was falling apart without her? He closed his eyes and sipped the drink. He couldn't stand the taste of the stuff, but the buzz it gave him numbed the emptiness. He gulped down half the mug and put it back down, then, picked it back up and finished it. He slammed the tin cup back down on the bar. "Another."

The barman nodded. "You'll need to play for it though and motioned to the stage. Sidawi heaved a sigh. He was too tired to play. Too tired to care. Too tired to... anything. Still, the fact that the barman was offering and already accommodating him was a surprise. It was the least he could do, he supposed.

He looked around the crowded room. Nothing ever changed at The Witch's Brew. Rough men and even rougher women drank, gambled and in one corner, even duelled one another. The Witch's Brew was not one of the better places in town and since the fire, with no more students from the neighbouring Dorbe Manor came, they didn't seem to feel the need to take care of the place. He sighed again and turned back when he heard his cup placed back down.

He drunk thirstily.

"Is the thought of marrying me so repulsive?"

He spluttered, the drink going down the wrong way so that he was choking. A man beside him slapped his back until he could breathe again. "Can't handle your drink, my friend."

"Handle it just fine," Sidawi almost snarled. He didn't want to look beside him. "Jayashree!" He gasped, turning to the girl. She could not be there. What in the names of all the gods of all the realms would she be doing in a place like The Witch's Brew? The pious and beautiful girl his parents were in the process of betrothing him to. She did not look like the girl he'd met only two nights earlier at a dinner, his parents had been so eager for. That night, the girl had stood from where she'd been sitting. Her peach-coloured dress shimmered down her body to the floor as it shifted down her legs. Long, black hair fell in curls to her waist, and she had smiled at him with a docile, almost placid expression. What was she doing here, in the Witch's Brew of all places?

That dinner, and in fact that night, with Jayashree and her family had gone on and on, especially once Mayur, her father, had started to describe the house he had planned for Jayashree's family. It had included what sounded like a spectacular mansion estate, complete with an entire compliment of Dökkálfar slaves. Sidawi couldn't tell what any of them were thinking. He'd looked anxiously at his mother and father, wanting to ask her what was happening, but his mouth had been unable to produce any sound, and his silence had been taken as acquiescence.

The man looked over him at the girl and grinned. "Can't handle your women then," he chortled with delight and slapped Sidawi heartily on the back. Sidawi cringed with every blow. Now, standing beside him, in this dingy, hole of a bar, she was dressed in tight-fitting leather leggings, with a billowing tunic top that just barely crested her behind. That was cinched around her torso by a tight and extremely low-cut vest. The outfit left nothing to the imagination, and he scoffed, remembering his mother's words.

"You're looking beautiful tonight, Jayashree. You will make a wonderful addition to our family," she had beamed in delight while inspecting the girl. Oh, how his mother would just love to see the respectable and docile Jayashree now!

"That bad?" the girl asked, arms crossed over her chest.

He scowled at her, not deigning to answer. He finished his drink, picked up his instrument case from where it lay at his feet and went to the stage. He strummed at the balalaika and conversation dimmed around the crowded bar. A game of dice continued, but other than that, most eyes were on him.

The song was slow, mournful, telling the story of a girl forced into a marriage of convenience, one that helped cover the shame of the man. Did his parents know? Were they using Jayashree as a pawn to protect him before the news came out? No, it couldn't be, but the reality for the girl was true enough. Maybe in time he'd have been able to learn to tolerate her. Maybe with time he'd have found a way to extract himself, but his mother was talking of marrying him off to this girl as soon as the school year was over. He couldn't do it. He couldn't pretend. He couldn't drag someone else down with him.

Then, amidst the crowd he spotted a man who stared up at him. The rest of the crowd were preoccupied with drink, games or companions. This man, stared intently at Sidawi, a dark clack with a large, enveloping hood around his shoulders.

"I can help you bring her back."

Those words stuck in Sidawi's mind, and he missed a chord. People looked up at the awkward sound, but no one said anything. They looked up, didn't see anything of interest to them and then looked away once more, but to their own lives. It was him. Sidawi was sure of it. He rushed his way through the rest of the song, eager to catch the man.

As soon as the last chord was strummed, Sidawi lurched from the stage, barrelling through the crowd. He only had eyes for the man, standing there, completely still amidst the chaos of the bar. A large man lumbered before Sidawi, cutting off his route and blocking the hooded man from view. When he finally managed to pass him, the man was gone. Sidawi spotted Jayashree staring at him, and he cursed. He sure hoped that she didn't say anything to his parents about this. Then again, maybe it would be a blessing if she did. Then he could out her and his parents would break off the betrothal before it was finalised.

He hurried outside and looked around. The man wasn't there though, if he ever had been. The road was empty as he turned around wildly, hoping to spot some sign of him.

Dejectedly, he returned inside and went to the bar. As if knowing what he needed, the barman slid a tin mug across to him as he approached. With a small nod of acknowledgement, he took the ale and drank it, lifting the glass high and swallowing it all. The cool liquid slid down his throat, "Another?" he asked.

The bartender nodded, filled the mug and passed it back. Sidawi slammed it back on the bar after draining the whole mug once more. "Go perform."

Sidawi sighed and stared down into the inky depths of the mug. "Not at the moment," Sid murmured. "Just... Another? Please?"

"Romijn," the bartender called out, waving to someone Sidawi couldn't see. "Get up there!"

A man clad in a cloak, the cowl pulled over his face so that it was in shadow appeared by Sidawi's side. "I thought the kid was playing. Besides, Prosha's not here."

The bartender nodded, a smug expression on his face that looked like he had solved all the world's problems. "Kid, go play with Romijn and his group."

Sidawi grimaced. He had no interest in playing with a group he'd never even met before. "No thanks."

Romijn placed a heavy case on the bar and pushed it towards Sidawi. "Look."

Sidawi sighed heavily. He wasn't interested. He just wanted another drink, although maybe he'd already had too much, because this man's voice was familiar. He regarded the man beside him, trying to get a look at him but the cowl of his cloak hid any identifying features. So where had he heard that voice before?

"I can help you bring her back." Sidawi's eyes narrowed as the voice in the back of his mind taunted him. Could it be?

He glanced pointedly at his mug and the bartender nodded, filling the mug halfway. Sid glared angrily at him, but he just pointed to the instrument case that Romijn placed beside him.

"I have my own," Sidawi said, motioning towards the stage where his balalaika waited for his return.

"Just take a look at it," Romijn insisted.

Heaving a second, pained sigh, Sidawi opened the case. The lamplight glinted off the luminescent surface. Leaning in, Sidawi realised that he could see his face shining back at him. It was a beautiful instrument. The exterior of the instrument was black, but it reflected everything. He wasn't even sure if he could identify the material, it had been lacquered in, because he didn't think he'd ever seen anything like it before. He reached out tentatively and stroked a finger across the smooth, warm surface. How odd. Instruments were usually cool to the touch. Maybe it had been placed near the fire. Nothing too strange there.

He strummed a chord, then another. The sound vibrated though his body, resonating with his core.

"Sidawi..."

He whirled around. "Ziva?" He croaked.

Beside him, Romijn watched without making a sound, his mouth twitching somewhat as he waited eagerly. Sid leaned against the bar, dizzy and disconcerted by the feeling. He strummed the balalaika again and he could hear it. Her voice seemed to carry on the breeze that flowed through the bar when the door opened, letting more patrons in. He strummed it again and closed his eyes, imagining that she was there beside him. She smiled that shy smile of hers, her cheeks burning a deep mahogany colour as the firelight danced in her hair, changing the stark white of it to dancing shades of yellow and orange. With his eyes closed, he could just about believe it, especially as his fingers strummed the chords of the balalaika.

All the while, Romijn waited.

"Ok..." Sidawi said slowly, drawing the word out. He would play with them, if only for the chance to feel her beside him for one song.

Romijn grinned. "Horak!" he called jovially, "The boy's in. Get our instruments! We're going up!"

"Great!" The other man called back over the din of the bar.

Romijn wrapped and arm around Sidawi's shoulder. "Bring it," he said motioning to the instrument with his free hand. As soon as Sidawi had closed the case and picked it up, Romijn directed him away from the bar and towards the table where Horak was hurriedly pulling other instruments from cases. He assembled a silver flute and handed a lute to Romijn, who accepted it with a nod.

Within minutes, they were up on the little stage made of old crates playing for the crowd. Sidawi knew a wide range of songs and they started out with some jaunty, but slightly off-colour songs, but bit by bit, the songs got slower, darker and more depressing. He patrons drank more, ordering more from the bar and the barman, despite the sombre music, looked ecstatic.

~ * ~

Sidawi returned home feeling lighter than he had in months. As he had played, it had been as though she was standing at his side, cheering him on, just as she had always done.

"Where have you been?" His mother chided as he entered.

"Out," he said, heading straight for the stairs.

"Out? We had guests. I thought you said you were feeling unwell and were going to bed," she pressed.

"I felt better and decided to get some air." He started up the stairs, but his mother would not be deterred and followed him, asking where he had been and who he had been with.

"Out Ma, I was out. I just needed some air."

She came closer, sniffing. "You reek of cheap booze. Go and get cleaned up. That is no example to be setting for your sister or your future wife."

"I don't want a future wife!" Sidawi cried. "I just want to be left alone!"

He ran up the last few steps and to his room, slamming the door behind him. He leaned against it, the energy seeping from his body as he slid down, cradling the instrument case against his chest and trying to ward off tears that threatened to fall. He looked down at the case, his brow furrowing. Why did he have it? He didn't remember Romijn saying he could take it, but at the same time, he didn't remember packing it up.

"Sidawi?" His mother called, "Sidawi? We're not done talking about this!" When he finally heard her footsteps retreat, he extracted the instrument from its case and thrummed the chords tunelessly. Her voice carried to him again and now he couldn't stop the tears as each time he ran his fingers over the chords, he heard her call his name.

QUEENETTE DORMITORY

The house ghost hated her, and Saga knew it. She had known it since she had first stepped foot in Queenette Dormitory two weeks ago when the holidays had started. Having nowhere to return for the holidays, Saga Joy Carolle, like many other students had been forced to relocate from her usual student residences to the dormitory for the holidays. It had been a nightmare ever since and she just wanted to go home.

"You coming?"

Saga peered up from where she was searching under her bed and saw Navi standing in the doorway, looking harassed, white locks already falling out of the supposedly neat bun that the girl had tied her wild hair into.

"As soon as I find my gloves!" Saga called back.

Every day it was something new with this ghost. Cordelia Queenette, house ghost and namesake of the Queenette Dormitory had been startled to discover that she could still see her. At the beginning of the year, the Choosing Ceremony where the ghosts argued with one another to select the students for their house, it had seemed obvious to Saga at least, that Mistress Grimaldi and the House Prefects had been able to see the ghosts. From what she could tell though, for the Prefects, it extended only to their own house ghost, not the others, but she couldn't tell about Mistress Grimaldi though and she'd not approached the Residence supervisor to ask about it. While her own house ghost, Tremblay Jimpsee had never mentioned talking to Tymberlee, the elegant faeric girl often seemed frustrated and would mutter their ghost's name in dismay. There had been some evidence though, when Mistress

Grimaldi was almost brought to tears at the end of term assembly, that she was still able to see the house ghosts. Dina Bess, Jemima's aunt, and their religious studies teacher was a former Angel of Death, and she too had been able to see the assembled gathering of house ghosts and the students who had died during the tragic house fire. Cordelia Queenette though, was livid at having to deal with Saga.

Arms crossed over her chest Navi watched with little amusement as Saga crawled on the floor, digging around under her bed. "And is this helping?" Navi asked.

"No!" Saga griped, "because that damned ghost hates me! She keeps stealing my things!" She started to crawl back out from under the bed but grunted in pain when she hit her head on the underside of the bed. "I hate it here!" She sat up beside the bed and stared across it at her friend.

On her first night in the dormitory, after their friends had left for home, Saga had attempted to initiate a conversation with Cordelia Queenette, only to somehow offend the ghost woman with her mere presence. That night had seen the fire in the first-year dorm room blown out repeatedly by the ever opening and banging of the windows, rattling in the wind. Those windows had most definitely been locked before they had all gone to bed. The hostility of the Queenette house ghost had come as a surprise given that the house ghost over at Jimpsee House was always up for a good chat. He was always up for a good dose of gossip or ready to impart a small amount of wisdom... But not Cordelia Queenette.

Cordelia Queenette had been a spiteful woman in life, looking down upon the masses and Saga was glad that the other students could not see the female ghost for whom the Dormitory had been named after. It was a real wonder how she selected anyone for her house. She seemed to dislike everyone, including her own students, students she had chosen to reside within her house herself. There were constant arguments about missing items since the beginning of the school holidays, with items from Queenette students often being stolen and later located in the belongings of students from other houses.

"You have got to be kidding me!" Saga fumed when she located the textbook from Vampire Lore and Law that had gone missing the week before from Illeana Tair's belongings. The vampire girl was a second year from Vitillon Hall, the residence of choice for Vampire students. She was also certain that there was a thief amongst the students and there was, it was just the damned house ghost. Still, if that book was found amongst Saga's belongings, she would be named the thief and that would cause all kinds of problems that she did not want to face again.

"What is it?" Navi asked as she waited anxiously in the doorway to the room. Saga reached up from under the bed, waving the book for her to see. "Ohhh... She does hate you."

Never before had she had a home that she wanted to return to, but Jimpsee House, where the house ghost, had chosen her to come live in the house that bore his name, that place had become home. She loved the house and her roommates and everything about the place. She had never once in her life, not ever, wanted to 'go home.' She had never had a home that she had wanted to return to, or where she had been wanted. The beginning of the new school year had seen her welcomed into Jimpsee House and she realised, as she searched for her winter gloves, - Where had that blasted ghost hidden them this time? - that she had not thought about the old world all that much. She had even stopped referring to it as 'the real world,' to herself and to others.

Navi fidgeted anxiously in the doorway. "Navi cannot afford to be late for work. They already hate this one there."

Saga knew that her friend was right, and they still had to go past the magical animal stables to check on their Animal Husbandry partners, Pingu and Ephyra, as well as Jemima's and Tasso's partners Kia and Cronin, with them out of town for the holidays. She remembered that Emory had been horrified to find out that his partner, Hermes, the little leathery, gargoylesque homunculus who had instantly bonded with him was going to go home with him. Despite the fact that they hadn't been talking at the time, the rant he had given to Mistress Anhora about the unfairness of it all, had continued long after class as they made their way back Jimpsee house and to anyone and everyone who would listen. Whether they wanted to or not. Tymberlee had eventually begged him to be quiet and just deal with it. The bond between homunculus and carer was magically intertwined with their souls, and he was stuck with it. That had not gone down well. Hopefully, for his sake, they had found a way around that, because she could just imagine Lady Harding's reaction to her son bringing home the grotesque little creature.

Saga grabbed her horse care kit, then with a sigh, she also grabbed the vampire textbook and deposited it on a hall table outside the dorm room.

"Just one second," Saga called as she detoured from their path to the front door of the large building. She ducked away from Navi and into the large dining hall. With its large, long tables with benches down the lengths, the room reminded her of the great hall at the school of witchcraft and wizardry, but it wasn't that interesting. No floating candles or magically changing roof displays. She quickly located the fruit bowl and selected a bright red apple. She dropped it into her pocket and quickly ran back to join Navi.

"Can we please go now? " Navi asked, her anxiety growing with every delay.

"Yeah, sorry," Saga said as she shoved her hands in the pockets of her winter coat and trudged after Navi. "Why does it have to snow here? It never snowed back in Melbourne. It's cold, it's wet. It gets everywhere!"

Navi just shook her head in dismay as she led the way down the stairs of the large old house that served as the dormitory. She was out the door, walking hurriedly across the snow-covered ground, with Saga in quick pursuit.

From somewhere behind her, she could hear laughter. Saga craned her neck and saw Cordelia Queenette standing on the porch of the house, waving Saga's gloves at her.

"Hey!" Saga cried. "You filthy thief!"

"Saga!" Navi called.

"She's got my gloves!" Saga called after her. Navi was halfway to the end of the street, but Saga stepped up to the porch of the house. She reached for her gloves, but the ghost whirled backwards, taking the gloves with her. Saga leapt after her, but Cordelia cackled in delight. Saga stopped and stared at the ghost, a thought coming to her. Something from some random daytime television show that seemed to always be on in the afternoons after school. They were soldiers and doctors in a medical camp during one of the wars. She didn't really know, but one scene had stood out to her, mainly because one of her foster siblings at the time had been grounded and everyone had chanted the words every time, they'd left the house. Saga's grin widened. "I can go in." She stepped back onto the porch, "I can go out." She jumped off the porch, then bounded up the steps again, "I can go in. I can go out."

"Thee will rue the day you crossed Cordelia Queenette!" The furious ghost screeched.

Saga laughed as she jumped from the porch, minus her gloves because the wretched ghost hadn't surrendered them. She ran after Navi, who was miraculously still waiting for her.

Suddenly, she was falling, arms flailing and her bag flying, the contents landing all around her as she fell to the ground with a heavy thud. "Ow..." She groaned. Laughter erupted from the porch. "At least I can go outside!" Saga shot back at the ghost, half-heartedly, craning her neck to catch sight of the woman.

"Saga!" Navi whirled around, scurrying back carefully over the icy cobblestones. She offered a hand to Saga and hauled her up. Despite her tiny stature, Navi was deceptively strong, and she held Saga steady as she swayed, getting her bearing once more.

"I hate the snow!" Saga muttered, moving to bend down, and groaning in agony.

"Here!" Navi said, helping Saga pick up her things. Saga stuffed them in her bag. From the porch, Cordelia laughed and laughed and laughed, her arms wrapped around her belly as she hooted about telling 'that stupid daemon boy' about his 'useless Valkyrie.'

"Why do you have to have to antagonize her? You know she hates you. You know she's a thief. Ignore her until we can leave here! And, to make it worse, there's a good chance Navi is going to be stuck here once the new semester starts and she already hates this one because of well... You know!" She waved her hands at herself as if to indicate there was something wrong with her, "And now you!" She huffed angrily, then to Saga's surprise, Navi's tirade ended, and the slight girl stormed off, leaving Saga standing there, shocked by the girl's outburst. Having never stayed in one place long enough in the past to make friends like she had found in Nýr Ásgardr, Saga stood there, uncertain as to what to do. Did she run after Navi, apologise and plead her case? Did she trudge along slowly, go about her day and hope that come nightfall and the return to Queenette Dormitory that all would be forgiven and forgotten?

She had no idea, so she went with the latter plan and avoided the situation.

~ * ~

It was awkward as they entered the stables, Saga tried to say something to Navi, but she disappeared through the stall doors to see Cronin, Tasso's blink dog and Ephyra, her own project animal before Saga could find the words. Cronin always enjoyed a good game of catch, which took time. Ephyra, a catlike creature who looked to be made of shadows, preferred to lounge by Navi, luxuriating in the presence of her person who would feed her, brush her, and tell her how pretty she was. It wouldn't be long before Cronin would be running around and panting before Navi, then blinking back and forth, trying to guess where the ball would wind up. She would play with him as Ephyra, slinked around her, cleaning her delicate, shadowy paws as she watched the dog with a disinterested eye.

However, Navi had not said a word to Saga since her explosive comments during their walk. Saga sighed as she trudged off towards Kia's stall. The Dragonne put up with Saga's presence, but it was obvious that the intelligent animal was not going to make anything about their forced companionship enjoyable. She stalked and huffed the entire time Saga was there, as such, Saga made sure to feed her, check her over after the injuries she had sustained at the end of term and clean out her stall, as fast as possible, allowing her to spend more time with Pingu.

Kia snarled as Saga tried to pull back a bandage and inspect the site where she had been speared. She raised her clawed paw, swiping towards where Saga was standing. Saga jumped out of the way, rolling as she neared the ground, but not wanting to land with the inevitable thud the creature had been wanting, which would allow her to prowl over and eat her prey. Saga came back to her feet, several feet away, hair askew, with hay sticking out at various angles. Kia stared at her, mouth opening, and Saga saw her rear back, as though readying to pounce or unleash her devastating roar that would likely blow out her eardrums. Neither option would be good for her own ongoing health.

"Stop it!" Saga ordered. The Dragonne, paused, cocked her feline head to side and huffed angrily, leathery wings rippling with dissatisfaction. "I know you don't like me. But Jemima entrusted your care to me and I'm going to make sure that wound doesn't become infected whether you like it or not."

Kia huffed again, the frigid air making her hot breath steam up. Eyes locked on one another, Kia lowered one paw, long claws extended to the ground and slowly swiped backwards. Saga gulped. She wasn't going to charge, was she? Would she have time to call out to Navi? No, it wouldn't matter, she would be in with Cronin or Ephyra, through the magical portals that lead to their habitats. No, worse would be if she emerged and Kia was charging around like a wild beast, and she was unprepared.

Saga held her hands up before placatingly, "Good kitty..." she said slowly, in a sing song voice, trying to calm the animal down. "Good dragon?" What platitude did you use on a half dragon, half lion creature?

Kia swiped her paw through the hay again, snarled angrily, lunging towards Saga. Saga jumped backward, slipping on the hay and falling to the floor. She landed hard on her butt. Kia snorted, then turned, presenting her bandaged side to Saga.

"Oh, I bet you're pleased with yourself," Saga muttered, moving to take care of bandaging the injury. When she was done, she was glad to move on and finally see Pingu.

Pingu, the small black and white pegasus, unlike Kia, loved to see Saga. The young animal had grown in depth and personality since they had first met and as soon as she was at his stall door, his head was over the side, nudging her, eager for cuddles, treats and if he was extra lucky, a ride out in the pasture behind the stables.

"Hey boy," Saga said, as one arm wrapped around his large snout in an affectionate hug. He whinnied at that, his nostrils flaring as he pushed against her harder. "Hang on there," she murmured to him. "Let me get this open, then we can cuddle more."

The pegasus nudged her again, but then stepped back from the stall door, allowing her to concentrate on the mechanism that kept it closed. With a grunt of effort, she hauled the heavy wooden door open to allow herself in. She closed the stall door behind herself. "Ok boy, let's see about brushing you down, huh?"

She set the horse care kit down on a small stool and opened it up. She extracted his brush and set to work brushing down his mane and tail before getting started on his coat. Pingu stepped back and forth every so often, his eagerness for something more exciting than a brush evident. Unfortunately, after the glove crises earlier, Saga didn't think that there would be time for a ride tonight. Pingu's head kept searching out her pockets as he moved.

"Oh, I know what you want," Saga said into his ear as she gave him a scratch in his favourite place. "You want that juicy red apple I picked up for you, don't you? You cheeky boy. You know that you have to wait for me to check your hooves and feathers first!"

Pingu snorted in disagreement; his nose still angled towards the offending pocket of her coat. After ensuring that he had received a good brushing, Saga replaced the brush where she found them and went after the hoof pick, but it wasn't here. "You have got to be kidding me!" Saga swore. "That stupid ghost! I bet she stole it!"

Pingu nickered in her ear, hot bursts of air blowing her hair around. "Let me have a look. I can always get one from the office..."

Pingu resisted her first effort to pick up his front leg and inspect the underside of the hoof. "Come on boy," she cooed, "the sooner I do this, the sooner you get your apple."

Pingu stamped his hoof, then settled and allowed her to finish her exam. She brushed at some dirt gathering near the edge of the horseshoe but found that she didn't need the shoe pick. She was going to have words with that ghost when she got back to the dormitory.

The awkwardness continued as Saga cleaned up after her time with the dragonne and the pegasus. She pulled strands of straw from her hair and dusted off her clothes, hoping that she would be presentable for work. Navi was cleaning up, preparing to head to work for the night. Neither girl said anything to the other as they locked up and walked toward the town square and the Saffron Heart. Saga had come to dread stepping foot into the kitchen for any reason, especially when she would see Navi, alone in her corner of the kitchen washing everything that came her way, trying her hardest to ignore the words spewed at her by the ignorant and racist Ljósálfar that thought that they were so much better than everyone else.

When the night of tedious work had finally ended though they had left the restaurant, still having not spoken a word to one another.

Saga fell into step beside Navi, and they walked in silence for several moments before Saga finally spoke. "I'm sorry."

Navi heaved a huge sigh. "No... Navi is sorry..."

"Tremblay said that you could come back to Jimpsee with us," Saga added, wanting to fix things between them as quickly as possible, but not have to go over her own selfishness and irritations. Navi was having a hard enough time without Saga making it harder on her.

"Only if the school allows it and Jimpsee's maxed out. There's no way they'll allow it... Besides... What about Annis and Edun?" The world of the Jensyn siblings had been rocked only two months earlier when their student residence had burned to the ground killing seven students, including their oldest sister, the house Prefect, Ziva. "Where would they go? Where are any of us going?"

In the aftermath, students who had not returned home to their parents had been rehoused throughout the various student residences wherever there was a bed. Not having anywhere to return to, Navi and her siblings had remained in Nýr Ásgardr, all being separated into various houses. Navi had come to Jimpsee House, bunking with Saga and Jemima in their tiny room. Edun, her brother had found accommodation at the boys' dormitory, Knightrich and Annis had wound up in Queenette, the girls' dormitory where they were now spending the school vacation because the school forced all students remaining in the city over the holidays to stay in the two dormitory buildings instead of their own houses.

"I don't know," Saga said softly. "Have you heard anything from your patron?"

Navi shrugged. "Not that this one has heard... Maybe the school has..."

The insecure nature of their remaining at Toserra Sorose had been wearing on Navi and Annis. Edun seemed indifferent to what was happening, but he had, to Saga at least, always been a little aloof. Navi and Annis loved school and the chances being there afforded them. Being Dökkálfar, they had been enslaved since infancy, their mother also being a slave. Ziva had once been caught in the library of their master's house, teaching herself to read. Perhaps out of idle curiosity as to what a Dökkálfar could achieve or maybe genuine kindness, Ziva had been educated and when she had turned fourteen, had been accepted into Toserra Sorose Academy, the first Dökkálfar to attend. A year later, Annis had followed with their master's blessing. There had been some hesitancy about Edun. Being young and strong, he would have garnered a high slave price or been able to undertake huge quantities of menial work. As it was now, Edun, while not the best student in the school as Ziva had sought to be, was a talented fighter, often winning at the school Tourneys, despite an obvious level of aggression and cruelty on his side.

"What will happen if you don't hear back from them?" Saga asked softly.

Navi shrugged again, obviously not wanting to voice her fears. They continued walking, biting wind whipping at their faces. Saga was sure hers was turning red with the cold. She had, up until only recently, never seen snow before and its majesty had worn off and left her irritated with the constant cold and wet.

The lights that burned on the porch of Queenette Dormitory seemed to blow out as Saga and Navi stepped up, dropping them into a darkness that the streetlamps could not permeate. Light from the house was little too, with the big heavy drapes having been pulled over the windows, preventing any light from spilling out.

Saga cursed when she kicked a heavy wooden bench, jumping around on one foot as she waited for the pain to subside. Beside her, Navi walked confidently to the door, ready to push it open when she stopped. She stooped and picked something up.

"Are these your gloves?" she asked holding the wet, dirty items that Saga barely looked at. She attempted to put her foot back down, but cringed, knowing that the cold was making the pain all the worse.

"Huh?" She asked.

"Your gloves. From earlier, are these your gloves?"

Navi waved them in front of her face, but Saga shook her head. "I can't see anything!"

"Oh yeah..." Navi giggled softly. Of all the things Saga could do, seeing in the dark was not one of them. A fact Navi often forgot. Still giggling, Navi pushed the door of the dormitory open. It seemed to stick and when they managed to pull themselves through the apparently stuck door, Saga saw Cordelia Queenette leaning against it trying to keep it closed.

Saga raised an unimpressed eyebrow at the ghostly aristocrat. "That is so unbecoming," then slammed the door closed. She wished though that the ethereal being of Cordelia Queenette would have fallen as a solid person would have.

"Here," Navi handed Saga the wet, dirt crusted items she had been holding.

"Oh, gross!" Saga exclaimed, staring at the ghost. "They're all frosted over and trodden on!"

Cordelia Queenette straightened out her red velvet gown, before standing up straight, arms crossed over her extensive bosom and attempted to stare down her nose at Sage. She steadfastly refused to speak to the girl.

"Is she here?" Navi asked, looking around.

"Yeah, being just as petty and snobby as always," Sage replied, holding her gloves in front of her by the tips of her fingers. "Petty little witch…"

"How much longer do we have here?" Navi asked.

"Too long!"

~ * ~

"Mail call," Ellora Tayyip, the prefect of Queenette Dormitory called. She walked around the common room. "Illeana," the Vampire girl reached out her long, pale arm to claim the offered letters without a word. "Sarabia," the former Dorbe Manor resident took her letter, on top was what looked to be an official letter from the school. "Caoimhe," a faerie girl with hair as bright orange as the sunrise leapt up, giggling, her wings a flutter to embrace Ellora as she took her mail.

"Ta!" She exclaimed, before flopping herself back upon the couch she had originally been sitting on and tearing open her first envelope.

Ellora, who Saga thought was some kind of Were, but wasn't sure what kind, shook her head. "Moise." Moise was easy. Her long face, tall, lanky frame and often, uncoordinated movements reminded Saga of Mannish. The girl was a hyena. Her laugh confirmed her thoughts. "Saga," the Prefect continued, handing Saga a single envelope that also looked official.

Saga took the envelope from Ellora tentatively. "Thanks," she murmured, staring down at the letter with apprehension. Official letters were not a good thing in her experience, at least it was smaller than Sarabia's.

"Annis and Navi," Ellora said, handing both girls large envelopes similar to Sarabia's.

The two sisters looked at each other, then at Sarabia. Across the room, Alvina Blackledge, a werewolf who had also been a Dorbe Manor resident was receiving a similar letter. By some sort of unspoken agreement, the girls who had once boarded at Dorbe Manor rose from their seats and disappeared into one of the smaller rooms. Saga watched them go, hoping that somewhere in those letters they all held, that there was good news.

She looked down at her own letter. It wasn't half as big as the ones received by the Dorbe girls, but how big did it need to be to expel someone or reveal that this whole charade had been a joke? She bit her lip. What if the school had realised, they'd made a mistake admitting her and were sending her back to Midgard? What would she do then? The letter in her hands, with the school emblem on it seemed to taunt her.

Across from her, Caoimhe was giggling at her own mail. One of Saga's best friends was a faerie and neither he nor his sister were anything like this bubbly, flighty girl. Tasso was actually pretty stoic. Come to think of it, so were Tymberlee and Onorati back at Jimpsee House, but they were fourth years with lots of exams and the previous semester's disasters had worn on them.

"You not going to open yours?" Caoimhe asked. She had a thick Celtic brogue similar to Siobhan's, the female leprechaun who lived at Jimpsee House.

Saga looked up and shrugged, the letter waving before her awkwardly. "Official letters usually mean bad news."

Caoimhe bounced up from her seat and flopped back down beside Saga, extracting the letter from her hands in her shock. "Hmm, official school stationary, but not like the others... It's thin, so that's probably a good thing." Hope swelled in Saga's chest. "Or not, you never know." Saga sighed and stared at the girl despondently.

"Thanks..." Saga said, not really sure if Caoimhe was trying to make her feel better or not. She held her hand out to the older girl, trying to take her letter back.

"Here," Caoimhe said, starting to rip the letter open. "I'll open it for you!"

"I-," Saga tried to object, but before she could, the faerie girl had already extracted the single piece of parchment from the envelope.

"Huh," Caoimhe said, staring at the letter.

"What?" Saga asked tentatively.

"You didn't start your musical studies last term?" She asked. "You've got to choose an instrument this semester. Better find some time to get back to Yggdrasil City... One thing we miss here in Nýr Ásgardr is a music shop!"

Saga groaned. If there was one thing she had always hated at school, it was music class. It wasn't that she didn't like music. She could kick back and listen or put her headphones in and go for a run at any time, but she had no talent, skill, or interest in making music herself. "Do I have to?" She asked, a whining groan edging into her voice.

"Mandatory for Elves, Angels and Sirens," Ellora added, coming over to have a look at the letter. "But you're not an angel, why would they make you do this class?"

"Because they enrolled me as one..." Saga muttered. At the beginning of the year, Astrid Grunborg, Weapons Mistress of Toserra Sorose and apparently friend to her mother, had wheedled and cajoled the headmaster,

Hadar Gotts to enrol Saga, despite the school not running a program for Valkyries, stating that the role was similar enough to that of an Angel, that the angelic studies program would suffice for now. This was one such area of study that Saga was certain she did not need.

"Huh…" Caoimhe hummed. "Well, what are you going to play?"

Saga stared dumbfounded at the girl. "Huh? I… Well… Umm… I don't know… The recorder…" When forced into music at her old school, everyone had been made to buy those silly plastic musical instruments that they would attempt to play as a cohesive group. That never actually happened.

Caoimhe shook her head adamantly and waved her hand in front of her. "No, absolutely not. Nothing lamer than those who play recorder."

Saga's eyes widened in surprise. Usually, people never understood what she was on about when she mentioned something from home. Was the recorder an old instrument or something?

"Take that back!" Priscilla Geldred, a third-year angel called. "I play the recorder!"

"And she makes my point for me!" Caoimhe exclaimed excitedly. She turned back to Saga. "Promise me that you won't play the recorder!"

"I don't want to," she said, "but I don't know what else to pick!"

"Clarinet, oboe, bassoon, flute," Moise inputted, looking up from her mail.

"Violin, lute, harp, hurdy-gurdy," Illeana added.

Everyone looked at her. "What the hell is a hurdy-gurdy?" Saga asked.

The vampire looked at all of them and sighed. "Heathens. You are all heathens! I swear!" She put her mail down on the table and got up. She left the room, muttering about their cluelessness.

"How about horns or trumpets?" Ellora suggested.

Saga sighed. "I…"

"Of course," Ellora continued, "There is a way out of music lessons."

Saga's eyes widened in surprise and anticipation. "Really?" Saga asked, straightening up from her seat and looking intently at the prefect of Queenette Dormitory. "What? How do I get out of it?"

Ellora's grin turned wicked. Caoimhe giggled, obviously aware of what Ellora's theory would be.

Illeana stormed back into the room, a strange instrument in her hand. It looked like some kind of weird, mutilated violin, The strings were oddly spaced, keys were situated to one side of the board and a hand crank at its base.

"What the hell is that thing?" Caoimhe exclaimed, drawing everyone's attention to the girl.

"A hurdy-gurdy," Illeana said. "I play a little…"

"I don't think that I can play that…" Saga murmured.

Any further conversation was prevented when the Dorbe Manor group returned. They looked almost as they did in the days after the fire, lost and as though they were adrift in the world. Annis had her arm around Navi as they passed through the common room without a world, Sarabia and Alvina in their wake. Saga tried to catch the attention of either sister, but when she tried to follow, Ellora shook her head.

"I know she's your friend, but that's about them right now," she said softly.

Saga nodded. "You're right… I just…"

The older girl clasped Saga on the shoulder and nodded. "I know."

Beside her, Caoimhe bounced up and down, her gossamer wings fluttering and giving her far more lift than anyone bouncing on a couch needed. "Ellora was going to tell you how to avoid the dreaded music lessons."

Ellora looked away from the departed group and turned her attention back to Saga. "Well…" The Prefect started, that eerie, knowing grin returning to her lips.

Illeana hefted her ungodly-looking instrument. "Music lessons aren't dreaded," she exclaimed. "I signed up to do them voluntarily."

"Why?" Moise asked, "it's not like you have to."

"I wanted to!"

Caoimhe sighed loudly. "No one wants to know about Illeana's fetish with that abomination of an instrument, we want to hear the words!"

Saga sighed and looked up at the older girl. "How do I avoid music class?"

Eyes sparkling with delight, Ellora said, "Pentathlon," and it seemed to Saga, as though everyone in the room said the dreaded word with her.

THE SAFFRON HEART

Saga weaved her way through boisterous diners of The Saffron Heart, wishing that someone had arranged the tables as less of an obstacle course. There wasn't a straight line anywhere for her or the other servers to make their way down without constantly having to try avoiding another diner... or three. The Saffron Heart was the fanciest restaurant in Nýr Ásgardr, everyone was dressed in their most luxurious gowns, their finest suits and jewels in every colour sparkled from the ears, fingers, wrists, and necks of the women. Even some of the men had donned their sparkliest accoutrement for their night out. A few men and women had even decided to wear coronets. It was all a little ostentatious to Saga.

The night was long, and Saga didn't think she had ever given much thought to the work done by waiters before, but if the average restaurant diner at The Saffron Heart was anything like the people back home, each and every one of them deserved a raise... And these people were meant to be high society, not the riff raff that frequented places like the Rolly Polly Kitty Eatery with her all-time favourite meal, Lucuma pie. Maybe next holidays, she would work there. Surely, they would treat Navi better... Even if there was that slight issue of them both being banned from the Kitty...

"You," a man from a table of young noble lords called, his finger pointing directly at her. Saga sighed, then plastered on the fake smile she had been taught to use when addressing the most annoying of patrons. "Yes. You, girl," the man echoed as she approached their table.

"What can I get for you?" Saga asked, her brightest, fake smile, beaming at the men.

One of them, a boy, maybe a year or two older than her looked her up and down with a crooked smirk. She was sure that she had seen him somewhere before. His ginger hair accentuated his pale face and freckles. He was even kind of cute, until he spoke. "How about you?"

The smile she had been showing them slipped slightly to a bland expression that she once again covered up. "I'm afraid the that the wait staff are not on the menu sir."

"More the pity," he said, his smirk only growing.

The man next to him elbowed him and looked at Saga. "I apologise for my cousin. He's hopeless with women." The rest of the men at the table laughed uproariously. The orange haired man who had originally spoken seemed to go as red as his hair and she could have sworn that in his embarrassment, that cat ears had sprouted from his hair, just as she had seen in so many different Anime. Maybe he was a weretiger? She smirked at him. He was kind of cute after all.

"Another round of drinks and perhaps a recommendation for dessert?" The older of the men asked. Eyes lit up around the table and Saga guessed that this man was in charge. Perhaps he was their Alpha? She had heard that term thrown around a bit by various members of the Were community and maybe in a fair few books before coming to this strange and magical world. She presented to them that day's dessert options and waited as they discussed.

"I think we'll take a round of the steak tartar for dessert," The leader said after contemplating the options. It had not been one of the dessert options she had presented, but then again, maybe she had been right about them being weretigers.

"Very good sir," Saga said. As she walked away though, the young orange haired boy reached out and grabbed her. Without hesitation, she reached behind her as his fingers still gripped her butt, gripped his hand, and twisted. The boy cried out in pain as he fell from his chair.

"Harian!" The leader of the group exclaimed. He stood up, eyes on Saga as she bent the boy's hand back. She eyed him, willing the older man to tell her off.

With a defiant look at the older man, Saga released the boy and walked away. "I'll be back with your order, sir."

Behind her, the boy stumbled back into his seat, cradling his hand.

For a fancy restaurant, people sure got rowdy, and it wasn't just occurrences like the young weretiger. Saga had no objections to rowdy, but rowdy patrons meant less tips and more trouble. Unfortunately, that meant that they had to put up with all the crap that the patrons put them through or the Lord almighty who ran the restaurant would take the complaints of his guests as gospel and fire them in a heartbeat. She would hear about what she had done to the young Were, she was sure of it. Lord Harmeet was all about appearances, after all.

She sighed in relief as she made it back to the kitchen without dropping the tray of dirty dishes. A patron had run into her on the first day she had started working at The Saffron Heart and Lord Harmeet had taken the cost of replacing those dishes from her pay.

"This one hates the weekends," Navi whispered as she helped Saga unload the dishes so that she could begin washing them. "It seems to bring out the crazies."

Saga shook her head. "You have no idea."

Navi sighed and stuck her hands back into the boiling water she was using to clean. "Yeah... Navi wishes she did."

"No, you don't," Saga responded, placing the last of the plates beside her friend. "I've had my butt pinched five times tonight alone." She cringed. "I kind of lost it on the last one... Not to mention the insults... I mean, one of the women out there actually insinuated that if I didn't stop eating, I would never be dainty enough to catch a man... Like, seriously?"

They laughed.

"What are you doing?" The harsh voice startled them, and Saga almost dropped her empty tray. They turned meekly to the stern, older elf who was standing behind them.

"Dropping off dirty dishes, Mr Harmeet," Saga replied, eyeing Navi out of the corner of her eye. The other girl had her eyes down, looking at her soap covered hands and was trembling.

"Dropping off dishes does not require conversing with the Ash-Face," the blond haired, blue eyed, pixie-faced elf stated harshly. Saga felt her hands ball into fists beneath the tray. "You would do well to remember that." He directed the last comment to Saga, before turning on Navi. "And you," he sneered. "You are only here because my son insisted that you were a good, quiet, worker. Do what you are told and stay out of sight. Do I make myself clear?"

Navi nodded, her shoulders hunched, "Yes Sir," she said in toneless voice that Saga had been hearing more and more and did not like. It had only been two weeks since they had started at the Saffron Heart and in that time, she had seen the delicate elf girl recede further and further into herself. Not so much away from work, but it had been good to hear her laugh. With everything that had happened in the last few months of the school semester, the instances of Navi's laughter had been far and few between. For all of them really, but perhaps Saga was better at faking it.

"What was that?" Saga whispered as the old elf lord walked away.

Navi shook her head and turned back to her pile of dishes. "Life as a Dökkálfar..." She murmured. "Now go!"

With a tray loaded with precariously balanced dishes in her hands, she made her way over to a table of diners. The women were dressed richly, with fine velvet dresses that seemed to glimmer in the faerie lights of the restaurant. Their jewels only adding to the effect of their etherealness. It was a party of six, two adult women, two adult men and a girl and boy around her own age.

"And we will see about getting you out of that atrocious residence," a woman was saying. "Bridelow Cottage or at least Timbergard Hall... But Jimpsee House? What in the name of the moon did we do wrong for you to wind up with those-." She had been about to say freaks. Saga just knew it. The woman huffed at Saga's appearance. "It's about time," The women announced, interrupting her own tirade as soon as Saga placed the tray down on the table, ready to unload their dishes. "Do you have any idea how long we have been waiting?"

"I apologise ma'am," Saga said, looking up from the table to address the woman. "Lady Harding," she corrected herself, remembering her first encounter with the woman earlier in the year when she had been in the Tree City before Astrid had brought her to Nýr Ásgardr and the school. She took a quick, surreptitious look around the table, recognising the man beside her as her husband. With a growing sense of dread, Saga realised exactly who the young man was at the table. Emory Harding, a fellow roommate at Jimpsee house. He too had described the residents of the house as freaks when the assignment had been made, almost alienating him from their other housemates.

"Saga," Emory said looking at her in shock. It had been two weeks since she had seen him and even longer since they had spoken to one another. She didn't think they had even been alone together since that day in the hospital when he had sat by her bedside as she had pretended to sleep. After that, it was almost as though they had avoided each other except when absolutely necessary.

Saga nodded to him in response but knew better than to show any familiarity with the customers here. Lord Harmeet did not want any familiarity between the staff and his diners and given that Saga either went to school with them or they were her teachers, that was hard.

She turned her gaze quickly to see who the younger girl was and was surprised to see Bindi Billingsley, a classmate of theirs. She was also a werewolf like the Hardings. The two other adults must have been her parents. With a look if confusion, Saga turned her attention back to Emory's highly strung mother. "If there is anything I can do to make your meal here more to your liking, just let me know," she said, careful not to lay any blame for the time the meal had taken on her or on the staff of The Saffron Heart. The woman had ordered rósmarín og öndufyllt ugla or for those whose Norse was a little rusty, rosemary and duck stuffed owl. A dish that the chefs in the kitchen had complained endlessly about making. She had also ordered six of them. It didn't seem like a dish that Emory, who like Saga, enjoyed a trip to the Rolly Polly Kitty for Lucuma pie, would like. She had also seen Bindi there plenty of times before with her own group of friends.

The other woman, with her shimmering blond hair, so like her daughter's spoke up. "It smells divine. We should eat and not let the chef's hard work go to waste."

Emory smiled appreciatively at the other woman. Saga knew how he hated the way his mother made a fuss of everything, often for no reason.

As soon as she had placed the dishes down before each of them, Lady Harding huffed and waved her hand in Saga's direction. "That will be all, girl."

"Of course, madam," she replied. "Call on me if you need anything at all, " and with that, she walked away.

"As I was saying, we will get you situated into a proper Were residence and all this Jimpsee nonsense can be swept right under the rug to be forgotten about," Lady Harding said as she started on her meal.

"And the betrothal?" Bindi's father asked.

The sounds of cutlery clattering against plates followed the question and then the sputtering of protest from both Emory and Bindi. Saga couldn't help herself. She looked over her shoulder at the table. Emory was staring not at his parents, but her, his face as pale as one of the house ghosts. He looked panic-stricken as his eyes slowly left Saga's to turn to an equally distressed Bindi.

Saga hurried out of the main dining area, not wanting to hear what was said next, not really looking where she was going until she collided with someone. He looked up from her feet to see the bemused smile of Sidawi

Harmeet. The smile couldn't reach his eyes and Saga didn't think she had ever seen it do so since the fire at Dorbe Manor.

"Saga?" He asked. "Something wrong?"

She shook her head. "No, not at all. I'm so sorry!"

Sidawi was an amicable boy, well, he was a man now. Perfect of his school residence and a mere six months off graduating. "You look as though you've seen a ghost."

Saga wanted to laugh at that. Seeing a ghost at that moment probably would have been easier than the encounter with Emory. "Nothing like that," She assured him. "Just someone I know..." Saga really did not want to elaborate on what she had heard Emory's mother talking about. At least not with him, maybe with Navi later, back at the dormitory... Assuming Cordelia Queenette gave them a chance to talk. Saga took a moment to compose herself, before taking in the lanky Ljósálfar appearance. "Are you going to play for the diners?"

Sidawi looked abashed for a moment, before holding up his balalaika. "Uh... Yeah... Tonight's musical act dropped out and my father is all in a rant that there was no one to fill in, so I said I would. Of course, that started a different tirade as to how I was better than some useless musician, but here I am."

Saga shook her head. She did not like Sidawi's father, and she wondered how Sidawi had planned to break the news to his parents that the love of his life was a Dökkálfar. She supposed that didn't matter anymore, but given the way the man treated Navi, she could only imagine what might have happened if Ziva had lived.

"How's Navi doing?" he suddenly asked. "I haven't been able to get anywhere near her since you two started here."

Saga frowned. "She's retreating into herself. Your father insults her constantly and encourages the staff to avoid her, if not be outright cruel."

"Bölvun," Sidawi muttered under his breath. "Is she going to be, ok?"

"Yeah. Of course. It'll take more than a stuck-up Ljósálfar to get her down," Saga said. "And it's only another fortnight until school starts up again. Then we can get out of Queenette Dormitory and back to Jimpsee House."

"Cordelia Queenette being her charming self again?"

Saga raised an eyebrow at him. As a house prefect himself, during special events, such as the start of year choosing, he could see his own house ghost, but how had he known about Cordelia? Maybe Ellora had mentioned the Queenette ghost's tendencies to the other Prefects? Saga though, wasn't sure if he knew that she could see the house ghosts. "What do you mean?" she asked coyly.

Before he could reply though, Sidawi was called away. He brushed a long strand of golden hair from his eyes and put a smile on his face that did not reach his eyes. "I've got to go. Talk to you later?"

Saga nodded. "Yeah, of course."

Saga continued back to the kitchens to collect the next round of orders as Sidawi went into the main dining area. A few moments later she could hear the music from his balalaika start.

"I need these done first." The voice was harsh and accompanied by a loud clattering of plates being dumped in a careless stack.

"Who said you can cut in front? If we've got no pots to cook in, you don't need any plates to put the food in. She does my washing first!" Another male voice argued.

"You could always help," Saga suggested. "There's only one of her and everyone in this kitchen expects her to do everything."

The head waiter and one of the chefs stopped and looked at her and she could see the incredulity written all over their faces. Behind them, Navi said nothing as she worked away, washing the next plates on her ever-growing piles.

"But that's what Sla-," Saga held her hand up before the head waiter, a man by the name of Tavares, could finish that sentence.

"She's free. She's a student at Toserra Sorose. Not a slave. Start treating her like a person. The whole act of slavery is barbaric and the fact that a race supposedly as refined at the Ljósálfar engage in it is disgraceful. If you have a particular need for some items, either ask nicely or roll up your own sleeves and help."

"You listen here," Tavares said, stepping towards Saga. He tried to be intimidating, hands on hips, bolstering his height and taking an aggressive stance, but Saga, at half the man's age was half a head taller than he was. She saw his advance falter as he realised this, but to his credit, he kept going with his bravado. "The ash-face-"

"Navi," Sage interrupted him.

"The ash-fa-" Tavares tried to speak again.

"Her name is Navi."

"Saga, stop it," Navi said in a small voice. "Please... It's only two more weeks."

"I'll help her with the dishes and if Lord Harmeet doesn't like it, he can hire more dish staff," Saga said, pushing past Tavares. He stumbled as their shoulders collided, but he said nothing. The cook who had been a part of the original argument had backed off slightly, as though he was looking for an opportunity to run off and get help.

Tavares stormed away, with a muttered order of, "Just get it done."

"You shouldn't have done that!" Navi hissed under her breath. "You're just going to get us fired and Navi needs this job."

"You cannot work like this. These people are poison!" Saga insisted.

"They can't be that bad..." Navi insisted. "They liked Ziva, right?"

Saga looked at her friend and shook her head. "You think Sidawi actually introduced her to his parents? Did she tell you this?"

Navi's eyes widened in surprise. "Well... No... This one and Annis didn't even know about Ziva and Sidawi... Oh... They were a secret..."

Saga nodded. "Yes."

Together, they washed dishes together until Tavares returned, stating that one of their VIP diners was requesting her service at their table.

Saga glanced discreetly at Navi who gave a small nod. "Of course," Saga said, drying her hands off with a nearby towel. "Which table is it?"

"The Harding-Billingsley party," Tavares announced. "Try not to make a mess of it."

Saga sneered and rolled her eyes at the arrogant man as soon as he turned his back.

She headed out to the main dining room of the restaurant. Sidawi's haunting balalaika music floated over the room and people were taking small, surreptitious glances up at him when they could. Saga could tell that a fair few young women found the young light elf enticing. Perhaps it was the sadness he had been haunted by since Ziva's death that made him appear vulnerable and appealing to them.

"I hope you are all enjoying your meal," Saga said as she presented herself at the table.

"It was wonderful," Bindi's mother said.

"It was passable," Lady Harding said, talking over the other woman. Emory looked pained at his mother's behaviour and Lady Billingsley looked taken aback. She was probably not used to people talking over or contradicting her. Emory and Bindi shared a look with each other that Saga tried hard not to notice.

"Would you like anything else, perhaps the dessert menu? Chef Kenwyn makes Lucuma and truffle parfaits which I'm told are divine," Saga told them.

"How about Lucuma pie?" Emory asked eagerly.

"Absolutely not," Lady Harding interrupted. "We will not be having anything as common as Lucuma. How about a plate of fresh Hala?"

Saga could hear the complaints now. Within an hour, the entire restaurant would go from the light floral smell that most people liked to a horrible stink that would force them to stay late and cleanse the restaurant of the smell. She was certain that the only reason Lady Harding wanted it was because the fruit was incredibly expensive as it was imported from some far away isle that Saga could not remember the name of.

"Mother," Emory interrupted. "None of us like Hala," he hissed under his breath.

"Hush now, of course you do," she said. "Off you go now girl," Lady Harding stated stoically.

Saga glanced at Emory and Bindi. Neither one of them looked pleased. She passed the order on to the kitchen along with one slight alteration, where Tavares looked scandalised by the request. He shook his head, muttering about people with more money than sense.

She returned to the table with a tray of jewel like Hala smelling sweetly and as she placed it down on the table, Lady Harding's eyes narrowed in distaste when Saga placed a different dish before Emory and Bindi. "The kitchen apologises Lady Harding, but there was not enough Hala for a party of six. I hope that the young couple enjoy their Lucuma parfait."

Emory and Bindi look relieved, with Emory mouthing Saga a discreet 'thank you' that his mother didn't see. Saga walked away from the table, not wanting to look at Emory and Bindi together any longer.

On the stage, Sidawi strummed at his balalaika, the music drifting over the dining room, complimenting the low-level conversation that was going on around them. There was a hypnotic element to the music, something that seemed to ensure that Saga always noticed the music around her. Saga walked towards the kitchens when another table stopped her to ask for the dessert menu. She went through the menu with them and promised to return with their order.

A figure walked right in front of her, as if they had not even noticed her about to walk into them and continued past as though nothing had happened. Saga stopped short, not wanting to crash into a customer, but as they passed her, she had to look where they were going. Beside her was a table full of diners, but now as she looked, there was an ethereal being standing amidst the food, his body half through the table as he stared intently towards the stage. Saga blinked several times, trying to make the image of the being disappear but instead of disappearing, more seemed to appear, moving in towards the stage, their gazes intent upon the form of Sidawi and his music. Saga looked around, there were at least as many ghostly figures as there were diners.

A chair scraped somewhere in the distance. "What's wrong?"

Tension she hadn't even known she was holding seemed to flood out of her at the sound of his voice until she remembered why he was there. A betrothal. To Bindi. Bindi Billingsley, who was in their class and Saga would have to see every day.

"Nothing," She forced herself to say. Emory had always been the one she could be the most honest with. He had, in the past, been the one to get her to open up about the ghosts and the things she could see, but not now. Not anymore. "You don't need to concern yourself with me anymore... Moving over to Bridelow or Timbergard right?"

"Saga," Emory begged.

She shook her head. "Go back to your table Emory."

"Look at me," he begged softly, but Saga couldn't make herself do it. The ghosts were so intent on the music that Sidawi was playing that they seemed to take all of her attention. "What is it?"

Saga bit her lip, not wanting to confide in him, but needing to tell someone about what she was seeing. It couldn't wait until she saw Navi and that was assuming the kitchen staff let her anywhere near her best friend.

"Saga?" Emory prodded.

"Ghosts," she finally whispered.

"What?"

"The ghosts... They're attracted to Sidawi's music..."

Emory looked from Saga to the elf on the stage, his fingers caressing the strings of his instrument with grace and care. Emory couldn't see the ghosts, although Saga suspected that he might be able to in his wolf form. They had never talked about it though, so she wasn't sure. "Have you ever seen anything like this before?"

Saga shook her head. "No..."

"Think Sidawi knows?"

Saga shrugged. "Don't know."

"Stop chatting up that customer, Carolle." The shout came from across the dining room and Saga jumped. How she hated it when they used her last name. Not even in the way the teachers did, calling her Miss Carolle, just that harshly called word. She shook herself off. Tavares was glaring at her over the heads of the other diners, and she was pretty sure that this was one breach too many in the one night.

MUSICAL DILEMMA

The airship port was surprisingly busy, Saga thought. Sure, people were coming into town, with school starting on Monday that was only to be expected, but she was surprised by the number of people that seemed to be trying to find a ride on the ship out of town.

"Saga! There you are!"

Saga turned to see who was calling after her. "Astrid, what are you doing here?"

"Looking for you actually," Astrid said, coming up to her. "Well, actually, I was hoping Annis would be here."

"Annis?" Saga asked. "Uhh, she was looking for Edun. She and Navi went over to Knightrich first."

Astrid nodded. "Good. I suppose they need to do some school shopping. "

Saga nodded. "Yeah... And me too..." She dug into her bag and pulled out a piece of parchment. "I got this letter saying that I need to take some sort of instrument this semester and I have no idea... and Illeana's suggestion that I take up the hurdy-gurdy is not going to happen!"

"I should hope not!" Astrid exclaimed. "I'm not even sure what that is... But no, you should definitely not play one... Drums?" Astrid added helpfully.

Saga shook her head. "Apparently, not an option."

"I'm sure something will speak to you when you're in Yggdrasil city." Saga looked up at the older woman. Despite being her guardian officially, Saga rarely saw her outside of weapons class and even now, she had not been looking for Saga. Before she could say anything though, Astrid spotted the Jensyn siblings. "Ah, there they are."

Navi came running up, a rare smile upon her face. "Navi got mail from Tasso. He and his sister are going to meet us in Yggdrasil city!" She announced, waving the piece of parchment in the air before Saga. It didn't surprise anyone that the girl was excited of at the prospect of seeing the lithe faerie boy again. Despite a rocky start prior to the beginning of the school year, they had become fast friends, perhaps even something more, but neither would admit to anything.

"Tonya?" Saga asked, less than pleased at the prospect of the faerie girl.

"Oh, well, not her!" Navi exclaimed. "She'll go off with Amita and Gherree. Leave us to our own business."

Annis shook her head as she watched the girls. Astrid strode over to her, a warning look at Saga before speaking. "Annis, would it be possible for you to do me a favour?"

"Of course, Mistress Grunborg," Annis said. "What can I do?"

She motioned towards Saga. "I'm supposed to take Saga to Yggdrasil for instrument shopping and you know how the money still confuses her," Saga's eyes widened in betrayal at the comment and Navi glanced suspiciously between the two. First of all, they had always planned on going to Yggdrasil to meet with Jemima before the beginning of term. Navi had some shopping to do with money supplied by the school in the aftermath of the Dorbe Manor fire to spend to replace her uniforms and books. The only thing she had managed to save from the fire had been a beautifully engraved staff, similar to Saga's own that they had both won in a dual with Tasso's sister. It had been the moment they had first met, bonding them together in the midst of battle against a common foe.

"And this way you'll be able to take your time, spend the night in the city, cut loose a little before term starts," Astrid suggested. Saga thought the weapons mistress was laying it on a little thick. She knew Ziva would have seen straight through the attempt at charity. "I would really appreciate it."

"I... Umm..." Annis looked uncomfortable and glanced towards Navi and Edun, who as usual, was scuffing his feet at the ground, waiting as though he had no interest in being there. The prospect of a night in the Tree City though, seemed to perk him up.

Navi nodded excitedly and when even Edun nodded, Annis turned back to the weapons mistress and agreed to her job. They all knew that Saga could manage her money just fine, it wasn't like she wanted to buy a house or anything insanely expensive, but they appreciated Astrid's effort to make it look as though they were working for her.

"Can we go now?" Edun muttered.

"Yes, of course," Astrid said, passing Annis a small pouch of coins. "You all have fun now!" she said brightly before walking away.

"Mistress Grunborg is a terrible liar," Edun declared, pushing past them and making his way towards the ticketing booth. "We're not a charity case."

"No one thinks you are," Saga said. "And besides, she's right. I'm a mess at making decisions. Ziva had to practically tell me what to do last semester. I mean, how many times did she totally save me from being ripped off?" And now she was trying to sell Astrid's act. What was she doing?

Navi nodded in agreement, even though she too knew that Saga trying a little too hard.

The boat ride from Nýr Ásgardr to Yggdrasil was uneventful and they passed the time with far fewer nerves than when they had flown last time.

"They're children!" Edun complained about Saga and Navi.

Saga turned to the constantly grumpy boy and grinned. "It's a flying boat! It's still super cool to me!"

"What are we doing first?" Navi asked, almost bouncing on the spot. Annis looked to the large time machine at the end of the ship's dock and nodded to herself.

"It's still early, why don't we get some food? Then, if we can get everything done, we could go have some fun tomorrow!"

"The market or the inn?" Saga asked.

"Market!" Edun declared, taking the lead, "And if either of you dare mention pie, I'm going my own way!"

Saga and Navi looked from Edun, to each other, then back to Edun. "What? Why?" Navi asked.

"What's wrong with La-," Saga started to ask, but was cut off.

"Don't say it!" Navi and Annis cried together, knowing that their brother meant what he had said and that they would never find him before their booked departure from the Tree City if he did disappear on them. As much as he liked the pie, everyone did, the girls, and Navi in particular were slightly obsessed with the pie. So much so, that Edun refused to even hear about it.

As the ship drew into port amidst the highest branches of the world tree, Saga hung onto the side of the ship, her paralysing fear of heights somehow immune to the spectacular visage of the Tree City. Despite having spent plenty of time running up and down the central stairs, and exploring the many branches, which formed entire streets, Saga still could barely comprehend the sheer size of the tree.

The first time she had arrived, it had been after a harrowing experience hanging off one of the smaller rainbow discs that traversed the nine realms. The tree, bigger than any tree she had ever imagined, teemed with life. People dashed about or lived their lives and the lights and colours of their dwellings and street lighting looked magical... and many of them were. It had smelled sweet like a tree, and yet, the scents of people and animals and even cooking food had wafted towards her. It had been a heady experience and loved flying into the tree city.

They ate lunch as they walked through the market branches of Yggdrasil city. They would, between buying titbits of food from various stalls, duck into the shops where they needed to be and collect new school uniforms and books and tools. Tomorrow, regardless of any fun they had planned, would probably still include a jaunt down to the base of the tree in order to visit the stables and gardening shops.

"Navi also needs an instrument," Navi said as they sat outside the music shop, polishing off a packet of crispy lotus chips.

"We all do," Edun grunted.

"You hate music class," Annis observed. "Maybe you want to see if you can drop it. You would be able to drop it next year anyway and you did do first semester."

Edun looked over at her, wiping his greasy hands over his pants. "Hmm," was all he said.

"Navi wants to play the balalaika like Ziva did."

"Ziva only played that god's awful thing because Sid did," Edun put in disdainfully, having put their sister's choice of instrument together with Sidawi's reaction after her death and figuring out the reason, before being told.

Navi nodded enthusiastically. "This one knows that, but Sidawi has offered to tutor Navi."

"Really?" Annis asked in surprise.

"Yeah, he offered to tutor both of us," Saga confirmed, but some nagging feeling in the back of her mind had her resisting his offer. Aside from not wanting to do music to begin with, the night at The Saffron Heart had unsettled her and she didn't want to be around Sidawi when he played again. "But I just want to pick something and be done with it, then drop it as soon as possible."

Annis chucked, "Just like our Edun!"

The shop was bright, with walls of instruments lit up for the browser to view. Saga figured that the store owner must spend a fortune on the magic stones that provided safe lighting in the wood and canvas environment of the tree city.

Each section of the shop was separated by type; brass, woodwind, string, percussion and what was the last type? Saga had no idea. She was not looking forward to the next semester... And if Annis was right, she wouldn't be able to drop doing the instrument until third year.

"Oh..." Navi exclaimed. "Would you look at that," she pointed excitedly towards the strings section, where a display of various types of balalaika were on show.

"You're not serious, are you?" Edun complained. "Why must you play that thing?"

"Because Navi wants to!" she cried, storming over to the display to have a better look.

"Faerie boy would probably prefer a harp or a flute," Edun called after her. Navi's only response was to turn and stick her tongue out at her brother. Annis sighed and watched her younger siblings.

Saga wandered off on her own, meandering her way through the various shelves and stacks of instruments. Each one looked far more confronting than the last and every time she dared to look at the leaflet with the instrument and saw the description of how to play, she was faced with instructions and technical jargon that made her head spin. Give her a good routine in weapons class and she would feel far more confident.

"Pentathlon!" A voice whispered behind her.

Saga jumped and turned to the speaker. "Edun!" she exclaimed.

"You have an open invitation to join the pentathlon team," he elaborated. "Virtually unheard of in first year by the way. It's a sure way out of these ridiculous requirements. Use it!"

Saga shook her head. "I'm not joining the pentathlon team. Donetta said that the archery component is an aerial relay..."

Edun was nodding along. "Yeah, lots of angels and faeries do that bit. Some Griffin riders, but we don't have a good team because of the stadion. None of them run well and the Weres that enter the relay can't go full pentathlon because of the aerial component. You're probably the closest thing the school has to a sure thing with the way you run and that Pegasus."

Saga just shook her head the entire time he spoke. "I can teach them to run. Or at least help with tryouts or something like that, but there is no way anyone is getting me in the air." She pursed her lips and glanced out of the corner of her eye at the boy. "Plus... Pingu can't fly..."

Edun stared dumbfounded at her. "Say what?"

"Exactly what I said. He can't fly. No one knows why."

"Edun has seen you take him jumping," Edun pressed.

Saga nodded. "Yeah, Jemima was teaching me and Navi how to jump and it's like his wings twitch as though the feeling of air around him should be familiar, but nothing."

Edun followed her awkwardly as she browsed the instruments. It was as though he wanted to ask her something but didn't know how. Instead, he just stayed at her side, pointing out the positives and negatives of each instrument as he saw them.

After what seemed an eternity to Saga of looking at one impossible instrument after another, she turned to Edun. "Annis said you picked the easiest thing you could. What did you pick?" Edun was staring at her, but it was almost as though he wasn't seeing her. "Edun?" Saga asked again, giving him a poke on the arm.

"What about your wings?" He asked in a hoarse voice, his eyes glazed over as though seeing something else instead of the musical instruments that surrounded them.

The question told her exactly what he was seeing in his mind's eye, and she had little desire to remember that night. "What?" she choked out.

"You... You had wings..." Edun's ability to form full sentences seemed as offbeat as her own. "That night... Big, glowing wings..."

"I..." Before she could figure out what to say to him, a figure rushed at them.

"Saga!" Jemima cried. "What are you going to play?" She had come a long way from the quiet, shy girl who did not like to be touched at the beginning of the school year.

Saga frowned. "I don't know."

"The harp, then we could be in class together." As much as Saga liked the idea of being in the same class as Jemima for music, the harp was not for her. She glanced over at Edun who looked distressed by Jemima's appearance. He looked as though he wanted to say something but bit his lip momentarily before scowling. Instead of speaking, he turned on his heel and walked away without another word.

"Edun-," Saga tried to call after him, but he vanished between the racks and shelves of instruments.

"What's up with him?" Jemima asked.

Saga shook her head. "I don't know..." she said softly, she didn't elaborate though, because a part of her was worried about the boy but she couldn't put her finger on why she was concerned.

"He's always such a grump..." Jemima added, "And you've seen him at Tourney events..."

That was true. Edun often competed in combat related tourney events and had a reputation for violence that surpassed that even of the vampires and Weres. "He has his reasons," Saga said. Jemima, she knew, had led a relatively sheltered life before starting at Toserra Sorose, but Saga had seen many kids like Edun, angry with the world for their lot in it. Saga herself had been one of them for the longest time, getting into fights and hitting her way through frustrations. "He has his reasons," Saga said again, looking in the direction he had disappeared.

Jemima looked as though she was contemplating saying something else on the matter, but something in Saga's voice must have changed her mind because she turned her attention back to the instruments.

"So, what will it be?" Jemima pressed. Saga guessed that the young angel had selected her instrument months before school had even started and had always known what she would be doing. The girl was always organised, often going so far as to organise Saga's things for her.

"I don't know..." Saga said again, her eyes glancing over the myriad of instruments, each looking like it would be harder than the one before it. The harp with its long strings did seem like a good idea. She walked up to one, a big one, as tall as she was and plucked at the strings.

"Not like that!" Jemima exclaimed, scurrying over and situating herself at the curved end of the large instrument, her arms extended around both sides. She started to pluck delicately at the strings, a soft melody emanating from the instrument.

Saga sighed. "Right..."

Navi bounced up towards them, a smallish triangular looking guitar in her hands. "Look what this one found!"

Jemima frowned. "What is it?"

"A balalaika," Saga answered before Navi could start on her exposition on the instrument. "She's been fascinated with them because Sidawi has offered to teach her."

Jemima nodded. "A private tutor, that's great!"

"Navi knows!" she exclaimed excitedly. "What are you going to play Jemima?"

"The harp," The angel said primly, as though it was the only available answer.

"Are you girls done?" Annis asked walking over to them. "Oh, hi Jemima."

"Hello Annis," Jemima said

"This one is done!" Navi said.

"What about you Saga?" Annis asked.

Saga frowned, eyeing her two friends. She had no idea what to do. She shook her head. "Not yet... Maybe I'll come back tomorrow while you guys finish off your shopping or something..."

Annis didn't seem to like that plan. She took the responsibility given to her by Astrid very seriously and didn't think that separating was such a good idea. Jemima and Navi headed towards the kiosk to pay while Saga wandered around the shop some more.

A dark hand extended before her, holding out an instrument made of long hollow pipes, arranged from shortest to longest. They seemed to be held together by a carved band. The band was engraved with a pattern of flowers similar to that of her staff. Saga looked up the length of the arm to the owner. Edun stood nervously beside her, the instrument held awkwardly between them.

"What is it?" Saga asked, taking it from him and inspecting the instrument closely.

"A pan flute," Edun said. "It's what I picked when I had to do music in first year. It's easy to play and somewhat fun..." He swallowed nervously. "And that one matches your staff..."

Saga nodded. "I noticed. It's lovely." She looked up at him. "Will you show me how to play it?" Edun held up a second one with a polished black enamel and held it to his lips. He blew against it, moving the instrument left and right, depending on what sound he wanted to make according to the melody. A couple of people stopped what they were doing to look at him. Saga smiled at him when he finished. "That was beautiful!" she exclaimed.

Edun's black skin seemed to tinge the strange reddish, mahogany-like colour Dökkálfar turned when they blushed. Was he blushing? He waved awkwardly towards the instrument Saga held in her hands. "I could... I could show you how to play... You know, like, help you practice and that."

Saga beamed at him. "I would love that!"

He nodded and together they walked through the shop to join Navi and Jemima at the kiosk to pay. Annis looked at them both in surprise when they both presented pan flutes to the shopkeeper and paid but said nothing, eyeing her brother suspiciously.

So, Jemima, when did you arrive?" Saga asked as they walked out of the shop with their shopping bags.

"I've been in Yggdrasil for the holidays. My Aunt Gabrielle lives here and it's where the family always congregate for the holidays."

"Are you from Yggdrasil, Jemima?" Annis asked as they walked.

"Yes and no. My mother was from Andlang... But when she died, I came to my Aunt Gabrielle, except Aunt Gabrielle's job meant that she was always away," Jemima explained. "So, my Aunt Angelica came to stay with us, but everyone would visit often and as I got older, I would come with Aunt Dina and Aunt Raffi to Nýr Ásgardr."

"If you're from Andlang, why not go to Aquino Beccara?" Edun asked, as he walked just a little behind Saga, their arms occasionally brushing against one another.

Jemima grimaced and thought of how to explain, "My mother was Malakim. With her death, I am not quite Malakim, but because of my aunts, I am not quite Bene Elohim-."

"What is Malakim or Bene Elohim?" Saga asked.

"Ranks, within Angel society. Not very high ones. In fact, Bene Elohim is one level above the lowest rank in our society... As such, at Aquino Beccara... Well, if I would have even been accepted, my options would have been very limited."

"The Angel program here rivals Aquino Beccara easily, wouldn't the issues here be the same?" Annis asked.

"In Nýr Ásgardr Aunt Raffi is very highly ranked. She is Cherubim. Her skill as a healer revered by many... And Aunt Dina, as a teacher and a former Angel of Death is Tarshishim. My connections to them allow me to study as I wish towards being a healer, rather than a helper or worse. Aquino Beccara would not have allowed me these opportunities."

"Huh..." Navi said. "This one did not know Angels were so..."

"Uptight?" Edun offered.

"Structured?" Annis added.

Jemima nodded uncomfortable. "Well... Yes, there is that..." She agreed. "I hope that when I graduate, my exams and performance in my chosen field will elevate my rank to such that I might be selected into the Angels of Healing."

"But what's wrong with Malakim or Bene Elohim?" Saga asked. She'd never had much in her life and had never expected to have much or achieve much in her life.

Jemima looked towards the three Dökkálfar siblings uncomfortably. "Well..." She scratched the back of her neck awkwardly, her hand eventually taking hold of her long plait and skimming the length of it before finally speaking. "The Bene Elohim and in particular the Erelim have a status similar to that of the Dökkálfar in Elvan society," she finished hurriedly, her voice barely more than a whisper.

Annis stared at her, a look of complete incomprehension on her face, but it was Edun who spoke. "Angels keep slaves?" he asked pointedly.

Jemima shook her head. "No... It's not quite like that and it's a great shame upon our people. They're not owned in the same way as the Dökkálfar are owned by the Ljósálfar, but they are not afforded the same opportunities as those of higher rank, they have little to no rights... Getting out is... almost impossible."

"And you're getting out?" Navi asked.

"In a way... Had I wound up in an orphanage, I would never have been allowed to attend school and would have spent my life in servitude to another angel rather than the Gods."

Edun's fists clenched at his sides and Saga instinctively reached over to take one of his hands in her own. Nobody seemed to notice, but he looked at her, grateful for the contact. "I thought Angels were better than that," he breathed out.

Jemima looked around. A few angels passed them by, their regal clothes and lofty demeanour evident in their every move. "We like to believe that we are. And the existence of the Bene Elohim and the Erelim is not something that is widely known outside of our society. I trust that you will keep it to yourselves."

No one said anything, but Saga, Annis and Navi nodded their heads. Edun looked away but grunted in what they took as his agreement.

They kept walking from shop to shop, gathering whatever was still needed for the new school term for the three siblings, books uniforms, equipment, even a few non-school uniform items. The money from Astrid definitely helped, not that anyone said a word about what it was really about.

They were leaving the astronomy shop when a woman bustled up to them, taking Jemima's face in her hands and kissing both of the girl's cheeks.

"Aunty Angelica!" Jemima groaned, her face flushing in embarrassment. Jemima's Aunt Angelica was a short, stout woman with grey, spotted wings that reminded Saga of a pigeon. The woman gathered each of them up into a hug, not even batting an eyelash at the three dark elves.

"My, how absolutely darling you all are," she gushed. "Oh, I know dear Jemmy, what if your friends come and stay at ours for the night. Gabsey won't mind one bit!"

Saga looked at the group. They had money for one night at The Bore Tooth, but a night with Jemima's family would save them even that. The revelation about angel society though still hung heavily in their minds and Saga wondered what Annis would say.

"We wouldn't want to put you out," Annis started to say.

"Nonsense, nonsense my girl," she wrapped a plump arm around Annis's shoulders and started to direct the girl down the market thoroughfare. "Plenty of room at Gabsey's and a friend of our Jemmy's is a friend of us all!"

Navi, Edun and Saga glanced at each other wryly. Jemima hung her head, her hands covering her face as she followed, trying not to show her embarrassment. Annis looked over her shoulder at them, but no one stepped up to help them.

"Aunty Angelica, maybe they've already got their accommodation paid for-," she tried, but Angelica cut her off.

"Then we will get them their money back!"

The enthusiastic angel led them through the marketplace. As always, it was teaming with life as people bustled about their daily chores. A parting in the crowd caught Saga's attention. Her gaze focused there as she thought she saw someone she recognized... But no... It couldn't be... Could it? What would Vali be doing in Yggdrasil City? She hadn't seen the man since that fateful day in Valaskjálf when he had nearly killed Navi while trying to use Saga to claim Odin's vacant throne. He had this crazy idea that because she was a Valkyrie, the first to be seen since Ragnarök, that she was the key to his ascension.

Navi broke away from the group, running excitedly to stall that sold dried foods. For a moment, Saga was certain she saw the flash of the dagger, sticking from the girl's back as she fell silently to the floor. A shiver ran down Saga's back as she heard his voice in the back of her mind.

"Why don't you ask your father?" His words still taunted her. Her father. She'd never even considered that she had father until that day. Both her mother and father were just figments of her imagination, left by a letter scribbled by a woman who had abandoned her. "You look so much like your mother. It's remarkable, really." How had this madman known her mother and father? Why did he get to know them, and she didn't?

"Hackey Sack," Navi exclaimed excitedly, turning to her siblings. "Navi hasn't played since Edun went away to school!"

The store she had run to was overflowing with barrels and crates of grains, legumes, beans flours, wheats and even a few things that Saga couldn't even begin to identify. When she looked back to where the man had been, she didn't see him. It had been her imagination, that was all. A figment, nothing to worry about.

Edun's eyes widened, "You can't be serious!"

"Let's do it!" Annis said, "It's been even longer for this one!"

As the siblings talked, Saga's eyes scanned the crowd, trying to spot the man again. She couldn't help it, despite her certainty that it was just her own imagination playing tricks on her, but he had vanished. Jemima eyed Saga, not knowing what the three were on about. She elbowed Saga when the other girl didn't respond.

"What's wrong?" She asked softly.

Saga shook her head. "Nothing," she replied just as softly, not wanting to draw attention to herself. She looked around anxiously though, trying to spot the figure that sent shivers down her spine, but followed as they approached the stall to look at the offered goods. "We should figure out what we're doing." She scanned the offerings but didn't know what the others were so excited about.

"What are we doing?" Jemima asked, when it became evident that Saga wasn't going to ask.

"You fill a bag with your preferred insides and you… kick it around" Edun said, he looked at his sisters. "There has to be a better way of explaining it, right?"

"We'll make them and then we can show!" Annis declared. She glanced over at Angelica who was watching them. "Do you mind?" she asked.

"No, you children go right ahead," she said watching them with an intense fondness.

There was an argument brewing between Navi and Edun about the best filling for a hackey sack, Edun was for dried pinto beans while Navi preferred chickpeas.

"Rice," Annis said leaning over the barrels of supplies looking for the aforementioned ingredient. "It's rice," she said, getting in on the argument.

"Too small and soft!" Edun complained. "What about you two?" he asked looking back at Saga and Jemima.

Saga though was scanning the crowd once more and gasped, when she saw him. He was talking to another man. The man looked to be a musician and carried an instrument case, strung over his back. They were leaning in, talking to one another, a book held between them.

"I would probably use wheat," Jemima said. "Then I could heat it when I'm not playing and use it to keep warm."

"That's an amazing idea!" Annis exclaimed and the two descended into a conversation on the best way to heat the wheat sacks.

"What about you?" Navi asked, elbowing Saga to get her attention.

Startled from her observation of the two men, Saga looked over the ingredients as she thought about the beanbags she had played with back home and tried to find the ingredient that most reminded her of the small polystyrene balls that tended to fill toys of that variety. She pointed to tiny, wrinkled, green balls. "Peas, baby peas even."

"Really?" Navi and Edun of them said in unison.

Saga shrugged. "I guess…" She bit her lip and tried to spot Vali and the other man again. She couldn't find them though. If they were still there, the crowds blocked them from her view.

"How much do we need?" Saga asked, hoping that hadn't already been discussed while she'd been searching the marketplace for Vali and his new… What was the other man? Just an acquaintance? A colleague, maybe a new henchman, like Master Iacono had been?

"About a cup," Annis said. She called the shopkeeper's attention to them and requested her preferred rice. "Do you sell hessian sack scraps?" she asked.

"Sell it?" he asked. "No, but you kids are more than welcome to look over there," he pointed to an area beside his stall where crates, barrels and empty sacks were stacked high. "Take what you want. Making kick sacks, are you?"

"That's the plan," Edun said, "Can this one get a cup of pinto beans?"

"Coming right up," the man said.

When they had all bought their bag insides, they rounded the side of the stall and from a few of the hessian sacks, cut away pieces that they could sew together.

As they made their way back to Angelica, Saga scanned every face she could, craning her neck until it became impossible to see the people in the market. Together they made their way to the trunk at the centre of the tree city and Saga started towards the stairs, but Jemima pulled her back. "We're up too high for that."

Saga's eyes widened. "What?" She asked in a small voice.

"Ah, there's a large platform, all aboard!" Angelica cried, launching herself from the gantry that spanned the expanse of the tree's centre. Her wings flapped once before she landed on the rainbow platform. Jemima followed suit, landing on the platform before it reached the gantry, allowing the three Dökkálfar and the Valkyrie to board it. Saga stood there unmoving until Navi and Jemima reached out, took hold of her and dragged her onto the platform before it got too high.

"Ahhh!" Saga cried as she fell into them. "Don't do that!" she cried.

Edun raised an eyebrow at her, watching as she steadfastly refused to step closer towards the edge or even look anywhere near the edge of the platform.

"You really are afraid of heights," he exclaimed.

"You thought I was lying?" Saga cried. "Why would I lie about that? I mean, there's nothing keeping us on here. We could fall! We could die! Doesn't anyone ever fall off these things?" Saga cried in a hoarse whisper, remembering her trip into Yggdrasil city with Astrid, where she had spent a good portion of it, hanging off the rainbow disc as it transported them away from Walhalla and into this strange, magical world.

"Well," Angelica piped up. "It does happen, although very rarely. There are Angels and faeries hired to protect the trunk. They are supposed to catch anyone unfortunate enough to fall... Mind you, there is a story from a few months back about some oafish girl who managed to fall off one onto a gantry and loose half her belongings."

Saga turned red. She remembered her horse-riding helmet shooting across the gantry almost knocking over some poor leprechaun like a tortoise shell in a Mario kart video game.

Navi, having heard the story before coughed. It had been shortly after that that they had met. "Well, umm, it is very nice of you to invite Annis, Edun and Navi to stay with you," she tried, attempting to change the subject.

"No trouble at all, no trouble at all," Angelica beamed. "Now, I wonder whatever happened to that clumsy oaf. It would be a miracle if they made it out of the city alive, I think."

Edun looked from Saga's red face to Navi who was clumsily trying to change the subject. He leaned in, whispering in Saga's ear. "That was you, wasn't it?"

"I don't want to talk about it," she sneered, harsher than she had intended, but all Edun did was let out a loud, full belly laugh that caused his sisters to turn and look at him in surprise.

"What is it?" Annis asked, shock and confusion merging into concern when her brother just laughed louder. "Edun?"

"It was her," he gasped out between great gasping breath as he pointed at Saga. "It was her!"

CALL OF THE DEAD

Dinner with Jemima's aunts was loud. Dina Bess, the religious studies teacher at Toserra Sorose welcomed them into the house with a bright smile.

"Come in, come in," she beamed. "Eva's just got the food on to warm and Muriel's finishing the last of the salads."

Raphaella glanced at the extra house guests before taking one look at Edun and frowning. He kept her and her team of healers in a solid stream of work on Tourney days.

A woman, tall and lithe with white wings tinged in silver looked from Angelica and Jemima to the other kids. "Angelica, you brought guests," she said with a tight-lipped smile. They had not been expected.

"Aunt Gabby, they're my friends from school," Jemima said, stepping in. "Saga and Navi and her siblings, Annis and Edun," she pointed to each of them in turn.

Annis immediately stepped up. "We don't want to cause any trouble, we can just go-," but Angelica immediately cut her off.

"Absolutely not. I offered hospitality and hospitality we shall give," Angelica argued.

"But it was supposed to be our last night as a family," a small, diminutive angel said.

"And so, we'll have a few more!" Angelica declared.

Jemima looked at her two friends. "Just missing Tasso and Emory, huh?"

Saga coughed and looked away while Navi stared down at her feet, mumbling something incomprehensible.

Dina stepped in and guided the lot of them through to a large dining room that could have probably seated twenty if they'd tried. As they passed through, she heard a voice whisper to Dina, "I don't mind the dark elves, but the war maiden makes me uncomfortable."

"Hush, Evangeline," Dina said, crossing the threshold into the dining room with the rest of them. "Raffi, extra settings." As the matronly healing angel set about place the extra four places Dina disappeared, pulling the aunt identified as Evangeline with her. "Not one of those children is a problem, Saga in particular. Keep your opinions of Valkyries to yourself."

"But how can you stand it?" Evangeline pressed. As an Angel of death, you must be seeing all kinds of things around her."

"That is none of your concern Eva."

The other woman looked put out to not be taken seriously, but when Gabrielle declared the meal ready, they all settled at the table. Gabrielle said a grace of thanks for the food they were about to eat, something Saga was able to mouth the words to from her time in a religious household that, while it hadn't been all sunshine and roses, had left Saga feeling as though religion was not for her. Dina Bess's classes had gone a long way to showing her another view. Several other ways to think about religion, but it was unlikely that she would find her way back to the church.

After the dinner things were cleared away, Angelica put a large sewing basket in the middle of the table. "I thought you might have forgotten the small things," she said, looking at each of them.

"We have to sew?" Saga asked.

"How else did you think we would get the sacks?" Edun asked.

"I..." Saga bit her lip. She had done textiles in year seven but had never been particularly good at it. Her big fingers made her clumsy as the delicate work required.

"Just make sure your insides don't fall out and you'll be fine," Annis said. "Thank you, Miss Angelica."

Edun, far defter with a needle than anyone had expected, even his own sisters, leapt from his chair after what seemed like only a few minutes. He had a childish gleam in his eyes that Saga had never seen before. His pinto bean filled bag clutched in his left hand, he found a clear spot where they could all see him and toed off his boots, then lifted his right leg and placed the small hessian sack upon his foot.

Annis counted him down, "three, two, one," and with that final word, he kicked the bag into the air. It didn't go high, but it was in flight long enough for Edun to hop, catching the bean filled bag on his left foot. Momentum growing,

49

he kicked again, this time it went higher, over his head and Edun turned, almost on the spot. When it came back down, he was off centre, but he crooked his leg out to the side, the bag landing on the side of his ankle. He hopped once, twice. He wobbled.

"Come on, come on, come on," Annis chanted, her own sewing all but forgotten on the table, grains of rice spilling from her bag.

Edun kicked out, his bag launching into the air again. It flew far afield from him, but he chased after it headfirst. It landed on the top of his head, and he crouched, trying to get some leverage. He launched it into the air once more, trying for another full turn. His socks slipped on the hardwood floors and Edun fell to the ground with a thud, the bean bag landing beside him with a splat. The girls erupted into laughter as he lay there, sprawled on the floor.

Raphaella burst into the room, a look of panic on her face. "What happened? Are you all alright?"

The girls, clutching their bellies as they tried to choke back their laughter, were unable to answer, but Edun held his hand up from his position on the floor. "Fine! This one is fine!" He called.

"Edun!" Annis tried, pointing at him as if to indicate what she meant. "He..."

"Navi's turn!" The little dark elf declared, jumping up. She clutched her hessian bag filled with dried chickpeas tightly, toed off her own shoes and went to stand in place Edun had started. The boy scrambled to his feet and out of her way, going to perch precariously on the chair he had vacated and wincing as he tried to get comfortable.

Navi threw her beanbag into the air above her head. It landed on top of her right foot, and she jumped, launching it to her left. She kicked her legs out behind her, catching the bag just on her toes. She launched it back over her head in a wide, sweeping ark and mimicked the move on the other side. She was graceful, athletic, and speedy in her movements.

"Do something else," Edun cried when she had repeated the same manoeuvre four times.

Navi kicked the bag up higher, turned all the way around and caught the bag on her knee. They whooped and hollered in delight, bringing the other aunts into the room to watch as Navi sent it flying again. It went over her head, and she kicked her foot out behind her, catching the beanbag on the sole of her foot. Raphaella had joined in with their cheering as they waited to see how long Navi could go before, she dropped the bag.

In the end she misjudged a kick, and it hurtled across the room landing on a sideboard full of delicate knick-knacks. A vase wobbled and they all waited with baited breaths as it settled back into place, a collected exhalation of breath leaving them as nothing fell.

"Sorry," Navi said, ducking her head and dashing across the room to collect her bag.

Jemima and Saga both gave their own sacks experimental kicks, trying to keep them up for longer than two or three kicks but Saga found that she could barely do much more than move it from one foot to the other, while Jemima tended to over or under shoot the distance between her own feet.

Edun and Navi even did a joint showing, shooting a bag back and forth between them before the aunts suggested sleep before the next day. The night had been filled with so much fun and laughter, that Saga forgot about the marketplace and Vali and the man he had been meeting with.

There was some concern over sleeping arrangements as there were too many people to fit into Jemima's room and Aunt Evangeline had concerns about Edun being in there. Instead, Azrael suggested a big slumber party in the living room where the aunts could keep a careful eye on all of them. Angelica had even provided an abundance of snacks to keep them occupied throughout the night.

Jemima was strumming on her new harp as Navi inspected the things she had bought during the day, muttering to herself as she checked items off on her list. Saga eyed the items curiously and picked up a particularly tattered copy of 'Realities of Ragnarök' by Saoirse Taliesin. She put it back down after tracing the etching on the front cover with her fingers, then looked at the other items, including the uniform items.

"I thought the school gave you enough to cover all your expenses? " She asked.

"They did," Navi said, "But Navi and her siblings decided to buy as we normally do and save the rest of the money for the year and onwards..." She said it without looking up from her checking. It made sense and Saga felt dense for not realising the thought process that went into the decision.

"We could have gone all out, and Annis is sure that many will, but we do not have the ability to seek further money from our parents, therefore we must look out for ourselves," Annis added.

"Not sure why we're bothering," Edun said. "It's not like we've got anywhere to go when we return to school."

"I'm sure that Mistress Grimaldi will assign everyone from Dorbe Manor to new houses," Jemima interrupted. "They won't leave you all out on the street."

"But this one and her siblings will unlikely be rehomed together," Navi said softly, "and it makes Navi sad to think that."

Saga was frowning as they talked. Their absolute belief in Mistress Grimaldi was endearing, but what Saga knew about house selections made her nervous. House residents were selected not by chance or random assignment, but hand selected by the house ghosts. Amyra Dorbe had selected all of her students with

51

care, some of them because no other house would take them. They would all need to go through selections again.

"What is it Saga?" Navi asked, looking at her.

Saga shook her head, fiddling with the strap of the pan flute she had bought that day. "Nothing."

"Liar," Edun said, sitting up from where he had been laying, staring out the windows of the house. "What is it?"

"Nothing, really," Saga said, still fiddling with the instrument. She blew into it experimentally, releasing a piercing noise.

"Not like that!" Edun exclaimed, jumping up. He raced over, falling onto the cushions beside her and taking the instrument from her hands. He blew into the straight end delicately, moving the pipes across his lips, the notes coming out in a harmonious melody. He finished a jaunty little tune and handed it back to her. "Gently, not with such force."

Saga nodded and put the instrument to her lips, glad that her mortifying attempts at the instrument had distracted them from the conversation about the houses. She didn't know what to tell them. If the house ghosts had not chosen them last time, who would choose them now? Or had Amyra Dorbe simply gathered the siblings together, not allowing the other ghosts a decision in the matter?

She blew gently, a strangled whistling sound emanating from the instrument. She huffed a sigh. "This is going great!" she griped sarcastically.

Edun chuckled. "There's a balance," he said. "Gently, yet with some force."

She stared bleakly at him. "You promised that this would be easy."

"It is!" he exclaimed. "Even this one can do it!"

In the morning, they left Jemima's aunts' house and split up with Navi and her siblings heading for the base encampment to do the last of their shopping while Saga and Jemima went to meet with Tasso.

"I don't get it, though," Tasso griped. "If the school can afford to pay out the way they did to all the Dorbe Manor students, why don't they offer more support?"

"According to Aunt Dina, the school board doesn't think that it's their job to help and that they already do so by ensuring the funds to purchase new supplies," Jemima said. "It's not something she agrees with, but there's not much she can do beyond trying to fundraise some... It's never much, but it's there for anyone who really needs it."

"Not that anyone knows that," Tasso shot back.

Jemima scoffed. "Of course you don't know, you're a Bonnedras and Bonnedrasses don't need financial assistance." Saga started to open her mouth, but Jemima shot her down too, "and you have a school benefactor. You also don't need to know."

"Yeah, but do Navi and the others know?" Tasso pressed.

"Probably not, don't forget that Ziva was far too proud to a accept help from anybody," Saga concluded.

Jemima nodded adamantly, "That's true..."

Tasso dived in front of them, walking backwards along the branch-street. "So," he said rubbing his hands together enthusiastically, "Where are we off to?"

"Well," Jemima started. She and Tasso discussed their options while Saga was looking around, trying to come up with an idea. In the distance she saw a familiar lanky form. Strands of long golden blond hair escaped a hood that was drawn up over the wearer's head. It was odd, almost as though he didn't want to be mistaken as a vampire moving about in the daylight, with the short, elbow length cloak, but he didn't want to be recognised, so he kept the hood up. "What are you doing?" Jemima asked Saga, who was looking over Tasso's shoulder, her gaze following something in the distance.

"Huh?" Saga asked, trying to get a better view of the cloaked figure and spotting the instrument case they were carrying and trying to navigate the crowd with.

"Well, Tasso and I were just thinking of taking some griffin rides from the top of the city and you're all looking anywhere but at us."

"We also considered the edge of the tree obstacle course. That's always fun!" Tasso added.

"Like... the thin branches?" Saga asked, still staring over Tasso's shoulder. She started to walk towards the central trunk.

"What is so interesting down there?" Jemima asked, following.

"What?" Saga asked, distracted. The hooded figure disappeared into a crowd of people emerging from the trunk of the tree and Saga struggled to find him back.

"Saga are you even paying attention to us?" Tasso asked.

"I thought I saw Sidawi over there..." Saga murmured.

"Uhh... Who? Oh, Harmeet? The Prefect of Yeatwens house?" Tasso asked.

"Yeah," Saga said.

"Since when are we calling fourth year Prefects by their first names?" Jemima asked. "I mean, other than our own..."

"Sid's a friend... Well, no that's an exaggeration. The Harmeets own The Saffron Heart and well... He..." She didn't want to out Sidawi's secret. She knew that no one could know about his relationship with Ziva. "He was good to Navi and me... He's going to tutor Navi in the Balalaika."

"Ok…" Tasso said. "I'm still not seeing what the big deal is, so what if he's hanging around the Tree City?"

"Nothing… Really… But he said that he was staying in Nýr Ásgardr…"

"And we care that he lied, why?"

"Because he looked as though he was being secretive. Come on."

"How is he being secretive?" Tasso asked, trying to spot what Saga was looking for. "I mean, it's not like he has to answer to us or anything, right?"

"Right…" Saga said.

"Dinner here in town or do we go back to Nýr Ásgardr first?" Jemima asked as they gathered their belongings.

"Where would we go in Nýr Ásgardr?" Navi asked.

"The Kitty?" Tasso suggested. Navi and Saga looked at each other, then at the rest of the group. "Oh, right… Still banned?"

"Well," Saga murmured. "Yeah." During the previous half-term break, a group of Ljósálfar elves had pushed Navi out of line at the Rolly Polly Kitty Eatery and Saga had gotten into a fight with them when they'd manhandled the small elf. The lot of them had been taken in by the city guard and despite the guard being sympathetic to their plight, Navi and Saga had been banned from their favourite eatery in town. The lucuma pie was the best and their friends were starting to find the situation somewhat funny. Saga still thought it was unfair.

"Then here in the tree it is!" Jemima declared. "The Bore Tooth?"

"Isn't there anywhere else in this whole tree?" Saga asked.

"That we can afford?" Navi asked, looking anxiously into her coin purse.

"And is reputable?" Tasso added.

Jemima shrugged, her expression shifting from potential excitement to resignation. "Not really."

"There's a couple of places near the base that aren't half bad," Raphaella said walking into the room. "Perfectly respectable, just generally only known to the locals. Want a suggestion or two?"

"Sounds great," Jemima said looking at her aunt.

"Well, The Roots is pretty up and coming. Liked by a lot of the local kids too and there's Old Clementine's, that's pretty similar to your Rolly Polly Kitty. Personally, I would go with The Roots though. Good music there usually too. Just make sure that you make it to the port in time for the last flight to Nýr Ásgardr."

"We're just going to grab dinner," Jemima promised.

"Well, you kids have fun. You want to leave your bags here, go right ahead. "

"Thanks Aunt Raffi," Jemima said. "So, this Roots place?"

"Sounds good!" Tasso agreed.

~ * ~

"Ohh look, there's live music tonight!" Jemima exclaimed as they approached The Roots. The place was burrowed into a large root that extended out from the base of the Tree City and a line of people extended along the exterior, waiting to get in.

"We're never going to get in!" Tasso complained. "Not in time to make it to our ship…"

"No, look," Saga said. "It's a steady stream going in. We'll be fine!"

"Hmmm…" Tasso groused. "I can probably…"

"What about that place?" Saga suggested, pointing towards another place that people were going. A small sign was painted onto the root that ran atop what appeared to be a staircase leading down, beneath the root structure of the Tree City. People seemed to disappear into the depths of the place in small groups and there didn't appear to be a line to get in.

"What's it called?" Jemima asked. "My ancient Greek is a little lacking…"

They looked at each other but shrugged. Navi squinted at the characters painted on the root. "Ah… ga… No ge… see… loss. Ah-ge-see-loss! Or something like that…"

"Well, we're not going to get into The Roots tonight, so why not?" Tasso said.

"Let's go," Saga said leading the way. They descended the stairs, entering a narrow door that found them in a large subterranean room. The magic lights were dim, flickering to mimic candles around the cavernous room. The low murmur of conversation filled the space as a few people looked up at them, decided that they were of no interest and went back to their own drinks, food and conversations.

"There's a table," Navi declared, pushing through the crowd to the empty table she had spotted.

"They have lotus chips!" Tasso cried excitedly.

"Everywhere sells lotus chips," Jemima teased. "It's practically a crime not to sell lotus chips!"

"I'll go order," Saga said. "What do you want?"

"Cider!" They chorused.

"Jelly Melon, right?"

"D'uh!" Navi replied.

"Lotus chips!" Tasso added.

"Got ya!" Saga said, pointing at him in agreement.

"Pie!" Jemima suggested eagerly.

"I'll see!" Saga wove her way through the tables and chairs to the counter.

"Welcome to Agesilaus, what can I get for you?" the server asked.

"Well," Saga said searching the menu. "A pitcher of Jelly Melon and four glasses."

"Anything else?"

"A bowl of lotus chips, umm, do you have lucuma pie?"

The girl shook her head. "No, only place around here who does that is Old Clementine's. Can I make a few suggestions?"

"Go right ahead!"

The woman motioned to the menu board behind her. "There's Duffy's special, actually, I would totally go with Duffy's special if you don't know what you want."

"What's Duffy's special?"

"It's a share platter of just about everything on the menu."

Saga's eyes widened in delight. "Really? That sounds great!"

"Perfect... Still want that bowl of lotus chips?"

"Absolutely, you can never have too many chips... Especially with Tasso around... We're just over there," Saga pointed over to the table where the rest of the group was sitting. She paid and made her way back over.

"What'd you get?" Tasso asked excitedly.

"Don't worry, you got your chips," Saga said shaking her head. She sat down, just as a cloaked figure brushed past her, pushing her against the table. Saga turned to say something. "Sid?" she asked, recognising the half-cloak she had seen earlier in the day.

The figure said nothing as he hurried past her.

"Well, that's just rude," Jemima said, following the figure with her gaze. "You think that's Sidawi Harmeet?"

Saga watched the figure as he stopped by a gathering of musicians off to the side of a small stage. She saw him draw out an instrument, it was a balalaika, just like Sidawi played, but it didn't look like his. The instrument was dark in colour, almost black. Saga couldn't look away from it.

"Saga?" Jemima asked.

"Huh?" Saga asked looking back at her friends. "What?"

"Land of the living over here!" Navi declared waving her hand in Saga's face.

"Yeah, sure," Saga said, still eyeing the cloaked figure and his black balalaika.

"Hey, it's Sidawi!" Navi suddenly exclaimed and raised her hand, half standing in her seat. "Sidawi!" She called out. The figure flinched but didn't look up from tuning his instrument. "Huh... Maybe it's not..."

"No, it is," Saga said.

"You don't know that," Tasso said.

Their food was delivered, and all discussion of the cloaked figure was halted in favour of admiring the platters of food that seemed to take up most of their table. Tasso filled their glasses with the purplish jelly melon cider, his eyes wide as he stared at the food.

"You really have to admire his restraint," Saga said motioning to Tasso with a meatball coated in a sweet, sticky sauce.

Navi and Jemima nodded in agreement. "Really admirable," Navi agreed.

They tucked into the food and around them, music started to play. A small group had taken to the stage with a selection of instruments and were now playing. Saga still found the music here odd, but she had heard some of the tunes before on the phonograph at the house or when they were out in town. Sidawi's playing at The Saffron Heart had exposed her to even more.

"They're not bad," Jemima said waving a hand towards the group on stage.

They offered various sounds of agreement, their faces full of food. "Pass the chips, Tas!" Navi demanded as she tried to steal the bowl away from where he was hogging it before himself.

"Hey!" he exclaimed, trying to retain control of the bowl.

"Share!" Saga said, reaching over the table to dig into the bowl of chips.

"Hey!" Tasso protested again; his protests turning to squawks of indignation as Jemima's hands joined the assault.

The music died away, but the din of conversation filled the air once more. On the stage, the group was stepping down and a new one taking their place.

"You've spoken to Mistress Grunborg; do you know when the Tourney teams are being announced?" Tasso asked.

"Eager much?" Navi asked. "Why do you want to know?"

Tasso sighed. "My father made the tourney jousting team in first year. He expects the same from me..."

"And Tonya?" Jemima asked.

Tasso grimaced. "He couldn't care less what she does, apparently its family pride on the line..."

"Well, I know I'm not on the jousting team," Saga said, which resulted in the others laughing.

"I should hope not," Tasso said, "I don't think we can deal with another run of you in the ring..."

"I don't think I would live through another run!" Saga added sardonically. Just thinking about that traumatic run made her body hurt. "I don't understand the point of it..."

"This one would have thought that you were well acquainted with the point of jousting," Jemima said, licking her fingers from the meatball sauce and trying her best to look innocent.

"Oh ha, ha!" Saga spat sarcastically, even as she grimaced, not wanting to remember the fear she had felt before her joust or the feeling of the lance connecting with her body and then flying from Pingu's back. When she had landed, she'd barely been able to breathe and had not been able to move.

"Seriously though," Tasso said. He took a breath as to settle himself, "It's about overcoming fear, showing prowess in battle and..." Tasso talked with a mixture of excitement and obligation about the joust, but Saga thought that perhaps Tasso enjoyed it more than he was willing to let on. He probably just didn't appreciate the pressure put on him by his father.

"It really doesn't seem like that much fun," Navi said thoughtfully. "It's just a ploy to show off your manliness."

Tasso sputtered out protestations, but the three girls just laughed at him, agreeing with Navi.

"Well, I've never jousted for competition," Jemima said, "But I can see the connection between rider and horse. It's a partnership between the two."

"Exactly!" Tasso exclaimed.

A flute started to play, followed by a stringed instrument. In interest, Saga looked up. She was no music aficionado, but starting in the new term, she had music classes to take. The stringed instrument appeared to be the guitar like instrument they called lute. It seemed stubbier and rounder than a guitar and far bigger than a ukulele. The shape seemed more fluid compared to the instruments she was used to. It was the man though who drew her attention. He looked to be older than they were, maybe a few years out of school, though she was discovering that age and appearance was subjective in the Nine Realms, with many talking as though they had been around since before Ragnarök. His face. Where had she seen him before? She couldn't remember. It was like her head was full of cotton wool and they didn't even have cotton wool here.

The melody suddenly took on a morose timbre when a piccolo and a second stringed instrument joined in. She knew the sound of that instrument. She'd heard it before. She looked away from the naggingly familiar face and saw that a black balalaika in the hands of a hooded figure had taken centre stage. As the group played, several other heads looked up. She knew who was playing the black balalaika, but the name just wouldn't come to her.

"What's going on?" Navi asked looking around. "Saga?"

The music was enthralling, and Saga pushed her chair back. She stood up. Around the room, four other people were doing the same thing. The constant din of conversation ceased as Saga and the other four moved away from their tables and started to weave their ways through the mess of tables, chairs and people.

"Saga!" Jemima called.

Saga stopped at the base of the stage, an angel on either side of her and two more behind her. People were starting to talk quietly, pointing at them. A tug on Saga's arm had her looking over her shoulder at Jemima and realising that aside from the four angels that were as enthralled with the music as she was, a gathering of ethereal ghosts were crowding in around the stage. The angel to her left, a young man with copper flecked wings backed away suddenly with a gasp.

"Stop him," he gasped out, his panicked cry breaking through the haze. "Orson." She saw him tug at the arm of an older angel. "Stop him!"

"Sid!" Navi cried, waving at the stage.

Saga turned back to the stage and saw that the hood of the cloaked figure had fallen away from his face revealing what she had always expected. "Sidawi!"

The music washed over her once more. She shook her head, everything felt fuzzy, and she was having trouble thinking straight. "I... What...?"

Jemima reached for the young angel beside Saga. She heard the words, Jemima's concern. "Why are you affected and I'm not?" she asked him.

The angel with the copper flecked wings looked around at the gathered group. "We're... We're all angels of death..." He finally said. "Well, they are... I'm an apprentice..." He glanced down at Saga who was once again feeling the cotton wool thrall of Sidawi's music. "What about her?"

Jemima glanced at Saga then at the angel, "Valkyrie."

The man's clouded eyes widened in surprise and the news seemed to help clear the fog from his mind. "Valkyrie... Angels of death... and ghosts..."

"Lots and lots of ghosts..." Saga murmured, fighting to keep herself in the moment. Focusing as hard as she could on Jemima and the angel seemed to ground her, ever so slightly. The need to hear the words, understand them and process them, somehow stopping her from giving in to the cloudy feeling threatening to overtake her.

The song finished, the fog that had engulfed the angels and Saga seemed to lift as the last notes died away. Confusion set in as Orson almost fell into his younger companion. The other two angels disappeared, as though they couldn't stand the embarrassment of what had happened. The ghosts lingered longer, staring after Sidawi. Some even followed him, still lured by the haunting music.

"Saga?" Navi asked, tugging on her arm.

"Yeah?" Saga asked, still confused as she tried to figure out what to look at.

"What's going on?"

"I... I don't know..." Saga said. "Where's Sidawi gone?"

"There!" Navi said, pointing to the side of the stage where the group had disappeared to.

"Come on," Saga said, taking Navi by the arm to pull her through the gathering crowd.

Seeing them coming, Sidawi clipped his instrument case closed and pulled his hood up.

"Sidawi!" Saga called after him as he disappeared through the back entrance of the establishment.

"What's he doing?" Navi asked.

"I don't know..."

Saga stood there, staring after Sidawi. It wasn't until Jemima and Tasso rejoined them and pulled Saga away that she was able to look elsewhere. The cloudy feeling in her head was still there but was receding as they walked through town back to Jemima's aunts' place before getting their ship back to school.

COMING HOME

Morning was breaking over the horizon as the airship arrived in Nýr Ásgardr and people began disembarking. Students flooded out through the dock, hurrying away to their houses to get changed for the first day of the new semester. It would be a long day with the school assembly that night after classes and as long as Saga didn't make a repeat of last semester's first day of school detention, things should get off to a better start.

"Where are we going?" Navi asked Annis as they made their way through the throngs of people.

"Queenette for now to grab the rest of our stuff, apparently there should be information waiting for us there."

"I wonder where we're going to wind up..." Navi said nervously, wringing her hands together.

"It'll be fine," Saga said confidently hoping that Tremblay had managed to do as she had asked.

"Come on, we still have to get to our actual houses and then figure out what classes we have first," Annis said.

"We're off this way," Tasso said, turning in the opposite direction of the girls with Edun. Edun had to return to Knightrich to find out where he was going, and Tasso actually lived there.

"Meet you at Jimpsee?" Saga asked Jemima.

"Nah, I'll come with you," she said, pushing her bag between two groups of bystanders, seeing each other for the first time in a month. Annis, Navi and Saga followed in her wake.

They half ran, half walked through town, dodging carts, market sellers setting up for the day and other students hurrying to their residences before the start of the day. Queenette Dormitory was a dance of chaos of incoming students returning from holidays and outgoing students who had stayed in town and were now returning to their regular houses. Caoimhe ran past them, shouting her goodbyes as she caught the door before it could close. Ellora was doing her best to direct the traffic and return her house to order, especially with the overflowing basket of misplaced lost property thanks to the pilfering of their house ghost.

Jemima followed Saga through the halls of the dormitory, and they made their way into the long room where the first-year girls slept. Saga bypassed her own bed and followed Navi to hers, where a thick folder awaited her attention.

"Navi can't do it," she said holding it up for them to see.

"Do you want one of us to read it?" Saga asked her.

Navi held the folder out to her. "Yes." Saga reached out to take the folder from her and Navi suddenly pulled it out of her reach. "No." She sighed. "Navi doesn't know." She hugged the folder tight against her. "Navi is scared."

They waited patiently as the chaos of the first day moved on around them. Navi looked down at the folder against her chest and stood there, not saying anything.

"Where are you going?" Annis cried, rushing into the room. She paused. "Why are you all just standing there?"

"Navi's nervous about her placement," Jemima said.

"Where is it?" Annis asked, glancing over her sister's shoulder. "You haven't opened it!" She exclaimed.

"Where are you going?" Navi asked in a small voice.

"Here," Annis announced. "I'm staying here at Queenette."

"That wouldn't be so bad, would it?" Saga asked her, hoping that Navi wouldn't be left staying in the large dormitory with their awful house ghost.

"Give it here," Annis said, trying to take the folder from Navi.

"No!" Navi cried. "Navi will do it!"

"Well?" Annis said impatiently.

With a petulant sigh, Navi flipped the folder open and stared down at the papers inside it.

"What does it say? " Saga asked trying to peer over it and read upside down.

Annis squealed in delight. "Jimpsee! You're going to Jimpsee house," she cried excitedly.

"Jimpsee..." Navi said in a hoarse croak. "But... I... How?"

Saga breathed a sigh of relief. Tremblay Jimpsee had come through for her and Navi in the end.

"I wonder where Edun is going to wind up..." Jemima said thoughtfully.

"He'll land on his feet," Annis said confidently. "You three had better get moving if you're going to make it back to Jimpsee before classes begin.

"Oh crap!" Saga exclaimed, racing off to her bed to hurriedly pack the last few items into her bag. She looked around anxiously, hoping that nothing was missing, but with everything Cordelia Queenette had misplaced over the last month, she couldn't tell.

"Let's go!" Jemima said.

"See you later Annis!" Saga called. Navi hugged her sister, reached for her own meagre possessions and hurried after them.

The door to Jimpsee house was flung open before they could even reach the door handle. Tremblay hovered there, a wicked grin upon his ethereal face. "Welcome home," he exclaimed, the door opening wider to permit them entry to the house.

"Thanks Tremblay," Saga said.

"And tell Navi, welcome."

Saga looked over her shoulder at Navi and said, "Tremblay says to tell you Welcome."

"He's here?" she asked.

Saga nodded. "He's always here," she leaned over and said quietly. "He's also a bit of a perv, just a warning."

"He's what?" Navi asked in horror.

"Hey!" Tremblay exclaimed in disbelief. "I am not a perv!"

"Whatever you say," Saga said.

"There they are," Tymberlee announced coming out of the main living room of the house. "Navi, welcome to Jimpsee house."

"Thank you," Navi said in a soft voice.

"Here," Tymberlee said, placing something in her hand. "I hope that you'll wear it with your Dorbe Manor pin."

Navi looked down at the small shield shaped pin in her hand, embossed with the fire breathing chimera of Jimpsee house. "I will," she said.

"Come on," Siobhan exclaimed coming down the stairs. "Are you guys coming up or what?"

"Right, you three do still have to get ready for class," Tymberlee said more seriously. "Come on."

She led the way upstairs and when Saga and Jemima made to go to their room on the second floor the faerie girl tutted and motioned them towards the stairs to the third floor. "There's been some rearrangements," she declared, hustling the group up the stairs. They could hear the rest of the house following them.

"What is going on?" Navi asked in a whisper.

Saga and Jemima glanced at each other and shrugged.

"It's great," Tremblay said, hovering at the top of the stairs, "absolutely great! You're going to love it!"

"Shut up Tremblay!" Tymberlee ordered before Saga could tell the ghost off. Saga looked at the prefect in surprise and the older faerie girl said, "Yes, I can see and hear him when I wear my prefect's badge," she explained. "He has a reputation for being a pain..."

"Actually... Cordelia Queenette could give him a run for his money..." Saga muttered.

"Old Queenie up to her old tricks again?" Tremblay asked. "Girl always did have a little confusion as to what was hers and what wasn't..." he added pensively.

"Is that what happened at Queenette?" Tymberlee exclaimed. "The little thief!"

"Guess who lived at Queenette before becoming our Prefect?" Onorati asked coming up behind them. "You ready Tym?"

"If that ghost would get out of our way, yes!" Tymberlee said as she led the way through the small study area that formed the mezzanine area of the third floor. Three doors extended off the space, if Saga remembered correctly, one of them lead to the room Onorati shared with Siobhan and the other was Tymberlee's room. As prefect, she warranted a room to herself.

"What are we doing up here?" Jemima asked, looking around confused. The semester before, they hadn't wandered up to the senior's floor. There really hadn't been any point to after they had been given their house tour.

"Well," Tymberlee said stopping outside one door. "The house is rated for twelve residents, but we usually stick with eleven, allowing the prefect a room to themselves."

"Navi is sorry."

"No, no, no!" Tymberlee hastily added. "We regret nothing... But quite frankly, I did figure that you would have no interest in sharing a room with me and having you share with Perdita would make a mess with where to put Percival... Well, anyways, we found ourselves a glorious solution!"

"Oh?" Saga asked, wondering what she and Jemima were doing there.

"Well, we thought you three would like to share," Tymberlee announced.

"And I think we all know that your room was not going to work out for longer than you already did last semester," Onorati added. "That wasn't fair on any of you girls."

"Go on, open the door," Tymberlee said, her wings fluttering in excitement.

Jemima frowned. "But this is your room."

"Just open the door!" Emory groused. Saga turned. She hadn't noticed him amongst all the other residents of Jimpsee house. His eyes were set on her, and Saga couldn't help but look away. Things had been awkward between them since Valaskjálf. Whatever had happened at The Saffron Heart had not helped with any future hope of repairing their previous friendship.

"Go ahead girls," Tymberlee instructed.

Navi tried to shrink away from the focus of the others, but Saga stepped forward and opened the door. It swung inwards to reveal a large room, far larger than the small space she and Jemima had shared the semester before.

In the far-left corner was a bunk bed that had a bookshelf adjoining it, serving as the side table for both the lower and upper beds. Across from them was a single bed with a small side table with open shelves beside it. At the end of the single bed was a large wardrobe with space for the owner's trunk next to it. Behind the door they found another two wardrobes and space for the additional two trunks. Unlike their old room, there were no desks. Instead, the centre of the room featured a large coffee table surrounded by comfortable looking, colourful cushions that looked as though it could easily sit about six.

"Wow..." Saga breathed out.

"It's... It's amazing..." Jemima said.

"But... It was your room..." Navi added.

Tymberlee waved the comment away nonchalantly. "Honestly, it was always too much space for me and the room downstairs will do me just fine."

"As you can see, it's set out a bit differently, but that has a lot to do with all the houses rearranging to fit in the Dorbe Manor students."

"And we just couldn't fit three of everything in here," Mannish added. The lanky Werehyena leaned against the doorframe.

"Didn't stop us from trying," Percival added.

"When did you guys do this?" Saga asked looking around.

They all started talking at once until they heard a sob. Silence descended upon the room as they looked around the room trying to identify the person who was crying.

"Navi?" Emory said with uncharacteristic empathy and gentleness.

She sniffed, her hands swiping furiously at her face, trying to wipe away her streaming tears.

"What's wrong?" Jemima asked, "do you not like it?"

Another wet sniffle and Navi exclaimed, "No, no, Navi loves it."

"Then what is wrong?" Siobhan asked in her thick Celtic brogue.

"Navi is so happy!" she managed to get out and burst into a fresh bout of tears. She flung her arms around Tymberlee's neck, crying out her thanks in between gasping sobs.

Tymberlee awkwardly patted the small girl's back. "You're very welcome."

"It's the hope," Tremblay said, "That you three will be very happy here for the rest of your schooling."

"Thank you," Saga said to him, then looked at the rest of them, "All of you, thank you."

"Ok everyone," Tymberlee said awkwardly trying to extract herself from Navi. "Get dressed for classes," she motioned to the table in the centre of the room. "Everyone's class schedules are waiting for you in your rooms. Try to remember that there is an assembly tonight. Also," she looked back at the three girls, "All of you have music lessons starting in the afternoons from off next week, you need to return the form in your folders as to what instrument you're taking."

"Harp," Jemima said easily.

"Balalaika," Navi added, holding the instrument up for their Prefect to see.

"Pan flute," Saga looked away as she said it. She still felt ridiculous about the music requirement and for the first time, thought about what Edun had said about joining the Pentathlon team. She also didn't want to catch sight of Navi's instrument so similar to Sidawi's. The thing creeped her out. She just wished she knew what it was about balalaika music that seemed to space her out.

"Great," Tymberlee exclaimed. "Ok, go on everyone, breakfast in ten!"

It turned out that their class schedule was the reverse of their first semester schedule and from Jimpsee House they were able to head straight to the training grounds for weapons training.

Astrid stood in the centre of the field, hands behind her back as students trickled onto her field for the first class of the day. When no one stopped talking, excited to see friends again for the first time in a month, Astrid gave them two minutes before she called attention to herself.

"Alright," she declared. "I'm sure that everyone is aware that later in the semester selected students will travel to Yggdrasil City for the inter-school tourney. Much of those decisions will be based upon your Tourney scores from last semester and from further competition this semester. In this class I do not want to hear about Tourney."

"But you're a major decider in regard to who's on the team right?" Tonya asked. "Surely you're able to provide some indication as to who is on the team and who isn't."

Astrid paused and Saga witnessed her pleasant expression morph into a frown before turning her steely eyes upon the faerie girl. "That is the other question that I will not be entertaining. I will ignore it this time," she glanced towards Saga, "And any time I heard it during the break, but," she walked down the line of students. "From this point forward anyone who asks that question regarding the Inter-School Tourney will find themselves not only off the list, but the more frequently I am asked, the more frequently the penalty will grow, starting with cleaning all the staves, sharpening all the swords, restringing the bows and fletching the arrows. Any questions?" Saga looked up and down the line of students, trying to see if anyone would take Astrid up on her offer. No one did. "Ok, everyone get a bow."

~ * ~

"Anyone else wondering who the new Planarography teacher is?" Tasso asked as they approached the circular classroom at the base of one of the towers that accented Sorosian Hall. The hall had once been the manor house of the city's founders, but was now the main building for the school, where the majority of the classrooms were.

"No idea, the schedule didn't say," Jemima said, pulling her own schedule from her bag.

"Pity we still have Master Berfelan for World History," Saga muttered.

"And right before assembly too..." Navi said, peering into the planarography classroom. "Odin's beard!" she cursed, popping back into the hall and hoping that she had not been seen.

"What?" Tasso asked trying to pear around her.

"Umm..." Navi said, biting her lip. She sidestepped out of the way allowing the others to look in.

Saga's eyes widened in horror at what she saw, and like Navi, she tried to duck back out of the doorway before being seen.

"What's he doing here?" Saga hissed at the others.

"This one doesn't know," Navi hissed back.

"Miss Carolle." The voice from inside growled. "And I presume Miss Jensyn, Miss Dove, Mr Bonnedras and Mr Harding." Saga felt a pang at the mention of Emory's name, but of course it had to be this teacher who would start things off on the wrong foot. "I suggest that you lot get in here and take your seats."

They looked at each other quietly before stepping into the classroom one by one. "Yes Master Berfelan," Saga said, looking at her feet as she made her way to her regular seat. So, she didn't just have to make it through World History without getting detention, but Planarography too.

The grizzly old man waved students in as they all stopped in the doorway, confused by the sight of the old man in the circular classroom. "In," he ordered. "We will begin this semester with looking at the former realms of the gods. I see that last semester you looked at the nine realms and I won't be repeating the information regarding Asgard that would have been covered by Master Iacono last semester." He inserted a crystal into the centre of the central desk that dominated the middle of the room and a map exploded into life above them. "Asgard exists on the same plane of existence as what other realms?"

Hands raised around him, and his eagle eyes glanced around the room. His gaze hovered over Saga, who was waiting quietly for someone else to answer first. He finally selected Essa Izadi on the far side of the room.

"Wākea," she said.

"Good, the realm ruled by the god of the same name. Anyone else?"

Lorcan Kavanaugh raised his hand, his stout leprechaun form requiring him to wave his hand in order to be noticed. "Tír na nÓg."

"Good," Berfelan announced. "Something from this side of the room?" he asked waving towards where Saga was sitting. Jemima's arm was raised in eagerness, but as Saga had feared, he called on her. "Miss Carolle?"

She looked up at the map before them. What did she know about these other realms? She barely understood the Nine Realms and now she was once again put on the spot by Berfelan. She looked up as inspiration struck. Eyes wide with excitement she said, "Mount Olympus."

The look on Berfelan's face was priceless as he tried to extract another realm from the rest of the class. He took far too much pleasure in catching her out in front of the whole class. Saga settled back into her seat and reminded herself that she just had to keep her head down and do her work where Berfelan was concerned.

The afternoon was excruciating. After leaving Planarography, the entire group, including Master Berfelan, had made their way to his classroom on the second floor of Sorosian Hall for their history lesson. Somehow, Saga wound up with Berfelan right behind her. She could feel his eyes on the back of her neck as they made their way up the grand staircase.

Jemima and Tasso eyed one another around Saga as they walked. Saga was grateful that no one said anything though. Something about Master Berfelan made her uneasy. He watched her, even when they weren't in class, he watched her, whether it was at school assemblies, tourney events or just out and about in town. When she looked around, he would be watching her. Then in class, he seemed to always try to catch her out. At least she had made it through the first class without saying anything stupid.

Still, despite how uncomfortable he made her and his apparent need to aggravate her, she couldn't help but think about what Tasso had told her when she had been laid up in the hospital after the fight with Master Iacono in Valaskjálf the semester before. Berfelan had carried her unconscious body out of the hall while the others had tended to the critically injured Navi. Saga stopped short, Master Berfelan colliding with her from behind.

"Is there something the matter Miss Carolle?" Berfelan asked, almost snarling as he held his papers tight, trying to ensure that they didn't fall from their precarious tower in his hands.

Saga swallowed hard but shook her. "No, Master Berfelan," she said, except something was very, very wrong. She had just remembered where she'd seen the lute player at the Agesilaus and the thought made her blood run cold. She looked furtively towards her friends, but they were already making their way into the World History classroom.

"Then get a move on," Master Berfelan ordered.

She glanced surreptitiously over her shoulder at the grizzled old man. Trudging into Master Berfelan's usual classroom, with him right behind her, she heard him mutter about useless schoolgirls and the uselessness of having to change rooms between classes, but that wasn't the worst thing. The worst thing was that maybe she wasn't paranoid or delusional, because Sid's lute playing friend, had been the same man she'd seen talking to Vali in the marketplace.

~ * ~

"Who wants what bed?" Jemima asked that night as they entered their brand-new bedroom.

Navi looked around, bewildered by the choices. Saga, used to taking whatever she was told to take, shrugged. "No idea..."

"Navi doesn't mind," Navi added, looking between the two.

Saga put her book bag down on the table in the centre of the room and the others followed suit. She turned on the spot, taking in the whole room. Their trunks had been brought upstairs and someone had pushed them in beside the large wardrobes. "We can follow our trunks..." she suggested.

"Good idea," Jemima said, looking around and locating hers next to the wardrobe by the single bed. "I'm over here," she declared.

"Top or bottom?" Saga asked Navi.

"Bottom," Navi said, "You're taller than me and will hit your head on that top bunk every day!"

"But what about..." Jemima started, before pausing, not sure how to bring up Saga's paralysing fear of heights.

Saga waved her off. "Not my first top bunk," she stated, "but thanks."

"So... How are things done here?" Navi asked, going over to her trunk to start unpacking. Books made their way to the bottom shelves of the bookshelf beside her bed. On the other side of the room, Jemima was doing the same thing, placing her books on the open shelving of her bedside table.

"We have free study until dinner, then assembly," Jemima explained, moving on to arranging clothes inside the wardrobe. "Saga!" She suddenly called, turning around to find Saga rearranging things inside her trunk.

Saga looked up guiltily. "What?"

"Are you going to unpack?" she asked, watching her as though she already knew the answer.

Carefully and with purpose, Saga retrieved her schoolbooks from the trunk, taking them over to the bookshelf and arranging them on the higher shelves. "Yeah," she croaked out. "See!"

Jemima scowled slightly as Navi looked between the two girls, her gaze shifting from Saga to Jemima and back again. She had heard the rumours of Saga not unpacking the semester before and knew that it was something that had grated on Jemima's nerves.

Trying to distract herself from Jemima's ire and Navi's confusion, Saga looked around the room, confusion settling in. Where was Tremblay? They were settling in, he should be here, offering his own advice, unwanted as it might be. He was a known perv and he wasn't there. Finally, she shrugged and figured he must be hassling Tymberlee.

Making their way back from Jimpsee House to Sorosian Hall, Saga could barely keep her eyes open, and she realised that back at the room, she'd lost the opportunity to tell the Navi and Jemima about her realisation She should have tried harder to sleep on the ship from Yggdrasil City but sleep and travel had never been something that had gone together for her. She was feeling the effects of it now and she was exhausted.

They took their seats in the auditorium and when directed, stood to sing the school song before Headmaster Gotts took to the stage to welcome them back for the new Semester. He spoke of the school's mission to educate them and prepare them for the world, the fourth-year exams and of the most interest to everybody, the upcoming inter-school Tourney.

As soon as the event was mentioned, voices broke out throughout the auditorium as students stated talking about their chances of making it onto the school team.

"I have been asked by Mistress Grunborg and Master Everard to inform you all that there will be no tolerance to their being asked about your individual likeliness to make the team."

"I'll third that," Master Toshiji, the stable master and riding teacher called out.

"I know that excitement about the upcoming event has been and will likely be the talk of the school until the event. I will remind you all though, that first and foremost, we are an institution of learning. You are here to learn and to prepare yourselves for the future. The teams will not be announced until after our third Tourney this semester, so please take the time to lead balanced days. Take care of yourselves and set your priorities, not only for each day, but also for the whole semester."

He finished with the announcement of the construction of a memorial for the students lost at Dorbe Manor and his hopes that the survivors would spearhead the project. Around the room, the scattered students, identifiable by their double house pins, seemed to seek each other out, a sense of comfort from the announcement overcoming them.

INTERMEZZO

After classes were done for the day, life didn't end in the school buildings around town. The school Were Council met and the Vampires came out at night, but most importantly, students took to the practice fields to train, they saw to their animal handling projects and they went to classes necessitated by their specific learning programs.

For Saga, that was music. A group of about twenty students gathered outside a third-floor tower room of Sorosian Hall. They were a mixed group of Angels, elves and even one leprechaun.

"There you are," Edun said, coming up beside her,

"Here I am," she said looking at the others, all clutching at pan-flutes. She had been dreading this day.

"Have you been doing those exercises I suggested?" he asked.

Saga nodded. "Yeah... But I still sound like a strangled squirrel when I try anything."

"What does a strangled squirrel sound like?" he asked deadpan.

"You're about to find out," Saga muttered as the group filed into the classroom.

Unlike the planarography classroom on the ground floor, this room had no desks. The chairs were set up in a semi-circle, each accompanied by a stand just large enough to place their music books. Saga followed Edun and they took seats in the back row.

"Good afternoon everyone," a squat man said walking to the only stand that stood alone without a chair. It was also placed upon a small block like a mini stage. "Hurry, hurry, take your seats. For those of you who don't know me, I am Arias Aneesh and I'll be your instructor." He looked around the room, stepping back down from the little platform and walking slowly from one side of the room to the other. He eyed everyone in the room, taking particular interest in the new first years. "And given those who are starting in second semester and at pan-flute to boot, I will guess you are the 'we had to take music' bunch and that you're just bucking for the chance to drop this class." About five of them had the good sense to look abashed at this statement, obviously he was used to his students not wanting to be there. "Well, we will be stuck together for the next two years so we might as well make the most of it. Let's start with a simple question, who can read sheet music?" The only one who raised their hand was an angel girl Saga recognised but couldn't put a name to. "Brilliant, better than last year! Well then, before we can learn to play, you must know what it is you are doing Ok, first years pair up with a senior and let's see what we can do."

Saga frowned at the pages of the music book Edun had told her to buy back in Yggdrasil city. She had done music lessons at her old school, but it had always been one of those classes that she put up with. She knew that the little notes stood for A's, B's, C's, D's and so forth and that they correlated to the pipes on the instrument... and that was where it ended.

"Here," Edun said, changing the page of her book to one that displayed a picture of a pan flute with each pipe labelled with a letter. Around them, tentative blows were being made, some were loud and sent the unwary flying from their seats in shock. Others were like long, choking, gasping breaths that could barely make a squeak. "Give me a C," he instructed.

"Which one?" Saga asked staring at the image of the eighteen pipes, three of which were identified as Cs.

"That doesn't matter," Edun said, catching the look on her face though he sighed and pointed to the one on the furthest edge of the image. "Start there," he suggested.

Saga took a deep breath, eyed the dark elf out of the corner of her eye and blew. A gasping, rattling sound erupted from the instrument and sent the second-year girl on her other side flying from her seat in fright.

"What was that?"

Edun leaned around Saga to look at the girl. "Sorry Nassima."

She rolled her eyes as she hauled herself to her feet. ""No... It's fine," she groused as she searched the floor for her own instrument. "I should have expected it and avoided sitting near the first year."

"I'm really sorry," Saga said, before looking over her shoulder at Edun. "Someone promised me that this would be easy."

"It is!" Edun exclaimed. "Come on, give it another go."

"Less power," Nassima suggested.

"Right," Saga sighed. "Ok... Here I go..." She raised the instrument to her mouth and wrapped her lips around the pipe, then blew.

"No, no," Nassima said, taking the instrument and holding it away from Saga's mouth. "You're not blowing a blow dart, blow on it like you're cooling a hot drink or food."

By the end of the class and with much patience from Edun and Nassima, Saga could blow the scales across the instrument, something most of the new students in the room were getting a handle on.

"Ok, I want everyone to take this piece of music and at a minimum, write down the corresponding note on the sheet music. If you can, I want you to learn the piece as well."

Saga trudged out of the classroom, the pan flute packed away in its protective pouch. She looked around, wondering where Jemima and Navi might be. They too had been scheduled for their music classes, but as they were all doing their own thing in terms of their instrument selections, she had no idea where they were. Tasso, a faerie had no music class, but was either out practicing his jousting or maybe doing homework from his Arcana class, the mandatory class faeries and magically inclined elves did.

"Saga!" She turned to find Edun pushing past their classmates to catch up to her. He threw out apologies at anyone that called him out on his behaviour, "Wait up."

She slowed her pace and waited for Edun to catch up. "What?" she asked.

"You didn't seem all that confident with that assignment," he said as they headed towards the stairs.

Saga shrugged. "Music isn't my thing... I'll figure it out..."

"Want some help?" he asked.

"There's nothing in this world that is going to make this make sense," Saga muttered, staring down at the music book in her hands.

"Why don't I come over and help?" Edun asked, trying to keep up with her as her pace quickened on the way down the grand staircase.

"Not tonight," she said and looked up just in time to catch a crestfallen look on his face that he quickly smoothed back to his standard impassive expression. "I'll take you up on it," she said quickly, "But I want to get a hang on reading the music first and maybe try some things out on my own, practice what you've already told me."

He nodded. "Ok, sure. No problem," he said, still walking with her.

As they approached the clock tower at the centre of the town square, Saga expected Edun to say his goodbyes and head for his own house, except now that she thought about it, she had no idea where he had been placed in the aftermath of the Dorbe disaster. "Where are you this semester?" she asked, "Knightrich?"

"Uh, no, Warlins," he said.

"That's down that way, right?" she asked pointing down a street that led directly to Knightrich, but from there it would be easy enough to get to Warlins house.

"Actually, I've noticed that it's quicker going down that way," he said, not looking at her as he pointed down the street Jimpsee House was located on. Having run around town with reckless abandon, Saga highly doubted that going via Jimpsee was the faster route to Warlins House, which was in the opposite direction.

"Really?" She said.

"Yeah," he said as they continued on in a comfortable silence, neither looking at each other as they walked.

The door to Jimpsee House was clear before them when Edun spoke again. "How is Navi settling in here?" he asked.

"Good," Saga said. "She's sharing with me and Jemima."

Edun frowned as he looked up at the window that had once looked into her room. "Isn't that room awfully small?"

"It is," Saga admitted. Edun had seen the room the semester before when Jimpsee house had taken Navi in, in the immediate aftermath of the fire. The girl had spent the rest of the semester sleeping on a cot situated in the tight space between Saga's and Jemima's beds. There had been little space to move, but neither girl had regretted sharing the space with their friend. "That's why this semester Tymberlee moved us upstairs to a larger room."

"Really?" He asked. "That's..."

"Really nice," Saga said. "It's been a change but it's a lovely room that the others put together just for us!" She looked up at the building that she now called home. "It's funny you know..."

"What is?"

"When we packed up for the end of semester, I had this feeling that I would not be returning to that room again... I took it as a bad sign, that I had done something wrong and that all of this would go away... It never occurred to me that the three of us would be starting on something new together."

"And now?" Edun asked.

"Now?" she echoed. "Now I can see forever in that space." She shook herself off and turned to him. "What about you? How are things at Warlins?"

Edun shrugged. "Getting to know a new crowd. It's not bad. This one only has one roommate compared to three at Dorbe. It's all very quiet really, it's taking some getting used to really..."

"Well, you're always welcome in the madhouse of Jimpsee when you need some noise... Plus, it's almost impossible to stop Mannish from trying to feed you."

Edun chuckled. "I might just take you up on that sometime," he said. "I should go. It's almost dinner time."

"Thanks for your help today," Saga said before he could leave. He nodded and walked away, glancing over his shoulder to watch her enter the house. Saga caught him looking at her and watched as he hurriedly turned his gaze away and almost scurried down the street and out of sight. What was going on with him?

Saga let herself into the house. Smells of dinner cooking instantly assaulted her nose, and it wasn't a good smell today. Something was burning and the scent of over-boiled vegetables seemed to permeate the air.

In the living area, the twins Percival and Perdita were working on homework while obviously trying to cover their sensitive noses. Tymberlee was pacing, looking every so often at Onorati, before they both turned on Siobhan.

"You can fix this right?" Tymberlee asked.

"What?" the stout girl exclaimed jumping from the sudden attention of the two older girls, anxiety clouding her features.

"You can fix this," Onorati repeated.

The leprechaun girl shook her head. "That I doubt," she said.

"Wish us better food," Vespers suggested from where he lurked in a dark corner of the room.

"Where's Manish?" Saga asked, taking note of the unfolding drama and glad that Edun had not taken her up on her offer to join them for dinner.

"The blasted hyena got himself detention," Tymberlee almost growled, "and we have the backup cook today."

"He's not supposed to do more than prep for Mannish... Apparently, there's a good reason for that..." Onorati finished for the frantic prefect.

Tymberlee looked ready to pull her hair out, but stopped when she realised who it was that had actually asked about Mannish. "How was your music lesson?"

"When can I drop it?" Saga asked hopefully.

"Third year," Siobhan said.

"Or...." Vespers started.

"Don't say it!" Saga exclaimed, pointing at the vampire. "Just don't say it. Where are Navi and Jemima?"

"Upstairs, the burning smells... they weren't good for young Navi," Tymberlee said. "Emory disappeared to his room too."

"I have to admit, this isn't doing me any good either..." Onorati said. Onorati and Tymberlee had worked their Arcana at the fire scenes, including Dorbe

Manor the semester before. "Let's get out of here, we can take everyone out to dinner at the night market..."

"Or we can just go our own ways," Vespers suggested.

Tymberlee nodded, "Let's go. The house fund will pay for whatever you decide upon."

~ * ~

Thwack!

Staves collided as Saga and Navi circled each other. Their eyes focused intently on the face of their opponent. Saga breathed heavily as she waited, trying to spot a potential opening knowing that Navi was doing the same to her.

Saga spun her staff after several moments of neither of them making a move. Navi took the bait, coming in low for a strike to Saga's knee. The tail end of the spin caught the end of Navi's, deflecting the attack.

"Tricky!" she said, "Navi likes!"

Saga laughed, following through with a jab towards Navi's throat. She stepped back, the tip of her staff appearing from nowhere to defend the delicate flesh of her throat. She spun, her lightning speed taking her out of Saga's field of vision as she tried to come at her from the rear.

Knowing that she couldn't match the smaller girl's speed, Saga stabbed out behind her and the squeak of surprise and the clash of wood on wood told her that the move had worked. The moment of distraction allowed Saga to turn and once again they were face to face.

"Looking good," Sidawi said from the doorway.

"Sid!" Navi exclaimed, dropping her guard. Having not agreed to end the bout, Saga stepped in, raising the staff and moving for a strike to the side of Navi's head that stopped millimetres away from her white hair.

"Wha!" the girl cried in surprise, "Saga, that's not fair!"

"You let Sid distract you," Saga said with a shrug. "Sid," she added with a nod in his direction. She glanced towards the instrument case in his hands, it looked like his regular case, but did that mean his old balalaika was in there or the strange black one?

"Saga," he said with a curt nod. He glanced at her only for a moment before turning his attention back to Navi. "You ready for that lesson?" Saga frowned. Was he avoiding her now?

"Yes!" she exclaimed. "We were just about finished, weren't we?"

Saga nodded slowly. Did she really want to leave Navi and Sidawi alone together?. "Yeah, go ahead. I've got some word conjugations to do before languages today anyway." She said finally. She passed Sidawi. "We missed catching up with you in Yggdrasil City. The new band you're playing with. They're good, very... enthralling."

"Yggdrasil City?" He asked. She could see his eyes darting back and forth between her and Navi, as though trying to decide if he should try to lie or not. After a panicked moment he shook his head. "Uhh, yeah. Tight schedule." He said, then turned to Navi, "Ready?" he pressed. The small dark elf nodded and followed Sidawi into the house as he struck up a conversation with her about the piece of music he wanted to look at.

Saga stood there, staring at the two of them as they disappeared from sight. Something odd was going on with him and she bet it had to do with that new friend of his, the lute player and his new balalaika.

Later, when she came downstairs, Saga found the two packing away their balalaikas. Onorati was sitting in the room having obviously been watching them practice. Saga stepped into the living room on her way through to the dining room for breakfast.

"You going to eat with us, Sid?" Onorati asked, "you're more than welcome. Mannish always has too much."

"Mannish is only a second year, right? Why's he handling your kitchen? Don't you get someone in?" he asked. Part of boarding at Toserra Sorose included the provision of all breakfasts and dinners. Nothing stopped a student stockpiling for lunch, but essentially, they were on their own then. As such each house had a cook in the employ of the school who took care of the provided meals.

"We do," Onorati explained, "But Mannish gets in there as often as he can. Honestly, I don't think our cook does much more than the prep because Mannish seems to always be in there."

"He can cook really good!" Navi added. "Way better than our old cook at Dorbe."

"And don't get me started on the back up cook," Tymberlee growled. It was over a week later, still the smell of the burned food lingering in the kitchen and throughout the house. Between airing the house out and an almost sickening amount of herbs brought in to add their aroma to the mess.

"And just for that Navi, you can ask me for absolutely anything," Mannish said poking his head out from the dining area. "Breakfast is served."

Navi glanced at Saga and in unison they turned to the grinning Werehyena. "Lucuma pie!" they cried.

He sighed dramatically. "I don't even know why I asked!" he said, slinking back into the kitchen.

Feet on the stairs let them know that others were coming down, "Did I hear something about pie?" Jemima asked, rushing into the room.

"Mannish is going to make Navi pie," Navi explained excitedly.

"We can have pie here?" Jemima asked.

"Once," Mannish shouted from the kitchen. "Once. Are you guys coming?"

The group started to file into the kitchen, but as Saga passed Sidawi she peered into his instrument case, where the balalaika was nestled into soft velvet. It was his standard brown wood one, the one she usually saw him playing when at The Saffron Heart.

"How many instruments do you have?" Saga asked, peering into the case.

Sidawi slammed the case shut before he looked up at her. "Just the one," he said hastily.

"Oh..."

"Really?" Navi asked, looking back at him, "We could have sworn we saw you in Yggdrasil city with this amazing black one."

"I doubt that," Sidawi said curtly, standing up in a hurry. "Breakfast girls?"

"Yes," Navi said, "but are you sure? It was really weird, Saga and a bunch of Angels of Death got entranced by the music."

"And the ghosts," Saga added, following Sidawi as he tried to lead the way.

"And the ghosts," Navi repeated.

"Sounds like you girls had an eventful trip," Sidawi said. They strode into the dining room, Navi still talking animatedly about the scene at Agesilaus. Emory, often distant with Saga, seemed to be listening in and much to her surprise took his seat beside her.

"Like that night at the restaurant?" he asked, leaning in close so that he could whisper.

Saga glanced at him, before glancing towards Sidawi. She nodded. "Yeah, but worse..."

"What do you mean?" he asked.

"I... I couldn't stop myself, I just..." she shook her head. "I don't know. The music just washed over me, and I could barely think..."

Emory looked across the table towards Sidawi. He watched the older boy as he chatted away with Navi, Onorati and Tymberlee. The elf was one of the top students in the school, his status as house Prefect of Yeatwens House was a testament to that fact. His family was highly regarded in Nýr Ásgardr and as Ljósálfar, they held an additional position of status.

"It was a different instrument though," Saga added, pushing her food around on her plate. She would pick something up then put it back down again, the thoughts in her head distracting her from her breakfast.

"What do you mean?"

79

There was something comfortable about talking this out with Emory and she was tempted to answer, but then she saw him sitting with Bindi Billingsley and their parents at The Saffron Heart as their engagement was being discussed. The talk with him was like the semester before when she had been able to confide in him and then she remembered that they had barely spoken at the end of the semester. She bit her lip and debated her answer and wanted to kick herself when instead of telling him about the odd black balalaika, she said, "How's Bindi?"

Emory choked on his toast and dropped the rest of the piece to his plate. Out of the corner of her eye, Saga could see him staring at her. "What?" he managed to choke out.

"Aren't you two together?" she asked, pushing her eggs around until they mingled with the spinach and mushrooms, she had selected.

"Together? Me and Bindi?" He scoffed. "By the dark moon, no! My parents might want us to, but there's no way I'm taking Bindi Billingsley as my mate, not that it's any of your business!" Emory shoved his chair back. "I'm going to get my books," He said to Tymberlee, then stormed out of the room.

"What was that?" Navi mouthed across the table, but Saga shook her head not able to answer.

Various people around the table eyed her for an explanation, but Saga instead stared at her plate, which was now a mess of food that had been endlessly swirled around while they'd been talking. She pushed it away. "I think I'm going to get ready," She said softly, before escaping from the room and the questioning eyes of everyone there.

"Stupid, stupid, stupid," Saga muttered to herself as she let the door slam shut on her room. She was so angry at herself. Emory had willingly talked to her, and she'd had a chance to bring him back to the group only for her big mouth to get in her way and say something so incredibly stupid. What was she? Jealous of Bindi Billingsley? Absolutely not.

No. Bindi didn't bother her. Emory didn't bother her. It was just like she had told him. She didn't need him. She had never needed anyone. So no, she did not need Emory Stuart Leigh Nathanial George Harding. Who had six names anyway? Was there a shortage of perfect names in the world that his pretentious parents needed to pick them all?

She pulled her uniform out from her trunk quickly, setting out her formal uniform for the second half of the day. She double checked her homework for languages, located her astrology book and placed them together on the central table.

The door handle turned, and Saga hurriedly closed her trunk lid. The last thing she needed was Jemima or Navi realising that she had still not unpacked her trunk into the wardrobe. It was an argument that she did not need to get into, and it wouldn't take much for Jemima to lose it and unpack for her.

"What happened?" Jemima asked coming in.

"What happened where?" Saga asked, grabbing her herbal studies book, gardening tools and staff.

"With Emory," Navi added, dashing in behind Jemima to get her own things for class. "It was hard not to notice."

"Nothing happened."

"One minute you were talking and then you two were fighting," Jemima elaborated.

Saga sighed and leaned back against the side of the bunk bed as the other girls collected their belongings. "I said something stupid," Saga admitted.

"What do you mean? Jemima asked.

Slumping, Saga sighed. "I mentioned Bindi."

That caused Navi to look up. "Ohhhh..."

"Wait, what?" Jemima asked, stopping what she was doing and looking at them both. "What's Bindi got to do with anything?"

Navi, who had heard the story in the aftermath of that work shift shook her head. "This one does not want to hear that again."

"They're betrothed," Saga exploded.

"Navi does not think that the decision was finalised. Neither Emory nor Bindi have said anything."

"Well, I wouldn't, but Werewolves put a lot of stock in their pairings. A big announcement would have been made if it was finalised," Jemima said.

Saga glared at the angel. "Their parents were arranging it. Lady Harding was particularly enthusiastic about the match."

"Can we go to class now?" Navi begged. "This one already had to spend half the holiday hearing about Emory and Bindi. This one does not want to hear about how Saga does not care about it, but everything she says and does says otherwise."

"Yes, class," Saga stated. "Let's go. Maybe Ephyra or Kia will eat one of you," she added in a mutter, passing through the door in front of them.

LEIDAGR

Leidagr was Saga's favourite day of the month. In Nýr Ásgardr, Leidagr was the first Saturday of the month and it was the day of the School Tourney. It was the third tourney of the semester and the last before the team selections for the inter-school tourney were made official.

The first event of the day was the Joust and Saga was more than happy to sit on the sidelines and cheer Tasso on.

"What are you competing in today?" Saga asked Jemima, realising that she wasn't sure.

"The usual," Jemima said, spreading out a blanket on the ground near the side of the field. They had taken to sitting in this spot rather than the stands when they kept coming back injured from their bouts. The rug allowed them the chance to lie down, enjoy a picnic. They were also close to the tourney stables for when they needed to claim their horses.

"Nothing new?" Saga asked.

Jemima shook her head. "You've seen me in class. None of the weapons really suit me. No, I'm helping Aunt Raffi in the Healing tent. Speaking of which, as soon as they start running into each other with large pointy sticks at full speed, they're going to be inundated. I'll see you later," and with that, Jemima ran off, leaving Saga to finish setting up their picnic area.

"Hey!" Saga called after her, "Do you know where Navi is?"

She turned, running backwards as she spoke. "Went to wish Tasso luck before the joust, just like a real damsel with her knight!"

"Who's a damsel?" Annis asked, plopping herself down.

"Your sister," Saga said.

The last event before the lunch break was the Stadion and as always, Saga switched from the soft leather boots she wore to her old sneakers. People had stopped whispering about her magic shoes and the unfair advantage people thought they gave her, especially as time had progressed and their colourful patterns had tired and dulled with use, even if she only used them on tourney days. She trained in local shoes, looking to the eventuality of her sneakers falling apart and there being no opportunity for her to acquire new ones, but come race day... Race Day was all about running at her very best.

"Got it in you for another win?" Dayan asked.

Saga paused in tying her laces and thought. "Oh, I don't know Dayan, maybe today's your day."

"This close to the announcement of the tourney teams? Nah, you'd have to be cocky to think that you can always win," he stated. "And you are, especially after all your wins."

Saga cocked her head at him and put her foot down. "So, you think I don't have a reason to be cocky?" she asked.

"Oh, you have a reason," Dayan admitted. "Just don't think that the rest of us aren't watching and learning ready to show you up when it best suits us."

Saga chuckled. "I would expect nothing less."

"I still don't get the point of how you start," Javaid said coming up. He got down in a crouch, similar to what he had seen Saga do before every race, but she could see that his posture was wrong and that there was no way that he could get the spring-like action that was supposed to be gained from the movement.

Did she help or not? Dayan and Javaid were both Weretigers and had a natural strength and speed that gave her a run for her money. Up until this time her years of training had been her secret weapon, far more than her shoes had ever been.

"You're going to hurt yourself like that," she said.

Javaid stood up, "What's wrong with it?"

Saga bit her lip for a moment and hesitated for a moment before giving in. "When you're in animal form and you're going to run, not just a bit, but a real sprint, what do you do?"

"You get low and launch yourself," Javaid realised, "ahh, and that's what you're doing, you're loading yourself like a spring."

Saga nodded. "Exactly. Back home there's actually a block... Well, it's like a wedge or sometimes they have two, one for each foot, to get yourself into the right position."

"And then what?"

"Mmmm," Saga murmured, looking around. She found an empty space and tried to think about the lessons her coach had jammed into her head over the years. She got into position, trying to explain as she went, what she was doing.

Master Everard, the tourney commentator watched them. "Giving away your secrets Miss Carolle?"

"No, preventing them from hurting themselves," she said standing back up. "If Javaid had tried what he was doing during a race when he wanted to go full speed, he would have hurt himself."

Everard nodded to himself, before looking at the two boys. "You have yourself and honourable competitor there," he said pointing at Saga before walking away. "Competitors, to your marks," he shouted.

They lined up, Javaid on one side of her and Dayan on the other, each mimicking Saga's positioning. A trumpet sounded and they were off. Saga was surprised to find Javaid just barely in front of her when she finally looked forward. His larger size and longer legs allowing him to launch himself further. Dayan was right beside her and the rest of Weres in the line seemed to be left behind as the three of them sprinted forwards.

Javaid laughed gleefully, looking over his shoulder at Saga and Dayan and waving smugly. The move proved to be a mistake as Saga kept her attention on the track and as she passed him, she pushed herself onwards.

"Don't look back!" Dayan shouted. The two weretigers were relentless and Javaid put everything he had into reasserting his lead over Saga, but somewhere along the way, Dayan disappeared. Even though she didn't give into the temptation to look behind her, Saga wondered why she couldn't feel him there, right behind her. She loved the feeling of the challenge and competition that the two gave her. They wanted to run their best race and she loved racing with them. As they headed for the last few meters before the finish line, she listened for the cheering from the stands, but she only heard her name along with Javaid's.

There was no break between the race and the sword fighting and as soon as the fourth years had finished their stadion, people were emerging to collect weapons for the fight.

"That was close." Saga turned around to find Emory standing behind her, his sword sheathed at his side. "Javaid was right on you for the whole race, hell, he overtook you at one point."

Saga waved him off. "Dayan promises that he'll be up in the top next time too!"

"Dayan's performance was so bad he won't be competing next time."

"Nah, his yearlong scores will protect him," Saga said. "You in the sword fight?"

"Of course, it's the last tourney before the teams are announced. Every student still in with a chance is competing today... I think allowances have been made to go over tomorrow for any events that aren't finished."

"The fourth years are acting like loons too," Saga commented.

"It's their last chance to represent the school..." Emory said and Saga agreed wistfully.

"What?" Emory asked as they put on their leather armour. Without thinking about it, Saga adjusted his straps and Emory did the same for her. She shook her head.

"Come on," he prompted.

Saga sighed and looked around before leaning in to adjust another of his armour straps. "When... When I came here, back home, I was supposed to compete at a national competition, it was a bit hit or miss if I was going to be able to go, but I had qualified..."

"National?" he asked.

"It's like our country, I guess think of representing Asgard against competitors from Wākea, Tír na nÓg, and so forth..."

"Like the best in all of Asgard?"

"The winner? Yeah."

"Which if you were going to compete against the other level planes, then you were and then what?"

"Well, then the winners of that competition go on to compete at a huge international competition," she explained. "They represent their country, so all of the upper god realms, against the best competitors from the other realms."

"Wow," Emory breathed out. "Why... Why did you give that up?"

Saga shrugged. "It wasn't guaranteed that I was even going, the adults in my life were arguing about it. My coach thought I could go all the way and my foster parents..." she trailed off, "Well, ultimately, they didn't matter I guess, they sent me back to the group home and there was a lot of back and forth... I think... I think things are better here..."

Emory was about to reply when Astrid called the first-year competitors to order, and Saga was paired off with Etan Balmilero for the bout while Emory was paired against Alexa Vaccaro.

The elf glared at Saga with such hatred that she had to wonder if she'd actually ever spoken to him before. She didn't think so, but Etan's fingers clasped around his sword so tightly, his fingers looked to be going white. It was a in stark comparison to his face which could soon stand in for a tomato.

When the horn sounded, beginning the match, he leapt, his sword raised high for wide arcing blow to her head. He telegraphed his moves so early, that it was easy to defend against, even as the power of the blow seemed to ricochet down the length of her own blade.

"What's your problem?" Saga asked, defending herself from another powerful blow.

Etan moved from power strikes to a series of rapid moves as he pushed Saga backwards, across the field. He was unrelenting, a talented swordfighter, so why had he opened so recklessly? Saga was certain that Astrid would have words with him about that. His moves got faster, and Saga felt herself struggling to keep up while also maintaining a steady step. There was no chance to step forward, no chance to move from the defensive to offensive strikes and then a stone in the midst of the field sent her falling backwards. It was a relief, a moment away from him. She fell to the ground and rolled away before he could attack, the shock of her suddenly disappearing slowing his relentless attack. She came back to her feet a few paces away from him.

Etan stalked towards her, and they met, swords held in defensive positions, neither giving way for the other to find an opening as they circled each other. Around them, other matches were called.

"What's your problem with me?" Saga asked again.

"I'm here to win," Etan said and Saga wondered if that was all, but she seriously could not think of any moment where she might have made an enemy of him.

"So stop fighting like an idiot," Saga suggested as they continued to circle one another. Eventually time was called, neither one of them winning the match.

By the time the darkness fell, and the last events of the day were complete, the equestrian events had still not been held and neither had the Were fights or stick fighting.

"Another long day tomorrow?" Saga asked.

Jemima shrugged. "Depends, I guess. There's just a lot of competitors."

They joined the long line of students returning to the school stables. Tasso fell into step beside them, his black stallion nuzzling in at Jemima's Sir Hoofington. Pingu bucked, neighing in greeting at the bigger horse.

"There, there boy," Saga said rubbing his neck.

Tasso leaned over his horse's neck to crane round Jemima, "Why did you have Pingu out, Saga?" he asked.

"Jem convinced me to do the dressage competition. I wish I had waited until after the inter-school though," Saga said. "I never expected it to be this nightmarish."

"Well, with tomorrow morning being taken up by church services and the amount of time the equestrian events take..." Tasso contemplated. "Actually, I think they might have made a mistake putting the joust on first this morning."

Both girls nodded in agreement. "They could have definitely caused some issues," Jemima agreed.

"Maybe they should run multiple events at the same time?" Saga suggested.

"They won't do that because of people trying to make pentathlon and doing multiple events," Tasso said.

Saga rolled over, pulling her pillow over her head. Sunnudagr or Sunday, was her rest day usually. She avoided church, not really believing in gods and no one bothered to force her to go, despite being a part of the religious studies group.

She could hear Jemima moving around getting ready to head out. "Are you two coming? There're still events from Leidagr to do."

"What about church?" Navi asked, sitting up in bed.

Jemima held up a sheet of paper from the table in the centre of the room. "Events are starting in an hour, so I'm not going."

"An hour?" Saga asked sitting up. She was careful not to look down towards Navi who was scrambling out of bed and instead focused on Jemima. "When did this happen?"

"When Tymberlee dropped this off," she said, waving the parchment in Saga's direction.

Saga climbed down from the top bunk and headed straight for her trunk to find her combat leathers. Navi had her head deep inside her closet, but Jemima didn't miss the contents of Saga's trunk.

"I thought you unpacked at the beginning of the semester!" she said accusingly. She stalked across the room and stood over Saga and the full trunk.

Saga squeezed her eyes shut and hung her head. Every day for weeks she had managed to trick the angel into believing that she had fully unpacked. Jemima was pretty docile at times and avoided fights, but this one issue had been a bone of contention between them the semester before.

"Jem..." She tried.

"You've been lying to us," Jemima accused. "For weeks, you've been lying to us!"

Fear seized her as she witnessed the hurt and betrayal on Jemima's face. Navi came over, glancing first from Jemima to Saga. "What's this?" she asked.

"She never unpacked!" Jemima cried.

Saga had tried. She had managed to get her books onto the bookshelf, but as she had hovered over the trunk, her non-school clothes in her hands she had frozen. Fear of losing something had gripped her and she had hurriedly stuffed everything back inside the trunk, leaving only a few things in the wardrobe such as her weapons and kit bags.

"Jem," Saga tried again. How could she explain to the other girl how she felt? It was not something that either of the other girls should understand and she really hoped that they never did.

"No," Jemima said turning on her. "What is it? Don't you trust us? Do you think that if you leave your stuff out, we'll take it?"

"Jemima!" Navi exclaimed.

"I wanted to!" Saga cried. "I tried!"

"What does that even mean? You told me that you had. I trusted you."

"You don't understand!" How did she explain that feeling of fear that overcame her when she left the room and her things were not all in one place where she could, if need be, come in and pick them up, secure in the knowledge that she had everything?

"You're right, I don't understand you," Jemima cried. "I thought we were friends." Then she stormed out of the room.

"Jem!" Saga cried, trying to go after her, but Navi shook her head.

"Let her calm down," the little elf suggested.

"What's going on in here?" a voice asked from their door.

Saga sighed when she saw Onorati. The elegant faerie-angel girl looked concerned as she eyed them. "Nothing..." Saga said, slamming her trunk lid closed.

"Didn't sound like nothing. You girls alright?" she asked, stepping inside the room. There would be little traffic on this floor of the house, the only other person would have been Onorati's roommate, Siobhan, but Saga appreciated the older girl's discretion.

"Just... A misunderstanding," Navi finally said. "We'll sort it out."

Onorati crossed her arms over her chest and watched the girls in consternation. "Ok... Well, make sure you get to any remaining events you might have today."

"We will," Navi said and waited until Onorati left before turning to Saga. "Now what?"

"We go finish the tourney."

They were going to run the stick fighting when the equestrian events were being set up, so there would be little time between events to retrieve Pingu. Honestly, Saga wasn't even sure if she wanted to compete in the events still on that day.

She led Pingu out of the magical animals stable and saw Jemima brushing and saddling Sir Hoofington in the yard of the next stable. She started to head over to her, but as soon as Jemima had spotted her, she had turned away, concentrating on Sir Hoofington.

"That was cold," a voice said from the other side of Pingu.

"Huh?" she asked, walking around the large animal. "Edun?" she asked, seeing his lanky form leaning against the fence of the paddock.

"Yeah."

"What are you doing here?" she asked, tying Pingu to the rail and going to find his saddle and bridle.

"Y... Uhh... Navi's competing today," he finally said.

"That's down at the training grounds," Saga said. "Why are you here?"

He scratched the back of his head awkwardly, trying to think of what to say. "Well, it's Sonnedagr and I've got nothing to do..." He said, reaching up to help align Pingu's saddle from his side.

"Aren't you in the stick fighting?"

"Well yeah, but not until the second years and we've got to get through all you first years before then," then as if he had suddenly come up with the most brilliant idea, he said, "I came to hurry you up!"

"Uh huh," Saga said adjusting straps to ensure that they were secure. She fed Pingu half a carrot that he chomped on happily.

"So, what's up with you and angel girl over there?" he asked.

Saga sighed. She rubbed at Pingu's nose and looked at Edun. "She's mad at me."

"What'd you do?" he prompted.

"It's what I didn't do," she said, grabbing hold of the saddle pommel and putting her foot in the stirrup. She hauled herself up and onto the back of the great animal. Pingu shifted his weight slightly, adjusting to her presence.

"Forgot her birthday, right?" he asked.

"If only..." Saga muttered. "That would be easier to explain."

Impishly, Edun held his hand up to her. "Help me up and tell me all about it. This one has three sisters. This one can help fix anything!"

Saga was confused by the change in Edun. She had always assumed that he didn't like her but ever since their trip to the music store, he had been uncannily kind to her. She even found herself enjoying his company, which was really odd. Their pan flute lessons were something she was starting to look forward to. Edun's attitude on the battlefield painted a different picture from the patient and funny boy she was coming to know.

Saga rolled her eyes but held out her arm to him. Edun grasped her arm and allowed her to pull him up onto Pingu's back. "Strong," he murmured as though he had never really noticed and maybe he hadn't. Saga glanced over her shoulder at him, but he adjusted his seat and wrapped his arms around her. "So, what did you not do to upset Jemima?"

Pingu cantered out of the yard and Saga directed him to the road that ran around the town. The ruins of Jisook farm could be seen off a nearby side road and Saga directed the Pegasus away from it.

"How big a deal is it if you don't unpack?" she asked.

She felt him shrug against her back. "What do you mean?" he asked.

"Jemima was on me all last semester about unpacking things from my trunk," Saga explained, "But I didn't."

"Ok…" he murmured, but didn't go on, waiting for her to continue.

"Do you remember when I told you about the room change?" she asked.

"Yeah," he said nodding. "You were worried about what would happen coming back."

"My whole life, I've never had any say in how or why or when I moved and in the last few years that could be weekly…" she sighed and made sure that Pingu was still headed in the right direction. She also made sure that they stayed on the road rather than going through Rishi farm. "They might pack for me or I would be given a few minutes to get my things and things would get lost or left behind because I didn't know where they were. You never see them again and when you get to the new home and you don't have something, then it'll be your fault… You learn pretty quickly to always collect your washing and to keep your things together in as few places as possible…"

"And that's what you've been doing," he said.

She nodded. "I tried. I mean, my books are out and that's better than last semester when I would make sure that they were tucked away in my trunk when I was done rather than out on my desk!"

"Progress then," Edun said.

"I guess, but really I just wanted to make it look like I had. I still made sure at the end of the day that all the books are together and easily collected for packing…"

They were silent for a while, the only sounds coming from the jangling of Pingu's halter and bridle or his hooves along the ground. Around them, townsfolk and students hurried to where they needed to be whether that be church, the second tourney day events or somewhere else.

Edun broke the silence, his voice low and strained with memory. "Growing up there was always the fear that the next day might not come and even if it did, that we would not be together. They could reassign us, sell us, beat us, kill us, at their will."

Saga knew that the four Jensyn siblings had been slaves and the thought of her complaining about her life to Edun made her feel ashamed. "I'm sorry-," she started to say.

"No," he cut in. I don't tell you this to make you feel sorry for me… Nothing we owned was our own, even ourselves and our family. When Ziva was caught in the library, we feared that we would never see her again. Then she was sent here, to school. Free. We feared again when Annis was sent away. Both of them would have brought in a high slave price as workers or as breeders… Navi too," he added in disgust.

Saga tugged at Pingu's reigns, motioning him over to the side of the road and bringing him to a stop. She turned as much as she could to look at him. His eyes were downcast, concentrating on his grip of her, maybe focusing on her to keep him in the here and now rather than in the past. "Edun..." she murmured.

"When it was my turn there was a lot of talk. I'm not the scholar my sisters are. I'm strong and despite some issues with authority, I worked hard, if for nothing else than fear of what would happen to my sisters and mother if I didn't," she felt his fingers clench at her sides and resisted the urge to gasp out in pain. If she had, he would have stopped talking, she knew that. "When they did send me, I was relieved and terrified. There was no one there to protect Navi. It's not like we could write letters home and even if we did, the likelihood of a reply was minimal..." he sighed. "I'm very protective of what's mine. The things I own, and while there are few things I own myself, those that I do, I always know where they are. These last weeks, with Annis and Navi in different houses... That's been hard, hard not seeing them at the start and end of every day... Jemima has all those wonderful aunts and I know that she's an orphan and there's all those weird angel rules, but you could tell from the way they were that she never wanted or feared for anything... Not like we did..." In the distance they heard the ringing bells of the temples calling the time. Edun looked around and realised for the first time that they had stopped moving. "We're going to be late!" he exclaimed. "Come on, you can't miss your event!"

The road around them was almost completely empty of students. A few travellers and townsfolk went by, but the rush of the morning had passed them by as they had talked. Saga tightened her grip on Pingu's reigns and with a soft kick into his sides a crack of the reigns and word in his ear, the Pegasus took off, galloping down the road. People were forced out of their path as they raced by. Riding at speeds like this was almost as good as running.

They rode into the yard laughing like the schoolchildren they were. Mistress Anhora looked at them with dismay as Edun dismounted and held up a hand to her. Saga accepted the hand down.

"How long do we have?" she asked.

Edun looked around, trying to catch sight of a timekeeper. "Not long enough. Do you want me to settle him?"

Saga shook her head, her hand resting on Pingu's neck. "No, Tasso's the only other person he tolerates other than Mistress Anhora. Go, see if you can distract Astrid from starting the bouts."

"A... Oh, you mean Mistress Grunborg. Right!"

He started to run off, "Edun?" she called after him.

"Yeah?" he asked, looking back at her.

"Thanks... For the talk."

He nodded and ran off to try and halt the matches that were about to start.

As Saga set about loosening Pingu's straps and ensuring he had water. She noticed Emory standing on the far side of the yard. She started to wave, but noticed that he was scowling at her. She frowned as his gaze seemed to follow Edun for a while, before settling on her.

By the time she had finished settling Pingu and was heading out to join the other competitors, he was gone.

There was a jovial mood in the air as the combatants got ready. Somehow, it didn't feel like the regular bouts on Leidagr. It was Sunday and that just seemed to make everyone that little bit more relaxed. Out in the stands people were talking, laughing, even playing music. People were excited. It helped that the majority of students had already done their events.

Saga made her way out to the field, her staff in hand. Her thumb caressed the engravings, swiping up and down as she faced off against Elayen Eastwood, a Werewolf from Bridelow. She had seen him fight before in previous Tourney events but had never actually spoken to him. She saw Emory out of the corner of her eye, he stood opposite Tonya Bonnedras. He'd be fine. Tonya was no match for him. Across the field from her, Navi was set against Shaunette Anand. Saga didn't know her well and wondered what the Ljósálfar girl thought about being paired with the only Dökkálfar in their year level.

The bell rang indicating the start of the match. She allowed the world around her to shrink to nothing but Elayen and herself. She couldn't allow herself to be distracted by Jemima in the stands, Emory three pairs down or Navi and the light elf.

Elayen shifted his weight and spun, almost taking her head off with a circular sweep. Saga wanted to be fancy with her move, but he was too close, and she had barely seen him appear before her. She took the only option open to her and ducked. She shot her own staff out, tangling it between the Werewolf's legs. He fell to the floor beside her, and Saga rolled away from him, coming to her feet out of his range of attack.

They resituated and circled one another, waiting for an opening, an indication that the other was about to strike. In the background the music changed from a lively and upbeat tune that you could imagine in the background of a fun action film to something dark and moody. The music that had been invigorating and inspiring was now distracting, and Saga wished that whoever was strumming at their instrument would stop. Elayen's staff shifted ever so slightly and Saga misjudged his intended move. She moved to deflect, but out of seemingly nowhere, the point of his staff connected with her midsection.

"Oompf," she gasped out. She backpaddled, trying to reclaim her balance. She caught a concerned look from Astrid but tried to ignore her and focus on the boy in front of her. Her head was cloudy and the next thing she knew, the bout was over before she had a chance to really centre herself and she really had no idea what had happened.

"Good match," she said to Elayen. It was obvious that he had won. It wasn't the first time that she had lost a match, but it was the first time that she had been so out of it that she could barely remember what had happened. She thought back, but the last few minutes seemed to just be not there. She turned, taking in the sight of everyone in the stands. What had happened to her? She saw Dina Bess, the religious studies teacher and one of Jemima's Aunts standing in the aisle between seats staring in the direction of a group of fourth year students, mostly elves, with their instruments out. In the midst of the group, Saga could see Sidawi Harmeet, the black balalaika resting against his chest.

She turned back to find Master Everard consulting with Astrid. Every so often the Weapons Mistress would shoot Saga a furtive glance of concern. She shrugged at the Weapons' Mistress but looked back out to the stands. Sid was up to something, and it was like no one was noticing. She needed to talk to him.

"Are you alright?" Elayen asked, knowing that at the very least that Saga should have been a tougher fight than she had been.

"Yeah," she managed. "Just... Just not my day," she said. "Congratulations again."

ANTICIPATON

Saga slipped away from the house festivities that night. Jemima was still ignoring her, and Emory was always certain to be on the furthest side of the room from her. Her head hurt and she needed time to think about the day. Not the staff fighting event, that was just about all anyone could talk about, but about what had happened afterwards. She had needed to talk to Sidawi, needed to corner him and him to talk. Whatever was going on with him was getting ridiculous and it was as though nobody was noticing. Then there was her concern about his new friend. She hadn't seen him today, but that didn't mean he hadn't been there. Except the fourth-year Prefect was busy and it wasn't like she could walk into Yeatwens House and demand to speak to him. Also, not plausible at The Saffron Heart, but maybe next time he had a tutoring session with Navi? Would that put her on the outs with Navi too? She'd been trying for ages and after the staff fighting event, she'd had enough of trying, so she'd pushed through the crowds and almost had to fight her way through people wanting to confront her about her last event to make her way to where he'd been sitting.

He hadn't been there though, and Saga had almost retreated to the game stables to hang out with Pingu while she sorted out her stroppy mood. Then she had spotted the elf's golden strands disappearing down the back of the viewing stands and she'd chased after him.

"Sid!" He didn't reply, if anything, he sped up, as though trying to avoid her. "Sid? Can we talk?" He walked faster, breaking into run. He disappeared around a corner and Saga had to stop, wondering which way he might have gone, before spotting him talking to a hooded man.

"Everything is going to plan," the man said then his eyes were on her. "Who's she?"

Sidawi whirled around, spotting Saga coming towards him. "Saga!"

"Sid, we need to talk," Saga called to him.

"Gt rid of her," the man said, then pulled his hood further over his face and stalked away.

"Who's he?"

Sidawi looked anxiously over his shoulder at the retreating man, then scowled at her. "Why won't you leave me alone?" he cried, his beautiful, elegant face contorted in anguish.

Saga's heart broke for him. She hadn't known him the term before, but when she had seen him around school, he'd been so bright and happy, especially when with Ziva. "I just wanted to ask-."

Sid shook his head and turned to follow the man. "Go away, Saga. You're getting in the way."

"Getting in the way of what? Sidawi, what is going on with you? What's that instrument? Who's that man?" She reached for him, grabbing his arm to halt his escape.

The elf whirled back to her, the instrument case he'd been carrying flying up. The long, hard end hit her on the side of head, and she went stumbling backwards, releasing his arm. "Sid!" she gasped, arms pinwheeling as she tried to regain her balance.

"I'm sorry! Leave me alone!" Sidawi begged, then ran off.

Saga swayed slightly, leaning against the nearest wall, her head spinning. Had he really just attacked her? She could hardly believe it. That was not the Sidawi she had come to know.

Not sure what had just happened, she'd returned to the game fields and slipped into the stables, giving a carrot to Pingu so that he would keep her secret as she tenderly felt out. She then spent the rest of the day hiding out, keeping Pingu company. That far away from the action, she knew that Astrid would be too busy to come and find her to discuss her dismal showing during the staff fighting match further. What she did know was that whatever had happened, wasn't her fault.

When the dressage competition had come to her turn, she had ridden Pingu out to the field, past Jemima and Sir Hoofington and completed the complex array of manoeuvres. Her helmet and hair, likely covering the effects of her encounter with Sidawi. She and Pingu were slow, but the Pegasus had obeyed her commands and completed the sequence. Her horsemanship and her connection with Pingu had increased since the beginning of the year and despite her hesitation about competing, she was glad she had, even if she didn't think it was going to be a regular occurrence.

"You shouldn't feel bad," Perdita said, bringing Saga back to the present.

"Oh?" she asked, wondering what the older girl was talking about. What had she missed?

"We all have our good days and our bad days. You knew Dressage was something you still needed to work on."

"Ah…" Saga replied. "That… Yes… But you didn't see how badly I did in the morning…"

"Good days and bad days," the Wererabbit repeated. "And besides, you could at least try being happy for your friend."

Saga smiled fondly in Navi's direction. She was happy for her. Navi deserved top place for that day's staff fighting… or at least she thought she did. Saga could still not remember any of it. "I am happy for her Perdita… I'm just not feeling too good. I'm going to head up," she said. "See if I can shake this off."

Upstairs in their room, Saga changed for bed and managed to get three rungs up the ladder before she came back down. She couldn't fix whatever was going on with Sidawi, so she could try to fix what was going on with her and Jemima. She threw her wardrobe door open and pulled out all the coat hangers, dropping them to the floor beside her trunk and opened the lid. She sat down in front of it, crossing her legs and stared at the contents.

Or at least try to.

The contents of the trunk stared back at her. Saga picked up a couple of skirts and pants and laid them on her lap. She picked up a coat hanger and slipped pants on. She laid it aside, postponing the actual act of hanging it in the wardrobe.

She'd rather go another round of the joust than do this.

She started with school items. Maybe she could get her blazer and jacket and other winter gear into the wardrobe. Maybe her leathers and…

It was too much.

She had no idea how much time had passed when Navi entered the room and found her sitting there, clothes scattered around her and the coat hangers half used, but also laying around her.

"Saga?" she asked and Saga could hear the concern in the other girl's voice. "What are you doing?"

Saga swallowed hard and tried to choke back a sob that she refused to acknowledge. What was wrong with her? Everyone else did this. She was not, under any circumstance, going to break down in tears over something as trivial as finally unpacking her belongings. They were just things, right? They didn't matter. "Unpacking..." she choked out.

"Now?" Navi asked, coming to kneel beside Saga.

"I don't want to lose Jem over this... So, I have to, right?" Saga asked looking at her friend with tears glistening in her eyes that she swiped at angrily.

Outside they could hear people moving around the old house, getting ready for bed. Siobhan and Onorati talked loudly as they made their way to their room, and they called out their goodnights to Jemima.

Saga was startled at that and hurriedly started to pick up the full coat hangers intending to hang them up when she felt hands on her arms, stopping her.

"Stop," Jemima said.

"Jem..." Saga whispered.

"I'm sorry," Jemima said, dropping to her knees and hugging Saga from behind. "I'm sorry," she repeated.

"I shouldn't have lied," Saga said. "I do trust you, you know that right?"

"Yeah... It's just everyone else you don't trust."

Saga nodded slowly. Saga reached out, took Navi's hand in her hers and bit her lip, trying to find the words. Telling Edun had been one thing, but she did not want to make Navi feel bad or upset either of her friends. "I... I love that we're here together," she managed.

"So do we," Navi said squeezing her hand. "But the move up here unsettled you, didn't it?"

Saga looked at her. "Have you been talking to Edun?"

Navi leaned her head against Saga's shoulder, "A little... although he seems to spend more time with you these days..."

"What's this?" Jemima asked.

"I told her brother about this feeling I'd had when we packed up for Queenette at the end of last term..." Saga said. "How I thought I'd never see our room again..."

"And we didn't..." Jemima concluded.

"For all the right reasons and not the nightmares I was imagining!" Saga added hurriedly. "But yeah... I... tried Jem, I really did..."

"How about," Navi said after they had been silent for a while, simply just being there together in that moment. "We put your school stuff in the wardrobe and the you stuff in the trunk," she suggested.

Saga nodded thoughtfully. "I can do that I think..."

"Come on," Jemima said. "We'll help."

They got to work, hanging school blouses and blazers on hangers, getting the skirts and stockings and everything else packed away into the drawers.

Jemima carefully refolded the other clothes, placing them back inside the trunk.

There was a knock on the door, and it opened a moment later before they could reply. Tymberlee leaned in. "Saga, there you are!"

"What is it?" she asked.

"Have you seen Tremblay?" she asked, looking around the room as though she expected to find the house ghost hovering somewhere in a corner.

Saga frowned and handed the hanger she had been holding to Navi. She got up, "No..." she said slowly. She had been up here, alone in her room in crisis. That was Tremblay's favourite time to come and bother her. In fact, the house ghost hadn't been around much at all since the semester had begun.

"Yeah, that's what I thought," Tymberlee said. "The other prefects have said the same thing. Their house ghosts aren't around all that much..."

"Must mean things aren't going missing at Queenette," Navi said without thinking.

Tymberlee actually laughed at that. "It has been mentioned," she looked back at Saga. "I thought I saw him at the tourney, did you?"

Saga knew that the house ghosts could follow their house Prefects around thanks to the house badge they wore. "I..." Saga bit her lip. "I don't remember part of the day..." she admitted.

Tymberlee stepped into the room and closed the door behind her. "What do you mean?"

"Was it the music?" Navi asked.

"Yes!" Tymberlee exclaimed. "A group of elves were playing during the staff fights. I could have sworn I saw Tremblay then. He didn't seem to notice me."

"I didn't see him," Saga said, "but I also couldn't get a grip on myself while it was on," she looked at Jemima. "I saw your Aunt Dina at the end of the match... She was looking towards those elves... Sid was there. It was like she too had no idea how or why she was there..."

"That's why you were completely out of it during the match," Jemima said. Navi had been caught up in her own fight to notice, but Jemima had been on the sidelines watching. "Just like at Agesilaus,"

"And at The Saffron Heart," Navi added.

"This has happened before?" Tymberlee asked. "Tell me everything," she said, as the four of them settled in around the table in the middle of the room.

So, they did. Saga told her about the night at The Saffron Heart when she had been drawn into Sidawi's music and she had noticed the presence of ghosts, dozens if not hundreds of them crowding into the restaurant, trying to get to the Prefect.

"Did you see this?" Tymberlee asked Navi.

Navi shook her head. "I wasn't allowed out front, but Emory was there. He saw it."

"Ok... I'll talk to him later. What happened at Agesilaus? And where is this place?" she asked.

"Yggdrasil City, shopping trip before the term started. Saga and Navi came to stay with me," Jemima said. "We went out for dinner. We'd meant to go to The Roots, but the line was so long that we went to this other place instead."

"And what happened there?"

"They had live music, some sort of open mic night," at everyone's confused looks Saga sighed and said, "They were letting anyone who wanted to play or sing go up."

"Right," Tymberlee replied.

"Sid and a group of others went up to play. He was playing this weird black balalaika and this time it wasn't just me..."

"No, about four angels also got drawn into the music. They all got up from their seats, ignoring everyone and making their way to the stage," Jemima added. "No one could get through to them."

"A young apprentice angel managed to get a grip on himself, " Navi added.

Tymberlee nodded along, before looking at Jemima. "What about you?" she asked. "Anything odd?"

"No, but they were all Angels of Death according to the apprentice," she said.

"Just like Mistress Bess was," Tymberlee concluded. "And the ghosts?"

"Climbing on one another to get at the stage," Saga said, "by the time I finally saw them, anyway."

"Each and every time this happened, Sidawi Harmeet was there?" Tymberlee asked.

"Yes, but it's more than that," Saga said. "It's not Sid alone. He's been here with Navi and nothing. It's... It's that black balalaika." She patted her hair down, covering her temple where the bruise was forming from Sidawi's instrument case. Did she mention that he'd attacked her? She didn't want to and it was so unlike him. He was a prefect. If it came out that he'd attacked a first year... It would ruin him.

"He denies having another instrument though," Navi added, moving the conversation along.

Tymberlee frowned. "I'll think on this," she said getting up." "I remember thinking his instrument looked different. What class do I have with him tomorrow?" she murmured to herself. She headed for the door of their room. "Let me know if you see Tremblay, yeah?"

Saga nodded. "Of course," she said, glad that the older girl was leaving. With her gone, Saga wouldn't have to think about whether or not to tell her. Tymberlee would be honour bound to report the attack to their teachers and the repercussions would be dire.

When Tymberlee left the room, the three girls stared at each other. There was definitely something going on, they just had no idea what it was.

~ * ~

The next morning as they prepared for class, Saga had issues finding her uniform. She stared at her trunk, unable to figure out where her riding jacket or jodhpurs were. Her leathers were missing too. She heard Jemima shift in bed and hurriedly closed the lid of her trunk.

"Wardrobe," Jemima said getting up. "All your school stuff is now in the wardrobe."

"Right!" Saga said, opening the doors to the wardrobe and seeing everything hanging just as it always should have been. "Right... Sorry..."

It might make things easier not having to hide from her roommates any longer. She collected her belongings, taking longer than usual as she had to rifle through drawers to find socks and underwear, but eventually she was dressed.

Downstairs, Tymberlee had Emory cornered in the hallway and neither of them were looking happy. Emory caught sight of her and she could see the concern etched on his face as the three girls passed him by.

"I don't know," he said when Tymberlee prompted him. "One moment she was walking back to the kitchens and the next she was staring into space, walking towards the stage."

"Did she say anything?" Tymberlee asked.

Emory thought. "Yeah," he said. "She was still a little out of it, but she said that the ghosts were attracted to the music."

"Did you see anyone else get enthralled by the music?"

They passed into the dining room before he answered, but when Emory and Tymberlee followed, his eyes were on her.

"Seen him this morning?" Tymberlee asked stopping by Saga's chair. Saga shook her head, and the faerie girl patted her on the shoulder. "Ok."

Talk at the table turned out to be about the tourney and the suspected results of team selections.

"I think you can kiss your spot on the staff fighting team goodbye," Mannish said as he set the last dish on the table, a plate stacked high with his homemade bread.

Saga nodded in agreement, but it was Percival that spoke up. "Surely her performance over the past year speaks for itself."

"Team selection is open to the entire school," Onorati said. "They might not want to take the risk on a first year after that performance."

"Then I don't qualify," Saga said. "You're acting like I never lost a match before."

"Yeah, but it was like you were somewhere else," Vespers said. "The boy got several hits on you."

"That would explain all the aches and pains..." She murmured, tucking into her breakfast. "Ok, how about instead of reminding me that I got walloped yesterday, we talk about the break next week. What are your plans?"

Excited talks of family, travel and relaxation broke out around the table. Jemima was headed to Andlang city for a week with her nine aunts. Tymberlee and Onorati were staying at school to study, they had end of year exams coming up before they knew it. Siobhan was excited that her father would be passing through town and was hoping to spend some time with him. Mannish had an apprenticeship at a local restaurant and was planning on spending everyday cooking. Emory said something about his mother and father, but he sounded less than thrilled at the prospect of going home.

"They trying to set you up yet?" Mannish asked.

Emory nodded disdainfully. "Thankfully so far only the one. Hopefully Bindi and I can drag it out because she's not interested in me one bit and that's just fine with me. But the longer we drag it out, the more chance of not getting matched up again."

"Playing the system," Perdita said. "Does that ever work?"

He shrugged. "I can hope, because I know that I'll never be interested in anyone my mother chooses for me."

"And Bindi?" Jemima asked. "What does she think of all this?"

"Got a guy her parents disapprove of," he said and leaned in as though about to tell them a secret, "a traveller!" he said as though it was some great shame.

The twins and Mannish looked shocked. "Really?" The Werehyena said in hushed tones that was so unlike him.

"I didn't know that we had travellers around here," Perdita said.

"What are travellers?" Saga asked, not sure what all the fuss was about.

"Gypsies," Mannish said.

"Rats," Percival added.

"Rats?" Saga pressed; this conversation was getting even weirder. What did gypsies and rats have to do with each other?

"Wererats," Tymberlee clarified. "They are nomadic people, never in one place for long. Like the Wererabbits they're considered a prey race. They travel the realms in these brightly covered caravans, set up near towns, run fair like attractions... Honestly, the community gets a bad name. Don't call them Gypsies to their faces. Personally, I've loved the traveller encampments I've been to."

"There are Wererats too?" Saga exclaimed.

"There are a lot of races that don't attend the school," Onorati said.

"The rats don't even go to school," Mannish said. "They're a blight on the Were communities."

"Harsh words from our friendly Hyena," Siobhan said.

Mannish bristled. "In Sirtlan there's usually problems with the travellers when they come," but he didn't elaborate further.

"Hang on, if you're from Sirtlan, how come you're not at Ehras Magna?" Emory asked.

"Because my family dates back to The New World School here, like yours does," Mannish shot back.

Saga looked over at Emory. This discovery of a new Were race had come because he was not engaging in a relationship with Bindi Billingsley. She bit her lip, then remembered her food and ate her breakfast, letting the conversation flow around her.

"How long do you think you can hold your parents off?" Mannish asked.

Emory shrugged. "Depends on how well Bindi and I plan our stories... It's got to be believable enough that we're serious, but not so serious that they start planning our wedding."

~ * ~

The next morning as they prepared for class, Saga had issues finding her uniform. She stared at her trunk, unable to figure out where her riding jacket or jodhpurs were. Her leathers were missing too. She heard Jemima shift in bed and hurriedly closed the lid of her trunk.

"Wardrobe," Jemima said getting up. "All your school stuff is now in the wardrobe."

"Right!" Saga said, opening the doors to the wardrobe and seeing everything hanging just as it always should have been. "Right... Sorry..."

It might make things easier not having to hide from her roommates any longer. She collected her belongings, taking longer than usual as she had to rifle through drawers to find socks and underwear, but eventually she was dressed.

Downstairs, Tymberlee had Emory cornered in the hallway and neither of them were looking happy. Emory caught sight of her and she could see the concern etched on his face as the three girls passed him by.

"I don't know," he said when Tymberlee prompted him. "One moment she was walking back to the kitchens and the next she was staring into space, walking towards the stage."

"Did she say anything?" Tymberlee asked.

Emory thought. "Yeah," he said. "She was still a little out of it, but she said that the ghosts were attracted to the music."

"Did you see anyone else get enthralled by the music?"

They passed into the dining room before he answered, but when Emory and Tymberlee followed, his eyes were on her.

"Seen him this morning?" Tymberlee asked stopping by Saga's chair. Saga shook her head, and the faerie girl patted her on the shoulder. "Ok."

Talk at the table turned out to be about the tourney and the suspected results of team selections.

"I think you can kiss your spot on the staff fighting team goodbye," Mannish said as he set the last dish on the table, a plate stacked high with his homemade bread.

Saga nodded in agreement, but it was Percival that spoke up. "Surely her performance over the past year speaks for itself."

"Team selection is open to the entire school," Onorati said. "They might not want to take the risk on a first year after that performance."

"Then I don't qualify," Saga said. "You're acting like I never lost a match before."

"Yeah, but it was like you were somewhere else," Vespers said. "The boy got several hits on you."

"That would explain all the aches and pains..." She murmured, tucking into her breakfast. "Ok, how about instead of reminding me that I got walloped yesterday, we talk about the break next week. What are your plans?"

Excited talks of family, travel and relaxation broke out around the table. Jemima was headed to Andlang city for a week with her nine aunts. Tymberlee and Onorati were staying at school to study, they had end of year exams coming up before they knew it. Siobhan was excited that her father would be passing through town and was hoping to spend some time with him. Mannish had an apprenticeship at a local restaurant and was planning on spending everyday cooking. Emory said something about his mother and father, but he sounded less than thrilled at the prospect of going home.

"They trying to set you up yet?" Mannish asked.

Emory nodded disdainfully. "Thankfully so far only the one. Hopefully Bindi and I can drag it out because she's not interested in me one bit and that's just fine with me. But the longer we drag it out, the more chance of not getting matched up again."

"Playing the system," Perdita said. "Does that ever work?"

He shrugged. "I can hope, because I know that I'll never be interested in anyone my mother chooses for me."

"And Bindi?" Jemima asked. "What does she think of all this?"

"Got a guy her parents disapprove of," he said and leaned in as though about to tell them a secret, "a traveller!" he said as though it was some great shame.

The twins and Mannish looked shocked. "Really?" The Werehyena said in hushed tones that was so unlike him.

"I didn't know that we had travellers around here," Perdita said.

"What are travellers?" Saga asked, not sure what all the fuss was about.

"Gypsies," Mannish said.

"Rats," Percival added.

"Rats?" Saga pressed; this conversation was getting even weirder. What did gypsies and rats have to do with each other?

"wererats," Tymberlee clarified. "They are nomadic people, never in one place for long. Like the Wererabbits they're considered a prey race. They travel the realms in these brightly covered caravans, set up near towns, run fair like attractions... Honestly, the community gets a bad name. Don't call them Gypsies to their faces. Personally, I've loved the traveller encampments I've been to."

"There are Wererats too?" Saga exclaimed.

"There are a lot of races that don't attend the school," Onorati said.

"The rats don't even go to school," Mannish said. "They're a blight on the Were communities."

"Harsh words from our friendly Hyena," Siobhan said.

Mannish bristled. "In Sirtlan there's usually problems with the travellers when they come," but he didn't elaborate further.

"Hang on, if you're from Sirtlan, how come you're not at Ehras Magna?" Emory asked.

"Because my family dates back to The New World School here, like yours does," Mannish shot back.

Saga looked over at Emory. This discovery of a new Were race had come because he was not engaging in a relationship with Bindi Billingsley. She bit her lip, then remembered her food and ate her breakfast, letting the conversation flow around her.

"How long do you think you can hold your parents off?" Mannish asked.

Emory shrugged. "Depends on how well Bindi and I plan our stories... It's got to be believable enough that we're serious, but not so serious that they start planning our wedding."

~ * ~

"And swipe to the legs," Astrid ordered, then watched the different ways that people avoided the attack. She cringed as Seona backed away squealing in panic but nodded in approval as Dayan lowered his own staff to defend his leg, resulting in a resounding clash of wood on wood. Moving down the line of students, Astrid ordered the move again. "And Seona, defend yourself!"

The girl whimpered something, right before squealing in fright as Tonya attacked her again without regret or hesitation. Astrid shook her head, but moved on down the line towards her advanced students who were all vying for a place on the Tourney team.

Dayan struck out low at Navi's shin. The girl confidently blocked the attack before launching into an attack of her own. The end of her staff stopped just millimetres from the boy's throat when she was done. "Good Navi," Astrid praised. "Dayan, how do you protect yourself from that move?"

The boy stepped away tentatively from the end of the staff and Navi lowered it. "You never go up against Navi when Tourney is on the line?"

Beside them, Saga started to giggle, missing the attack from Emory and letting out a gasp of surprise as his staff managed to hit her on the side of the leg. "Saga, concentrate!" Astrid scolded, but despite the pain, the girl didn't stop giggling, in fact it erupted into full blown laughter.

"I'm sorry As- Mistress Grunborg!" she managed between bouts of laughing and rubbing her injured leg. I just... Dayan..." She shook her head in dismay. "Never mind... You wouldn't understand."

Around them, people were pausing to watch. "No, go on," Astrid insisted.

Saga looked around awkwardly, "It's close to a line from a movie..." she muttered.

"A what?" Astrid asked.

"Don't get her started on these movie things!" Emory begged.

Astrid sighed. "A Midgard thing?"

Saga nodded, "Yeah... One of the best."

Astrid turned her attention back to Dayan. "Aside from avoiding the fight altogether, how would you avoid the eventuality of getting your throat ripped out and no, you can't use your animal form."

Dayan growled at that but glanced at Navi and motioned for her to resume the start position. She did so and they went through slower this time and as she brought the end of her staff up to attack his throat, he shuffled backwards, pushing one end of his staff down at speed, allowing the free end to come up, blocking Navi's attack from reaching his throat.

"Right," Astrid said. "Now at speed."

As they repeated the sequence, Emory reset his position to start again, but Saga waved him off. "I'm going to get a drink," she said, before wandering off to the water bucket and scooping herself a ladle of water.

The last day of term arrived and with the free afternoon, it meant that their holiday started as soon as class broke for lunch.

"Where's everyone going?" Saga asked, standing on the steps of Sorosian Hall, watching as students seemed to file into the town square from every part of town despite the impending mass exodus of students heading home for the week. Saga herself had been invited by Astrid to join her for the week in the ocean town of Honah lee and she was excited, even if none of the others had been able to come with them.

"Master Everard is announcing the Inter-School Tourney Team!" Tasso exclaimed.

"You mean it's not posted on the message board like scores?" Navi asked, racing to keep up with him.

"It will be, but Master Everard always makes a big show of the announcement," Jemima said. "Come on, we don't want to miss it. They followed the rest of the students into the square, which looked even more crowded than it was on the day of The Choosings at the beginning of the year. Townsfolk ringed the exterior of the square, leaving plenty of space for students to file in and watch.

"Happy Mid break everyone," Master Everard exclaimed. His voice sounded strange, almost tinny, but Saga couldn't see any contraption that was amplifying the Elf's voice. "I'm sure that you're all eager to be off for the week, but I'm even more sure that you all want to know the answer to the biggest question of the semester..." he paused dramatically, waiting for everyone to subtly lean in towards him, "Who made the Tourney team!" he cried out. The students cheered excitedly; it was almost as if just by being there they had already won something. "Ok, ok, here we go."

He started to read the list, starting with the faeries and elves chosen for the Arcana Battle. Tymberlee and Sidawi had both made the team. Saga didn't recognise the names of anyone who had made the Archery teams, but Donetta who she knew was on the Pentathlon team had made the Equestrian dressage team and to everyone's surprise, so had Jemima.

"That's amazing!" Navi exclaimed. Unable to help themselves, Navi and Saga embraced the angel in a tight hug that she struggled to get out of.

"I... How? What just happened?" she asked.

"You made the inter-school team," Tasso said, wide eyed, almost as though realising that there might just be hope for him and the jousting team, which was announced after the hand-to-hand combat team that included Edun.

They waited with bated breaths as the first name, then the second and the third were announced for the jousting team. Saga didn't think any of them were breathing as Master Everard scanned his scroll for the fourth name. "Tasso Bonnedras!"

They cried out in excitement at the news, hugging Tasso and congratulating him. Boys from Knightrich surrounded them, thumping him on the back in hearty congratulations. Jousting was followed by the Pentathlon team and the two solo competitors who were expected to complete all five events were no surprise to Saga, Delucca Goett and Zibby Amin. Then there was the team Pentathlon and Saga was relieved to hear that Harian Mau, a second year Weretiger would be competing in the Stadion portion of the team challenge.

"And for the reserve Pentathlon member," Master Everard announced, "Saga Carolle!"

There were excited cheers and murmured whispers about a first year getting anywhere near the team. Saga just stood there, staring up at the Tourney coordinator. "What?" she asked, not sure that she had heard right. "I don't... I..."

There was no time to really think about it though as Master Everard went on, announcing the Stadion competitors. The Weretiger from the Pentathlon team was there and to her surprise, Saga's name was called again.

This time, there was no confusion as people around them started decreeing their upcoming win against Ehras Magna Were Skoli... Finally.

"Stick fighting's next," Navi whisper shouted to the group, her arms wrapped tightly around Saga's. They had some of the highest scores in their year level, but how did that compare to the rest of the school? Four names were read out and both girls felt themselves deflate as neither name was called.

"I guess I really messed up last week," Saga murmured. "But why isn't Navi there?"

"Wait up, there's still the paired completion team," someone from beside them said. Saga thought it was someone from Knightrich who hadn't yet moved on.

"And for the first time in a hundred and fifty years, we have a staff pair of first years!" Master Everard called out to oohs and aahs of anticipation. "Saga Carolle and Navi Jensyn!"

Navi screamed in delight, jumping up and down and forcing Saga to move with her or risk having her arm torn off by the over excited dark elf. "We did it! We did it!" she cried excitedly.

The team roster continued with the swordplay team and Were Battles.

"They have to have made a mistake," Saga murmured.

"About us?" Navi asked.

"No... About me..." Saga said. "Reserve?"

"It's just a placeholder," Jemima assured her. "The reserve never gets to compete in the actual event!"

THE TENT CITY

As soon as school returned from the break, it seemed as though they were off again after a whirlwind of classes, many of which gave out homework to be done while at the tournament, last minute training, and team meetings. Then they were bundled onto an airship and flying back to Yggdrasil city. It seemed to Saga as though she barely had time to tell her friends about her trip, before they were all travelling again. So much had happened, but the whole time back at school had been so busy. She'd also never got the opportunity to talk to Sid who had taken to actively avoiding her, tuning and disappearing every time she so much as entered the same room as him. "Why didn't we just stay in Yggdrasil City when we came back from Honah Lee?" Saga asked as she stood beside Astrid, slightly back from the railing so she wouldn't have to look down.

"You and me for that matter, needed to attend the team meetings. You also had training and classes that you couldn't just miss."

"It just seems like such a waste," Saga argued.

"It was two weeks, Saga. You can't just miss two weeks of classes and training. Besides, how much longer could you have gone without Navi and Jemima?"

Saga shrugged in response, not sure how to answer. It was true. She had missed them dreadfully. Navi in particular. Ever since she'd come to Asgard, they hadn't really been apart, even spending their breaks together.

When they finally landed in Yggdrasil city, there were so many of them trying to find a place on the floating platforms that Saga was able to squeeze herself into a position in the centre, meaning that she didn't have to risk seeing the sides or worse, over the sides as they descended through the trunk of the world tree from the airship docks to the base of the tree.

Navi wrapped her arm through Saga's, making sure that the Valkyrie didn't try to find her way to the stairs instead. They'd lost track of Jemima, who was helping Raphaella Damir and her healers with their gear and Tasso had disappeared with a group of boys who also lodged at Knightrich.

"Navi can't believe that the tourney is finally happening," the little dark elf exclaimed as they passed another floating disc of students, all wearing a uniform of blue and gold that looked like flowing magic robes.

"What school is that?" Saga asked, pointing them out.

"Aquino Beccara," Navi said. "The school for Ljósálfar, faeries, sirens and leprechauns. They might also have a demi or half god too..." A rowdy crowd in green and brown could be seen racing each other down the stairs that encircled the entirety of the World Tree's hollow trunk. "Ehras Magna Were Skoli," Navi said pointing towards them. "Weres."

"Obviously," Saga said, eyeing the rambunctious group as others leapt and fell out of their way, trying to avoid the staggering fall to the bottom of the trunk. "Who are the ones in red and black?" The group was solemn and far more disciplined than the students from Ehras Magna.

"Rinsunid Cantera, Vampires, Weres and daemons."

When they finally reached the bottom, they stepped out into an array of colourful tents and people. Everyone was being directed one way or another depending on which school they attended.

"Toserra Sorose?" A harried man with a scroll asked. When they answered in the affirmative, he said, "continue down the path to the blue and red tents, that's your area for the week. Do not go to other areas unless invited. There is a communal area at the centre of the camp in which to gather with other students."

They nodded and were ushered along before they had a chance to ask any questions. Saga looked around in awe, it was like a carnival, the segmented areas of tents were all in bright colours, much like the buildings within the tree city.

"Look over there!" Navi exclaimed, pointing towards the pale blue and green tents arranged around a lake. "There's a contingent from Kahawaiola'a Ocean," she said, and Saga could already see that several students were enjoying the lake, fish tails flicking water as they swam.

"I wonder if Hilina'i or Inoke made their team…" Saga said, trying to get a good look, but they were too far away.

Navi looked at her wide eyed. "How do you know anyone that goes there? "

"I met them in Hona Lee. Hilina'i helped us fight of the pirates that attacked." Saga elbowed her playfully as they continued on past a group of students in orange skirt-like Hakamas that billowed as they walked and grey wide-sleeved Kosodes. They looked like something from an old Japanese film. She spotted a few tails and other animal body parts as they passed her by. "What's that school?" Saga asked.

Navi cocked her head to the side and watched them. "They're from one of the far-off eastern planes… This one doesn't know what they call their school, but Navi thinks it is translated to something like The Two Worlds School… Something like that…"

Saga raised an eyebrow at that as she watched another group go by, their grey kosodes and orange hakamas making them stand out amongst the Toserra Sorose blazers and the straight lines of the black tunics of Rinsunid Cantera. They talked amongst each other, and Saga realised that it was not a language she could understand. Just how many languages were there? How many planes had they not yet learned about in Planarography?

They joined a mass of students heading into the camp. A group of girls dressed in identical purple and gold gowns pushed past them. They were trailed by a group of cloaked figures who carried their bags and weapons.

"We were standing there!" Saga called after them, but none of the girls deigned to reply to her. Navi circled around a small figure wheeling a heavy trunk, trailing behind the group. The trunk got caught and the cloaked figure was forced to stop and struggle with the unwieldy luggage. They were pulling and tugging, trying to get it over the obstacle and if not over, then around it. The hood of the cloak fell away, and Navi gasped at the sight of a young boy of maybe eight or nine years old with shaggy white hair and obsidian skin.

"Oh… my… God…" Saga breathed out, realising that all of the cloaked figures following the elegantly clad girls must have been slaves.

"Zaki!" A girl yelled. She had stopped and was staring at the poor boy as he struggled with the trunk, the other girls standing around her as some kind of entourage.

Navi stepped past Saga to go and help, but Saga laid her hand on her arm and shook her head. "No, you're no one's slave," she said with a venom in her voice. She handed Navi her own bag and weapons, before walking over to the boy and picking up the trunk with ease.

"I've got it," she said as the boy looked up at her with wide eyes full of wonder. Navi followed them as Saga picked the trunk up with relative ease.

She walked up to the collection of elves and dropped it at the girl's feet. "You ought to be ashamed of yourself, making a small child haul your junk."

"Junk?" the girl shrieked, her delicate pale features going beet red in anger. Zaki stood there, staring up at Saga, then at the girl who was obviously his owner, looking for instruction. "And who else is going to carry it?"

"You," Saga said. "Look around, you're the only ones too lazy to carry your own bags."

"We have servants," Another girl said haughtily.

"No, you have slaves. Servants have rights. Servants have pay and days off and they are treated like people."

Around them, people were watching the encounter, no one wanting to get in the midst of the confrontation. It was as though no one wanted to step up and do something about the blatant slavery on display.

The girl turned contemptuously to little Zaki, "Take my trunk boy." The boy bowed his head before her, not looking at Saga as he took the handle of the trunk. "If there's any damage to my trunk from that barbarian's handling, it'll come off your hide," she hissed.

Recognising the look on Saga's face, Navi intervened, stopping her from confronting the elf girl further. "You can't protect the boy forever, eventually they will go back to their school, and he will be at her mercy."

"But!"

Navi shook her head and tugged on her arm. "Navi doesn't like it either, but you cannot change them all."

"Listen to your doxie," the sneering elf girl said, taking Zaki roughly by the arm and repositioning the small child before the chest. The boy cringed, but said nothing, used to the treatment.

Saga stepped up to the girl and lowered her voice so that she was the only one that could hear what was said. "If anything happens to that boy, you won't see me coming."

The girl's expression faltered for only the briefest of moments, before she turned loftily to her friends and demanded that they follow her.

The tent was buzzing with activity when they arrived. Caoimhe, one of the second year Arcana competitors was arranging her belongings around her cot while Elfina, a master archer already, despite being only in her second year had dropped her bag and was already changing into her uniform. Saga had seen her name listed for both solo archery events. Tymberlee was staring at a roster that was pinned to the central strut of the yurt-like structure.

"Off already?" Tymberlee asked the elf.

"The hunt's on in less than an hour!" She exclaimed. "Apparently the grand idea is that we provide for tonight's opening feast!"

Tymberlee, still staring at the roster exclaimed. "They've got all four groups competing between now and tonight."

"Is everyone even here yet?" Navi asked, picking one of the free beds and dropping her own belongings on it.

"I hope so or it will be immediate disqualification," Tymberlee said. "Surely our teachers knew of the schedule in advance right?"

Elfina was quickly trying to get her boots on as the others discussed this. "I don't know, Mistress Grunborg said nothing to me about it and I have to wonder if any of the others even know."

"What group are you in, Elfina?" Caoimhe asked, peering at the list beside Tymberlee.

"One," she spat angrily. "That stuff have a map as to where I have to go?" she waved towards the pile of papers before Tymberlee.

"Here," Tymberlee said, flipping through the papers that were pinned to the tent strut. "We're here, you leave through that communal area and head towards the trunk, around the equestrian stables and out towards the forest… They'll use the portal system, right? Not hunt this entire area barren?"

"I don't know," Elfina admitted. "I just know that if I'm not there by the time the horn blasts, I'm out and Deluca will kill me."

Saga eyed the girl warily over her shoulder. "Deluca? As in Deluca Goett?" She wounded what the Pentathlon team captain wanted with the elven girl. Then, she remembered that Elfina was the archer for the team events, so of course Deluca would be interested in how she did during her standard events.

The girl nodded, slinging her bow over her shoulder, and coming over to have a look at the map Tymberlee was inspecting. "Yeah, and he won't be the only one. Ok, I'm off. Wish me luck!" Saga remembered then that the girl was also on the pentathlon team as their archer. Was there nowhere she could go without running into members of the team?

"What do we do for the rest of the day?" Saga asked.

Tymberlee looked at them and pursed her lips. "Where's Jemima?" she asked.

"Helping Matron Damir with her supplies," Saga said.

The Prefect nodded. "Ok. Well," she eyed them both, "Try not to get into any trouble and don't forget that all your teachers have also set homework that you've got to complete. Maybe you should get a start on that, huh?"

The two girls looked at each other. It wasn't that they had forgotten about the homework that had been piled on them in the week between the mid semester break and the start of the tourney. Master Berfelan had been particularly spiteful with those who were leaving for the week.

"You're such a killjoy," Caoimhe said, flouncing down on her cot and going through one of her bags.

"It wouldn't kill you to start on your work either," Tymberlee stated.

"Plenty of time," Caoimhe said.

"We could head up to the hospital when Jemima returns," Navi suggested. "Get the herbalism assignment out of the way first."

Saga nodded in begrudging agreement. "Oh yippee... Plants..." Saga still wasn't entirely certain that the lessons they were taught actually worked or not, especially when used without the healing magic of the angels running through the concoctions, but if she could at least memorise the facts she might get through the class until she was allowed to drop it in third year.

The arena was hung with banners from all ten schools that were present. In the air, faerie lights floated, bobbing and weaving in the night sky, just as they did higher up in the Tree City. The space was filling up already with staff and students from the various schools already mingling.

Or taunting one another.

They passed a group that included two of the fourth year Werewolves on the Toserra Sorose staff fighting team, in what looked to be heated argument with Weres from Rinsunid Cantera and Ehras Magna. They would change their heads and howl, as though seeing who could do it faster or louder, Saga wasn't sure.

"The teachers are going to love that..." Tymberlee said from behind them, eyeing one of the boys in the group with his gold trimmed blazer.

"They're getting along," Saga said. "What's wrong with it?"

Tymberlee looked at her disapprovingly but shook her head. "I haven't seen Emory all day. Would you make sure that he checks in with me?"

"Me?" Saga squeaked. "I'm sure he's fine."

"Tasso said that he's in with a bunch of the Knightrich guys," Navi added.

Tymberlee rolled her eyes. "That makes me feel so much better," but her over exaggeration of the word 'so' made sure that both girls knew exactly how their prefect felt about the situation. "Ok you two, don't get into any trouble, please!" She flicked her eyes towards the school of purple and gold.

"They look ridiculous in those uniforms," Tasso said appearing behind Navi, a plate of food already in his hands.

"Ahgh!" Navi screamed, not having noticed his approach. She jumped, causing the others to laugh.

"You have fun," Tymberlee said. "I've got some cousins that go to Aquino Becarra that I've got to find."

"Where's Jemima now?" Tasso asked, looking around.

"Probably still with Matron Damir to avoid the party," Saga said. "You know how she feels about the Aquino Becarra angels. "Oh, before I forget, tell Emory that Tymberlee wants to see him." At his raised eyebrow Saga added, "What? I saw the tent assignments! You guys are together."

"Come on, Navi wants food before this one starts taking Tasso's!" Navi exclaimed, pulling Saga in the direction of the food tables. Tasso hugged his plate of food to his chest dramatically.

"You can't!" he cried. They both turned on him, reaching for his plate and extracting juicy, sticky meatballs. "Uhhhh!" he wailed. "Come on guys!" With a laugh they ran off for the food.

"Catch us if you can!" Saga yelled over her shoulder at him, pulling Navi along with her as they wended their way through the growing crowd of competitors and teachers.

Raphaella Damir appeared, standing on the sidelines by the food tables as though she wanted to be anywhere but there. "Is Jemima here?" Navi asked her.

Raphaella frowned, then sighed. "Doesn't like big events, but she has to be here."

"I'm here, I'm here!" Jemima panted out, running up to them. "I had to get changed after spilling that pot of orange blossom and hibiscus salts all over myself. Have I missed anything?"

"Not yet," Tasso said, his plate having seemingly refilled itself as by magic.

"Are you feeding all of us Tasso?" Jemima asked, picking up a strange roll made of rice and wrapped in seaweed. "What's this?"

"I don't know, but it's delicious!" He exclaimed. "Here, try this one," he pointed to one that appeared to have a different filling at the centre of it.

"Sushi!" Saga exclaimed, reaching over to his plate, and retrieving a piece for herself. "Yum!"

"Guys!" Tasso exclaimed as everyone started eating from his plate. "Come on!"

Navi reached over, taking a sticky meatball from him and a delicate, fair hand reached out, slapping her hand out of the way. "What do you think you're doing?" A boy in the elegant purple and gold of Shamel Aiyeola said with a sneer on his face. "What are you even doing here?"

"N… N… Navi was… Navi is…" She stuttered, cradling her hand against her chest.

"How dare you!" Tasso exclaimed. "Just who the hell do you think you are?"

"He goes to that fancy elf school," Saga said, wrapping an arm around Navi. "They brought their slaves… Half of them are just barely babies."

"What is this?" the elf boy asked, staring at them.

Raphaella Damir stepped forward. "I would suggest you apologise and a move along, young man," the matronly woman said.

"Apologise? It was stealing his food. From his plate!"

"It?" Saga exclaimed. "Her name is Navi and she is a student of Toserra Sorose Academy."

At that revelation, the boy started to laugh. It was a full-bodied laugh, that had him bending over in fits. "School? They can't even read. Why would anyone waste their time educating a slave?"

"I said apologise and move along," Raphaella said. "You are not making yourself any friends here boy."

He scoffed, spat at Navi and walked away. Tasso dropped his plate of food to the table and ran after the elf, catching him by the shoulder. It took Saga, Navi and Jemima to stop him from following through on punching the guy.

"Don't Tasso!" Navi begged. "Please!"

"Get away from us," Saga told him.

"Wouldn't want to be near that thing anyway," he sneered and sauntered off.

Saga heaved out a breath. "I have no idea how we're going to survive the week without punching at least one of them."

"I wouldn't' do that," a voice said from the shadows. They turned to find a boy in the red and black of Rinsunid Cantera. He was bald, but his mahogany skin was streaked in black. Saga blinked in surprise. She thought that she had seen all the odd things already… Apparently there was still more. "It would mean instant disqualification."

They eyed each other warily before looking at him. "Thanks for the warning," Tasso said uneasily.

He looked Saga up and down and nodded to himself. "See you in the stadion," he said before walking away.

"What was he?" Saga asked under her breath.

"Daemon of some kind," Navi said.

"He's right though," Raphaella said. "If you let those taunts from Shamel Aiyeloa get to you, you will be disqualified. They don't tolerate fighting."

Somewhere in the distance the music changed, and Saga recognised the twang of the balalaika. Navi had been practicing with it incessantly. "Oh no..." she muttered as she turned and spotted Sidawi up on stage with the same group he had been with that night at Agesilaus, including the man from the marketplace.

"What is it? Oh..." Jemima spotted him too.

Saga moved away from the food table and started weaving her way through the crowd of students and teachers who were watching the performance. He was playing the black balalaika again. Saga glanced around and noticed the glazed look in the eyes of some of the angel teachers from Aquino Becarra. A few of their oldest students looked as though they were having trouble warding off the haze. Amidst a group of Rinsunid Cantera students, a girl with ash grey skin and mouse brown hair was also drawn in the direction of the music.

"Saga?" Navi called after her.

"Pinch me," Saga ordered.

"Huh?" the girl asked.

"Pinch me!" Saga ordered and gave a yelp of surprise as from her other side, Tasso did exactly that. "Keep doing it," she said, shaking her head to try and ward off the effect of the music. All night the music had been playing and up until now, nothing had happened. As soon as Sidawi and his group came on though, she felt the fog of confusion and the desire to follow him. She blinked in surprise when she saw the ghosts. Sure, there were the local ghosts to the area, but over the students from The Two Worlds School, it looked as though they were followed by all of their ancestors, then the students from Shamel Aiyeola were surrounded by angry looking dark elf spirits. She wondered how none of them could know that.

"Tremblay !" She gasped out, spotting the man wandering away from Tymberlee to get closer to the music. One of the leprechauns from Toserra Sorose also had a house ghost following him until the music seemed too much to ignore and the ghost of the leprechaun started to follow Tremblay. "The Ainsli house ghost is here too," she said. She could feel the foggy feeling trying to overtake her again and as she swayed, both Tasso and Jemima pinched her. "Ow!"

"You asked!" Tasso retorted defensively.

"I know, I know... Who else came that's a Prefect?" she asked.

They looked around, trying to catch sight of the distinctive blazers with the gold trim. "There's the prefect of Bridelow Cottage," Jemima said, having finally caught up with them. "Cashin Hasmuk."

Saga looked around, trying to discern living people from ghosts and unsettled dead from returned dead. She tried to remember the ghost who had so adamantly turned Emory away at the Choosings. "There!" she declared, pointing him out even if the others couldn't see him.

"What are they doing?" Jemima asked.

"Uhhhh..." Saga murmured, swaying as she walked. Tasso reached out again to pinch her, but Jemima stopped him.

"What are you doing?" she cried.

"She asked!" Navi cried, trying to get a hold on Saga as she followed the music towards the stage.

"Tymberlee!" Tasso cried. "Catch her!"

The startled Prefect turned from where she had been talking with a group of faeries with the pale blue and yellow of Aquino Beccara, along with Caoimhe and a few other Toserra Sorose faeries.

Unable to cross the distance, she started on what might have been a spell before a furry black body shot through the crowd, launching itself at Saga.

NOTHING IS A SECRET

"Explain it all to me again," Astrid said as she paced the length of the tent, her displeasure evident in her every move.

Saga, Navi, Tasso, Jemima, and Tymberlee all stared at each other, not sure who would start, but all hoping that someone else would. Shadow sat there, panting, his tongue lolling out of his mouth, waiting for someone to notice him again. Saga was picking bits of grass and dirt from her uniform and glaring at Shadow.

"The wolf came out of nowhere, Mistress Grunborg," Tymberlee finally said.

"Not about him. I know Shadow... I have no idea what he is doing here, but I know about him," Astrid said. "Tell me what happened with the angels." They told her everything, about the first time, the second time and then the time at the school tourney.

"It's not just the angels though," Saga said.

"What do you mean?" Astrid asked.

"It's the ghosts too," Saga added, scratching at a patch of dried mud on her sleeve with her nail. Instead of coming off though like other pieces that this move had been used on, the patch of mud disintegrated and instead of coming free from the material, was rubbed into it.

"The other prefects and I have been talking about it for a while now. Our house ghosts just aren't there. Usually, they're a constant presence in the houses. I mean, over at Queenette, nothing's gone missing in over a month!"

Astrid raised an eyebrow at that statement. Everyone at the school knew that Cordelia Queenette had an issue leaving personal possessions alone.

"And you can never shut Tremblay up, so it's been really noticeable," Saga added.

"Exactly!" Tymberlee agreed. She looked at Saga. "I know we talked about this before the break, but when was the last time you really saw Tremblay and actually spoke to him?"

Saga thought. She had caught glimpses of him at various events, but actually spoke to him? "The first day of school," she said slowly. "And I used to occasionally glimpse the other house ghosts either around their houses or following their prefects, like tonight, but… pass a fourth year class the halls or in the streets and there's not a house ghost to be seen these days. Except when Sid's around."

"It's the Balalaika," Jemima added.

"And the song!" Tasso said. "He was playing the same song both times I noticed him."

"The one he was playing tonight?" Astrid asked. "I didn't recognise it."

"Those other boys were with him last time we were here in the tree city too," Saga added.

Navi worried her lip and shook her head. "No, Sid can't be doing anything wrong. It has to be some sort of coincidence. What Navi means is, is that Ziva would-."

Saga elbowed Navi in the ribs, while Tymberlee coughed loudly. Saga eyed the older girl, realising that maybe her prefect knew more than she thought. Sid had made it seem like no one had known about his relationship with Ziva, but as Saga thought about it, she could see Tymberlee's hand on his shoulder that night, when Dorbe Manor had burned. Shadow looked from one person to the next, his gaze finally settling on Saga as silence descended within the tent.

"There's something else you should know," Saga added softly. All eyes turned to her. "I tried to talk to Sid about it, after the tourney event before break." She bit her lip, knowing that what she had to say next would change everything. "He attacked me."

"What?" Navi exclaimed. "Navi can't believe it."

"I was chasing him, and he was, I don't know, mad at me? Scared of me? Yeah, maybe that's more right. He seemed scared, but I don't know. He'd been talking to some guy I've seen around. He's a shadowy figure and I don't know who he is."

"Ok," Astrid said pensively. She was staring at Saga and Saga could tell that the Weapon's Mistress was trying to hold back her anger and frustration.

They watched as she took a deep breath, then waited as she tried to put the facts together. "I don't know what's going on with Sidawi Harmeet," she looked at Saga, "And you should have said something when his happened."

"It was my fault!" Saga argued, then hurried on when Astrid looked ready to go to battle with her. "Plus, he's not been himself. Not since..."

Astrid held out her hand, motioning for Saga to stop. "I understand that, and as an isolated incident, I would let it go, but it's not isolated. There's more going on. So for now, I'm going to suggest that you stay away from Sidawi Harmeet until we figure out what is going on with him."

"But!" Navi exclaimed, "He's tutoring this one with the Balalaika!"

Astrid glared at the girl. "Especially where that instrument is concerned," she said sternly. She looked back at Saga. He's already attacked saga. We have no idea what's going on with him. Stay away from him, Navi."

The girl pouted then, perked up as though realising something. "He's cancelled two of Navi's last three tutoring sessions."

"At Jimpsee? The one he did come to happened elsewhere?" Saga asked.

Navi nodded. "The music room at Sorosian Hall."

"He's avoiding me," Saga concluded.

"That's probably a good thing for now," Astrid said. She took a moment to look at each of them, before returning her attention to Saga. "Which of the house ghosts did you notice today?"

"Umm..." Saga thought. "Tremblay of course, and the Ainsli House ghost. I think the other one was from Bridelow Cottage? Jemima said that the guy I was pointing at was their Prefect."

"But Mistress Grunborg, it's not just us anymore. The angels from Aquino Becarra are also being affected," Jemima said.

"And the students from that Two Worlds School," Saga interrupted. "They look as though they are followed by every family member that has come before them... And the fancy pants elves from that other school, are totally being haunted by the spirits of their angry, dead slaves."

"Well..." Astrid said. "I did not expect that..."

It was interesting to not be the only one out for a morning run. Saga had awoken that morning to Caoimhe's snoring and finding Jemima and Navi still asleep, had decided to dress and get a run in before the morning meal. There was a lot to think about after the night before, like why Shadow had shown up? After Astrid had left them, he had slunk off into the night and

Saga would not admit, even to herself, that she missed him. Both in his wolf form and his... other form.

With a crowd though, she ran at a slower pace, more in line with what she had noticed the Weres capable of. It wasn't that she wanted to do this, but during the midday meal the day before, several fourth years, including Deluca Goett and her own house prefect, Tymberlee had cornered her, warning her not to let the Weres in on their secret weapon. She had of course argued the point, wanting to know how she was supposed to train if she was hobbling herself.

"In secret," Orsi Chuqiao, a fourth-year Weretiger on the Were Battle team had said.

Well, that had just cleared everything up, hadn't it? They were in a camp of several hundred other students, all their competition and they expected her to train in secret?

Still, despite the limitations, Saga still enjoyed the morning run. She would find somewhere to work on her sprints.

She allowed a couple of Weres and green and brown to rush past her in a heated competition with another group in red and black. It was going to be an interesting week.

To get anywhere, you had to pass through the central communal area and Saga tried her hardest to not look at awe at all the different races mingling with one another. She was passing by the entrance to the camp for Shamel Aiyeola's students when a brilliant shock of white hair caught her attention amidst a board of purple and gold clad students. Words like doxie, ash-face and slave being bandied about.

"Navi?" She exclaimed and pushed through the crowd. There delicate Ljósálfar seemed to fall out of the way for her and Saga was able to take the arm of the white-haired girl just before she lashed out at them. "Don't," Saga said, realising in an instant that the girl was taller and broader than Navi or any of her sisters and wore the red and black uniform of Rinsunid Cantera. "They're not worth it."

Then to her surprise she saw that the tall Dökkálfar girl had actually been defending another, smaller girl with ash coloured skin and mousey brown hair. With her other hand, Saga reached out and took her by the arm too. She was just on time too because the ash-coloured girl had a gnarly looking knife in her hand. "They're not worth it," Saga repeated and pulled both girls from the crowd. Amongst them, she recognised the elf girl from the first day, the one with the little slave boy named Zaki.

The ash grey girl without a uniform wrenched her arm free with surprising strength as soon as they were away from the Ljósálfar students. "Who are you?" She said angrily.

The other girl, older than both of them Saga guessed, reminded her of Ziva as soon as she spoke, her soft tones reminiscent of the Dökkálfar Prefect. "She was helping us Tena, it wouldn't hurt for you to be grateful once and a while."

"Why should this one be grateful? Tena could have taken those lilywhites easily!"

"This one is sure you could have, but Tani didn't bring you along for you to get into fights everywhere you went and what were you doing trying to sneak in there?"

The girl stopped her tirade and noticed that Saga had been herding them towards the Toserra Sorose encampment. "We can't go there. Who are you anyway?"

She had been about to answer when someone else screamed her name across the expanse of the camp.

"Looks like someone's in trouble," the girl, Tena said.

"What are you doing hanging out with the enemy?" An angry Deluca Goett asked stalking up to them, "do you have any idea who she is?" He asked, pointing at the unidentified dark elf.

"Uhhh..."

"The competition, Saga! The competition. She's their soloist!" He waved his hands up and down in front of the girl as though to indicate her uniform.

"Ok..." Saga said. "It's not against the rules to talk to them."

"How do you even know who this one is?" The Dökkálfar girl asked. "We were keeping it a secret."

Deluca's shouting had stirred a crowd and people were coming out of tents to see what was happening. The leprechauns on the racing team, Tymberlee and the other arcana combatants, then Navi and Edun, Tasso and Jemima hot on their heels.

"I do my homework," Deluca said, eyeing the girl and apparently not noticing their growing audience. "I will admit, I was surprised that you're not one of the vampires or daemons."

"Surprised?" Edun asked. "Is that all you have to say? We were told that Ziva was the first Dökkálfar to attend one of the big schools and," he said looking at Tani, "you're at least a fourth year, right?"

"Yes, this one is a fourth year, but this is Tani's first interschool tourney."

Navi had been silently staring at the two Dökkálfar girls and while Tena, with her unusual colouring was interesting, it was obvious that she was awed by the elegant girl in her black and red uniform.

Deluca frowned and tried to pull Saga aside, but she just shook him off. "Perhaps we should talk about asking first, huh?" She said to him, and he had the good sense to look embarrassed.

"This one is Tani," the Rinsunid Cantera girl said as she sat down across from Edun. Saga had led them to the dining tent where it was still relatively empty as people got ready for the day before coming in for breakfast. "And that is Tena."

Edun just stared at her, his gaze flicking between Tani and Tena. "You're Dökkálfar," he said dumbly as though he was unable to understand what he was seeing.

"Yes Edun," Saga said. "Just like you."

He shook his head adamantly. "No, not just like Edun..."

"How did you get to go to school" Navi asked the girls.

"This one don't go to no stinking school," Tena said instantly, but Tani gave her a playful, but insistent slap up the backside of her head. "Ow!"

"Be quiet, you heathen! My family are merchants across Svartalheim and-"

"Slaves for merchants," Edun interrupted.

Tani shook her head though. "No, they're merchants."

"But how did they get away from their masters?" Navi asked, her voice full of awe.

Tani looked kindly at Navi, "there are no slaves in Svartalheim... The Dökkálfar community at the school is small but growing. They do try to keep it quiet though to stop those old duddies at Shamel Aiyeola from interfering... But with Toserra Sorose presenting not one but two Dökkálfar to tourney, I stepped up," her eyes lit up with mischievous light, "we even have an entrant in the arcana battle this year."

"Really?" Jemima asked.

"Pah, Dökkálfar can't do magic," Edun stated, as Saga eyed Navi and Tasso who were looking anywhere but at the disbelieving boy.

Saga had caught Navi using a basic fire spell to light a fire and had been sworn to secrecy, explaining that Tasso had been teaching her.

"Of course, we can," Tena interjected, lifting her hand up before her, she muttered out a few words and a deep purple flame started to bob and weave on her palm.

"Perhaps you shouldn't do that so openly," Tani suggested. "Especially given how often you get those little misfires."

"But you're not the arcana entrant, are you?" Edun asked, watching the odd girl with interest.

"No!" Tena exclaimed. "Tena doesn't go to that stuffy school!"

"Tena lives in or around Dark Fields and the Dökkálfar at the school watch out for her," Tani explained.

"I can watch out for myself!"

"You were almost killed by a sequential killer," Tani shot back.

"He was my master!"

"So..." Saga said cautiously, "you were a slave then?"

"No, this one's ma lives in Nidvelir, but," she motioned awkwardly to herself, "Tena didn't exactly fit in so this one went to look for Tena's dad. This one hung out there for a while but..."

"Didn't fit in there either?" Saga asked.

The girl nodded solemnly. "Yeah, something like that. So, this one lived on the streets of Dark Fields for a while before Tena was taken in by this old man. He taught magic and then one day turned on this one. So Tena's back where this one started really."

A growing level of noise indicated that the camp around them was waking up and several students started to wander in.

"Foods up!" Tasso announced excitedly.

"Trust you to notice that," Navi said wryly.

"What?" He asked, pushing back from the table and getting up.

Saga looked around. She didn't spot anyone she recognised as she approached the staging area for the race. She had somehow managed to get herself into the first group and after the long conversation which she had left the others to, she had raced back to her tent in order to change for the official event.

Just before she checked herself in with the event coordinator, her arm was caught, and she turned to find that Emory had been following her.

"Emory..." She said, startled by his presence. "What... What are you doing here?" she asked.

"I just…" he said awkwardly, looking around as though trying to look anywhere but at her. "I just wanted to wish you good luck." He said hurriedly. "And give those jerks from Ehras Magna a run for their money!"

Saga nodded. "I'll give it my best."

Emory looked around. "Where are the others? I would have thought they'd come to watch."

Saga's eyes lit in delighted wonder. "Did you know that Rinsunid Cantera accepts Dökkálfar and have a whole community? Their pentathlon soloist is Dökkálfar."

"What?" he asked in wide eyed awe. "No…" He looked cautiously over her shoulder. "Not to alarm you or anything, but you're being watched by a big daemon guy in the Rinsunid uniform."

Saga surreptitiously tried to glance over her shoulder at what Emory saw. "Him again… I guess I'm racing against him today… I wonder how daemon's run compared to Weres…"

"Can't be too great, Ehras Magna usually wins this event unless Rinsunid puts up a Were," Emory said. "I'll let you go."

Saga nodded and started to walk away before looking back, only to find him looking for a place to watch from. She bit her lip nervously and went to check in for the race.

The daemon fell into place beside Saga as she signed her name on the check in form. "Can I help you?" she asked, stepping aside to allow him to sign his name.

"Rumour around camp is that Toserra Sorose has some sort of non-Were secret weapon," he said.

"Really?" Saga asked innocently. How much spying went on around here? Deluca had known the identity of the dark elf girl, Tani and now this daemon knew her.

"I watched you run this morning. You were holding back," he went on.

"Was I?" Saga asked.

He nodded. "Oh, yes." He said.

"I guess we'll find out," Saga said, allowing herself to be taken off by one of the judges to ensure that there were no magical or other methods of cheating in use. The daemon guy eyed her as he too was taken away for the same checks.

"Taken any herbal concoctions to increase speed or stamina?" a stern woman asked.

"No ma'am," Saga said quickly.

"Any sneaky little friends cast spells on you?"

"Not to my knowledge ma'am," Saga answered. She was pretty sure that no one would stoop that low.

"Any magical items?"

Saga looked down at her competition uniform, still regretting the shoes she was being forced to wear. "No ma'am," she said, recalling the meeting where Astrid had informed her of the rules. It had later devolved into near chaos when the Pentathlon stadion competitor, a Weretiger by the name of Harry Mau had objected to Astrid's decision to have Saga teach running skills.

"What do you mean I can't wear my shoes?" Saga cried indignantly.

"Saga there are school rules and uniforms that have to be adhered to," Astrid tried to explain.

"I know that," Saga said. "This isn't my first time representing my school, but shoes, shoes that work to your feet can greatly aide your ability to win!"

The other members of the stadion team and the two pentathlon soloists were staring at her. Astrid just handed her the outfit and said, "You've trained in your boots, right?" Worry etching her face.

"Yes!" Saga exclaimed, "But I haven't run a race in them!"

"Then we've got the rest of the week to make sure that you can and in that time, I want you to help coach the others. You've talked about how you were taught to run, I want you to share those teachings."

At that, there were objections from the other team members. The weretiger boy, Harry seemed particularly displeased at the prospect. "You can't teach running!" he sneered. "You either can do it or you can't!"

Where had Saga heard that before? "Oh yeah? Is that a tiger philosophy or something?" she asked, sure that either Dayan or Javaid had said a similar thing at the beginning of the school year, right before she had beaten them for the first time. "There's timing, there's posture, there's breathing, there's your starting position, and more. All of that plays into how you run," she looked at Astrid. "Suddenly training them now though could seriously impact their ability to win."

"How?" Deluca asked, he seemed genuinely interested.

"When you start trying something new, or you alter something to work on that something new, you forget other parts, parts that you knew really well until you figure out how to merge them, like in weapons class when you fix a bad habit."

"This is all nonsense," Harry groused.

The woman, a disgruntled Ljósálfar, cast a spell and Saga guessed that it checked to see if there was any magic around her. She nodded to herself and motioned for Saga to leave. "You can go," she said.

"Thank you, ma'am," Saga said, trying not to get on the woman's bad side. She hoped that when the time came for the staff pairs, this was not the woman doing the testing, because Saga wasn't sure what would happen with Navi. The elves they had encountered so far, had been vicious and cruel in their actions and their words.

There were ten of them in total. One competitor from each school. She saw one of the ostentatious elves in their purple and gold uniforms, his small servant cloaked at his side. In the orange and grey of the eastern school, Saga saw a boy that reminded her a lot of Harry Mau, but instead of Harry's tiger features, the boy seemed to be more dog like. What was he? She wondered, then he turned around and she just about squealed in delight when she saw his big, fluffy tail. She had to clap her hands over her mouth to stop herself from doing so. She had no idea what he was, but he was absolutely adorable.

"Something wrong?" The daemon from Rinsunid Cantera asked.

Saga eyed him. "Are you following me?" she asked.

"Just curious. All secret talks over at your camp about how the stadion is theirs this year. It has me intrigued as the only new racers are you and the tiger boy in group three... and there's nothing special about a tiger."

"Maybe he's really fast," Saga said.

"Maybe."

"Hey," Saga said sidling over to him. She still had no idea what his name was and had no interest in asking him or divulging her own. "The guy over there... What is he?"

The daemon eyed the boy in question. "Kitsune." Saga just raised a questioning eyebrow at him. "Fox spirit from Takama-no-hara... No, Tsuchi... No Yomi... No, definitely Takama-no-hara... Ugh! I don't know which realm," he finally admitted, "Tricksters. Be careful not to be set next to him."

"Competitors to your marks!"

"Good luck," Saga said to him just before one of the coordinators came to bustle the, off to their starting points.

"And to you," he called back.

Saga stood at the start line. Somehow, she had managed to get position one. Not a bad number, the racers were only to one side of her, but next to her was the trickster fox spirit. Next to him was a Were girl from Ehras Magna.

She closed her eyes and took a deep breath. This wasn't like Tourney back in Nýr Ásgardr. This wasn't like running in races back home. This was something new. She was racing against animal spirits and daemons. For the first time in a long time, she had no idea how it would turn out and she was excited. She could hear some people calling her name from one side. Apparently, the others had joined Emory. She was glad to have seen him before the race.

"Runners, are you ready?" A loud voice called, and Saga glanced down the line to see the others assume running postures. She did as she always did, lowering herself to rest her hands against the rough ground of the road. She heard the murmurs and the whispers. Beside her, the fox spirit reached out, trying to grab her.

"Leave me alone," Saga hissed.

"What are you doing down there?" he hissed back.

"This is my starting position," Saga said, shaking him off. "Leave me alone!"

A RACE AGAINST TIME

Saga could see the shuffling of feet as they waited. People were lined up along the road, waiting for the race to begin. The road encircled the tree city and usually connected the multitude of roads that lead to the centre of the nine realms.

"Go Saga!" She heard someone call out.

"Toserra Sorose for the win!"

Somewhere else, a werewolf howled and several other Weres joined in. Then the horn blew, and they were off. Saga pushed off from the ground, the world fell away as her body straightened up, the momentum from the push propelling her forward.

A loud, clear voice spoke out over the noise of the crowd and the pounding in her ears, "And they're off. Group one today features new runners from Toserra Sorose and Rinsunid Cantera. The rumour from Toserra Sorose is that this member of the heavenly host, their first-year student, Saga Joy Carolle has not lost a match yet this year! There's always time for a first. And from the depths of Svartalheim, comes Hymer Rendon, a third-year student at Rinsunid Cantera, Rendon is competing at his first Tourney event after injury pulled one of the runners from the team."

The fox spirit seemed to yip in surprise as Saga overtook him. Further down the line, the elf from Shamel Aiyeola seemed to vanish from sight altogether, as did the siren from Kahawaiola'a Ocean School.

"Our competitors today will run the length of the world tree circuit road, a length longer than the usual stadion events held at each school, this will be not only a trial of speed, but endurance. Look at them go."

The first turn came into sight. Saga was able to take the turn tight against the curve. This was where her track running experience showed, even if none of the others knew it. She stayed tight to the curve and the daemon from Rinsunid Cantera seemed intent of following her every move, was right on her heels. Unlike back home where running on a track meant that everyone stayed to their own lanes though, it didn't take long for the main bulk of the competitors to be running as a tight group, but those in the curve like Saga pulled ahead.

"Rendon is hot on Carolle's heels, just as Yen Makino from Ni Sekai-Ryu or for those of you not up with the traditional name of the school, The Two Worlds School. But these three should be wary, Margot Featherswallow a fourth year from Ehras Magna and the daughter of an Alpha, is catching up."

Eyes forward, she ran. Eyes always on the prize, her coach had been fond of saying. Shoulders up, back straight, chest out and pump those arms. One foot in front of the other. The rhythm was comforting as she put on speed. The kitsune was right on her heels as was the green and brown figure of the Ehras Magna competitor. She couldn't find the daemon anymore and she would not risk her position by looking back.

"It looks as though the only four worth watching at as per usual, Toserra Sorose, Ehras Magna, Rinsunid Cantera and The Two Worlds School. These four just can't seem to escape from each other."

The track turned again, and the cheering was getting louder. The side of the road was filled with spectators, students from the ten schools, residents of the tree city and visitors alike were there. She could catch flashes of the various school colours as she passed. There were hoots and hollers as she ran. Another group jeered at her intermittently as they cheered and howled for their runner. When had running become so popular? Back in Nýr Ásgardr almost no one came to watch and those that were there took the races as the time to get food breaks, rest or visit the amenities.

"Kahawaiola'a Ocean School always puts up a good fight, but their Sirens just can't compete against the raw animal speed of the Were."

The finish line was coming into sight now and Saga dug deep for that one last push. She had no time to look for the others. Her only thought was on the line that awaited her. Crossing it first was her only goal. Arms pumping and legs hitting the road, one after the other, again and again was all that she could think about along with her breathing.

Closer. That finish line was within her reach. There was a flash of green beside her and the Were from Ehras Magna was there. She didn't dare to look to confirm that. Instead, eyes to the goal, she kept on running.

"Would you look at that, Featherswallow and Carolle are neck and neck for the win. Does one of them have that drive for the win?"

She barrelled past the line, trying to slow her momentum, the other runners coming in around her. They waited for the last two runners to appear at the finish line. The Siren from Kahawaiola'a Ocean School and a pretty elf boy from Shamel Aiyeola. Probably used to getting his slave to do his training, Saga thought uncharitably.

"And with that the last runners are in. It looks as though the judges are entering into a heated debate," the announcer commented. "Make sure to stick around to find out who won!"

Skins of water were handed out to the competitors as heavy discussions went on with the judges. Saga drank her fill and worked on reclaiming her breath. The daemon, Rendon, sauntered over to her and held out his hand. "Good run and you put the dog in her place," he said with a glance over at the Werewolf. She was staring at them in disbelief right before her eyes went as wide as saucers and her demeanour changed.

"What in the ever-loving hell was that?" Someone shouted and all heads swivelled to an angry, bear of a man stalking towards the gathered competitors. They scattered out of the way as the man went directly up to the werewolf girl and towered over her as she cowered. If she'd been in wolf form, her tail would have been between her legs.

"Sir we've not announced the winners yet, please get back behind the line," one of the coordinators asked. Saga spotted Tilson Everard amongst the race adjudicators and wondered what he had seen. The dismay in the faces of those in the uniform of Ehras Magna kind of told her everything she needed to know though, even if the fury of the man had not. Whomever had come in first, it had not been the werewolf girl.

Saga glanced over at the girl, cowering before the big man, before returning her attention to Rendon. "Kind of wish I hadn't... I raced against kids like her back home... It's never good for them when they lose."

The daemon raised a curious, but hairless eyebrow at her. "You're concerned about her?"

Saga shrugged. "Who knows what their punishments are for losing... The way she's cowering there, it says a lot to me."

The daemon shook his head. "Softy," he muttered.

"Attention competitors, attention guests," a Siren, her voice and clear over the racket of hundreds of people called out. "What a most exciting race, I'm sure you'll all agree. If this is the capability of this year's competitors, then we are in for a week of wild surprises and exciting events."

"Who won?" Someone called from the crowd and the Siren announcer held out her hand to placate the crowd.

"In third place, Yen Makino, in second place, Hymer Rendon." Saga nodded her congratulations at the daemon but could see a look of consternation upon his face. "You all saw how close it was. It was a tough decision," she went on, "but in first place, we have Margot Featherswallow from Ehras Magna."

"Oh..." Saga breathed out, glancing over at the bear like man who had been berating the girl. There were boos from the crowd as the blue and red uniformed students of Toserra Sorose made their opinions heard. Had she really run that badly that she had not even made the top three? "Then why-," she started to ask no one in particular.

"AND," the announcer said, placing significant emphasis on the word to try and quiet down the disquiet building in the crowd. "And Saga Joy Carolle from Toserra Sorose."

"A draw?" Rendon asked incredulously.

"Wow..." Saga said.

Her name was getting louder as she noticed her friends running to the side closest to where she was standing. Behind them, she saw Tymberlee wave and Saga waved back. Her prefect looked proud.

"Nicely done," Rendon said holding his hand out once more. This time, Saga took it.

"Thank you," Saga said. "You too."

"I will race you again next year," he said. "And maybe by then, I will have discovered your secret."

"Good training," Saga said. "There's no secret, just good training."

He scoffed. "And if you're one of the heavenly host, I'm a faerie godmother. Till next year Story Girl."

"Strange guy," Saga said to herself before going to shake hands with her co-winner. "Good race," she said holding her hand out to the girl.

The girl snarled at her. "Get away from me! You must have cheated. There's no way anyone out runs me. Anywhere!" and with that, she stormed off.

Saga stared after the werewolf girl but was inundated by people hugging her. She cried out in surprise.

"You were amazing!" Navi exclaimed. Her arms wrapped around Saga's neck. People were trying to get at her, and Saga couldn't figure out why.

"You did it!" An awkwardly long-limbed girl Saga thought was the older sister of a boy in her own class. "Those uptight mutts at Ehras are going down!"

Saga leaned back against Navi and said, "You all do realise that I drew against the girl from there, right?"

"Right!" Donetta Coccio declared before pointing at a well-muscled boy nearby that Saga knew was supposed to have been Toserra Sorose's best runner... before her. "He could barely manage fourth last year! Never made the final."

"Hey!" the guy exclaimed. "Give me a break!"

"I thought that had more to do with the fact that his ex-girlfriend was running," Tymberlee called out, which caused the older students to jeer and taunt the weretiger in question. "I don't remember the last time we even made it to the finals!" She wrapped her arm around Saga's shoulders. "This one's mine!"

"Jimpsee!" Jemima called out.

"Jimpsee!" they shouted.

"You rang?" Tremblay exclaimed, swirling up from the ground and twirling before them.

"Tremblay!" Saga and Tymberlee exclaimed together.

He swirled, slightly more tattered than Saga was used to seeing him. He seemed faded too and that just did not fit with his flamboyant personality. He looked around. "This isn't Jimpsee House... This isn't even our beloved Nýr Ásgardr," his eyes widened and he gasped dramatically. "Are we at the interschool tourney? Did we just have a win?"

"Where've you been?" Saga asked.

"Oh, uhh..." Tremblay glanced from her to Tymberlee and around at the others who were gathered there. He turned back to the two girls with a smile on his face that was meant to light up his entire countenance and instead seemed only to show off exactly how dull his eyes appeared to be. "Here and there," he said with the idle swish of his hand. "Things to do, places to be, you know."

Tymberlee crossed her arms over her chest and Saga was certain that she was about to start tapping her foot. "No, I don't," the Prefect said. "Enlighten me."

"Us," Saga corrected. "Enlighten us!"

As Tremblay attempted to make his excuses, Donetta leaned over to Navi, Tasso and Jemima. "What's happening?" she asked.

"What?" Jemima asked. "Doesn't your Prefect talk to your house ghost?"

"No..." Donetta said, "And that doesn't explain Saga."

"Valkyrie," Tasso said. "She can see all the ghosts."

"The library is this way," Jemima said confidently as she led the way through the clustered buildings on what had to be the largest branch of the world tree city. It felt larger than the market branch which was full of bustling shops and stalls selling anything and everything from across the nine realms and the extended planes.

The branch, which to Saga's way of thinking was just a street, was lined with well-built wood buildings, properly roofed with tile and thatching unlike other buildings in the city, which usually used brightly coloured, and patch worked canvas.

"Everything seems so fancy here," Navi said, pointing out beautifully engraved adornments to the buildings.

"What else is here?" Saga asked. "Theatres?"

"Yes, but also museums and galleries. The religious gardens are also near the end of the branch. It is said that there is a statue there of every god who has ever lived throughout the nine realms and the extended planes."

"All of them?" Navi asked in disbelief. "But Zeus and Odin alone had enough children to overflow a single branch..."

Tasso laughed. "That's true. A little prolific..."

"Well.... You know," Jemima said defensively, "not the children they had with mortals!"

"What's that place with all the angels?" Navi asked.

"The Hall of Guardians," Jemima said. "Well, no, not the hall itself. That's on a cloud above Alfheim. That's the 'quick' way to Yggdrasil City. Look, it's my Aunt Muriel!"

The pretty, but haggard angel was there, talking to another angel, not noticing their approach.

"Aunt Muriel!" Jemima called, causing both women to turn. Muriel beamed, but the woman beside her went a shocking shade of white and looked as though she might faint.

Saga stopped and stared. she couldn't believe what she was seeing. Jemima ran towards her Aunt Muriel, but Saga's feet just wouldn't move anymore. She never thought that she would see the woman standing there again. That last day seemed so long ago, and she had barely given the woman another thought since the new school semester had started.

"Ms Roskin," she said just standing there as Jemima launched herself into her aunt's arms.

The woman seemed just as stunned as Saga, frozen to the spot. She opened and closed her mouth a few times as though she was trying to say something, until finally she managed to choke out, "Saga."

Muriel untangled herself from Jemima and looked between the angel and the Valkyrie. "Shari?" She asked cautiously.

"You're an angel," Saga said, still standing, rooted to the spot. Her friends were now all staring at her, the gazes occasionally peering at the angel, but concern glittered across their faces as they waited for something to happen.

"Uhh... Yes," the angel said.

"So, you always knew," Saga said.

"No," Ms Roskin exclaimed. "I didn't."

Saga shook her head. "That's not possible. Why else would you have taken me to Walhalla that day? Astrid said that she was meant to meet my mother there on that day."

"I..." The woman looked to Muriel for support, but she seemed to have no words of support for either of them. "Saga, I..."

"All those years..." Saga went on, "all those years of people telling me that I was making things up for attention or that I was a freak, and you knew. You knew what I was and you said nothing!"

"I didn't Saga, I didn't know!" The woman exclaimed. "I didn't know!"

"My mother's note, the blanket with the scene of Valkyries on it by Oji Kamal... I mean, Master Berfelan had the exact same picture hanging in his office! How did you not know?" Saga cried. "Why did you let them do that to me?"

"Saga," Tasso said. "Who is she?"

"Perhaps we should take this somewhere else?" Muriel suggested, looking around ay the people were starting to take notice. "Gabrielle's house isn't far from here, why don't we-."

"No," Saga said interrupting her. "I'm sorry Ms Muriel. I... I can't..." Muriel looked at her, her kind face creased in concern as she watched Saga.

She took several steps back from the group, backing away from a situation she didn't know how to handle.

"I didn't know," Shari said again. "I didn't know!"

"I can't," Saga said and turned. "I can't do this!"

"Don't!" Shari called after her, but it was too late. Saga was running along the branch, needing to be anywhere but there. She had no idea what was happening in that moment, and it was easier to revert back to form and run away then try to figure it out.

"Go after her!' Muriel exclaimed.

"She's beaten every Were she's been up against in running," Navi said. "You can't catch her!"

Saga had no idea how she managed to do it, but she found herself in a garden with statues set within small alcoves made of flowers and bushes. The Garden of the Gods she guessed, but how had that happened? She could have sworn that Jemima had said that the garden was at the end of the branch, and they had been making their way to the library which was supposed to be somewhere in the middle...

She stopped running. She didn't see anyone, but she was certain that running in such a place would be frowned upon. She also felt a similar feeling of reverence to when she entered the temple complex back in Nýr Ásgardr for class. There was something sacred about this space and despite her lack of religious beliefs, she still felt the need to respect the space.

The garden was peaceful and the further on she walked, the more she realised that she was actually not alone. Flower Angels were quietly tending to the plants and statues of the garden. Reverent believers were bowed in prayer, hidden from sight by immaculately tended bushes. Sound seemed to be dampened too and Saga wondered if that was a natural effect of the garden or of a spell had been cast over the area, because she could barely hear the rustle of the leaves in the wind or the chattering of small animals that surely called this garden home.

Sharon Roskin was an angel. The thought hit her like a tonne of bricks all over again. If Ms Roskin was an angel, then surely, she had to have known about Saga's heritage, right?

It didn't make sense that the woman would have let her be ridiculed for all those years if she had known...

So, had she known?

Did it matter even if she hadn't known exactly what Saga's story was? The unsettled dead and the returned dead were a part of life in the Nine Realms. Angels of Death could see them! It was a known ability here. The average person could also be given the ability to see the dead. The Prefects badges which allowed them to talk with their house ghosts were proof of that!

Sharon Roskin had always known that there was something different about Saga, something not of that world and she had said nothing. That was unforgivable.

Saga sat herself down on a stone bench in one of the flowered alcoves and buried her head in her hands. It wasn't long before she felt the wet, snuffling nose of a large animal nuzzling at her, trying to fit its big nose in under her arm.

"Hey," she said, looking down. "Shadow?" She asked, surprised to find his big, soulful eyes staring up at her. "What are you doing here?"

She didn't know what to think. She gave Shadow a scratch under his chin before he started to lick her face. It took a moment to realise that her face was wet, and she wanted to curse. She was crying! No, that was just embarrassing. She had a reputation to keep up.

"Don't you go telling anyone about this," she said firmly, then sighed and leaned her head on his.

Walhalla. It was still there, still prominent in her mind. That day, in that small town, nestled deep within the mountains of The Great Dividing Range. What had been her point in bringing her there if not to meet Astrid?

And why was this all coming up now?

She had occasionally thought about the predicament she must have left the poor woman in when she had found herself in Yggdrasil city and later in Nýr Ásgardr, but Saga was somewhat ashamed to admit that Sharon Roskin and all the people she had left behind had barely come to mind. Her life had been, not to be too cliche about it, magical since her arrival and there was always something new happening. In fact, she hadn't thought much about 'home' since the beginning of the semester because home was Jimpsee House.

But she could remember, standing there in that Bandstand with Ms Roskin telling her about the day she had been found as an infant. She had told her about the Valkyries on her blanket and the similarities of the town name. Walhalla. Valhalla. Instead of listening though, she had run off.

Just as she had now.

Just as she had when the ghosts had ridden over Jisook Farm when they had been in the library. Running had been so much easier than admitting to her friends that she could see the dead. Running, it was really all she ever did, wasn't it?

"I think I messed up again," she said to the wolf.

Maybe that was the real secret behind her speed on the track. Her need to always escape. She looked down at Shadow, perhaps that had been her biggest mistake. Nothing much she could do about it now. She didn't even know what he was doing there. She hadn't seen him since the race that morning.

She should go back. She should apologise. Apologise to her friends for abandoning them again. Apologise to Aunt Muriel for being so rude. But most importantly apologise to Sharon Roskin for running away.

Again.

She looked up at the statue of the Goddess and sighed. "Thanks for the insight," she said. She got up, took a moment to see who it was that she had been sitting with. "Frigg," she nodded to herself and looked up, inspecting the face of the female god. She looked familiar. Long, beautiful curls and an ethereal beauty that Saga recognised from somewhere. She shook the feeling off, even as a raven landed on the statue's shoulder and cawed at her.

"You're right," Saga said. "I need to go find them." Then she turned and left, Shadow on her heels as she tried to remember her way out of the garden and try to find her way back to the Hall of the Guardians or maybe the library if the others had continued on there.

The bird stared after her as she left, then proceeded to preen its feathers.

The area outside the Hall of The Guardians was buzzing with activity when Saga returned. There were angels everywhere, including a few in the pale blue and yellow uniforms of Aquino Bacarra.

"What's going on?" Saga asked. Sidling up to one of the students.

The girl glanced at her, barely taking her eyes off the angels at the front of the crowd and not noticing the big black dog at her side. "Seamus is missing," and as though realising that this inquisitive girl wouldn't know who that was, she went on. "Seamus Hiram, my staff pairs partner."

"Oh..." Saga said. "When did anyone see him last?"

"Last night at the party. A couple of our older students and a few of our teachers started acting strange. Mind you, that's not half the fuss, given the panic going on over in the camp next to ours."

"What do you mean?"

"Weren't you at camp this morning?" the girl asked, eyeing Saga's uniform.

Saga shook her head. "I had my race this morning and then we had to go to the library because our teachers set so much homework..." Realising that she was going on and on, Saga said. "Uh, no... I wasn't."

"Ohhhh! You're the heavenly host that tied with the Were at the races," she eyed Saga up and down. "But you're not an angel."

"No..." Saga said awkwardly. "It's a long story. What was going on in the camp next to yours... That's... That's... What? That Eastern school, right?"

The angel nodded adamantly "Yes, they apparently have their ancestors' ghosts following them around, something about family honour and all that, I don't understand it, but apparently, some of the ghosts have vanished."

"Huh... Our house ghosts have been acting strange too," Saga murmured. "This Seamus of yours and those teachers... Anything to do with the Angels of Death?"

The angel girl thought for a moment. "Seamus's whole family are in the field. I believe he did his work experience with the Angels of Death last year... And Sister Libitina was an angel of death before she started teaching, she now runs the learning program for angels interested in the field."

"What about these other people?" Saga asked looking around at the flustered group of angels.

"Apparently they're not the only ones who are missing."

13

BEAR VS RAT

The missing angels were all anyone was taking about, except for the students form The Two Worlds School, who were more interested in their missing ancestral spirits.

"Saga!" Saga stopped her purposeful trek through the common area between the school camps and looked around, trying to spot who was calling to her. "Over here!" The girl was wearing a mismatched collection of Rinsunid Cantera uniform items.

"Does that actually work?" Saga asked as she approached, Shadow at her side. His big body, rubbing against her leg as he sidled in front of her, as though protecting her from the unknown person. "Do the teachers really believe that you are one of the students there?"

Tena shrugged, eyeing Shadow warily. "Not when they get up close, but from a distance and I generally get enough time to hide then," she admitted. She peered around Saga. "Where are your friends?"

"Where are yours?" Saga shot back, bending slightly to give Shadow a scratch behind the ears. "Calm down, she's a friend."

"Tani has a match now," Tena said. "He a dog, a wolf, a werewolf, right?"

"Ummm," Saga said glancing down at him. "Wolf, I think." She didn't want to give away Shadow's secret.

"He seems very protective of you," Tena said, tentatively reaching a hand out towards Shadow from him to sniff. Shadow eyed Saga, before giving in and sniffing the girl's hand, then licking at it.

Saga tried to hold back a laugh. She could feel Shadow's tail, which looked to be wagging in delighted excitement, start thumping against her legs, harder than was really necessary. He eyed her warily before stepping back from Tena.

"So, what are you doing now?" Saga asked.

"This one is trying not to hang around the camp too much without Tani," Tena said. "Tena doesn't want her to get into trouble and this," she motioned to her uniform, "doesn't really work inside the camp with everyone."

Saga nodded in understanding. "Want to come with me?" Saga sked, not really sure why she was asking, especially when she still had to apologise to her friends, but the girl seemed a little lost without her friend and Saga didn't want to imagine the trouble if the stray Dökkálfar girl was found.

The girl lit up momentarily, before schooling her features to one of casual disinterest and shrugging as though it didn't matter to her. "Ok."

Saga led the way through the Toserra Sorose encampment, asking as she went if anyone had seen Tasso or Navi or Jemima.

"Mess tent," Harry Mau said as Saga passed him. He eyed Tena oddly, but a snarl from Shadow prevented him from saying anything.

"Thanks!" Saga said, hurrying past him. Tena followed close on her heels, keeping her head down to try and avoid drawing attention to herself.

"Firstly, I want to say I'm sorry," Saga said as soon as she found Navi, Jemima and Tasso down, earning an odd glance from Tena. They were set up to study in the mess tent, like many others were. Saga slipped onto the bench beside Jemima, Shadow sitting beside her and testing his snout on the edge of the table.

"Shadow!" Navi exclaimed, sliding out from her seat, to kneel beside the large dog and engulf him in a hug. "Where'd you come from?" She asked, rubbing his chest and under his chin enthusiastically. Tena hovered awkwardly until Navi pointed out her own seat. "Sit, sit, this one is going to play with Shadow!" Tena shook her head, but took Navi's vacated seat, beside Tasso.

Saga coughed, trying not to laugh. It only occurred to her sometimes, but she knew his secret and she couldn't help but wonder what Emory thought of Navi's affectionate greeting. "I didn't handle that well," she went on.

"Aunt Muriel's friend seemed quite upset," Jemima said, closing her book.

"That was Ms Roskin," Saga said. "She was my social worker..."

"Your what?" Tena asked.

"Umm," Saga thought, Tena knew nothing of her past and even if she had, the concept of a social worker was foreign in the Nine Realms. "She was like my guardian. She would make decisions for me and..." Saga shrugged, not knowing how to explain the relationship to her or the others, who were eyeing her with, "I was with her the day I met Shadow and Astrid in Midgard.

"You met the dog in Midgard? Wait, you're from Midgard?" Tena asked, "And who's Astrid?"

"Yes, I met Shadow in Midgard," she waved Tena off, "None of that is important though. I've known that woman for years... I... I just... That last day... Well, those last days before I came here, they were really tough, and I wasn't in a good place. And now, finding out that she's an angel, that she knew about all this, the Nine Realms and ghosts and everything that exists here and said nothing..."

"It felt like a betrayal," Jemima concluded, and Saga nodded. "If it helps at all, she feels really bad about how things happened."

Saga sighed. "It shouldn't, but it does." Tena grinned at that. She had no idea what was happening, but she was familiar with the feeling.

"Have you heard about the missing angels?" Tasso asked, leaning across the table and speaking in a low voice after a few moments had passed.

"Yeah," Saga said, "I went back to the hall looking for you guys, people were everywhere... Aquino Beccara lost a student and a teacher."

"And that school from Takama-no-hara is in a serious panic too," Tasso added.

"They share a strong connection with their ancestors," Tena added. "Especially the warrior classes amongst them. That connection forms the very essence of their beings."

Saga nodded to her. "I can see that when they're near. They're completely surrounded," that got her a strange look from the odd-coloured girl, but Saga went on. "But I heard that several other angels are missing too, not just the two from Aquino Becarra. Tymberlee and I have been talking about how strange the house ghosts have been, you know that." They nodded in agreement. "And the common factor..." she trailed off, giving the others a chance to fill in the gap. Shadow stared up at them, his eyes looking up at Navi as she hugged him close. She refused to look at them.

Finally, Tasso said, "Sidawi Harmeet," Navi looked up, displeased. They all knew how fond she was of the older elf boy, even if not everyone in the group knew the whole story, but there was no denying that he was at the centre of whatever was happening and it had now escalated to the disappearance of living people.

"So, who knows which tent he's in?" Saga asked, leaning across the table.

"No!" Navi exclaimed, hugging Shadow tighter. Saga would have to find a way to apologise to Emory later.

"Yes," Saga hissed. "He's up to something."

"But is it really up to us to figure it out?" Jemima asked.

"Probably not, but who knows what's going to happen the next time I go into one of those hazes. Ghosts and angels are disappearing... And we think we know the cause."

"Is that what happened at the party?" Tena asked, biting her lip. "When people were trying to get to the stage and," she glanced down at Shadow, "He attacked you?"

Saga nodded, thinking about Shadow tackling her to the ground to prevent her from following. "The music, angels of death, me, ghosts... We're attracted to it and we just follow it aimlessly unless someone stops us."

"Huh," Tena said, as though she wanted to say something else, but Jemima spoke up first.

"So, we tell a teacher."

"We did that and now look, people are missing." Saga argued. "I don't like it anymore than you do. I like Sid. He was good to Navi and me during the break, but he's doing something wrong."

"It could be some sort of death magic," Tena suggested.

"What? Like necromancy" Tasso asked. "Isn't that outlawed?"

"No..." she said hurriedly. "I just, no, I don't think he's doing Necromancy... Wait, is this Sid guy an Arcana practicing elf?" They nodded.

"On the Arcana Battle team," Navi added.

"Ok... So... maybe necromancy, but probably not the darkest forms of it because that is the raising of the dead. Using the dead, their bodies or their spirits to do your will."

"The dead are compelled when the music plays," Saga said. "I can see the ghosts, they're..." she paused for a moment, looking for the right word, "enthralled by the music."

"You're not much better when it happens," Navi said and Shadow barked his agreement.

"And neither was your Aunt Dina," Saga said to Jemima.

"You said something about that at the last tourney," Jemima said.

"Yeah, and now an Angel of Death teacher from another school has gone missing," Saga concluded.

"He's in my tent," Tasso finally admitted. "But you heard the strict rules about boys and girls in each other's tents."

"Then we'd better not get caught unless you want to look yourself?" Saga said.

Tasso shook his head adamantly. "He's a Prefect! Are you crazy?"

"So, you'll keep a lookout while I search?" Saga suggested.

Tasso rolled his eyes, but eventually nodded. He looked at Navi who shook her head.

"No," she said. "This one does not believe that Sid has anything to do with anyone going missing. Navi won't help you."

"Navi!" Saga exclaimed.

"No," she insisted. "He's a Prefect and he was Ziva's friend. He is Tymberlee's friend too. No."

Saga sighed. If she didn't know better, she would have thought that Navi might have had a crush on the older boy. He was, if what everyone suspected, completely her type. Tall, blond, willowy and perfectly beautiful. She glanced at Tasso, who also fitted that description. Sisters could be so alike. Not that Saga would know anything about that. She'd never had a sister. Navi and Jemima were as close as she had ever been to having sisters. Still if everything they had heard was true, Sidawi and Ziva had been close, perhaps even in love. They would never get to find out how real it was now and given how Sidawi's father had treated Navi when they were working at the restaurant, perhaps for Ziva's sake, that was a good thing.

"Just don't tell him anything," Jemima said.

"This one never said anything about telling Sid. Only that Navi would not help you riffle through his belongings!" Navi said, obviously hurt by the accusation.

"No one said you would," Tasso intervened, trying to settle things.

"Yes, she did," Navi exclaimed. "Navi is not a gossip!"

"Guys," Saga whisper shouted, "Voices. We don't want the entire camp knowing what we're doing. Will you at least go in first and make sure no one else is in there?" she asked Tasso.

Tasso rolled his eyes dramatically again, imitating his sister in the moment before finally nodding. "Yeah," he said, "I will.... But how are you going to know what you're looking for?" he asked.

Saga frowned. "I don't know, but... It's music right, so what, sheet music? That black balalaika he's playing when it happens? Books about the dead, I don't know!"

"If you don't know, then don't go!" Navi said, crossing her arms over her chest.

"Navi," Saga said.

"This one might know," Tena said softly. They all looked at her. "What? Tena does magic. Tena's last magic master was a sequential killer and into the dark arts. This one might recognise something."

"No, Navi doesn't want to know about this!" She exclaimed, standing up from where she'd been crouched beside Shadow and slammed her books closed. "No. No, no, no!" She insisted. "This one is sorry." She picked up the books, looked down at the big animal, who was staring at her, then back at Saga. "Come on Shadow," Navi said. Shadow looked mournfully at Saga, before following Navi out of the tent.

Saga started to get up and follow her, but Tasso shook his head. "Let her go," he glanced around awkwardly and leaned in closer across the table. "I know why she's so protective of Sidawi."

"Do you?" Saga asked.

He nodded. "You saw him that night... When... Well..." he sighed. "You know when... It didn't take a fool to see that he was in love with Ziva."

Jemima's eyes went as wide as shields. "What? But... But... Sidawi's Ljósálfar..."

"So?" Tasso asked. "Love's love. You can't control that."

"I did not see that coming," Jemima said. "And you both knew?"

"Sid told Navi and me during the school break."

"Navi told me after I figured it out," Tasso admitted. "Ok... I heard Sid and a couple of older boys say that they were going into town. Now might be a good time for us to go search his stuff."

As they exited the mess tent, they caught sight of Navi in the distance. She had stopped her flight to talk to Edun and Saga hoped that maybe her brother could talk some sense into her. Edun, while he knew Sidawi, had never liked the elf boy and didn't like the influence he was garnering over his youngest sister.

"Which way?" Tena asked.

"That way," Tasso said, pointing in the same direction as Navi had gone.

"Are we avoiding her or..." Tena asked when they just stood there.

Saga sighed, "Let's go. She knows where we're going."

"And the guy she's with?"

"Her brother?" Jemima asked. "He'll be fine, but I might... Wait with them..." Jemima suggested.

Tasso grabbed her arm. "You practically accused her of going to tell Sid what we're doing. Give her some space."

"That wasn't what I meant!" Jemima shot back.

"We know that," Saga said, stepping between them. "Let's just get this done before Sid or anyone else in the tent comes back, hey?"

They walked through the camp, looking for all the world as though there was nothing special to look at other than the odd girl in the red and black of Rinsunid Cantera, even if the uniform seemed to not fit her or match.

Tasso ducked into the tent, leaving Saga and Tena outside. Tena leaned against the stack of trunks and crates that were everywhere through the camp.

Tena clicked her fingers excitedly as though an idea came to her. "This Sid of yours, he lost his love?"

Saga nodded. "Yeah."

"This Ziva you guys were talking about, who is she?" Tena asked. "You guys mentioned her when we met earlier."

Saga looked away, her thumb rubbing roughly at the scars on her hands from the night of the fire. "Ziva..." She stopped, shook her head, trying desperately to find the words without descending into fits of wailing sobs. "Ziva was Navi's sister. Last semester there was a series of fires around Nýr Ásgardr... The... The last one..."

"Destroyed Dorbe Manor," Tasso said, appearing from between the tent flaps. "The house where Ziva was prefect... They all lived there..."

"She didn't make it out of the fire?" Tena surmised. She glanced from one to the other, taking in their sombre demeanours.

"No..." Saga said, her fingers still rubbing harshly at the scars on her palms, as she stared seemingly into space "Seven students died that night, eight if you include the boy who died a few weeks earlier in another fire..." Tasso reached out, taking Saga's hands and trying to get her to sop irritating the scars. They shared a look as his own thumb ran over the rough flesh.

"Come on," he said after a moment, "coast is clear." They slipped into the tent. "That's Sid's stuff over there," he said pointing across the mess strewn tent that stopped Saga and Tena in their tracks. The tent, which they had occupied for maybe a day was strewn with clothes and weapons and books.

"Tymberlee would kill us if we made this kind of mess," Saga said, rooted to the spot, this one, miraculous place within the tent that was completely free of debris.

"This one has lived in flea houses cleaner than this," Tena added, stepping an inch closer to Saga as a wrapper from a food vendor fell from its precarious position atop a stack of books to the floor by her feet. "This one's old master kept body parts around the house and that was cleaner than this!"

"Body parts?" Tasso asked, taking a surreptitious look around the tent. "You know what, I don't want to know. I'm going outside to keep an eye out for Sidawi or anyone else..."

"Oh sure..." Saga called after him, "leave us in here while you get to escape to the great outdoors!"

"Shhh!" was his only reply.

"How are we going to find anything in here?" Tena asked.

Saga pointed over to where Tasso had said Sidawi's bed was. "We start there."

They stepped over someone's discarded leathers, around the pile of bags and trunks that had once held all of the belongings now scattered across the floor and narrowly missed the edge of a falling sword. Thankfully, it remained sheathed. Saga hoped for their sake, no teachers entered this tent, because she could see them all being sent back to Nýr Ásgardr, regardless of whether they'd competed yet or not.

"Are they usually like this?" Tena asked, tentatively lifting up a nightshirt from the bed to look under it.

"I..." Saga bent down as to get a better look at the books stacked beside the bed. "Well, Sid's a Prefect and from a noble... No I don't actually think they are noble, but they like to think they are. They're rich."

"Maybe he doesn't know how to clean, always had servants and the like," Tena suggested.

"No... The family works hard. They run a fancy restaurant in town. They're no strangers to work, not that they might not have a maid or two, I don't know," Saga said, running her finger of gilt embossed words. "Plus, he's a Prefect, never would have made Prefect like this... I think..."

"And the faerie?"

"Tasso?" Saga asked. "He lives over at the boy's dormitory. I have no idea what the rules are there, but I spent the holidays in the girl's dormitory and let's just say, you didn't leave anything out and about if you wanted to find it back again!"

"Overbearing house mistress?" Tena asked.

Saga laughed. "No, the house ghost is a thief! And she likes to set people up by hiding the stolen items in their things."

Tena laughed softly. "Kind of sounds like fun..." She said, picking up a workbook. "Your elf really loved your friend's sister," she said, holding it out to Saga. Saga took the book from her and in it, Sidawi had written of Ziva, their plans, their future. How much he missed her and there were sketches of her. Saga ran her fingers of one sketch. Ziva's eyes were bright with laughter, her face almost aglow with delight. "She was beautiful," Tena said in a near whisper.

"Yes..." Saga murmured. "She was..." Saga took a deep, steadying breath, trying to reclaim her balance.

"You took her death very hard," Tena said.

Saga shook her head, "No, I just... Emory and I couldn't get her to leave the house... We uh..." She shook her head. "We should be looking for whatever it is that Sid's been doing..." Tena nodded and they returned to the search in silence.

"Are you two done yet?" a hiss came from the front of the tent.

"We might have been if you guys didn't live like wild pigs!" Saga shot back. "Now quiet! A day, we've been here a day! And Jemima yells at me for not unpacking!"

Tena shot her a weird look but said nothing as opened up an instrument case. "He plays well," she said, "What Tena heard of it anyway..."

"Tena?" Saga said, coming over to have a look.

"Yeah?"

"Why were you affected?" Saga asked.

"Ohhh..." Tena said, picking the instrument up from its case. Sheets of music and notes were scattered in the interior of the case and Tena's tentative hands traced engraving on the back of the balalaika. "This is not good..."

"What is it?" Saga asked.

"This one knows what he's doing..." She breathed out, shoving the instrument into Saga's hands and grabbing at the papers, one after the other. "No, no, no... This is bad... So bad!"

"What is it?" Saga exclaimed.

"Saga!" Tasso called. "Incoming! Sid and Cathal are on their way here right now!"

Both girls halted what they were doing, looking around for somewhere to hide or a way out of the tent. Saga put the balalaika in the case and darted to the tent side. She tugged at it, but the material was pegged down securely. She could take her knife to it, but that would take time and their presence would be known.

"Come here," Tena ordered, crushing several pieces of note paper into her jacket pockets. She slammed the balalaika case closed and tried to put it back where it had been found.

Saga went to her, but her foot got caught on something and she went sprawling across the room, landing amidst a pile of smelly clothes and weapons. "Ugh!" she groaned, crawling to her feet to see exactly what she had tripped on. "Tasso!" She cried. "Why is your damned lance laying across the floor of your tent?"

"Saga, get out of there!" was his only reply from outside.

Saga scrambled over to where Tena was. "You have a plan?" she asked.

"Maybe," the girl said. "You uhh... Can't shape change, can you?"

Saga stared at her. "No! Why? Can you?"

"Yes..." She said. "Ok... This one can hide you and change shape. Yes, that will work."

"Guys!" Tasso called again and now they could hear Sidawi's light, lilting voice and Cathal's big, booming voice.

"If you've got a plan, get on with it," Saga hissed at the girl.

"Go where they're unlikely to go," Tena instructed and Saga looked around. There wasn't really anywhere to hide.

"What about sitting on faerie boy's bed?" Tena suggested.

"I'll be seen for sure!" Saga said.

"No, you won't," Tena insisted, "Just don't move once I've cast the spell."

"Spell? What spell?"

"Just stay still," Tena insisted, pushing Saga down onto a bed. It wasn't Tasso's though. Of that, Saga was certain, she recognised the scent. "Tena means it, you cannot move until they are gone," Tena insisted.

"Yeah, yeah, of course," Saga said.

"I bhfolach i radharc soiléir," Tena murmured and watched as Saga seemed to melt away into her surrounds. The messed-up bed, the canvas siding of the tent. Then, satisfied with her work, Tena glanced around as Tasso's voice loudly greeted Sidawi and Cathal. He engaged them in idle talk about the competition as Tena's form started to shift. The ash grey skin and mousey brown hair gave way to short, brown hair as she started to shrink down. Saga stared wide eyed as a rat stared back at her, its grey tail and brown hair twitching as its little head looked first left, then right, before darting under the bed as the tent flaps were thrown open sand the two fourth year boys entered.

Tena was a wererat? Well, wasn't that something that answered a lot of questions. Half Weres, Saga still hadn't figured them out.

"And then, just like that, that little Magna tiger was all over Javaid. I seriously thought he was going to get his neck ripped out before the referee stepped in," Cathal was saying. "Turns out though, that they're cousins."

"Really?" Sidawi asked, "I thought the whole family had gone to Toserra Sorose, since the first students."

"Mother's side," Cathal corrected. "Major internal family rivalry apparently."

"We're all guilty of it, my mother's family goes to Aquino Beccara and before that, there were ties to Shamel Aiyeola."

Cathal slipped out of his school blazer and Saga's eyes went wide, hoping that the boys were not planning on changing clothes. Cathal tossed the blazer across the tent, where it landed on the bed, right beside her.

Oh boy... She sure hoped that Tena hadn't put her down on the large Werebear's bed. That would cause so many problems, but no... The bed clothes smelled too familiar to be the werebear's.

"Careful!" Sidawi admonished, kicking his way through the stuff that littered the floor. "We have got to clean this up. Tent meeting tonight, this is ridiculous. I don't even know how this happened. Get your blazer off Emory's bed for crying out loud."

Emory's bed. Of all the places Tena could have forced her down, why had it been there? Why had Tasso not mentioned that Emory was one of his tent mates? She tried to control her breathing, especially as Cathal came closer to retrieve his blazer. The werebear had a keen sense of smell, but she just hoped that the mess of the tent would cover her presence. She heard the skittering of claws against the debris and wondered what Tena was doing. That had been a surprise, but one she had been forced to watch in silence.

The blazer was picked up and Saga had to hold in her relieved breath as Cathal stalked across the room, only to trip on the lance, just as Saga had.

"Blasted faerie boy!" he roared, trying to get to his feet. Then he went still. "Sid!" he said hoarsely.

"What?" The elf asked, looking over at his friend and shaking his head.

"R-r-rat."

"What?" Sid repeated.

"Rat," Cathal croaked out. "We have rats!"

"Already?" Sidawi exploded. "How can we already have rats? This mess! That's how! Get up and do something about it."

"I can't," Cathal said, his voice trembling.

"Why not?" an exasperated Sidawi asked, putting down the books he had been trying to search through.

"I hate rats," Cathal said. "Just... Just do something, Sid!" Cathal begged. "Get rid of it!"

Saga felt the giggle bubbling up inside of her and struggled to hold back a snort of laughter. Tena had repeated several times that she should not move and that left her without the physical restraint of putting her hand over her mouth in fear that the spell would fail.

Shaking his head, Sidawi picked up a sword and stalked over to Emory's bed. Sagas eyes widened, as he said, "What are you doing there?" The sword held out in front of him. Could he see her? She had no idea, and he hadn't said her name. She would be in serious trouble if he was talking to her and not the rat beneath the bed.

Below her, Tena squealed in fright and darted from beneath the bed. Sidawi took a wild swing at her, but thankfully missed as she darted across Cathal's head and down his back.

The huge boy started to scream, "Get it off me! Get it off me!"

"I'm trying to kill it!" Sidawi cried.

The tent flap flew open, and Tasso stood there, staring in shock as the small rat jumped from Cathal's backside, onto a chest, Sid chasing it, sword raised above his head. Tena darted for the open tent flap, running as fast as her tiny little legs would take her.

Another head appeared behind Tasso and Saga didn't know if the appropriate response was to laugh or to cry as Tasso and Emory watched Sidawi and Cathal in silent disbelief.

"Get that rat!" Sidawi cried, then noticing the two boys, said, "We're cleaning up, do you hear me? We're cleaning up!"

Dumbfounded, they moved out of the way as he charged out of the tent, swinging the sword as Cathal scrambled back to his feet and chased after him.

"What was that about?" Emory asked, looking over his shoulder after the two fourth year boys.

"Why don't we ask the culprits?" Tasso suggested. "Saga? Tena?"

Emory sighed. "Why am I not surprised?"

"Saga?" Tasso asked again.

"Here," Saga said, getting up from the bed.

"Where'd you..." Emory started to ask.

"No time!" Saga said, bending down to pick up the pieces of the red and black Rinsunid Cantera uniform that Tena had been wearing before her shift. The uniform had been unnoticed by Sidawi and Cathal as they had tried to fight the tiny rat. "That rat was Tena."

"Huh?" Emory asked.

"No time! She found something and then the guys came. We have to catch her before Sidawi and Cathal do!" Saga exclaimed, racing for the tent flap.

BE THE JACKIE

They were gathered in Jemima's bedroom at her Aunt Gabrielle's house. Tena was behind a painted screen, hurriedly putting her clothes back on as the others waited for her.

"Why am I here?" Emory asked.

"I don't know," Saga said, trying not to look at him. He had been staring at her ever since she had emerged from the spell Tena had cast over her. She had clambered from his bed, picking up Tena's clothes before running out and he had been unable to look away from her.

"What did you find?" Jemima asked, sticking her head out of her bedroom door, to make sure that none of her aunts had returned.

"I don't know," Saga admitted. "Tena seemed to know something though."

"There isn't anything, is there?" Navi said, hope blossoming in her voice as she looked from Saga to the screen where Tena was.

"No," Tena called out. She came out, tightening the metal straps of the uniform shirt she was wearing. "There was something." She sat down and while pulling on stockings, she struggled to pull the crumpled sheets she had stolen from Sidawi's instrument case out from her shirt. She handed them to Tasso. Can you read Arcane Runes?"

He nodded. "Yes," he said, taking them from her. Navi sidled closer to him, to have a look.

"Your friend, Sidawi," Tena said cautiously, "Tena thinks... He loved your sister very, very much," she said to Navi. Navi looked up in surprise as she pulled out a sketch he had done of her sister.

"Oh..." she gasped, hand to her mouth as she tried not to cry. Tasso wrapped his arm around her as she stared at the picture.

"What this one caught of his notes, he mentions her a lot. Then there was his instrument," Tena said. "Is there some ink and paper this one can use?"

"Of course," Jemima said, jumping up and retrieving some for her. Tena began writing instantly. Her writing was wobbly and slow, but she kept scratching at the paper and they waited. Tasso got up and went to stand over the girl's shoulder as she worked, the frown on his face deepening as he watched the words and runes appear on the page.

"What is it?" Emory asked.

"I... I can't read it all, some of these runes are considered deep, dark magic, but... This is about gates and..." he shook his head. "I don't know. Navi pass me those papers back," he asked. She handed him back everything but the sketch of Ziva, which she continued to stare at.

"Your elf friend is trying to bring your sister back from the dead," Tena finally said as soon as she finished her writing.

"He's doing what?" Navi exclaimed, looking up from the picture.

"This," she said taking one of the papers from Tasso, then pointed between her own writing and the paper said, "is a portal spell to the underworld."

"What does that have to do with the ghosts and the angels?" Jemima asked.

"This spell is dark, dark magic. It opens the doors to hell and as such, requires a sacrifice to do so... A big, big sacrifice..."

"Hell? What makes Sidawi think Ziva went to hell?" Emory exclaimed. "I mean, don't we all know that Ziva went to Valhalla?"

Tena's headshot up from the papers that she was inspecting. "Say what?" she asked. "Really?"

Saga nodded. "We were there with her." Emory grabbed her hand, stopping her from going back to rubbing at the scars. Their matching scars met as he held her, and they shared a look.

"Tena doubts that your friend knows what this really is," Tena said. She looked up at Tasso. "Is it likely that you learn these runes? Because this one's friends at Rinsunid Cantera do not learn them."

"Then how did you?" he asked.

She pursed her lips nervously for a moment before answering. "Tena's magic master was a necromancer..."

"Was this the one that tried to kill you?" Saga asked.

The girl nodded. "He would kill his apprentices before they got too good... But he used the zombie bodies of the past apprentices to kill the next one..."

"How did you escape?" Navi asked, distracted for a moment from her grief.

"Tena never told him that she was a Were."

"So... You're a necromancer?" Tasso asked.

Tena shrugged. "Not a very good one. But Tena did do lots and lots and lots of reading. This spell... It won't do what he wants..."

"What do you mean?" Navi asked.

"Opening the doors to hell is not the same thing as resurrecting a lost love," Tena said. "Can it be done? Yes, and perhaps that is what he was told-"

"We can have Ziva back?" Navi asked, her voice so soft it took a moment to realise that she had interrupted the other girl at all.

Tena looked uncomfortable for a moment. "Tena thinks that you might want to ask an Angel of Death or the Valkyrie more, but this one does not think that such spells are a good idea..."

"Why not?" Saga asked. "I know where Ziva is..."

"Valhalla," Tena said, "But that would make her one of the Einherjar... Wouldn't it?"

"But the Einherjar fought in Ragnarök, they're no more..." Navi objected.

Saga shook her head. "That's not what Mimir said when we were there..." When they all just stared at her, waiting for her to continue, Saga sighed and continued. "Mimir said that the gods were fighting over Odin's throne. Vali's servants even confirmed that he thinks that possessing Odin's spear will guarantee him the throne."

"You're forgetting the part where he also possesses the world's only Valkyrie and that old man's head," Emory said, staring at her, his look displaying exactly what he thought of that. "And that that, would allow him to rule all the Nine Realms."

"Well... Yes... There's that too..."

Tena just stared at them. "Huh?" It took a moment for her to get her bearing. "And this one thought Tena's lot in life was hard..." she said. "This one will do some research on these runes and the instrument that Sidawi was playing. Ooh, Tena remembers! The ghosts and the angels, they are attracted to the music, yes?" Saga nodded. "There is a story of an unscrupulous and lazy werewolf who could not be bothered hunting his prey and the Wererabbits were really very wily little people..."

"What are you getting at?" Emory asked.

"The Rabbit Piper," she said and Emory's eyes widened.

"Myth," he insisted.

"What, like a guy playing a pipe and leading the Wererabbits to their demise?" Saga asked. "Huh..."

"What?" Navi asked.

"Well... It's just that I heard a story about a piper who would lead the rats away from the villages..." she glanced at Tena, "Rats get a bed rep where I'm from, bringers of disease and stuff like that... Well, then he took the town's children because the villagers betrayed him or something..."

Tena nodded. "Yeah, similar thing!" she agreed. "But it was um... a pan flute!"

"A pan flute!" Saga said at the same time as Tena. They stared at each other for a moment before Saga went on, "But Sidawi plays the Balalaika and it was on that black balalaika that you found those runes."

"Magic instruments are as old as time itself," Tasso said. "There's really no reason why the magic of those pan flutes, if they really existed, couldn't be cast upon any other instrument."

"I thought I heard voices," Gabrielle said, standing in the doorway to Jemima's room. "Ah, some new faces. Are you children staying for dinner?"

"Aunt Gabbi," Jemima said with a squeak. No one had heard the woman come into the house, let alone into the room. "Uhh..."

"We wouldn't want to impose Miss Gabrielle," Saga said quickly.

"Nonsense, besides Angelica would never let me hear the end of it if I didn't at least ask. I don't believe we've met before," she said looking from Emory to Tena.

"Emory Harding, ma'am," the werewolf said. "I should probably," he started to pint towards the door.

"Stay," Saga said, not looking at him. "Please," she added softly.

"And you dear?" Gabrielle asked, looking at Tena and taking in the uniform from Rinsunid Cantera.

"Oh... Tena," she said. "This one is Tena."

"Lovely to meet you both. So, dinner?"

"Yes, Aunt Gabbi," Jemima said, "We'll stay."

"Good, I'll let Muriel and Evangeline know," Gabrielle said.

"Miss Muriel's here?" Saga asked tentatively, biting her lip as she thought about the way she had behaved earlier in the day.

"Even Dina's here," Gabrielle said happily.

When Gabrielle left the room, Tasso turned to Tena, the only one out of them that seemed to have any idea of what was going on. "So, what do we do?"

Tena appeared ready to answer but glanced at Saga before speaking. Saga nodded and motioned for her to answer. "Tena needs to do some research," the girl said. "Maybe some of you could help this one with that and we can figure it out together.'

"And we should try to keep eyes on Sid," Saga suggested, find out who those guys are that he's been playing with. They're not from Nýr Ásgardr I think and might be at the centre of all of this."

The next day, they were off on a homework mission, trying to get work for Master Berfelan's Planarography class completed before their next matches.

"What's this place?" Saga asked pointing at a shadowy section of the map that seemed disconnected from the rest of the Nine Realms and the extended planes.

"Tartarus," Jemima said, barely looking up from her note taking. They were standing in cavernous room behind the ticket booth of the air ship port at the top of the World Tree. The walls were painted with a map of all the known realms, connected at their centre by the world tree. Further into the extended realms of Tír na nÓg, she could see that the realm existed across both the upper god realms and the upper light realms, while Takama no hara was connected by a bridge to Tsuchi, which seemed to be not only the human realm but also a part of the upper dark realm.

"Hmm," Saga thought. She was certain that she had heard the name somewhere before. "That's like a prison, right?"

"Aye me lass," a stocky little leprechaun in the smart black uniform of the air ship service said walking over to them, "Tis where they locked away the evilest of all evils."

Saga nodded along thoughtfully. "Zeus created it?"

"Nay lass," the man said. "Tartarus was once one of the primordial deities, along with Lady Gaia and Lord Chaos. Many others, including the great Titans came before Zeus. It just so happened that the realm of Tartarus was one of the few places one could imprison a primordial deity or a titan."

"I've heard that there's no way out of Tartarus. No way in or out and it's not just Gods who are imprisoned there, but any evil creature that could not be killed, right?"

The leprechaun paced before her for a moment, his finger tapping against his fiery bearded chin. "It's thought that perhaps Zeus also just put people he did not like down there too, but I didn't say that!"

The others stared at Saga, "What?" she asked. "I know stuff!" It was just probably better not to admit how she knew some of the stuff she managed to piece together at times, because no one ever seemed to understand her.

"But," the little leprechaun added, "there's been rumours that it is, indeed possible for the gates of Tartarus to open."

"How?" Navi asked.

"Time!" Tasso suddenly cried, before the leprechaun had a chance to answer.

"Time?" Jemima asked, looking surprised by the faerie's sudden outburst.

"Paired staff. Navi and Saga are competing today!"

The two girls stared at each other, realisation dawning on them. How had they forgotten? "When does it start?" Jemima asked.

"After the lunch hour," Saga said, looking around, trying to locate a timekeeper somewhere in the room.

The leprechaun reached into his pocket and extracted a pocket timekeeper. "You must get moving then, time is ticking away from you all."

"We'll never make it," Saga said. They were all the way at the top of the great tree and getting down would require more than a run down the central stairs.

"Jemima and I could fly you down," Tasso suggested.

The response was instantaneous, Saga's voice just a fraction before Navi and Jemima's responses. "No!"

Tasso stepped backwards, hands raised in surrender. "Ok, ok, don't shoot the guy with the idea!"

"Come on," Navi cried, "We can still do it," She grabbed Saga's hand and pulled her along until they were running through the cavernous space of the tree path museum.

"Oh!" The leprechaun called after them. I just remembered something." Saga held Navi back, wanting to hear what the little man had to say. "When the dead march upon the great, fifty headed hydra which guards the gates, there is nothing it can do, and the gates of Tartarus will open in Hell."

Astrid was waiting for them when Saga and Navi finally appeared in the waiting room of the arena.

"Where were you?" she exclaimed as she hustled them both inside. She started double checking the straps on their armour as soon as they were still, forcibly turning first Saga then Navi around so that she could get at every strap and buckle, making sure everything was tight and secure.

"Homework assignment for Master Berfelan," Saga said.

Astrid groaned as she tugged roughly on Saga's leather straps. "I knew that would be trouble."

"Breath!" Saga gasped out. "I can't breathe!"

"Oh, sorry," Astrid said, quickly readjusting the straps once more.

"Saga!" A voice called and the three of them looked up to find a girl with coral pink hair coming towards them.

"Hilina'i," Saga exclaimed. "What are you doing here?"

"Oh, Well, that's a long story that starts with Inoke opening his big mouth about pirates and everything that had happened in Honah Lee over the break." The girl said, flipping her coral coloured hair over her shoulder. "I wound up being the staff pairs reserve and now I have to work with Ho'okano and..."

"What about the tripping over your own feet thing?" Saga asked, remembering that the mermaid could barely walk a few steps on her legs before getting her feet tangled in one another and falling over. She sidestepped another of Astrid's attempts to get at her armour, at which she turned her attentions on Navi, who shot Saga a bitter look.

"Oh, well, I'm not half as bad at that anymore... I mean, you even taught us a few things..." the girl said, her confidence slipping. She groaned, "I'd rather be in the water but that little cuttlefish of a selkie went and got pushed into the ocean the day before we left, didn't she? And now she's trapped under the water for the next seven years! She knew the rules, no sea water, so what does she do? She practices on the pier of all places and now I have to do this, and I don't know what I'm doing!"

In the far corner of the room, a group of elves from Shamel Aiyeola were giggling as they stared at Hilina'i, then broke out laughing even harder when they saw Astrid fighting with Navi's armour.

"Oh, my crab claws," Hilina'i exclaimed, "What does it take to shut them up?"

"Knuckle sandwich would be my guess," Saga said.

"Saga!" Astrid warned.

"Ok, ok, but they're seriously irritating me!" Saga retorted, "And they need to be taught a lesson!"

"Angry warriors, Saga," Astrid said.

"Are dead warriors," Saga and Navi chorused in reply.

"Good, remember that. Good luck, show me some of that spunk from the beginning of the year, right?"

"Right," Saga said.

"Wish me luck," Hilina'i said, grabbing a staff and running it through her hands experimentally. "I'm better with tridents..." she whined as she walked out towards the field.

Navi and Saga followed her and watched as the girl met up with a boy of indeterminate race. Ho'okano, Saga guessed.

"There will be five bouts today, all drawn randomly," the tourney battle master announced, as he walked up and down the twenty students gathered there.

Out in the stands, people were moving around, finding seats, getting snacks or talking to one another. Children ran up and down the stairs and the students from the school competing that day, gathered as close as they could to the edges to call out to friends.

"Miss Thyra Bodil," the battle master said, "will be drawing the pairings." This caused the students all around them to start whispering to each other, especially the boys who were eagerly eyeing the woman.

"Who is she?" Saga asked.

"Thyra Bodil?" Navi asked, "Only the greatest singer of our age. "Her most famous song is this one about a Valkyrie selecting her dead for Ragnarök," she started to hum, before softly singing in Saga's ear, "Down on the battlefield, the Valkyrie, doth choose the slain, to serve the Gods, The brave and the true are called to serve, In the hall of Valhalla."

"I've heard it," Saga said, eyeing the woman with far more curiosity than she had before. "Vespers loves her... He's going to be so jealous!"

Navi giggled at that. "Navi can believe that!"

A leprechaun bounded across the arena field, before bowing before Thyra Bodil and taking his hat off to hold it out before her. Thyra reached her hand in. The audience erupted in laughter as her arm disappeared all the way to her shoulder, before she remerged with a slip of parchment in her hand.

"Ehras Magna Were Skoli," Thyra announced, reading the first name. She reached in again, this time, not going so far, "Versus The Two Worlds School." There were oohs and ahhs from the audience as the two teams went to positions assigned to them by the staff for the match.

"And our second match?" The battle master called to the singer.

"Aquino Beccara Holy and Fae School," She said, her hand remerging once again from the leprechaun's hat. "Versus Toserra Sorose Academy!" she announced gleefully.

Saga and Navi were directed away from the rest of the competitors to a bench where they were seated beside the two competitors from Two Worlds. Across the field, the competitors from Aquino Beccara were led to their waiting area. They were two Ljósálfar elves, a boy and a girl. The girl was eyeing Navi but leaned into her partner's side to whisper in his ear.

"We will be the Jackie," Navi said, with a sure nod of her head.

"What?" Saga asked.

"Be The Jackie," Navi repeated, at Saga's look of confusion, the girl laughed before saying. "The first day we met, you said that you could beat Tonya and her friends because you believed in this Jackie Chan. Navi decided to try and be The Jackie."

Saga had to press her fist to her mouth in order to stop from bursting out in laughter. "What?" she exclaimed.

"Did this one say it wrong?" Navi asked.

"Uhh..." Saga answered, not quite sure what to say. "Well... let's just say, I've never heard it like that before... but I like it!" She held her free hand out to Navi, fingers clenched in a fist. "Here, follow me," she instructed, and Navi did so, holding her hand out in an identical fashion. Saga bumped her fist against Navi's. The girl looked confused but watched Saga's movements intently. "Pow," Saga hissed out in a low and guttural whisper as she rebounded her fist against Navi's and allowed her fingers to uncurl and waggle as she pulled back "Be the Jackie!"

Navi fist bumped Saga, "Pow," she hissed out and copied the waggling fingers, saying "Be the Jackie!"

"We've totally got this!" Saga said with a grin.

"And by default, the final match will be between Kahawaiola'a Ocean School and Shamel Aiyeola Hall," Thyra announced.

The excitement from the Shamel Aiyeola contingent was infectious, it was as though they thought they had the win secured and nothing would or could get in their way, especially not students from Kahawaiola'a Ocean School. Hilina'i waved excitedly to Saga from the far end of the field and Saga waved back.

The first match between Ehras Magna Were Skoli and The Two Worlds School was over almost before it had started. In typical fashion, the two competitors from Ehras Magna had gone into the fight with strength as their first strategy, but Saga watched in amazement as the two slight girls from the eastern school moved, almost as though one second, they were there and the next they were somewhere else. The larger, heavier Weres would hover over them, only to find themselves on the floor moments later. She leaned forward, eager to observe them as closely as possible, trying to figure out timings, foot work and even the angles they held their staves at, but the match was over as soon as both Weres were flat on their backs, staves at their throats.

"Wow..." Navi whispered.

"No kidding," Saga added. "They were amazing!"

"Navi hopes that we do not have to go up against them!"

"That would require us to win this match," Saga said as the two girls, Koale Sakata and Suzuki Anh-Ly were announced the winners. "Their teachers must be absolutely amazing!"

Then it was their turn as they were called to the centre of the arena, across from the team from Aquino Beccara. Saga and Navi assumed their fighting positions and waited as the two elves across from them did the same.

Beside her, Saga could hear Navi mumbling under her breath, "Be the Jackie," again and again. She wondered how she was going to clear up this confusion as to who or what the movie action star was.

"Navi!"

"Saga!"

"Toserra Sorose!"

The calls rang in their ears as the gong hammered its sound across the arena. The girl elf launched herself towards Saga, her staff coming around over the top of her head in a sweeping arc. Telegraphing her movements so far in advance made her easy to read and with merely a glance at one another, Saga and Navi moved, much to the surprise of the elves. Saga ignored her and instead attacked the boy, who had been going in for a straight-line attack towards Navi only to have his staff met with resistance from an angle he had never expected.

"Yes!" they heard someone from the sidelines cry and out of the corner of her eye, Saga saw Astrid looking particularly pleased with herself. The boy's surprise had him stumbling backwards as he tried to find his footing. Saga didn't wait for him though. She swept her staff up and over his head. Instinct kicked in for him and he attempted to reach for it, his own staff following for it, trying to defend or block the anticipated attack, right until her dipped behind his head. He couldn't follow it any further and his staff was so high up that he'd been left wide open and then, without warning, swept his legs out from under him. He fell to the floor with a thud, his staff rolling from his hand.

To her side, Navi was part of a back-and-forth range of movements as she struck out, and the elf girl defended, then they swapped. Navi though, noticed that Saga was free of her attacker and orchestrated her own opponent to the point where Saga was behind her.

Navi raised her staff and started in on the girl, but she must have noticed something in their movements, because before either of them could attack her, the girl shot her staff out to her side, forcing Saga back, right before she drew it up with lightning speed, swinging it around her head, forcing both Saga and Navi away from her and providing enough of a distraction for her partner to regain his footing and regain his staff.

The four of them reset, once again going for starting positions. Saga eyed the girl, looking, waiting, watching for that slightest of movements that indicated a drop in her guard. She had apparently learned from last time because she didn't come charging at full speed.

And then the elves surprised them. The girl went low, dropping to her knee and sweeping at Saga's feet while the boy shot his staff straight out over her head towards Navi. Saga knew how much it hurt when a staff made contact with the legs, especially the side of the ankle where the girl was aiming. Saga waited until it was close and there was no changing their minds. She tucked into a roll, holding her staff tight to her body and launched herself into a roll. She came up on her feet facing their backs. Neither one had thought to turn towards her in anticipation of her retaliation. Instead, they were focusing on Navi as their only target.

Saga grinned to herself, knowing how futile this act would be. Astrid had drilled them on multiple attackers. They could, if the situation call for it, defend themselves against three of even four attackers. Those two elves didn't stand a chance and they didn't even know it. Navi's slight form and nimble speed made her the perfect person for such a technique and as much as Saga wanted to watch her friend get the better of the two, she needed to get back in there.

The boy stumbled back after a straight shot at his gut. His arms clamped around his middle as he groaned in pain. They'd made the mistake of ignoring him before when they thought he was out and it didn't take much to distract the boy from reclaiming his place in the fight, before Saga shot her own staff out between his legs, allowing the boy's feet to get tangled with the staff, sending him sprawling to the floor once more, before taking the last step and miming a killing move to his throat, Saga looked back at Navi right as the Ljósálfar girl tried to grab hold of the end of Navi's charred, floral staff, only for the momentum to send her flying across the field in an uncontrolled roll. The staff she had ben wielding went clattering across the field when she was unable to find a way to land safely with it. The staff rolled to a stop at Saga's feet and as she levelled the tip of her own floral staff at the elf boy's throat, she rested her foot on the other.

PAST AMENDS

Saga embraced Navi in the centre of the field. "And the winners of the second staff pairs is Toserra Sorose Academy in Nýr Ásgardr represented by first years, Saga Carolle and Navi Jensyn!"

"We did it!" Navi exclaimed. "We became The Jackie!"

Saga burst out laughing as she hugged Navi tighter, "Yeah!" she agreed, "yeah we did. We became The Jackie!"

On the sidelines, they could see Edun, standing in the background by Sidawi. Emory was standing nearby Tasso and Jemima, a look on his face that Saga could not identify, but the only person the field who perhaps looked happier than they were, was Astrid. As soon as they were clear of the field, she wrapped them both in her arms.

"Oh, you two!" she beamed, almost at a loss for words. "I knew that you two were the right pick for this!"

"Thank you, Mistress Grunborg," Navi said, trying to hold back tears, likely of pure joy.

The last paired fight was between Kahawaiola'a Ocean School and Shamel Aiyeola Hall and the elves from The Hall looked as though they thought the fight was theirs for the taking.

"You go get them Hilina'i!" Saga called out to the coral haired girl. Hilina'i waved excitedly and pulled Ho'okano along with her to centre field. She sighed and leaned into Navi, "I don't know about this," she said.

"What do you mean?"

"Hilina'i is a mermaid," Saga whispered.

"Ohhh..." Navi agreed. "Footwork isn't really her thing..."

"Well, her brother thought it was great to announce that she could barely walk without tripping over herself," Saga groaned and dropped her head into her hands as Ho'okano grabbed Hilina'i, preventing her from falling to the ground as she tripped over something, which Saga thoroughly believed to have been her own feet.

"Navi sees what you mean," Navi whispered. "Is her partner also a Mer?"

Saga shrugged. "I don't know him."

The fight began and the two Ljósálfar from Shamel Aiyeola went in hard and fast. Their over-brimming confidence evident as they moved without any real strategy. They thought that they had every advantage.

"Woah!" Navi exclaimed, when Hilina'i shot the tip of her staff up in-between her opponent's arms, forcing him to duck his head out of the way. She then turned and launched the unsuspecting elf across the field. "That's Astrid's move!"

"Go Hilina'i!" Saga called out as the girl turned her attention to helping her partner. Saga grinned. "I taught her that one!"

The noise of the arena was explosive as the winners were announced. Hilina'i beamed, taking in the cheers. Ho'okano stared in disbelief, it was obvious that he had gone into the fight fully expecting to lose.

Over on the side of the field, the two elves were standing before a taciturn looking elf, their shoulders slumped as they listened to him. He held out his hand to them and they handed over their staves. With a shake of his head the teacher turned and walked away, leaving them standing there with their heads bowed.

Hilina'i grabbed her partner by the arm and ran over to where Saga and Navi were sitting. She grabbed Saga up and wrapped her in a hug, jumping and forcing Saga to join her in her excitement. "We won, we won!" she cried excitedly.

"You were amazing!" Saga said, allowing Hilina'i's excitement to sweep her away.

"Hi." The four of them turned to see the fair-haired Ljósálfar girl from Aquino Beccara standing there. Navi stepped backwards, almost sidling herself behind Saga. Then they waited for the girl to make the first move. She held her hand out to Navi. "You were amazing," she said simply.

"T... t... thank you..." Navi stuttered out, staring at the girl's hand for a moment before hesitantly taking it.

"I wasn't sure what to think when I heard we were up against first years..." she paused, "And yes... I was surprised, but you move like you were born with a staff in your hands."

"Uhh..." Navi stared at the girl, dumbfounded and unable to speak.

Saga elbowed her in the ribs. "Say something," when Navi didn't though, Saga looked at the girl, "This is Navi."

"It's a pleasure to meet you Navi. I'm Consuela," the girl said.

"N... n... nice to meet you," Navi said.

"I have never seen two people more in sync with each other than the two of you. How long have you two been fighting together?" Consuela asked.

"About seven months-ish," Saga said, trying to figure out the time that had passed since her arrival in the nine realms.

Hilina'i looked surprised. "Really, isn't that when you told me you first came here from Midgard?"

Saga nodded. "Yes."

"W...w...when we met, N... Navi was being bothered by some faeries."

They were walking towards the stands, when a man stopped Consuela, "Want a staff just like theirs?" Consuela frowned at the man, before turning and looking at the staves the two girls were carrying. Her eyes lit up when she finally realised that both girls carried staves with engravings on it, but before she could answer, the man gasped in horror, then reached out and grabbed Navi's staff. "What happened to it? What did you do?" he wailed, inspecting the charred ends of the staff.

Navi's skin went as grey as Tena's as she reached out to try and grab her staff back. "G... g... give it back, it's Navi's!" she cried.

"My staff, what did you do?" the man cred, then reached for Saga's as well, but she dodged his grip and in the flash of an eye, she had the point of it at his throat.

"Give it back," she said in a low voice. The man gulped, his Adams apple just touching the tip of her staff as he did. Tentatively, he held his arm out, extending the staff towards Navi, who took it from him, then cradled it against herself, stroking the engravings as everyone watched them. "Who are you?" She asked, stepping back and sighed, lowering the staff to her side when she recognised him. "You're the weapons merchant from the market," she exclaimed.

The man nodded. "Yes."

Navi's eyes went wide and she held her staff against her body tighter, as though afraid that he would try once again to take it away from her. "Oh... Mister..." she whispered, her voice quivering as she tried to hold back tears. "Navi is sorry..."

"No," Saga said. "You're not sorry, not for that. Nothing could have been done that night." Around them, Consuela and the other competitors were watching them. The man eyed her fury and perhaps recalled the first time that they had met when she had challenged three faeries to a duel with his weapons without a second thought. She looked around, she wasn't going to tell everyone gathered there what had happened the night of the fire at Dorbe Manor. They had been forced to relive it enough times already.

One of the slight, eastern girls from The Two Worlds School came up beside Navi, "May I?" she asked, her hand held out to the small, trembling dark elf. Navi looked at her with wide eyes but nodded and slowly allowed the girl to take the staff, which she did reverently. "This is exquisite craftsmanship. The balance is superb and the detail second to none," she said. Then her eyes flashed from reverence to fury, "Every weapon's scar tells a story of hardship, battle and of overcoming. This weapon has overcome much hardship in its time. It is an honourable weapon in the hands of a young master," she glanced at Saga's matching, though undamaged staff, "they both are."

The man nodded. "Yes," he said, not daring to say anything else, surrounded as he was by the best staff fighters of the great schools of the realms.

The girl inspected the ends of Navi's staff once more, where fire damage had caused scales of char to crack the end. "My weapons master could fix this," she said looking at Navi.

"N... Navi does not want to lose the burn," she said softly.

The girl nodded, "Of course, but like this, the staff will chip away and die. It can be protected from such a fate while preserving its history."

"Really?" Navi asked, brightening.

"Yes. Shall we go see what Sensei says?" the girl asked.

Navi looked at Saga hesitantly, but she had no qualms about letting the other girl help," Go!" Saga said, "Get it fixed."

Navi beamed. "Navi will!" she exclaimed and turned to the girl. "Thank you, thank you so much!" The eastern girl led Navi away as her partner stayed with the group, listening.

"We heard about the student residence that burned down at Toserra Sorose," Consuela said, "Did she live there?"

Saga nodded. "Yes," she said glaring at the man. "And the staff was damaged when Navi tried to rescue a trapped student..."

"She did she manage?" the second eastern girl asked.

Saga nodded. "Just barely... But we lost a lot that night... Including Navi's oldest sister."

"Ziva?" the merchant asked, horror flashing across his face. "I... I'm so sorry. I never should have..."

"You are a craftsman who is proud of his work," Consuela said. "You couldn't have known. I would be interested in viewing your stock though."

The man brightened. "I sell the finest decorated staves in all the nine realms that don't compromise on quality!" he announced. "Ladies, get a weapon that matches your personality."

Saga shook her head and let the man advertise his wares. His staves had been good to them. She leaned in and whispered to him. "Do you still have that matching set of leathers?" she asked.

He reeled backwards in surprise. "Yes."

"Good," Saga aid. "Don't sell it, I'll try to come by sometime this week."

"For you?" he asked, but Saga shook her head and looked out in the direction Navi had gone with the orange and grey clad eastern girl.

Saga retreated to the side of the arena to collect her belongings. She was feeling hot, sweaty, and tired. It had been a good match and not just because they had won. She started on the straps and buckles of her armour, wishing that Navi was there to help get at some of the more awkwardly placed straps.

"Do you need some help?" a tentative voice asked from a few feet away.

Saga looked up and froze. "Ms Roskin," she said and sort of stood there, her mouth opening and closing as she tried to figure out what to say next.

"I'm sorry, I didn't mean to startle you," she said coming closer, hands out to help. Saga turned, giving the woman access to a strap on the back.

"No," Saga said. "I'm the one who should say sorry."

"I got your message from Muriel." She expertly released the strap, then helped Saga loft the leathers over her head.

Saga had wanted to speak to the woman, apologise for running off and had, when they'd had dinner at Gabrielle's house asked the Guardian angel to pass the message along. "I'm glad."

"Me too," She watched as Saga adjusted her shirt, pulling the sweaty fabric away from her skin. "Can we talk?"

Saga concentrated on grabbing a ladle of water from a nearby drinking bucket to giver self a moment before answering. "Sure," she finally said. "I just need to bring this stuff back by my tent... You could... walk with me if you wanted..."

The angel looked relieved and fell into step beside Saga as she lead the way from the arena and out into the chaos of the school tourney. Visitors and students and vendors were everywhere. "Did you run in the stadion?" Shari asked after a moment.

"Yes, on the first day... Right before we saw you actually," Saga said, concentrating on where she was going rather than looking at the woman.

"Right... One of your friends did mention that you had beaten all the Weres."

"Actually, it was declared a tie," Saga said. "The girl from Ehras Magna was not pleased."

"The Weres very rarely get beaten. Usually there's some relation to Mercury or one of the other messenger gods when they are," Shari said. "It would be a new experience for them. I saw your staff fight," she paused and when Saga didn't say anything, she went on, "Saga, you're amazing."

"So's Navi," Saga said.

"Yes, your friend is certainly very good, but Saga, you didn't know any of this existed a few months ago and you just competed successfully at the inter-school Tourney, and Aquino Beccara have a very good staff fighting program... I should know."

"Is that where you went?" Saga asked, wending her way through a line of people waiting for food from a cart offering the juicy, sticky meatballs that she and her friends liked so much. She paused, considered getting some for a moment, then shook her head and went on.

"Yes, with Muriel," Shari said. "Though that was a long time ago." Saga bit her tongue to stop herself from sprouting the first thought that came to her mind and ruining the moment. Shari must have picked up on the awkwardness of the moment and looked around for something to say. "I would have expected your friends to be around somewhere."

"Navi got an offer she couldn't refuse, and Tasso and Jemima went to work with their horses and..." She trailed off, not wanting to mention Emory. "Well, the others had to get back to their own school groups."

"Other school groups?"

"Consuela had to go explain how she lost to us and Hilina'i and her partner had to go bask in the glory of their win and I have no idea where Tani and Tena are..."

"A first for Kahawaiola'a," Shari said. "Some impressive moves that I'm pretty sure didn't come from their instructors."

Saga shrugged. "I met Hilina'i in Honah Lee over the mid semester break. I showed her and some of the other some things that Astrid had taught me. Came in handy when the pirates attacked the town."

"Pirates attacked Honah Lee?"

Saga turned to her, her eyes glittering with excitement, "I met the dragon, Ms Roskin. It's all real, the dragon of Honah Lee and the little boy who was his friend. He really did slip deep inside his cave to mourn the loss of his friend... And all he did was grow up."

"You saw a dragon?" Shari exclaimed. "Saga, no one's seen a dragon in... Oh, I don't know how long... But then again, I was on Midgard for almost fifteen years..."

"His name was Nihi and we went sailing together because I wouldn't let him take me flying... well... except that once..." she shivered at the thought.

"Was it on a ship with billowed sails?" Shari asked, her face alight with the same childlike glee that was on Saga's.

Saga beamed. "Oh yes!"

Despite the infectious nature of Sagas mood, they walked in silence as they passed the entry to the Toserra Sorose encampment.

They were passing the mess tent, which was mostly empty at this time of day and she stopped.

"You can't do this alone." She heard someone say.

"What is it?" Shari asked. Saga held her hand out towards her to stop her speaking and went back to listening.

"I don't need your help," the second, lilting and lyrical voice said.

"She wouldn't want this," the first, harsher voice said.

"What would you know?"

There was the shuffling of feet and Saga tried to peer into the tent without being seen.

"If you won't stop, then at least let me help."

"Help?" the lyrical voice asked. "Please, you've never helped anybody in your life."

There was the sound of fabric being grabbed and scuffling feet followed by a pained grunt. "You're not the only one who loved her!" The harsher of the two voices said before angry footsteps started towards the entryway. Saga scrambled backwards, pushing Shari back and turning her own back on the mess tent so that it wouldn't look like she had been listening.

"What is going on, Saga?" Shari asked again.

Saga glanced over her shoulder to see Edun stalking out of the mess tent. Sidawi watched him go and Saga frowned. What was Edun doing getting involved with Sidawi? Sure, the rest of them liked the elf boy, but Edun had never shown anything but contempt for the older boy. She watched as Sidawi ran his hands down his shirt, flattening out wrinkles caused by Edun.

"Saga?" Shari asked again.

"Nothing," she said, looking around for where Edun went. She spotted him heading towards his tent but frowned to herself. "Come on."

"Do you know those boys?"

Saga nodded as she hurried down the aisle of tents. "Sidawi's a Prefect and Edun is Navi's brother."

"Is there anything else going on?" Shari asked, almost tripping on a tent wire to keep up.

Saga stopped and turned to her, she looked around and didn't see anyone, but who knew who was in the tents. "Sid was dating Edun's sister," she said in a low voice.

"Bad breakup?"

Saga eyed the woman with disdain for a moment before she shook her head. It wasn't Shari's fault if she hadn't heard. "No. Ziva died last semester. Dorbe Manor burned down when the Wild Hunt rode through it. Ziva was killed..."

"Saga," Shari gasped. "I'm so sorry..." Unconsciously, Saga was rubbing her fingers against the burns on her palms. They didn't hurt anymore, but whenever Ziva was mentioned, she felt herself doing it. Shari reached out suddenly, taking Saga's hands in her own and turning them over to look at her palms. "When did..." she stopped, realisation dawning on her. "You were there..."

"That doesn't matter!" Saga snapped, taking her hands back from the woman. She turned and resumed her path to her tent. Shari followed her, finally coming to a stop as Saga stepped into one of the many tents. Saga dropped her armour on one of the beds and unslung her staff from over her shoulder, setting it up against a bench between two of the beds.

"Are we going to talk now?" Shari asked.

"What do you want me to say?" Saga asked, feeling resigned. She was tired and didn't know if she had the energy to deal with her feeling about their interactions in the old world. She located her brush and pulled her hair down from the ponytail it had been in to brush it. She shrugged. "You knew about all of this the entire time I knew you and you said nothing. I don't know what to do with that."

"You weren't the first of my charges to claim that they saw or heard things and I'll have you know, one of them was a pathological liar, another was making up fantasies to hide from their trauma and the last was going through the early onset schizophrenia, so no Saga, I did not know what it was that was going on with you. I was your guardian angel, and we work on Midgard, there was no reason to ever suspect that you were from here."

"Mum's letter? The blanket?"

"Saga, for all I had known your mother was a Norse mythology enthusiast going through a mental break. I didn't know. I never got to meet her. I didn't have anything to work with other than what I was told," Shari said, trying to come closer, but the cot got in the way. They stood there ,staring at one another, tension building as Shari didn't attempt to move closer again.

"You had what I said, but you always went with what everyone else said," Saga shot back. "You never once believed me and you never once stood up for me when they were kicking me out and when I tried to argue the matter, you let them label me as troubled and now I look around and I find out that not only was I not crazy, but that you knew that ghosts were real and that there are people that actually can see them too. That there was a reason for it."

Shari sat down on the cot and patted the place beside her. "Sit down Saga." Saga sighed but picked up her armour to put it away in her trunk. She pushed some things around before closing the lid and fiddling with the locks. "Saga," she said again, this time using the voice and tone Saga remembered from when she'd been younger and didn't want to talk to her. The girl sat down but didn't look at her or say anything. Shari sighed. "I'm sorry," she finally said and Saga looked at her, an unreadable expression on her face as her fingers scratched at the scars. "I'm sorry I didn't even consider that there was something more. I'm sorry that even there in Walhalla, where I knew that the Rainbow bridge came by, that I still didn't think of it, I'm sorry that I didn't come to find you here when I came back and I'm sorry that I failed you."

"You didn't..." Saga murmured softly. At her confused look, Saga said louder, "You didn't fail me..."

Shari reached out and took Saga's hands, stopping their nervous rubbing of the scars. "Has one of the healer's looked at these?" she asked.

"Raphaella Damir," Saga said. "She says they're fine... It's just me..." She bit her lip. "Ms Roskin?"

"Yes?" she asked.

"What do you know about Valkyries?" Saga asked.

Shari thought for a moment. "Firstly," she said, "My real name is Shari. Shari Rose."

Saga held out her hand and Shari took it hesitantly. "Nice to meet you Shari Rose," Saga said.

"You too, Saga Joy Carolle, you too," Shari said, "because you my girl, are a totally different girl then I knew back on Midgard."

"I feel different," Saga said, "and it's not just the acceptance of my weirdness..."

"You're not weird."

"I am weird," Saga insisted, "Just ask my friends... I mean, you should hear Navi's new catchphrase before a bout because she heard me reference Jackie Chan..."

Shari laughed, "What's that?"

"Be The Jackie," Saga said.

"Well, you did that!" Shari said with a laugh. It felt good to have this moment. Perhaps to finally have that closure from what had happened that day and in the days leading up to their trip to Walhalla. "I don't know all that much about Valkyries to be honest," Shari said after a moment, "No one knew that they still existed. When you disappeared and I told the Seraphim everything I knew... It was like there was a reckoning... I don't know exactly what happened, but I think this is something we will all have to learn together."

"Look, look, look," Navi cried, running up to Saga with her staff in her hands. It was close to dinner and Saga was feeling emotionally drained after the talk with Shari Rose, but she put a smile on her face for her friend and took the offered staff from her. The crumbling charred parts of the end had been encased in a solid resin-like substance, that coated the entire staff, filling in the holes and protecting it from falling apart further.

"It's amazing," Saga said, "And it's already finished?" she asked.

Navi nodded. "There was magic involved but look at it!"

"Those girls really came through, didn't they?" Saga asked and Navi just beamed, taking the staff back from her and running her hands up and down its length in awe.

"Navi loves it," she said happily, almost skipping along as they walked.

"We should celebrate," Tasso said, coming up between Navi and Saga and wrapping am arm around each of them. "Two wins for Saga, and epic win for Navi, and my word, look at that staff," he exclaimed, getting a look at it. "How did that happen?"

"One of the girls from The Two Worlds School said that their weapons master would be able to fix it," Navi said happily, completely ignoring the near scene with the weapon's original creator and his accusations right before the girl from the eastern school had put him in his place with her own weapons theory. "Sakata and Anh-Ly invited us to train with them before the finals."

Saga's eyes widened in surprise, "Really? That would be amazing!"

"Even more reason to celebrate," Tasso said, "Then there's my joust tomorrow."

"And Shamel Aiyeola got smashed by a couple of mermaids!" Another voice said. They turned to find Edun standing there, Tena at his side.

"That they did," Saga agreed.

"I'm up for a night out," Jemima agreed,

"Perfect, count me in," Tymberlee said, pushing Tasso out if the way so that she could get to Saga and Navi.

"Ok, great. Where are we going?" Tasso asked.

"How about Agesilaus?" Saga suggested. With nods of agreement, she seems on. "Why don't we grab Tani and Consuela and Hilina'i too. Ooh, what about... Sakata and Anh-Ly, was it?"

"Navi can go and ask!"

"Wait, can we leave camp at night?" Jemima asked.

"You can if you have a Prefect with you," Tymberlee said with a wicked grin.

"And the guys from the other schools?" Saga asked.

"Their camps have their own rules, but people like Tani who are fourth year, they're not going to need permission, I'm sure."

"Tena will get Tani!" the ash-coloured dark elf said.

FALLING FEAR

Everything seemed blurry as she opened her eyes. Around her, the figures were tattered and frayed, fading away into nothingness as their spirits waned.

"Help me," An old woman in an intricately decorated kimono called.

Saga looked around, several of the people around her were dressed similarly to the old lady. Amongst them were the bedraggled figures of small Dökkálfar children, who looked up at her with sad, mournful eyes.

Saga pushed herself up from where she had been laying, only to find even more people staring at her. They were dressed in everything from the rags of the poorest peasants to the glorious gown of a noblewoman who fanned herself delicately. She looked around, their threadbare appearance told her everything she needed to know though, they were ghosts, each and every one of them.

She saw a familiar figure pass through the crowd, and she pushed herself to standing position, looking down at herself, she saw that she too was looking worn out, faded and almost moth-eaten. "Help," she gasped out.

"You help us," the old woman said, reaching out to Saga. She reached out, taking Saga's hands in her old, gnarled hands.

"Where are we?" Saga asked, her gaze trying to take in any feature of her surrounds. She could see the giant base of the tree city and people were walking purposefully, engaging in day-to-day tasks. Saga walked away from the old woman when she recognised the nice faerie woman from the gardening shop who had put Tonya in her place on the day she had gone shopping for school supplies. She went up to her. "Miss, miss," she called, not able to remember her name, but wanting to get her attention.

There was no response.

Saga ran ahead, trying to get in front of the woman, but she stopped short when the woman wound up walking right through her.

Fear gripped her as she looked back to the old woman. "Where are we?" she asked.

The ghosts started to gather around the old woman and Saga stared as familiar faces appeared in the crowd including the Ainslie ghost, Tremblay right behind him

"Tremblay!" She called out, trying to get his attention, but he said nothing. She noticed a few others, feathered wings rustling in the breeze... except when she actually looked, she realised that it wasn't the wind moving the feathers in their wings, they were twitching, ever so slightly. The wind, it had no effect on their feathers or their hair. She her hair up into the gentle breeze and nothing happened, the strands hung there, limp.

"Tremblay," she begged, "Talk to me!" When all he did was look at her wordlessly, she glanced around looking for someone, anyone other than the old woman asking for her help. An angel caught her attention and Saga stopped short. Dina Bess stood there, staring at her as everyone else did. "Miss Bess!" she cried out pathetically.

A loud rumbling sound shook them all. The real people didn't seem to notice, but the bedraggled ghosts looked at her, no, behind her in absolute terror and fear.

The old woman, the only one who had spoken to her stepped forward, her hand pointing towards what they were all staring at, her whole-body trembling in fright. Slowly, Saga started to turn, the rumbling sound growing louder as she did so. An odd glow was starting to illuminate the area and suddenly a roar bellowed all around her, the shockwaves of the roar full of spittle.

A portal of reds and blacks and oranges and any number of swirling hues was like a gaping wound in the air behind her, but even that wasn't the most startling thing as ghosts from inside it screamed, while trying to break free from the portal. No, that wasn't surprising, what was surprising was the creature that was coming from within the door. It had heads.

Not one or two, was that ten heads? No, more heads appeared from the portal. Fifteen, twenty, twenty-five... They just kept coming and the body that was slowly stepping through...

"Ohhh..." Saga trembled. "Help me..." She turned and tried to run, the ghosts crowding her as she tried to get around them, the old woman, reaching for her again and again as Saga would change direction and try once more to escape them.

Suddenly, she felt herself being hauled backwards and the more she struggled, the tighter the grip got. She glanced over her shoulder, trying to turn, trying to break the grip, but she was confronted with one of the many heads of the creature, it's teeth clamped into her clothes as it lifted her into the air.

As her feet left the ground, Saga screamed.

A pain shot through her hand as though something was biting her. Saga struggled to wake from the dream and the pain helped to do exactly that.

"Hold on!" a strained voice cried and Saga looked up, spotting Hymer Rendon above her, his arms down, reaching around the straining figure of Shadow, who was belly to the ledge, his body hanging over the side, his mouth wrapped around her wrist. Teeth were digging into her skin as Rendon tried to take over, holding onto her as she realised that just like in her dream, she was hanging in the air. The strong arm of the daemon, taking over the bite of the wolf to become the only thing holding her arm. Panic set in and she started to struggle. "Give me your other hand!" Rendon ordered and Shadow barked as though echoing Rendon's order, but the beating of her heart in her ears and the desperate need for air seemed to take all her concentration. That and not looking down. She stared up at them, still half fogged from sleep, wondering how she had gotten to where she was.

"Help!" she tried to choke out, but her voice was weak with sleep and fear.

"Give me your other hand Story Girl," the big daemon ordered again. Shadow was leaning over the edge, his paws right over the side as he looked down at her, concern in his eyes. Rendon looked around awkwardly, as though he was expecting help to come, but they appeared to be alone until several other Rinsunid Cantera students arrived. They seemed to take stock of the situation and immediately dived in, holding on to Rendon and keeping him secure as he struggled to hold on to Saga.

"I can't," she cried. "I can't move!"

"You have to," he said. Saga felt him try to haul her up, then she was unbalanced and after his attempt, she felt herself slip, the blood from Shadow's bite making it hard for him to keep a hold of her. "Saga! Come on!" She tried to reach her arm up to him, but she couldn't get it up to where he could reach it. "Come on, you can do it! Give it a bit of a swing!" he insisted.

"I'll fall!" Saga cried fear gripping her as she imagined her body falling through the air. She had no idea how far it was because she still had no idea where she was, it looked like one of the branches of the tree city, but that could be any number of flights high. She could be falling for an eternity before finally splattering against the ground.

"I won't let you!" The boy promised. "Come on, give me your hand!!" She could hear Shadow's panting and he shimmied closer to the edge, until one of the Rinsunid Cantera students put a hand on him, stopping his forward progress.

Saga took a deep breath, then a second and a third and she felt them becoming ragged and panicked once more so she forced herself to try and slow them down, imagined a staff fight, breathing in and out with the move in her mind... and then she did as Rendon asked and tried to swing herself higher.

As she did so, she felt hands, not just his, but others grabbing for her, helping to haul her up until finally, she felt her body slide onto the flattened surface of the branch where the others stood. Shadow broke free from the hands that were holding him back and he launched himself at her, nuzzling her face, before turning his attention to the bite on her wrist that he had inflicted upon her and licking away the blood. She petted at him, trying to convey without words that he didn't have to do that, be he kept on going.

"Saga, what were you doing?" Rendon asked from where he was sprawled out beside her.

"I . . ." Saga tried, but her breathing was too ragged to construct a sentence.

"Saga!" The panicked voice seemed to part the small crowd as Navi collapsed beside her, Jemima and Tymberlee right behind her. Navi pulled Saga in for a hard embrace as everyone watched. "What happened to you? Why are you here?"

Saga looked around and noticed that she was primarily surrounded by the red and black clad students of Rinsunid Cantera. She looked up at Rendon, noticing Tani standing beside him and Tena standing with Jemima and Tymberlee, panting hard as though she had been running. "What happened?

"You happened," he said.

"I don't understand," Saga said, trying to remember what had happened.

The night out that they had been considering had wound up being postponed until the night afterwards, when Jemima and Tasso had completed their matches. Instead, they spent the night in the common area of the camp, mingling with their newfound friends as the campfire roared and they told stories of life at their various schools. It had finished with Tymberlee policing her first years back to their tents, reminding them of their commitments the next day.

So how had she wound up here? Wherever here was. . .

Tani was busy waving away the other Rinsunid Cantera students who had come to watch. Others were brushing themselves down, as though they had been on the ground, and maybe they had given Rendon's ability to use both hands to pull her up. Maybe they had been holding the daemon boy steady, preventing him from being dragged down with her.

"Go on, go," Tani was saying.

"Saga," Tymberlee said, crouching down beside her, "what happened? How did you get here?"

"I don't know Tymberlee, I went to bed and then I was here..." Saga said.

"We called out to you, but you didn't respond," Tena said.

Saga got to her feet, setting Shadow down beside her and with the dissipating crowd she now realised that they were in fact on a branch of the tree city, but she wasn't sure which one. She cautiously looked over the side where they had just pulled her up from and felt her head swim, even in the darkness of the night, she could see just how far down the encampment was. "Where are we?" She asked.

"The market branch," Navi said.

"The market branch?" Saga parroted, then realisation struck her, "that's thirty floors up from the ground!" She cried, her heart beating faster and her breath coming in ragged, shallow exhalations that did nothing to calm her.

"Saga," Tymberlee said, resting both hands on the girl's shoulders. "It's alright. You're alright," she looked at Navi and Jemima for help.

"She's afraid of heights," Jemima said softly, which caused everyone to stare at the young angel.

"She's what?" Tena asked.

"Afraid of heights," Jemima repeated and the oddly coloured Dökkálfar girl stared in amusement at Saga, as did Tani and Rendon.

Saga looked back at Rendon, "What did you mean when you said that 'You... Well... I happened?'"

He shrugged, motioned to Tani, "we were out by the bonfire. My matches are done, and she was psyching herself up over the upcoming pentathlon..." He glanced towards Tymberlee with a grin, "and we didn't have anyone trying to tell us what to do either. We saw you run by and like Tena said, you just didn't respond.

"And you were in your nightshirt and on your bare feet," Tena added.

Saga looked down and realised that they were right. "Then what? How did I get from the camp all the way up to the market branch?"

"You ran," Rendon said with a grunt. "And that wolf went running by after you."

"Ren was the only one who could even remotely keep up with you, so he followed you and the wolf and because we figured that something was up, so I had a couple of our Weres follow you, while I sent Tena to find these guys," Tani motioned to Tymberlee, Navi and Jemima.

They were slowly walking back along the closed market branch as Saga tried to put her thoughts together. "I was dreaming..." She said. Shadow stayed close to her side, his body rubbing up against her legs as they walked.

"About what?" Jemima asked.

"Ghosts... Ghosts everywhere... Tremblay and Ainsli and the ancestors of the eastern school... angels too..." She looked at Jemima, "Your Aunt Dina was there... No one could talk to me except for this one old lady... And then..."

"And then what?" Rendon asked, curiosity getting the better of him.

"There was this big, gigantic portal opening and from it these ghosts were trying to escape, but it held them tight… That wasn't it though…" Saga said, stepping tentatively and realising that her bare feet had borne the brunt of her midnight run up the stairs of the world tree.

"What was it?" Jemima asked, watching her friend as she walked hesitantly.

"It was the creature…" Saga said. They bustled her onto one of the floating discs going down, despite her protests about the floating death traps. Rendon chuckled loudly, the louder her protests got.

"Tell us about the creature," Tymberlee insisted, trying to distract her.

"Uhh…" Saga said, "It was… It had a lot of heads, like snakes or something, really, really big ones…"

"Like a hydra?" Tena suggested and Saga whirled around, trying to find the small girl.

"Yes," she exclaimed. "It must have been a hydra, then she paused, a thought occurring to her. She turned back to Navi and Jemima. "What was it that leprechaun said?"

"Which one?" Jemima asked.

"The one at the port museum, what was it he said about a hydra and the gates of Tartarus?" Saga pressed, getting worked up.

"Umm…" The girl murmured as she thought.

"Did it have anything to do with an army of the dead marching on the guardian hydra of Tartarus?" Tena asked.

"Yes," Saga cried excitedly. "Yes, it did. That… That there's nothing that the hydra could do to ward them off."

"And the gates of Tartarus would open," Tena finished. "That was where my research was heading!"

"One of you might want to start at the beginning," Tani said interrupting the conversation.

"Is this to do with Sidawi?" Tymberlee asked, dread in her eyes.

Saga nodded, "Yeah…"

Tymberlee shook her head. "Ok, we need to talk to Mistress Grunborg and the other teachers about him. Navi started to protest, but Tymberlee shot her down. "No, Saga could have died tonight. Someone needs to stop him."

When they returned to camp, Tymberlee thanked Rendon, Tani and Tena for what they had done, then directed her girls back to their tent. "Jemima, have a look at Saga's feet and that wolf bite, make sure Matron Damir doesn't need to have a look at them."

"No!" Saga cried. "Matron Damir won't let me run!" She didn't even want to think of what consequences Emory might face if someone realised that he was Shadow and that he had bitten her. She knew that it was his attempt to save her and given time, Rendon, Tani and the other Rinsunid Cantera students would be able to back him up, but she also knew that the Were community took such infractions very seriously.

"We'll cross that bridge when and if we come to it," the faerie girl said. "Let Jemima take a look and I'm going to go look for Sidawi Harmeet."

Shadow set himself down beside Saga as Jemima inspected the wounds. Tymberlee frowned at him but said nothing as she left the tent.

The next day, Tymberlee reported that Sidawi was nowhere to be found. His things were all still in his tent, all except the black balalaika and no one had seen him all day. He had also not returned overnight.

"Do you think he knows about the break in?" Tasso asked over breakfast after Jemima and Navi had finished filling him in. Saga sat there silently, pushing her food around on her plate as she thought. She still did not have a clear image of the night before and she didn't want to ask again. Instead, she listened as the others talked, speculating about what was known and what wasn't before Tasso had to leave for his jousting match.

Saga had refused to go and watch Tasso joust, just as she always tried to avoid it. He thought it was funny and let her go. Instead, she had gone to check in with Tena and her research, before going to watch Jemima compete.

Tena was waiting for her with Rendon and another dark elf, a boy around Tani's age. "This is Gaten," Rendon said, "Our arcana candidate."

"Nice to meet you," Saga said. The boy nodded stoically, and Saga noticed that he seemed to keep his distance from Tena.

"What is it with you and dark elves?" a haughty voice asked, and Saga cringed as she recognised Tasso's sister. "It's like they multiply whenever you're around!"

"Shouldn't you be watching your brother joust?" Saga asked.

"Why would I do that?" she shot back. "It's not as though he came to my arcana battle."

"He didn't?" Saga asked. She remembered the day, but that had been when they had gone up to the garden of gods and she'd been distracted by seeing Ms Roskin... No, Shari Rose, again. She had no idea what had happened after she'd left the group. Still, as they were on a homework mission, there was little chance Tasso had intended to watch his sister compete. "I'm sorry, " Saga said.

Tonya looked surprised by this for a moment, before sneering, "What's it matter to you?"

Saga shrugged. "It doesn't. I just think it's sad that you've pushed your twin so far away that he would rather go do homework than support you."

Tonya huffed but stopped herself from a repeat of the time before when she had stopped her foot like a child about to erupt in a tantrum. She flicked her hair over her shoulders, fluttered her delicate gossamer wings and stormed off.

"Nice girl," Rendon said dryly.

Gaten, the Dark elf boy coughed, as though to draw attention back to himself. "I have study to do, so if you don't mind," he said slowly. Saga stared at him for a moment, she wasn't sure that she had ever heard a dark elf refer to themselves in that way. Did the free nature of dark elf society in Svartalheim result in a different speech pattern or had the boy learned to speak as those around him did? It was something she wanted to explore further, but there was no time.

"Right, yes," Tena said excitedly. "Gaten specialises in protection magic."

"Unlike some people," he said, with a glare at the girl.

"But we needed both of you to make this," Rendon said, reaching out and taking from Gaten an amulet. No, it wasn't an amulet she saw, although it was held on a leather thong intended to be worn around the neck. It was a hessian pouch that had several herbs sticking out from the top of it.

"It is a protection against the call of the dead," Gaten said. "Wear it and when the music plays, you will not be called."

"Thank you," Saga said as Rendon handed it to her. "Did you make one for Tena too?"

"Tena?" the girl echoed. "Why this one?"

"Because at the party on the first night, you too were under the music's thrall."

The boy sighed dramatically. "I will do so. Come Tena."

"Bye," Tena said with a wave as she ran off with the boy.

"Thank you," Saga said to Rendon, "For this... and for last night..."

The big daemon nodded. "Pleasure."

"And thank those two for me, would you?"

Tasso was sitting in the stands nursing injured ribs but talking animatedly about the match and how everything would be different next year. He looked surprisingly well for someone who had been knocked from a galloping horse by a large, pointed stick and Saga wondered what his secret was given how disastrously her first and only attempt had gone.

Navi was hovering by Tasso, trying to make him stay still as his arms flew about wildly as he spoke. Then, predictably, winced when he became too enthusiastic. "Matron Damir did not want him to leave her tent," Navi said, "But he thought he was as tough as you."

"Fool be you," Saga said, sitting down beside him. "I spent every moment of that afternoon regretting that decision."

Navi's eyes went wide in horror. "You never said anything," she exclaimed.

Saga shrugged. "I thought I was tougher than I was."

Tasso laughed. Or at least tried to, "Well... Yeah... I get that now..."

"It's not your first jousting injury," Saga said. "You'll be just fine," she said patting him on the shoulder, despite his grimaces.

"Just fine," he echoed in a low voice.

"Do we know what number Jemima is?" Saga asked, looking out at the field, and trying to locate their friend amidst the array of competitors, staff and horses.

"She's on third, we think," Navi said.

They watched as the horses and riders went through the complicated array of commands and movements. Saga thought that Sir Hoofington looked like he was right on the mark with his every move, but she was far from an expert on the matter. Her own presentation with Pingu had resembled a disaster and she was pretty sure it would be a while before Jemima managed to convince her to go out at Tourney for the event. She had too many events as it was.

"There she is," Navi exclaimed as the angel led her horse to the starting mark.

Like at school, they ran the event, two-by-two, as a skill and time trial. The failing participant was immediately disqualified, then scores were assessed and the top two were then sent through to the finals on the last day.

They cheered when Jemima beat out her adversary from one of the smaller schools based on time alone, then waited, the tension palpable as the judges assessed the precision of her presentation to see which of the two competitors won the match.

There was a lot of waiting, which left a lot of time for thinking and gazing towards the Tree City, the high branches alive with the hustle and bustle of daily life.

"You alright?" Navi asked, catching her faraway look.

"Yeah," Saga said, playing with the pouch around her neck.

"But?" Tasso asked.

"I'm wondering where Sidawi is," she said, not admitting that she was really thinking about how close she had come to falling to her death without even knowing what was happening. Hopefully, the magical pouch around her neck would prevent that from happening again. She could only hope, right?

"Are we still going out tonight?" Tasso asked.

"If you can move, yes," Saga said. "I think that we could all use it."

"Is everyone coming?" Navi added.

"I saw Rendon and Tena earlier, neither of them said anything, but I would say that they are," Saga said. "Oh, they're about to announce."

They leaned forward, waiting for the announcement, their gazes shifting from where Jemima stood with Sir Hoofington, beside her competitor.

Master Toshiji and the event announcer stepped forward to the centre of the field. "Jemima Dove, Toserra Sorose Academy."

If they were excited for their friend, then the gathering of Aunts over on the far side of the arena were ecstatic for their niece. Raphaella, Dina, Muriel, Evangelina, Cassiel and who were the others? Saga couldn't keep them all straight. They were cheering as though their lives depended on it.

Jemima beamed as she petted Sir Hoofington's nose. The horse stomped at the ground and shook his head, as though he intrinsically knew that he had done well.

"And now we celebrate," Tasso said excitedly.

"You're awfully happy for someone who lost their match," Saga said.

He shrugged, then grimaced before saying, "I competed and went down honourably. My father has nothing to complain about. I can be happy."

"Then celebrate we shall," Saga said, even if she didn't feel like it. She was wondering where Sidawi was and what her dream of the hydra had to do with his disappearance.

Halfway through the tournament, Agesilaus was overflowing with students from the various schools. Groupings around the various tables, dancing to the music and talking in loud, excited voices. Weres were running around in their anthropomorphic half animal forms, roaring and growling to the music while Angels and Faeries had left the dance floor to swirl and dance around above the heads of the club guests.

What bothered Saga the most, was how crowded with ghosts the space seemed to be. Tremblay wandered off from Tymberlee to join a group of ghosts, but they were everywhere.

"It's a mad house in here," Tymberlee said as she looked for somewhere to sit.

Saga wanted to tell the older girl that she didn't know the half of it, but there were so many ghosts filling up every free space, Saga wasn't even sure where they could walk to find their table.

"Thyra Bodil is playing tonight," A siren said, passing by them, her Kahawaiola'a Ocean School jacket hanging open. She already looked particularly dishevelled as she wandered up to a male angel from Aquino Beccara and draped herself over him. "Fly with me," she instructed and the boy, obviously besotted with the beautiful girl did exactly that. He wrapped his arms around her, flapped his powerful wings and launched them from the ground, almost colliding with a dancing pair above them as they went.

"Well, that explains a lot," Tasso said, looking around. "There's Rendon and the others."

The large daemon was looking particularly uncomfortable as an angel poked at his horns with a delicate finger. Tani was too busy laughing at him to help and Tena was giggling along with Consuela, the pretty light elf surprisingly accepting of their weird group.

Navi waved excitedly before noticing Sakata and Anh-Ly. "Navi will be back!" she said, rushing over to meet with the two eastern girls. Today though, they were letting their animal sides show with long tails and ears visible. Sakata looked to be some sort of cat, although different than the Weretigers Saga was used to and Anh-Ly was some sort of dog... or, she was a fox.

Saga's eyes went wide when she caught a good look at the two girls between a horde of their ghostly ancestors. "She's a Kitsune, isn't she?" she asked no one in particular.

Tymberlee glanced in the direction Navi had gone and nodded. "Probably and her friend is probably some sort of Bakeneko or maybe Nekomata... It's hard to tell when they're young and their tails haven't forked yet."

"Wow!" Saga gasped out. "Just when I think you can't surprise me anymore..."

"The extended planes beyond the Nine Realms hold many wondrous things," Tymberlee said. "Many we have no idea about."

"Table!" Jemima declared, and together they surged forward to claim it, Saga following in their wake, unable to see the table Jemima had seen. To their luck it was even near Rendon and Tani's table and in minutes, their tables were combined.

"No Gaten?" Saga asked, looking around, desperately trying to see anything despite the hundreds of ghosts that occupied every free space of air around her.

Tani laughed. "You have to excuse him, he's not very sociable. All study, study, study that one."

"We know the type," Saga said, "Well, the unsociable part, not the extra studious part..."

"Navi's brother?" Tena asked and they all nodded in agreement. "Where is he?" she asked, looking around, as though he would magically appear.

"Actually..." Saga said. "I haven't seen him... Not today anyway..."

"Food and drinks," Tasso declared as Navi returned to the table, the two eastern girls with her, along with their countless ethereal ancestors. Saga rubbed at her eyes, trying to clear them, but she knew from long nights and days of trying, that there was no way to make them go away. She really wished that she could turn off the ability to see ghosts. The room was feeling overly claustrophobic with them filling every singly free space, and even half sticking out from the walls, furniture and other people.

"Has everyone met Sakata and Anh-Ly?" Navi asked.

"Not yet," Tani said, holding her hand out to the girls. "I've heard good things," the dark elf said.

"Likewise," Sakata, the cat girl said.

"Is this normal?" Saga asked, "Everyone letting their animal sides show like this?"

"Away from school and when having fun like this?" Tasso asked, "Absolutely. The Weres and the Yokai and any of the shape shifters really, they personify the term 'Party Animal.'"

People were everywhere, but a certain head of orange hair caught Saga's attention and she watched as Harian Mau limped past with a group of second years, several ghosts laughing at him as he went.

"No," Saga exclaimed, "No, no, no, no!" She kept going, starting to stand from her seat, to get a better view of where the Weretiger was going.

"What is it?" Tani asked, trying to figure out what was going on.

"Harry bloody Mau is limping!" Saga cried, apparently loud enough that the Weretiger heard her. He glanced over his shoulder at her and seeing her glare, he seemed to limp away faster.

"Oh him?" Rendon asked. "He got run over in his stadion run by a Were from Ehras Magna. It was a spectacular cat fight with both of them changing and starting to brawl in the middle of the track."

"He did what?" another voice cried.

Deluca Goett was standing there, a drink in his hand and his face as white as a ghost's. "What did he do?"

"So he's injured and disqualified?" Saga questioned. "I wasn't allowed to punch out those horrible so-called noble elves from Shamel Aiyeola, but he can get into a fight in the middle of the racetrack?"

Rendon nodded. "Yeah, that's the way I heard it. He got a real yelling at from one of your teachers… If it helps any, the Were he got into it with, also got disqualified."

"It doesn't help!" Saga and Deluca chorused together.

Saga looked up at him. "No!" she exclaimed.

"Yes!" he shot back.

"No! You didn't even ask!" With Harry disqualified for brawling, even if he recovered from his injury, she would still be forced to race in the pentathlon even on the last day of the tourney. Once Deluca got her into an event, neither he nor Donetta would let her go.

"Many, many times," he declared. "You're running in the pentathlon team challenge Saga," he declared.

"Deluca!" she cried as he walked away in the direction Harry had gone, a scowl on his face. "Deluca!" Then she turned on Jemima, the ghosts suddenly clearing away from their table. "You said it was a formality. You said the reserve never competes!"

Jemima sunk back into her chair and shrugged. "My bad..." she said in a small voice.

MARCH OF THE DEAD

The atmosphere went positively electric… or was it magical? Saga had no idea what the appropriate colloquial terminology would be for the atmospheric shift when Thyra Bodil stepped onto the stage, replacing a jaunty instrumental group that had been keeping up a lively set of dance tunes.

There were people crying out her name, wolf-whistling and just screaming in delight. It was, Saga thought, just like a concert back on Midgard not that she had ever been to one, but she had seen them on tv.

The band that came on with her began to play and Saga recognised the tune. It was a song that Vespers really adored, the one about the Valkyrie on the battlefield.

"Here we go, to war again, all the heaven sent soldiers
When they fight they shall have all the weapons they're proud to wield
Arrows and bows, maces and swords, all the weapons for them to wield,"

The screams of delight as her melodic voice carried across the excited crowd. The dancing had slowed and couples huddled together, arms wrapped tightly around one another. The ghosts seemed to also quiet down, their voices dying away as they gave into a gentle swaying motion, in time to the music.

"Down on the battlefield, the Valkyrie,
doth choose the slain, to serve the Gods

The brave and the true are called to serve

In the hall of Valhalla,"

The music seemed to lull everyone into a calm demeanour and as Saga looked around, she noticed that everyone... Or almost everyone was watching Thyra, her music drawing them in, much as Sidawi's had been drawing her into a thrall. The sirens all loved her, was she a siren too? Her music was able to manipulate and control those who heard it, or was it just her fame that had everyone watching her in awe and Saga's paranoia getting the best of her?

And then she spotted him. Sidawi was standing to the side of the stage, watching Thyra while talking to a man Saga recognised all too well and to her surprise, Edun was with them.

"Here we go, to war again, all the heaven sent soldiers

When they ride they shall have all the weapons they're proud to wield

Arrows and bows, maces and swords, all the weapons for them to wield."

Saga pushed her chair back, trying to stand up amidst the crushing crowd of onlookers.

"What is it?" Navi asked, her voice slow and slurred as though she was coming out of a trance.

"Vali," Saga breathed out and suddenly, Jemima seemed not so entranced by the music either, as though the name had been a jump start to her brain. Saga's hand clenched at her side, ready to grab a knife from the table, to summon to her the blade tat always seemed to come when she needed it most. She glanced at Navi. There was no way she was letting that man anywhere near her friend again, not after she'd almost died last time.

So what was Edun doing with him?

"What's he doing here?" The angel asked.

"Why don't we ask Sidawi and Edun?" Saga suggested, still struggling to get up from the table. Tasso and Rendon seemed completely enamoured with the song of the woman and neither so much as looked away from her.

Tena looked around climbing onto the table for a better vantage point. "This one can get to them," she said, locating where they were. Her form started to shift and elongate before shrinking down, leaving her clothes on the table, along with the pouch of herbs.

The small brown rat then peered up at them with beady eyes. She searched around frantically before grabbing the herb pouch in her mouth, then jumping onto Saga's shoulder and scurrying down the length of her body, jumping to floor and disappearing between the feet of the patrons of the club.

"Tena!" Saga called out, but the rat girl was gone.

"What just happened?" Navi asked, staring in awe at the mess of clothes that were spilled across the table.

Saga shrugged. "Tena's half Wererat."

"Huh? She's what?"

"Half Dökkálfar, half Wererat," Saga said. "It explains her colouring, yeah?"

"Navi supposes it does..." she murmured. "Let's go after her."

Jemima flapped her wings, allowing their lift to pull her out of the chair. "How are we going to get through them?" She asked.

Navi poked at Tasso, but the boy was completely enthralled by the singer, his eyes glazed over in fascination. Around them, all the men were affected and some of the women too. "Tasso!" Navi hissed, but nothing seemed to faze the faerie boy. "Vali's here."

The song died away and Anh-Ly shifted uncomfortably in her chair, but her attention, like Sakata's, Consuela's and even Tymberlee's, was taken up by the siren.

"Why aren't you two affected?" Saga asked, looking at Navi and Jemima.

Both girls reached into their shirts and retrieved similar little ouches full of herbs to the one that Tena had given her, and that Rat Tena had run off with.

"So, do we think Thyra Bodil, one of the Nine Realms most famous bards, is in on this... Whatever this is?" Jemima asked.

"No," Navi said pointing at the band, "Some of those guys are the ones who have been playing with Sidawi."

There was a confused and dazed shuffling as people started to move again. Tasso looked up at them, his eyes still glazed over. "What... What just happened?" he asked in a slurred voice.

"The music," Navi said, pinching him.

"Ow!" He exclaimed, rubbing at his arm. "What was that for?"

At their table, like at the others, people were starting to talk and eat, complaining that their food was cold or their drinks warm and any would be fizz, gone. "Come on," Saga said, "we have to catch up with Tena. Come on, while people are milling around."

Navi grabbed Tasso, hauling him to his feet with surprising strength. "You heard her," she said, and they slowly began to push their way through the packed club, leaving behind a table full of confused people.

The only just head Tani ask, "Where did Tena go?" before they were enveloped by a pack of half transformed Weres.

A new tune was starting up on a lute, the pan flute joining in, just as Thyra began to sing again and Saga grinned as she recognised the Dragon of Honah Lee. A group from Kahawaiola'a Ocean School started to sing along, followed by the proud voices of the students' The Two Worlds School. Obviously, this song was as well-loved in the Nine Realms, or more particularly the Extended Planes, as it was back home and Saga found herself singing along, a rare occurrence in this world where the music seemed entirely foreign to her.

As they moved though, getting jostled by the crowd, Tasso seemed to fade away once more, his gaze focusing on the woman on stage.

Navi tried to pull him along with her, but he was stuck still, as many others were. "Forget him," Jemima ordered from above them. Saga had rarely seen either of her winged friends fly around, despite Tasso's suggestion to fly her and Navi down to their match, neither of them relied on their wings all that much. Other angels and faeries dashed around town, wings flapping over the heads of those stuck walking. It was even more prevalent in the Tree City, where the winged beings would fly from level to level instead of using the stairs or the rainbow shards.

"Can you see Tena?" Saga asked, as she tried to limbo herself under the arms of two Werewolves. She came up between them, their breath hot and heavy and unbearably smelly. "Ugh…" she cringed trying to find a way to best past them.

"No," there's too many people and she's too small. We might have had a chance if they were conscious and could get scared at the sight of a rat."

Then, the balalaika started up and the ghosts started to swarm in a mass of energy, surging towards the stage.

As soon as The Dragon of Honah Lee finished, they were straight into a new song, Thyra's melodic, hypnotising voice entrancing the entire crowd while the instruments garnered the attention of the dead.

"What is Edun doing there?" Navi asked, "Why is he playing with Sidawi?"

"I don't know," Saga said, the sound of his pan flute actually soothing, despite the enthralling effect of the balalaika and the siren's song. She remembered overhearing Edun in the camp, arguing with Sidawi about Ziva. Had he been trying to join him? Working with him on this foolhardy plan to bring Ziva back from the dead?

A crack of thunder bellowed throughout the club, startling everyone, even the dazed, from their reverie. Murmurs and questions started to flow as Saga ducked under a flailing arm in the midst of a wild conversation.

Nearby, but separated by the crowd, Navi was keeping low, using her small frame to her advantage as she ducked and weaved between the people.

Another thunderous crack echoed, forcing many people to cover their ears in surprise. The ghosts were starting to look worried and as behind the band, a fissure started to appear, creating a crack in the air. It swirled with orange and red and black and every hue in-between.

"No!" Saga cried, no longer caring about being nice as she started to push people aside. Some stumbled and others fell as she tried to barrel herself across the room.

"Sid!" She cried out, "Sidawi!" But it was as though he couldn't hear her and maybe he couldn't over the music and the portal and everything else that was going on around him. "Edun!" she cried and she could hear Navi echo the call towards her brother. Instead, though, both he and Sidawi kept on playing, the fissure of swirling, ominous light breaking the air behind them open.

The ghosts were staring at the fissure, their attention on it as though expecting something to emerge from it, when one of them turned to her. An old woman in a delicately embroidered kimono and bright, summery colours. Images of dragons and cherry blossoms covered her as she held out her hand to Saga.

"Help us," she said, echoing the old woman from her dreams... And then Saga realised... She was the old woman from her nightmare the night Shadow and Rendon had prevented her from plummeting to her death from the market branch.

"I don't know how," Saga said.

The old woman pointed behind Saga and she turned to try and see what she was pointing at. A large black dog... or wolf was bounding from table to table. "Shadow!" she breathed out.

"You and him. Help us." The old woman said, right before a deafening, booming sound exploded throughout the room, a shockwave emanating from the fissure, knocking everyone in the club to the floor. Glasses and bowls and windows shattering.

Saga struggled back to her feet, only for the angels and faeries and other flying races who had taken to the air to dance the night away to come falling back to the ground. There were bodies falling all around her and she only just barely managed to catch Jemima, as the young angel came crashing back to the ground, dazed, and confused from the shockwave.

"Jem?" Saga asked.

"Fine," she muttered as she struggled to get her feet on the ground until Saga put her down finally. "Fine..."

"What was that?" Saga asked.

On the stage, the band still played. Thyra singing, Sidawi on his balalaika and Edun on the pan flute and the other band members all still in the correct time and tune. How had they not been affected?

"I don't know," Jemima said, before spotting another form struggling to get to get to her feet. "Navi!"

They clambered over bodies, two and three, even four high after the collapse of the flyers. As they fought their way through the bodies they were met with grunts and groans of pain and grogginess.

"Watch it!" a Weretiger growled as Saga trod on his tail, but she ignored him, reaching Navi and helping the small dark elf up from where she had been caught under a couple of boys from The Two Worlds School with crow wings and jet-black hair.

"Thanks," Navi said, shaking her foot free from where it was tangle amidst clothes and feathers. A hand that had been wrapped around her ankle fell loose, thudding back to the ground.

Behind the band, the crack in space was still growing, the music seeking to feed it as they played. Slowly, an angel got to her feet from where she had fallen and started to walk towards it, her feet surprisingly sure in their movements as she made her way over the half-dazed forms of the club patrons.

Growls of discomfort or pain did nothing to stop the girl's movements, nor did whimpers and cries of fear.

Jemima was suddenly climbing over the large, half transformed form of a werebear, screaming out for the angel to stop.

"Azrael!" She cried. "Aunt Azrael!" The young Angel of Death didn't seem to hear her though.

Nearby, another angel was making their determined way towards the stage.

The ghost of the old woman reached out to Saga. "Help us," she begged, and behind her, Saga could see that the ghosts, like Azrael, were all single-mindedly, making their way towards the fissure. She saw it just in time to see a couple of ghosts get sucked in, their pale, already tattered forms being dragged in as they screamed, consciousness returning to them for a brief moment if time before they were sucked in, like water down a gurgling drain.

The old woman seemed to be fighting against some invisible pull, the strain ripping holes and tears into her ethereal form, "Wolf's ho..." She managed before she was flung across the room and engulfed by the fissure.

"What about the wolf?" Saga cried. She looked back to where Shadow had leapt onto the bar, his eyes searching, taking everything in. The cries of the ghosts being sucked into the fissure was becoming deafening and she could see Shadow cowering against the bar surface, paws over his ears.

He could hear them.

Shadow could hear the deafening cries of the dead.

"Saga!" Jemima cried, pointing towards Azrael and the other angels. They were nearing the fissure, the crack into some unknown hell.

Saga gave up caring who she hurt and ran toward the fissure. She grabbed for one angel, but he kept on walking, dragging her along with him as though her strength meant nothing.

Somewhere at the back of the club a door opened, and new noises filled the air. A gust of fresh air that seemed to for a moment at least, wake those closest to the door.

But through the door came more angels, more ghosts and few that Saga couldn't place, but maybe necromancers like Tena or other creatures and beings that Saga did not yet know the names of.

Wolf. What had the old woman meant? Shadow looked as though he was in agony, unused to the screaming, wailing cacophony of noise going on around them.

Saga stepped on the tail of a hyena and then the wing of a strange, half bird like boy. She reached the stage, Jemima just ahead of her, trying to grab a hold of Azrael and stop her from getting closer to the fissure, but like the angel boy that Saga had tried to stop, Azrael persevered, Jemima's attempts to stop her, ineffective.

Instead of going for an angel, Saga went for Sidawi. "Sidawi!" she cried, but the boy seemed completely absorbed in his music. To the side of the stage, the man they thought was Vali was reading from a book, chanting. Edun, the gentle notes of his pan flute soothing against the rush of energy the balalaika caused also didn't respond when called for.

Should she go for Vali? Should she go for Sidawi or Edun? Or should she stop the angels from going into the fissure? She didn't know.

A bellowing roar erupted from the fissure, large drops of spittle exploding, right before a giant, reptilian head appeared.

"No! No! No! No!" Saga cried. Decision made, she grabbed at Sidawi who was the closest to her. His fingers slipped on the strings of the black balalaika and with the break in the music, the fissure fluctuated with the change. Sidawi tried to resituate himself, to continue playing, but Saga tried to wrestle the instrument from his hands. "Sid, stop it!" Saga begged. She looked, trying to find Navi. "Get Edun!" she ordered and the girl leapt gracefully from the nearest table to the stage.

Behind them, a second roar drew their attention as a second head emerged from the fissure. The bellowing shockwave threatened to knock Saga from her feet, and she saw Navi get thrown backwards, falling from the stage. She scrambled right back up onto the stage, trying to get at Edun. Looking at him, Saga realised something odd. Unlike the other members of the band, Edun did not look to be absorbed in the music, in fact, he looked panicked. The look in his eyes as he watched his little sister trying to get to him. He tried to shake his head, the end of pan flute, pointing towards Saga as he tried to communicate something. He kept on playing though, as though stopping would be the worst thing he could do.

Azrael was closer to the fissure and Saga made to go and help Jemima, when a wave of ghosts were ripped out of the club and into the fissure. The screams echoing in her ears as the sight of the shattered forms being ripped apart was burned into her mind. "Tremblay!" She cried, trying to reach out to him, but her hand went through his ethereal form. The ghost looked dazed as he was drawn towards the gaping hole with the two gigantic snake heads emerging from it. There was a swirling of colours and a rippling in the shape of the fissure. "There's another one coming!" she cried.

The ghosts were going in faster now and Tremblay was so close to the fissure that his ethereal form was being drawn towards it, the tattered edges being ripped away slowly.

Edun let out a loud, wailing note from the pan flute and Saga whirled around, looking for Shadow. Realisation of what the old woman had been trying to say finally hitting her. "SHADOW!" she cried. "HOWL!" The large animal looked up at her from across the room, his ears still down, not liking the noise and confusion etched on his face. "HOWL!" she cried again over the noise of the screaming ghosts and the whirring of the fissure.

Shadow sat up fully and lifted his head up before howling as loud as he could. Those closest to him, streaming in through the door stopped. The sound of his howling filled the space and the ghosts started to come back to themselves. Angels stopped moving towards the fissure and ghosts started floating backwards. The ones closest to the fissure though were still being pulled in.

"Jem, get Azrael away from there!" She called, but the bellow of the third head emerging from the fissure made it hard to hear, the shockwave from the sound knocking the two angels from their feet. Saga crouched low, pulling Sidawi down with her, the air blowing over them. It was hot and smelled of rotten eggs. Behind her, she heard someone choking, trying not to let the stench get to them. She looked up and realised that it was Thyra. The siren looked positively ill at the stench as she stumbled away from the band. The first head, the one in the middle reached out before she could get two steps and swallowed her whole.

The man to the side, playing some form of drum screamed out as the woman vanished headfirst into the creature's mouth. Saga could only stare as the man, finally free from whatever enthrallment the music had caused.

"Thyra!" He cried in an agonised tone that even as she stood beside him, was barely audible to Saga over the sounds of the beasts, Shadows relentless howling and the nose of the fissure itself.

One ghost stood out. He stood still, taking in everything around him and he seemed to be unable to move. It was as though Shadows howl, which called to him the unsettled dead, had no effect on this ghost. Saga spotted another ghost that also seemed unable to move, the fissure still dragging in parts of his ethereal form as they were torn away from him. The small leprechaun ghost of Ainslie House hovering over a group of stunned Weres was another.

The returned dead were unaffected by Shadow's howl...

With Thyra's disappearance, Saga could hear Vali's chanting now. It was so strange how some sounds she could hear, and others seemed so far away, no matter how close they were.

A fourth head emerged from the crack in the air this one stinking of rotten fish left out on a warm day. Its roar seemed to awaken those who had been enthralled by the siren's song and atop all the noise, people began to scream. People ran for the door, climbing over one another to get out. With everyone moving again Saga couldn't find anyone. Navi was still trying to get Edun to move, but Jemima and Azrael were hidden from sight. Their friends, somewhere in the midst of all the chaos, were completely hidden from sight. Hopefully, they would be getting out, but Saga suddenly felt very alone.

Shadow's howl stopped, and a relentless barking started up. Saga remembered that barking. She had heard it before, back on Midgard, locked in the solitary room at the group home. The barks were getting louder. He was coming closer.

The drummer who was crying after Thyra suddenly stopped, his cries for the woman cut off in a gurgling screech of fear.

Navi pulled on Edun and his flute playing went loud, the screeching sound piercing the air. He shook his head again and kept on playing. Navi looked distraught that he wouldn't come, but the moment was short lived when the beast doubled its efforts, multiple heads coming out to swallow members of the band. Navi screamed when seemingly at once, Sidawi and Edun were taken up with the rest of the band, their instruments falling to the floor with unheard clattering. "Edun!" Navi shrieked, before running and launching herself so that she wrapped her arms around the neck of the best.

"NAVI!" Saga screamed.

Edun was gone. Sidawi was gone. Navi was gone. Saga froze where she stood, all thought abandoning her. What was she supposed to do? Her friends were... were... She couldn't even contemplate the thought. There had to be another answer, another something. Anything.

She looked around, but amongst the chaos and carnage of the bar, she didn't see anything or anyone that could help and she needed help if she was going to her Navi, Edun, Sidawi and anyone else back. She tuned back to the swirling portal and the beast that was emerging from within it. She gulped. There was only one thing to do... Wasn't there?

A black streak shot past her, snarling and barking, it jumped, launching itself at the head of the beast that had taken Sidawi, its teeth sinking into the scaley flesh of the creature. The other heads weaved and bobbed, baring teeth and snapping at anyone who came to close. Which head was it that had taken Navi? Was it the same one Shadow was now engaging with, or had it been another? Was that the same one that had eaten Edun? She didn't know. She couldn't tell. They all looked the same and with the way they moved, it was worse than keeping track of a game of find the shell.

"Shadow!" She cried as the head bucked against the weight of the wolf, held in place by the strong teeth digging into the flesh. All thought of Shadow fled from her mind when she saw the Ainsli House ghost, there because the house Prefect had apparently performed exceptionally well at the horse speed racing event was suddenly torn apart and swallowed up by the fissure.

She stood, panic continuing to freeze her to the spot as she tried to decide what to do, tried to find the will to move. She knew Tremblay was so close to the fissure that he was likely to be pulled in any moment now, the wolf's howl having done nothing to bring him back to his senses like it had the unsettled dead. The monster was retreating back inside having feasted on the band and drawn in angels, ghosts and other spirit beings from beyond the nine realms...

And where was Tena?

Behind her the stampeding crowd was desperate to escape the monster and the fissure and whatever delirium had made them a potential feast. The area immediately around the stage was now clear and Saga could clearly see Vali, his head still in the book as his voice now carried clearly to her ears.

She could go for him. Get him while he was distracted. Stop whatever it was he was doing from coming to fruition...

But what would happen if the fissure closed with Navi and Shadow and all the others still inside it? Where did it even go?

The Lower Realms of the Dead? But there were so many of them, from Hell the lowest of the nine realms and named after the goddess of the afterlife or to Hades, one of the extended planes that bordered Hell... And was also named after the God of the afterlife... How many others were there? She had no idea, but tried to make a mental note to ask Master Berfelan when they returned to school... If they returned to school.

She shook her head, she didn't need Planarography now, she needed common sense. What did Vali want in The Lower Realms of the Dead?

He didn't want anything in the lower planes themselves... He wanted what was under Hades. The titans, the evil entities trapped in Tartarus. Did he think that they would help him take Odin's throne? She didn't know, but it wouldn't be good for anyone if he succeeded. Tartarus existed for a reason, to lock beings so powerful and so evil away from the rest of the world...

So that left the question...

Did she jump in after Navi, Shadow and the others... Or did she stop Vali from opening the doors of Tartarus?

HELL

The last head of the beast was retreating into the fissure and Saga jumped, grabbing hold of the massive beast. Stopping Vali would mean nothing if Navi, Shadow, Edun and Sidawi were trapped in the depths of Hell.

"Nooooo!" The cry surprised her, but with her arms wrapped tightly around the serpentine neck of the beast. It was too late to let go.

Vali dropped his book and dashed up the steps of the stage. He tried to grab her by the ankle and haul her back into the ruined club. Saga kicked at him, and Vali tried desperately to grab a hold of her other ankle, stop her from kicking him. Instead, he caught the heel of her boot to his chin, and he stumbled backwards.

"Not her!" He yelled at the beast, his hand to his jaw.

The fissure was closing, the head dragging her in after the others. Someone, she didn't know who, called her name. The head reared up as it tried to avoid Vali pulling her away again, then in the last second before the fissure closed, Vali's hand wrapped around her in leg once more and he was dragged in with her.

The serpentine beast reared up, bucked against the weight of Saga and Vali around its neck. Nearby, another head was screeching as Shadow's sharp teeth and claws held in place. It reared, threshed, thrashed, and swirled in an effort to get rid of the weight of the large wolf. On her other side, Navi was holding on to the head of the beast, kicking at it relentlessly.

"Give him back! Give him back!" She screamed, again and again.

Suddenly, the head Shadow was latched onto surged wildly and the wolf went sailing through the air, only to collide heavily with a pillar that was nearby... And moved...

"Oh crap!" Saga muttered as she tried to see around the neck she was hanging on to. Shadow yelped in pain before tumbling down the length of the supposed pillar before another head came up, colliding with Shadow's body and sent him flying in another direction. "SHADOW!" she screamed when she lost sight of him amongst the heads that just seemed to keep on coming. She couldn't move though, not with Vali hanging on to her. "We're in Hades, aren't we?" she called down to the man.

He didn't answer though. She could feel him, scrabbling unpredictably at her feet. Every time he moved, she was sent off balance and her grip on the neck slid a little. Then he slipped, his hand coming away as her boot fell away from her foot. The change in his weight sent her swinging off to one side and she lost her grip. With one hand, she tried to hold on, but her fingers slipped, unable to bare her weight, Vali's weight and the constant movement of the beast.

She let out a scream that pierced the air as the tips of her fingers slid away from the beast's neck.

And then she was falling...

Falling...

Falling...

Navi screamed her name, but there was nothing the dark elf girl could do to help Saga.

And she fell...

Her greatest fear becoming a reality as she kicked and reached and nothing she did found anything to hold on to. How long would she fall for? She did realise in a moment of clarity that Vali had let go. They were falling independent of one another. In the end it wouldn't help. The ground was still hurtling towards her at an unprecedented rate...

She thudded against something hard and as it moved, she was sent flying through the air, much as Shadow had been. Her descent had slowed though with the addition of forward momentum.

If she could just get a hold of something...

A head reared up in front of her eyes. It seemed larger than the heads she had seen before... The ones that had eaten the members of the band. Its's eyes glowed red as it looked at her. Suddenly, it darted towards her, and Saga tried to turn, to change direction, to fight, anything to protect herself from the fangs of the beast.

She swung in the air. Her descent suddenly halted. She let out a breath she hadn't been aware she'd been holding... Well, no, not holding. She had screamed right until the fear had turned it silent and now, she took great gasping breaths of air... And coughed. There was a smell, similar to that which had permeated the club through the fissure. It wasn't the deep breath of clean, fresh air she had been anticipating.

Nearby, another head was holding Vali up and the man was screaming epithets, demanding to be put down, demanding to be respected. Saga just concentrated on not looking down... And that turned out to be pretty easy with the view that she was facing.

Head, after head, after head, after head, after even more heads stared back at her. She tried counting them, but after twenty or so, she lost her place as they moved, wrapping around one another, and then unwrapping themselves in continual motion.

Something moved. It caught her attention amidst all the other constant movement because it was small and seemed to skitter along the surface of the beast's skin. The head that had it bucked and reared, trying to dislodge whatever it was.

"Put me down!" Vali yelled, but the beast wasn't listening. How could it with everything going on?

She needed to get down. If she could find the ground, she would be able to think and then she could figure out how to get Navi and Shadow back. Then... then they could try to discover what had happened to Sidawi and Edun.

The head with the small movement running along it suddenly came crashing towards the one holding Vali, head-butting its' twin. Vali went flying as the creature screamed in agony.

"Oh no," Saga cried when she saw the head shake off the impact and redirect its attention on her... Or more accurately, the head that currently held her by the scruff of her clothes. "Oh no, oh no, oh no..."

The impact of the collision sent her flying backwards before the creature erupted in a roar of pain and Saga started to fall. The scream that was trying to come out was trapped in her throat and she wished that she could be anywhere but there in that moment. She collided once more with the thick, solid neck of the creature but instead of rebounding off it and going flying through the air, she seemed to proceed down by sliding down the twisting, turning neck of the creature. It might have been fun if the thing hadn't of eaten the band...

Chittering in her ear had her turning her neck ever so slightly to see the small, tawny coloured rat sitting there, its claws, digging into the shoulder of her clothes to hold on tight.

"Tena!" Saga gasped. She reached up, to cover the little rat with her hands. They were nearing the end, and it was likely to be a very brutal dismount... It's not like one practiced dismounting from hell borne monsters in class... Master Toshiji or Mistress Anhora should really consider it. It might come in handy the next time this happened.

Oh, let there not be a next time, she thought as she came hurtling off the end of the beast's neck where it connected to rest of the massive body. She flew through the air briefly, before falling to the ground and tucking in tight, little rat Tena held protectively against her chest as she rolled, once, twice, three times before sprawling against the ground at the feet of an army of ghosts.

Except they weren't ghosts. They were solid. The tattered, faded remnants of souls that Saga usually saw didn't look like that at all. She saw the old woman who had spoken to her in her dream and in the club stand there, in front of all the gathered ghosts... people... souls... What were they now?

"You," the woman said, holding her hand out to Saga, wide kimono sleeves of intricately embroidered silk hanging almost to the ground. Saga took it and allowed the woman to help her to her feet. "You are the answer."

"I don't understand," Saga said, settling rat Tena on her shoulder. One roar started behind her, then a second and third until it was loud cacophony of incessant roaring, one head after another, some going again and again to make themselves heard. Saga turned on the spot and for the first time got a full look at the beast that had dragged them into this strange, dark world. "Where are my friends?"

"The little valiant dark elf still battles with the head that holds her brother," the old woman said. "She could use some help, as could the wolf boy, you will need him."

"How do I help her?" Saga asked. "How do I help any of them... or any of you?"

"We will come to that, for now," The old woman said, "Do you know what that is?"

Saga started to shake her head, when she saw a leprechaun out of the corner of her eye. It wasn't Cillian Ainsli, the ghost of Ainsli House, but another one in the black, formal uniform of the airship service. Saga gasped. He wasn't the leprechaun they had spoken to that day, but she remembered. She closed her eyes, bring the sight of the little man to mind. They had been doing their planarography assignment. They had gotten into a conversation with the museum caretaker about Tartarus, the prison created for all powerful gods, titans, daemons and other unkillable, but unredeemable creatures before the realisation that they were going to be late for the paired staff fights and rushed off. But not before the leprechaun had uttered out the words, "When the dead march upon the great, fifty headed hydra which guards the gates, there is nothing it can do and the gates of Tartarus will open in Hell," she said, repeating his warning word for word. The old woman nodded and appeared to wait for something. "We can't kill it," Saga said under her breath.

"Exactly," The old woman said. "To kill the hydra, for any reason..."

"Would leave that hellish prison without protection," Saga finished for her. The old woman nodded again, the wide sleeves of her kimono flaring in the breeze caused by the roaring of the fifty headed hydra. "What do I do?" She asked.

"You must find the wolf boy," she said. Saga frowned at that. What could Shadow do to help? "The wolf boy stopped the ghosts back in the world tree from descending into Hades and now he can aide you in returning these spirits," she extended her hand out delicately, motioning to the restless crowd behind her, "to the realms in which they belong."

"I don't know how," Saga begged.

"Yes, you do," The woman pointed to Saga's heart. "The answers are there. Who else was brought into this impending doom?"

Saga looked around. The sold forms of the dead were everywhere, but a rustling feathered wing caught her attention.

"Angels!" She breathed out. "Angels and faerie ghosts."

"Call them to you. Close your eyes, clear you mind and summon them to your side," the old woman directed. Saga did as she was told, but her thoughts were a mess. Navi was in danger. Edun had been eaten. Shadow was hurt. Where was Tremblay? The ghost would be solid here. How was she going to do this? "Calm," the woman ordered. "Empty your mind of every worry and concentrate on what you need. The ghosts and the angels to come forward and aide you. That is your only thought. It is the only thought that will save your friends. Breath. In… Out… In… Out…"

Saga did as the old woman instructed and felt something she had never felt before… no… She had felt it, or at least something similar the night of the Dorbe Manor fire when they had hung in the night sky, high above the carnage and chaos.

She opened her eyes and saw, surrounding her were the solid forms of faerie ghosts, a few angels that she wasn't entirely sure if they Angels of Death that had been sucked in like Azrael had almost been or Angels who had passed on to the next life. Amongst them were also the Toserra Sorose House Ghosts, Tremblay Jimpsee and Cillian Ainslie.

"Tremblay!" She gasped out and hugged the man. He was startled for a moment before ever so carefully and tentatively, wrapping his arms around her.

"Saga," he said, his voice low and almost reverent as she let go and held her out before him.

"I've missed you," she said.

The young ghost canted his head to the side and beamed with pride. "And here I thought you detested my poking my nose in everywhere."

"Oh, I do," Saga said without hesitation, "So does Tymberlee, but I've missed our talks."

"What do you need young Valkyrie?" a wizened old man asked, dull and wrinkled faerie wings, lay loosely against his back. She was sure that this man had been dead for many eons, but it was possible, that he had yet to pass on to the realms of the dead.

"There are people trapped up on and in the Hydra," she said. "I need you to find them for me."

"In?" a young angel in the uniform of Aquino Beccara asked.

Saga nodded. "They were... I believe, swallowed whole and well, with everything as weird as it is around here, they might have... survived..." She said, her certainty giving way to hesitation as she spoke. What if she was wrong? What if Edun and Sidawi and Thyra Bodil and the other band members were dead?

No, she couldn't think like that. She would not allow Navi to lose two of her siblings within the one year. She touched the black pan flute, which was still, amazingly, slung across her body on the strap Edun kept it on.

Tremblay frowned. "I can sense Emory and Navi nearby."

Saga's eyes widened in surprise. Did he know that Emory and Shadow were the same being? Who was she kidding, of course their house ghost knew, right? She nodded. "Yes... Shadow...Emory... He was hurt and... and... I need him Tremblay..."

The ghost nodded thoughtfully, then motioned to two angels. "Come on. Let's go find my boy."

Tremblay, a half angel, half daemon who could manifest tails and horns and halos at will, suddenly grew two wings from his back. One that was made up of the pure white feathers of a dove and the other, of the thin, dark leathery flesh of a bat. He beat down hard, a gust of air billowing out as he did so. The two angels he had summoned to his side followed suit and they took off, flying into the air, amidst the fifty heads of the beast.

"DON'T KILL IT!" Saga called out to him.

"I'll do what I can," Tremblay called back, and Saga wondered what that really meant by that.

"What about us?" Another angel asked.

"Navi," Saga said. "She's trying to get her brother out... Or at least she was when I last saw her. Edun was swallowed up by one of the heads."

The angel nodded and with a faerie at his side, they took off in search of the young dark elf siblings. Saga sent another group to try and locate the head that had swallowed Sidawi and even more after the ones that had swallowed Thyra Bodil and the rest of the band. She had no idea if any of them were still alive, but she had to hope… She had to because Edun and Sidawi were in there.

She was about to ask after Vali, if she could capture him, surely there was something someone like Astrid or the guards could do with him, right? But the sounds of battle and the hydra screeching in pain flooded the area.

"He has started the march," the old woman said. "You must stop him."

"How?" Saga asked again, still not knowing what the woman wanted.

"Without the wolf it will be no good," she said. Well what use was that? Saga wanted to scream. "Hold them off," and with that, she held her hands out to her side, before creating a large, circular movement and when both arms were raised above her head she said, "Shisha no senshi no seishin ga kite, watashi ni anata no chikara o kashite, gijin no ha ni nari nasai." Saga had no idea what it meant, but men and women dressed similarly to the old woman and the members of The Two Worlds School contingent were drawn to her. The offered low, reverent bows of greeting before their spirits were drawn into her hands, the form of a curved blade taking shape with every soul that leant its power to its creation.

"What are you?" Saga breathed out in awe as the woman lowered her arm, holding out a curved blade of impeccable craftsmanship.

The old woman just smiled and presented the weapon to her, hilt first. There seemed to be some form of ritual to the way she was presenting it and Saga didn't know what to do, except that she was pretty sure she shouldn't simply reach out and take the beautiful weapon. "For the warrior class, to be reborn within the blade is a great honour. Do not feel bad for those that have taken this route. It will serve you well."

"I… I don't know how to wield a katana…" Saga said. She had practiced with one slightly in Honah Lee and knew that the style was different from what Astrid taught with their straight blades.

"No, but you do know how to move, and weapons come instinctually to you."

Tentatively, Saga took the blade from her and inspected the surface. It was so shiny that she could see her face reflected back at her. "It… It's beautiful…" She whispered. It was so different from the Norse blade Astrid had given her the semester before after the fight in the street. In the surface of the blade, she could see the faces of the people who had given up their second lives to make the blade and were to make up the spirit of this weapon.

"Hold him off until the wolf is by your side… Then… Then you will know what to do," the woman said.

"Hold him off she says," Saga said angrily as she started to lead a group of armed ghosts around the body of the hydra to where Vali and his horde of the dead were attacking the beast. "Hold off the crazy god guy and a horde of dead warriors. She says it like it's easy!"

Cillian Ainslie tapped his shillelagh against the ground and from the tip emerged a beautiful and bright rainbow bridge. "It'll be quicker," the leprechaun said as he started to wave people across the bridge. Angels and faeries and other winged beings took to the air, but those restricted to use of their feet stepped aboard the rainbow and were transported across the expanse of space at a magical speed. Saga took the brief moment in time to take in her surrounds. The realm was dark and heavy, purplish clouds hung heavy in the air obscuring anything far off in the distance. She could see the shadows and outlines of leafless trees, as far as the eye could see.

The hydra screamed out in pain as a fire spell lit up the darkness, illuminating an army of faerie and elf arcana users.

"Stop the magic users," Saga called out and a group of the dead diverted from Cillian Ainslie's rainbow bridge to do exactly that. They separated into two groups. One to defend the hydra and the other to directly fight the arcanists. She didn't want to fight these people. They were only doing what Vali had told them was the right thing to do. She hoped that Tremblay would return soon with Shadow so that she could miraculously find the answer to all this.

The bridge of rainbow light crested downwards, and Saga's army of ghosts flooded onto the field, focusing on the other ghosts that had been dragged into the vortex by the lure of the music. It was like those big movie scenes where the two armies clashed in a mess of colours and chaos, and you could never tell who was winning and who was losing until the army of one particular colour was left standing amidst a field scattered with the dead of the opposing side.

Except they were all the same. Angels. Weres. Faeries. Strange creatures from Wākea and Takama No Hara and worlds that she had not even heard of and that she could not even begin to fathom. They were on both sides. When the two sides collided, those trying to kill the hydra and those trying to protect it... There was no difference... They were all the same.

Saga approached Vali; the sword made of warrior spirits clutched in her hands.

Too tight... Something said, and she relaxed her grip, her fingers unclenching just a little and the sword seemed to settle into the new grip.

Vali's attention was on the destruction of the giant serpentine beast before him. He was adding his own magic to the chaos of the fight. Each impact of a spell or weapon sent the heads screeching and wailing in pain. Saga raised the sword up, high into the air above her head... Astrid would probably kill her for the poor form, and she could feel the disapproval of the weapon's spirits as she did it. She sighed and lowered it, bringing the hilt closer to her, her hands almost touching her forehead. That seemed to settle the sword, except for one word that echoed inside her head.

Honour...

There was no honour in striking a man down when his back was turned. Saga sighed in frustration. Who needed a judgmental weapon when they were on a deadline? Who knew what would happen if the hydra died and the gates were opened?

"Vali," she called out and the man whirled around, surprised to see her there.

"You," he exclaimed.

Saga sure hoped that Tremblay and the others located Shadow soon, because her sword skills were not good enough for a confrontation like this. Maybe if Navi was at her side she could hold on a little longer, but she too was gone... At least until someone located her.

A fire ball came flying towards her and Saga darted out of its path. This was followed closely by a bolt of lightning and then a blast of freezing snow.

Saga dodged the lightning bolt but was caught up in the swirls of freezing wind. The small icicles of snow cutting into her clothes and skin leaving her covered in what looked like dozens upon dozens of tiny paper cuts. She tried to attack, but the sword resisted her attempts to control it. She wasn't going to get anywhere if she had to fight her own weapon and Vali. She went flying backwards, tumbling across the ground until she was stopped at feet of what looked to be a horse man... Was he a centaur?

Oh, you just had to be kidding! Centaurs were real too?

The centaur offered Saga a hand and she staggered back to her feet with his help. She knew that she should be grateful for the weapon, but why did it seem to be more trouble than use at the moment?

"A mounted warrior beats a foot warrior in any battle," the centaur said.

That was true, or at least mostly true as far as Saga knew. The centaur, long dead probably as she had never seen a centaur in or around any of the cities so far, guided her to his back.

"Are you sure?" Saga asked. She knew nothing of these people and wasn't really sure if he was allowing her to ride him. The centaur nodded and Saga sheathed the sword for a moment, freeing her hands to allow her to mount the centaurs back.

She wrapped one arm through his, so that it grasped his shoulder and redrew the spirit blade. The centaur reared up and charged. Around them, the ghosts fought against one another, but the parting of bodies created an unobstructed path for the centaur to charge down.

He galloped, gaining speed as they closed in on Vali who was once again casting his spells of destruction at the many, many headed hydra. Unable to stop, they rode right past him Saga's sword sweeping down at the right moment to slice through Vali's outstretched hand.

The man howled in agony, clutching the mutilated limb to his chest as the hand fell to the floor with an unheard thud.

Echoing his howls of pain came that of a wolf. The wolf's howls brought an end to the fighting as the spirits of the dead came to a standstill and stared up towards the hydra's body, where, standing on the main torso of the body, between the numerous heads was a black wolf howling at the moon.

SPIRIT BLADES

It wasn't silent, not with the howling, but every other noise just ceased and with that, it seemed like a deafening silence had descended upon the battlefield. The hydra hissed and moaned, stamping its feet in agitation. A few feet behind where the centaur had come to a grinding halt, Vali fell to his knees, the handless limb clutched against his chest as he screamed silently, the agony too much.

Everywhere, the spirits of the solid ghosts stood still, staring up at Shadow, even the centaur, who had come to such a sudden stop that had Saga not been holding on to him with all her might, she would have surely been thrown from his body.

"The wolf," the old woman breathed out, walking towards where Saga still sat astride the centaur.

"You're not a ghost..." Saga said in awe.

The old woman stared up at her. "Who said I was?"

Saga climbed down from the centaur's back. He was too busy staring up at Shadow to even notice her leaving. She walked over to the woman. "What do I do now?" She asked.

"You send them back to where they belong," the woman said.

Saga frowned. "But... They're all..."

"The unsettled dead, yes. Let's just say that the time has come for all of these lost souls to make their way to the next life," she said, her arm sweeping around the battlefield to indicate everyone there. When Saga just stood there, the old woman turned on her. "Well, go on. The wolf is doing his part! Do yours."

"I..." Saga started but didn't get a chance to finish as the sound of flapping wings started to kick up the dust around them, moments before a figure with one leathery bat wing and one feathered angel wing landed before them. "Tremblay!" Saga gasped out, wrapping her arms around him in a hug. "You found him!"

"Wolf boy's fine," the house ghost said. He looked behind her and nodded to himself. "Huh, looks like he can be useful."

Saga shoved him playfully. "Be nice."

"Come on," he said.

"Come on where?" Saga asked tentatively.

"She is a Valkyrie. She can get to her hound," the old woman said, obviously frustrated with how long it was taking for everything to get done. Well, if she just gave out instructions instead of half riddles that she expected Saga to understand, things would work so much easier!

Tremblay pulled her close, wrapping his arms tight around her before he stretched out his wings and gave them a powerful, downward flap, pushing them up from the ground.

"TREMBLAY!" Saga shrieked, her feet kicking in desperation to be released. "Put me down! Put me down right this second!" Below, the old woman was shaking her head in dismay. "Trem, stop this! Please, stop it!" Saga begged.

"If you grew your own wings, I wouldn't need to," he said, flying towards the hydra's body. He hovered above Shadow before depositing her beside him. "Valkyrie and wolf. A powerful combination," he said, before flying away. "I'm going after the group that went for Navi."

And then he was gone, one of the heads of the hydra, nipping at his tail as he went.

Shadow looked up at her, confusion as to what was happening showing clearly in his eyes. She could see pain too. He seemed to be sitting awkwardly. "Oh Emory..." She murmured, reaching down to touch him and ruffle his fur.

Light erupted from them.

It was blinding and Saga felt as though she was going to explode with all the light that wanted to come out. Wings erupted from her back and Shadow howled. Looking out over the mass of spirits below them, she was confronted with the knowledge of what it was that she needed to do.

She cringed in anticipation and closed her eyes tight. Then, experimentally tried to move the wings on her back. She stumbled backwards and she was sure that she could hear Shadow laughing. She would get him back for that later.

She tried again but stumbled again. Then a thought came to find and since nothing else was working, she didn't see a reason not to make herself look like a bigger fool than she already did. She stood with her feet wide, set her left hand on her hip and raised the sword into the air above her head. "I do believe in faeries," she said under her breath.

And just like that her feet left the body of the hydra. Shadow's howls turned gleeful as she lifted higher and higher. She tried once again to flap the massive wings on her back and this time it worked, she felt herself dip and raise with the movement.

From the air Saga could see everywhere the light touched. The spirits of the dead started to congregate into groups and vanish in in hazes of different colours indicating the location of the second life. On the ground, the Angels of Death were organising people. Having come back to their senses they were able to engage in the job of putting the unsettled dead to rest. The sight, from so far up was making her dizzy and she desperately wanted to squeeze her eyes shut and block it all out.

"Noooooo!" the wailing cried echoed in tandem with Shadow's howls and Saga whirled around to see who it was, her body dropping as he wings forgot what to do. Vali, far in the distance, was watching his army of the dead vanish as above him, the hydra seemed to be recovering itself, the injuries it had endured were healing.

Where were Navi and the others?

The thought distracted her from the flying, and she could see everyone that still remained below her. Near Vali, she could see a person standing, feminine in shape with a head of long, luxurious, white hair and beside her, a delicately formed boy with golden locks of hair. Tena? No, the girl was still in rat form, nestled deep into Saga's clothing... Or at least she hoped that the small rat was still there... Who could it be? And who was that beside the mysterious girl? Tremblay had gone looking for Navi and if it had been her, Edun would have been beside her, not this strange light elf...Or at least she assumed he was a light elf... No... Could it be? Who was this? She had to find out...

She collided with the ground, tumbling head over feet until she came to a stop, the sword tucked tight against her as Astrid had taught her... No idea how she had managed to remember to do that, but she didn't allow the sudden crash to stop her. She scrambled to her feet and ran. The crowd had almost completely vanished with the only ones remaining being the angels of death, the returned dead and the few odd people like the old woman. She came closer to where Vali was, to where the white-haired girl was standing beside him.

The girl's hair covered her face, but Saga knew the clothes. That was a Toserra Sorose uniform, but not the uniform Navi had been wearing that night when they had been pulled through the vortex. No... This one was edged in gold trim.

"Ziva!" The girl didn't look up at her. "What is this?" she asked Vali.

The man cursed at her in old Norse, and she was pretty sure that she should be glad to that she couldn't understand the language well enough yet to know what he was saying.

Shadow appeared at her side. She had no idea how he got there, but when he barked angrily at the thing pretending to be Ziva.

Vali grabbed the dark elf girl who didn't resist. It seemed as though there wasn't anyone in there. Her eyes looked towards the man and there was no fear or surprise or even pity or concern for the state of his injury. She was just... Empty...

Vali muttered something that Saga didn't catch and then suddenly he and the Ziva look alike were gone. Shadow dashed forward, barking at the empty space, but all that was left was a pool of Vali's blood. Shadow howled once more before curling in on himself.

"Shadow!" Saga said, anxiously, reaching out to catch him by the fur in the back of his neck. "No!"

Tena crawled out from Saga's shirt, chittered something angrily the scampered down the length of Saga's body before jumping down to the ground. Her little head looked around as though she was trying to figure something out, then her body began to shift and change.

The small rat grew, and the fur receded until it was only the head on her hair and her ash grey skin replaced the mousey brown fur that her rat form was covered with. She looked haggard and as though she was in pain. Saga started to remove her jacket while looking towards Shadow to make sure he wasn't doing the same thing. She knew that the others wasn't know he was Shadow, and it wouldn't be her that outed him. Not today anyway. The old woman seemed to appear once more from nowhere and waved Saga aside. She draped Tena's body in a beautiful kimono of red and black. Little mice were embodied on it in silver thread, scurrying up and down delicate flower vines. Tena looked up at the woman gratefully. "Thank you," she said.

"Shape shifters," the old woman said with a shake of her head. "If only you could figure out how to do it with your clothes on. She walked over to Saga as Tena busied herself tying the belt around the kimono and hung from Saga's shoulder a small bag. "For the other one."

Saga nodded in understanding. "Thank you."

The woman nodded but didn't say anything as the frantic flapping of wings alerted them to the arrival of Tremblay and the other angels and faeries who had gone looking for Navi and the swallowed band members. Tremblay landed, letting Navi to her feet.

"Ground! Solid ground," she gasped out. "Navi now understands why you do not like heights," she said, bending over, her hands on her knees as she tried to catch her breath and stop shaking.

"You alright?" Saga said, going over to her and resting a hand on her shoulder.

The girl nodded. "Yes... fine..."

"And Edun? And Sid?" Saga asked.

Navi pointed backwards towards where the others were landing. "Yes, we got them all out."

Edun stood beside an angel, their contrasting appearances even more stark due to the angel's pale skin and dark hair. It was almost as though the woman was Snow White personified with skin as white as snow and hair as black as ebony. And yes, her lips were painted in a red the shade of blood. Saga stalked past Navi and straight up to him. She shoved him hard and he stumbled backwards in surprise.

"What were you doing up there?" she cried.

"Watch it!" Edun shot back, brushing down his clothes.

Saga shoved him again, adding in several additional, angry hits. Edun struggled, trying to catch her hands. "Do you have any idea what you did?" Saga cried. "What were you doing up on that stage?"

"Saga!" Tena cried, running over, her kimono only half secured. "Wait!"

"You almost got us all killed!" Saga continued, not having heard Tena.

"Let me explain!" Edun said, catching her hands as she hit him again. "The one was helping you!"

"Helping-," Saga started, but Tena cut him off.

"Tena told him to!" The rat girl said. Saga stopped, her arms still held tightly by Edun. She glanced over her shoulder at Tena, trying to ask the girl what she had meant to do, but her mouth just seemed to open and close in disbelief as nothing came out. "Tena never got to tell you that this one found a passage about the talismans working better with music. You and Navi and Jemima were not affected, yes?"

"Right..." Saga said tentatively, not sure what to believe.

"The story you know, about the rats and the children," Tena hurried on, her voice pitching almost to a squeak.

"The Pied Piper?" Saga asked, not sure where this was going. It didn't explain why would Tena have Edun playing with the band? They didn't know the girl. Essentially, they knew nothing about her, but she had admitted to being trained in the magic of the dead, necromancy. Wasn't that what part of this was? Those runes that Tena had understood when Tasso hadn't and her innate ability to always be around... What was the girl hiding?

Or was Saga being paranoid? "The Rabbit Piper?" Navi added.

"The pipe. Yes. The story is always a pipe. Not a stringed instrument. Always a pipe. Like a snake charmer or that one they tell of that makes the ghosts dance. It's always a pipe that controls."

Saga stared at the rat girl, confusion etched over her face. Edun threw his hands into the air. "This one was counteracting the effect! That's what Tena thought that This one's pipe could help!"

Edun's pipe! Saga thought about the moment she'd been close to the band. The panic she'd seen in Edun's eyes. Had he struggled with what to do? To keep playing or go after his sister?

She shoved at Edun again, but his grip held her arms strong. "You should have said something!"

"Edun never got the chance!" He argued. "Everything happened too quickly."

"So..." Navi asked tentatively. "Edun is not practicing dark magics?"

"Necromancy isn't evil or dark," Tena interrupted. "It was corrupted by those that used it. Necromancy uses the dead, communicates with the dead, but hordes of Zombies and murdering gigantic hydras was not the reason for its use."

Saga wrenched out of Edun's grip and turned from them. She looked up at the hydra, the beast was still mewling in pain. In addition to the assault lodged against it by Vali and his men, Edun was wet and slimy. Had they cut him out of the hydra, or had it spat him out? She shook her head and paced.

"Who was that who vanished with the man who looked like Vali?" Navi asked.

"Huh?" Saga asked, drawn out from her thoughts.

"The Dökkálfar with the Vali look alike," Navi said.

Saga bit her lip. "It was Vali..."

"Did you really injure him?" Tremblay asked, coming over.

Saga nodded. "The blade... I cut off his hand."

"But who was that with him?" Navi pressed. "A girl with white hair."

Saga looked from Navi to Edun. How was she supposed to tell them who it was? Or at least who the thing had been made to resemble. No, it would be better not to mention Ziva's name to them at all. "I don't know," Saga said.

"I didn't see her clearly." The lie clawed at her gut as Shadow looked up at her and Tena raised a questioning eyebrow. Saga shook her head. Edun looked as though he wanted to say something, but he looked at Navi and his mouth snapped shut. Saga looked around. "Where's Sidawi?" she asked, searching the group that had gone to retrieve the band. The drummer was there. Thyra Bodil was there. The guy who played an instrument Saga didn't know the name of was there... But there was no Sidawi.

"We couldn't find him," Tremblay said, speaking for the group.

"D...d....d...did the hydra..." Navi swallowed hard, the next words almost impossible to say. "Eat... Him?" she asked, her voice barely a whisper.

"No, we believe that someone got to him first," Tremblay said, resting a hand on the small girl's shoulder.

"Perhaps Vali's people?" Edun suggested.

"Can Tena ask a stupid question?" the small rat girl asked.

A throat cleared behind them and Saga jumped. She turned and saw an older angel standing there, his hand behind his back as he attempted to appear regal and in charge. "If one of you would be so kind as to firstly, tell us how we got here and secondly, how are we getting home?"

"And where are we?" another called out.

"Umm, ok," Saga said, looking at the others for help, but Navi just shrunk back behind Edun, and he shrugged. She raised an eyebrow at Tena in question, but the girl shook her head adamantly and backed away. "Right... Easy question first, we think... And I have to stress that we only think that we are in Hades." That started a cacophony of noise as all the angels started trying to talk over one another. Shadow barked, but they seemed to not hear him, so he began to howl and the piercing sound of it caused them to stop screaming and calling out. "As Angels of Death..." she paused, "you are all angels of death, right?"

"Yes," the old angel said. "Current or former or future," he said eyeing a small group in Aquino Beccara uniforms.

"So..." Saga said thinking. "Does that mean you have the ability to cross the barrier between the realms of the dead and the realms of the living?"

The older angel nodded. "Yes, those of us that are active in the field, yes. "

"Good," Saga said decisively. "Then you can take everyone back to Yggdrasil City..."

"It's not that simple, but we can get out of here, yes," The man agreed.

"Good," Saga repeated, then pointed at the others. "Then you can take them with you?"

"No!" Navi cried. "Navi stays with you!"

"Not leaving," Edun stated firmly.

"Seeing this through to the end," Tena added.

Saga stared at the three Dökkálfar but sighed. Edun wanted to say something else but was holding himself back because of Navi. She was sure of that. Saga looked down at Shadow and the wolf cocked his head to the side as if to say, 'They're your friends.'

"If you lot have finished caterwauling," the old, mysterious eastern woman said approaching them once more, "That man is still in Hades. That man is going to resume his assault on the guardian beast here. You must stop him."

"How do we do that?" Saga asked.

"You must visit Hades."

"But we're..." Saga started to say, "Ohh..." she said, realisation setting in. "That Hades..."

She nodded sagely. "Yes. He knows everything that goes on in his realm. Only he will be able to guide you to where Vali is camped out.

"Ok, we'll go for Hades..." Saga said, not quite sure of what she was saying. "And the rest of the angels and the others who were dragged in will leave here."

"Good," the old woman said, she gazed at the old Angel. "I will ensure your destination," she assured him. "Choose."

He looked at the others and they conferred amongst themselves. "Where we departed from."

"Done," he old woman said. The angels arranged themselves with those who could not transport themselves. The apprentices, the retired and those connected to the realm of death by some other connection, but unable to freely travel between the realms. Slowly, in small groups of two and three, they started to vanish. The angels would unfurl their wings, surrounding the person or people that they were taking with them, and they would be surrounded by a glow of light that seemed so pure and good and... Saga had no words to describe what it felt like to watch, but when the light died away, they were gone.

Saga looked up at Tremblay. "What about you?" she asked. "Are you going back?"

The house ghost shook his head. "I am able to come and go," he said. "I will return when you return."

"What about Mister Ainslie?" Navi asked.

The small leprechaun man let out a grunt, but knocked his shillelagh against the ground, causing it to emit small flecks of rainbow sparks. "Staying."

"So..." Saga said to the old woman. "How do we get to Hades?"

"You cross the river Styx," she said.

"Like the ferryman and one piece of silver... All that?" Saga asked.

The old woman nodded and handed each of them a large silver disc. "Give that to the ferryman," she instructed, then looking at them all, she frowned. "None of you are armed for a confrontation."

"We went out to a party," Tena said, as though that answered everything.

Instead, the old woman shook her head. "In my day, a warrior was never without their weapon, even at a party." She looked at Navi and nodded to herself before extending her hands out. Spirits seemed to flow to her, from where, Saga had no idea as all of the unsettled dead who had been called into Hades had been sent to their second lives. A long stick began to emerge, glowing like a fluorescent light tube or a light Sabre. Then, from the end of what Saga had assumed was a staff, a strange, curved blade appeared. She handed the long weapon to Navi. "I believe you will find some ease with this."

Navi stared at the weapon, her gaze travelling the length of the magnificent creation. The blade at the end of it, seemed to have the same odd colouring as Saga's katana. Navi experimentally swung it around. "it's amazing. What is it?"

"It is called a Naginata," the old woman explained. For Edun, the woman created a wickedly cruel looking set of brass knuckles and for Tena, a set of delicate throwing knives. The girl's eyes twinkled in delight as she spun them expertly through her fingers.

Shadow stared up at her and the old woman crouched down before him, her hands cradling his face. "And we cannot forget the valiant hound."

Shadow's face was covered in a shining helm that shimmered and moved with him. Chainmail extended down his neck and covered the majority of his body. Shadow stared up at her and the old woman crouched down before him, burying her face against his fury snout. "Take care valiant hound."

Like Saga's katana and the blade on Navi's Naginata, the armour seemed to emit this strange, but comforting light amidst the dim air of Hades. The wolf looked up at the woman gratefully, and yelped in surprise when from his long, already powerful paws, emerged a set of metal claws. He bounded back and forth a few steps, the claws digging into the hard ground with barely a noise.

"Who are you?" Saga asked as the woman straightened from her crouch.

She looked at Saga, then allowed her gaze to take in all of them. "Someone who has a vested interest in the outcome of Vali's actions..."

"What will happen to the hydra?" Navi asked. "We cut people out of it..."

"In time, it will heal," the old woman said. "Fear not, the gates of Tartarus remain sealed today."

"And now what will Vali do?" Edun asked. "We've sent his army away."

"There is more than one way to open the gates of Tartarus and you forget, Vali still possesses the lovelorn boy."

"Sidawi," Navi said.

Tena tentatively raised her hand. "This one knows Tena already asked this and all... But who is Vali and why does he want to open the gates of the deepest, darkest depths of hell?"

"Vali is one of Odin's sons," Saga said. "He believes that with his father's death during Ragnarök, and that of many of the other powerful gods, like Thor, that he has the right to assume Odin's throne and ultimately rule the Nine Realms." Shadow's nose snuffled at Saga's side, and she move slightly, allowing him to stick his nose between her waist and he arm.

"What does that have to do with your or Tartarus?" Tena asked.

Shadow barked. **Tell them.**

Saga looked down at the wolf, eyes wide. What was happening between them? "Uhh," She murmured, trying to get back on track. "He thinks that if he possesses Odin's spear, Gungnir, the head of the advisor Mimir and... the only known Valkyrie, that he can ascend the throne."

"Tartarus's forces must be his latest plan," Navi concluded. "After the Wild Hunt failed last semester."

"The Wild Hunt didn't fail," Saga said. "Valhalla opened for the worthy. That was his goal. He just didn't find Gungnir there. But you're right, without the Einherjar and without Gungnir, maybe he plans to use the beings within Tartarus to take the throne by force."

"So, killing Ziva wasn't enough." Edun spat.

"And all the others," Saga murmured. She could still recite the names of the dead. "But Ziva... She was the one who opened Valhalla... She was the worthy one."

"But that happened the night of the fire," Edun countered. "What happened after that? The day you guys came back injured."

Saga, Navi and Shadow all looked at each other. "He was still trying to possess me. He was going to kill Navi and Emory and convince me that he was right. But we bested him, and we bested Master Iacono, who was working for him."

Tena shook her head in amazement. "Tena... Well... Tena had not been expecting that. We need to stop him!"

"Saga nodded in agreement. Whomever wound up taking Odin's throne, if it was ever occupied again, it would not be Vali. Not if she had anything to do with it. She looked towards the old woman who had gifted them the weapons. "Which way?" She asked and the old woman pointed to the line of fire she had spotted earlier.

"Follow the River Phlegethon to where it meets with the rivers Styx, Cocytus, Lethe and Acheron," she instructed. "Cross the River Styx and you will find Hades. He will direct you to your missing friend and Vali." Saga stared where she pointed and took in the sight of the what the woman had called a river and tried to find its end, but it disappeared into the depths of the misty, eerie forest of leafless trees... Who knew what else awaited them along the river. "Do not cross the River Phlegethon. Do not step foot within the river."

They looked at each other, then at the woman, the concern evident on their faces. "W...W...why?" Navi asked.

"The blood which flows through the River Phlegethon will boil your soul alive," she stated, and Navi clutched at Edun's arm. The woman seemed to fade away, first into the faded form of the ghosts and then into nothingness. They were left standing there. Shadow leaned against Saga's side but didn't deign to let out the whimper that she was sure he wanted to. Hell, she wanted to curl in a ball and forget all of this.

"What do we do?" Tena asked, her arms wrapped tightly around herself.

"We can't go home without Sidawi," Saga said.

Navi nodded in agreement. "Ok."

"Let's go then," Edun said.

LOVER'S FOLLY

It was, to their surprise, cold in Hades. The burning river that they followed seemed to emit nothing but light and shadows unless you came too close to it and it wasn't even like a regular fire where the close you got, the warmer you felt... No, there was something odd about it in that they could be standing three steps away from the riverbank and feel nothing but the chill air around them, but if they were two steps away from the riverbank, it was like a raging inferno threatening to suck up all the air and... Maybe even boil you alive like the old woman had said would happen if you fell into the river.

Saga wasn't sure what she had been expecting, but the cold, wet mist of the realm wasn't it. Honestly, she had been expecting something closer to the effect near the river. She had been certain, that it would be all fire and brimstone... But as she had learned, Hades and Hell were not the same places... And apparently, Hades had seasons. Who knew?

The mist seemed to sizzle on the river, creating a billowing steam that added to the damp and misty surrounds. For a realm of the dead, where the spirits of those who had once lived in one of the many realms above, Hades was surprisingly quiet.

"Navi does not like this place."

"No," Edun agreed. "It's too... Too..."

"Empty. Silent. Eerie. Creepy. Freaky. Barren. Weird, -" Saga said, listing words off the top of her head. "Oh yeah, and I mention scary?"

"No," Edun said dryly. "You hadn't gotten that far yet..."

"Hades is quite populated. Like the lands of the living, there are cities and social hierarchies," Tena said. "But being where we are close to that beast and the raging fire river and this incredibly creepy forest... It surprises this one little that there is no one around."

"And what about you Tremblay?" Saga asked. The ghost had been surprisingly quiet. Odd, now that he was solid, he could surely act on some of his more annoying habits.

"What about me?" He asked, his eyes not looking at her, but quickly scanning around them, keeping a lookout for possible attackers or strange animals.

"You've said that you can come and go between the house and the realm of the dead. Where do you live?"

"Upper Realms of the Dead," Tremblay said. "The realms of the dead work differently to the living realms. One cannot simply come and go as they please, yet some of the boarders are open. Such as between Hades and Helheim. Nothing stops a resident of one, travelling to the other, yet that might not be true for a resident of the Mourning Fields..."

"Why not?" Saga asked.

"The Mourning Fields are for those suffering from unrequited love!" Tena jeered. "Fools who loved someone who could or would never love them back. They wasted their lives, and their second lives will be no better."

Saga scratched the back of her neck awkwardly and didn't look at any of them as she strode ahead of the group. She definitely didn't look at Shadow. She knew he would be shooting her that plaintiff looked that was twice as bad with those adorable doggie eyes. Ugh... He's not adorable...

"Saga," Edun said, and she turned back to him.

"Yes?"

"Is that this one's pan flute?" he asked.

Saga looked confused, before he reached for her. She stepped back slightly, not sure what he was on about, but he took the strap from her shoulder and held it up for her to see. "Oh..." she said. "I forgot that was there..." He raised an eyebrow at her, and she just shrugged. "What? I picked it up after you dropped it in the club and then it was all trying not to be killed by a giant hydra and stopping Vali from killing the hydra and dissipating an army of the unsettled dead..."

"She has a point," Tremblay said.

"Don't you start, "Edun shot back at him. He took the pan flute from her and draped the strap across his own body.

"Play for us," Navi suggested, looking up at her brother with big, pleading eyes. Edun tried not to look down at her, but as soon as he did, he relented and took the flute in his hands. He raised it to his lips and after a glance at everyone else to ensure no one disagreed, he blew into it. Gentle, haunting notes filled the air. With Edun's music to accompany them, the continued waking along the flaming river.

"Did anyone realise that the water in it is red?" Saga asked.

"The river Phlegethon flows with blood," Tremblay said.

"Blood?" Saga exclaimed. "What is wrong with this place?"

Tena laughed but kept on walking beside Navi. Shadow would run ahead and run back to them, much as he had that day on the mountainside above Walhalla.

Edun's melody was soothing despite everything that had just transpired. They had been held by a hydra, protected the hydra and now they were walking through the Lower Realms of the Dead. Who knew what awaited them when the flaming river beside them met with the river Styx.

In the distance they could see a great tree emerging from the landscape. Unlike the trees by them, this one was lush and gorgeous with beautiful autumn leaves in all the colours and hues of the season. With the fire of the river creating dancing lights and shadows against it, the tree looked as though it too was on fire. At the base of the tree, the Phlegethon passed in front of it, before the fire gave away. Saga squinted and raised her hand to shield her eyes in the ineffective way people do in the assumption that it will increase their range of vision.

"There's another river passing by that tree," she said.

"The river Styx?" Navi asked.

Saga shrugged. "I don't know."

"We'll need to cross it regardless," Tremblay said.

A chorus of screeching caught their attention and Tremblay's pale face went white, whiter than he usually was as a ghost. It was weird seeing him with colour definition like this. The ghost looked at Tena and the girl was looking around, trying to figure out where the noise had come from. "Harpies?"

"They sound like Harpies… There's a colony that regularly flies over Dark Fields. One even teaches some of the Daemons at the school how to fly… But they're so creepy!" Tena said with a shudder.

"Harpies…" Saga muttered. "When will these things stop surprising me-."

Talons as big as her head grabbed Saga by the shoulders and her feet left the ground before she could finish speaking. Edun's music came to an abrupt halt with a sudden, piercing note and then... Nothing.

"Down!" She cried. "Put me down!"

There was no response though. "Tremblay!" She begged, sure that it was the playful house ghost who was playing tricks on her. "Put me down!"

Tremblay's protestations were drowned out by the screeching of someone above her.

"Harpies!" Edun called out, his hands going for his pocket and drawing out the nasty looking brass -spirit- knuckles he had been given by the old woman.

He never got to use them as another harpy came swirling down in a whirlwind of air and feathers and dust. Nearby, the flames of the fire river danced maniacally with the added wind pressure.

"What's happening?" Tena squeaked, her inner rat coming out in her high-pitched voice, right before a third harpy grabbed onto her.

Despite the fear and the height and the panic and gods only knew what else was going through her head at the time, Saga saw Tena's tail start to appear. "Don't!" She cried out. "Don't shift. You'll be too small, and the fall will kill you!"

Tena stared up at where Saga was being held above her. Adorable, rounded rat ears extended from amidst her hair and whiskers seemed to adorn her pointed face. Her tail lashed back and forth. She was halfway through her change. Could she stop it? Saga had no idea and no time to figure it out. Navi was fighting off the harpy that had attempted to snatch her into the air, the blade at the end of the Naginata keeping distance between her and the feral winged woman.

Tremblay had taken to the air, his miss matched wings beating powerfully against the air and propelling him higher and higher into the fray. Shadow barked and snarled at the harpy attacking Navi, but it wouldn't come near enough to allow him to attack, even as he jumped and leapt at it.

What could Saga do? She had no idea. With her feet so far from solid ground panic ate at her and she didn't even dare try to attack the harpy carrying her, because the fall would surely kill her.

"Wolf Boy!" Tremblay shouted down as he tried to wrestle Tena from the harpy's grip. "Do what you did before!"

Shadow's barking and snarling ceased, and he sat staring up at the daemon ghost, trying to figure out what he meant.

He ran and came to a skidding halt beneath Saga, lifted his head and howled. The sound carried across the expanse of the realm and Saga felt that feeling deep within her that she had felt before, only recently at the hydra when the ghosts had been sent to their second lives.

"Not again!" Saga wailed as the harpy screeched in surprise as large, feathered wings sprouted from Saga's back. The harpy's enormous, strong claws suddenly released her, and Saga went plummeting to the ground, screaming.

"FLY!" Tremblay ordered.

"I DON'T KNOW HOW!" Saga screamed back, terror lacing every word as the ground came hurtling towards her. What was it about this week that she spent so much time up in the air?

"Concentrate!" Tremblay ordered, but she felt herself jerked backwards by the scruff of her collar. Obviously, Tremblay didn't trust her to figure it out before colliding with the ground. "They're like extra limbs, think and move."

"But the ground," Saga wailed, "It's so far away!"

"Just try!" Edun shouted as he struggled in the harpy's grip. He tried punching at the clawed foot that held him tight but could not get the strength or momentum to make the creature release him. "We need you!"

Saga tried to concentrate on the extra appendages that were supposed to give her flight. They twitched and feathers rustled.

"Saga!" the half-turned Tena cried out.

Why was she the only one they thought could do something? Navi was still holding her own against the harpy that was trying to grab her up into the air. What was their reasoning?

The wings flapped, beat down against the air which felt so strangely solid. She did it again and she felt the grip on her clothes release as Tremblay let her go. She tried again but dropped heavily towards the ground. Vali was going to pay dearly for all the times she had found herself in the air this week. She would get him this time, she vowed.

A screech from Edun's harpy as the spirit knuckles seemed to make contact with a delicate part of the clawed foot. He swung precariously from one taloned foot, the injured one releasing him.

"Edun!" Navi cried; her attention distracted as her brother fought for his life. The harpy dived in, taking the moment to grab her up in the air. She screamed in shocked surprise.

Saga beat her wings harder but was torn between Navi and Edun. The decision was made for her when Edun was suddenly released. Navi's scream cut through the air and Saga put every ounce of concentration she had into getting to Edun. She scooped the dark elf into her arms, his extra weight forcing her down as she tried to adjust. She beat her wings harder, trying with all her might to keep them up.

Now what? She had no idea.

"Saga!" Edun gasped, his arms were wrapped around Saga, with him looking over her shoulder. "They're taking Navi and Tena!"

What did she do? How did she stop them? She started in the direction that the harpies were flying off towards, but with Edun she was too slow, weighed down by him. Below, Shadow barked as he ran along beneath her.

"Tremblay!" She called, "Help!" The angel-daemon flew towards her and took Edun from her. Saga took off, the wings on her back propelling her forward towards the harpies. The harpies carried Navi and Tena across the river that intersected the land before them, the water flowing through it at an unnaturally slow rate.

Suddenly, there was a blast of purple fire from Tena and the harpy carrying her screeched out in agony, right before Tena plummeted towards the ground. There was no way Saga was going to get there on time.

Shadow ran, his strong legs eating up the distance as he neared the river of water, without stopping, he leapt. His body flew over the bank of the river and as it did, he started to change, the long wolf form being replaced by the strong, muscular boy as Tena was grabbed in his arms and they both collided to the ground, rolling in the dirt as Emory's momentum sent them rocketing across the ground, where they both lay still.

"Emory!" Saga screamed, not caring if Navi or Edun figured it out. With him there, there would be no hiding the fact that Shadow and Emory were the same. She dove in after them, but Navi's cry had Saga looking for her.

Edun was deposited next to Tena and Emory before Tremblay took off after the young dark elf, Saga right behind him when something caught her attention. Under the elm tree that sat between the river of burning blood and the other, slow running water river were two people. A boy with long, golden hair and a girl with flowing white hair.

"Sid," she breathed out. Tremblay was getting Navi. Tena and Edun were safe. She looked around. She needed Emory... Not that she was ever going to tell him that. She dropped the bag that the old woman had given her, not wanting to stop, but when Emory didn't move, despite Tena and Edun prodding at him. She would have to trust Tremblay. She came down, trying to land with some sort of grace, but as her feet touched the ground, something caught and she went tumbling, headfirst into an awkward roll and she fell, flat on her back, her wings changing the dynamics of the fall until she was sprawled out on the ground.

Tena was trying not to laugh, but Saga didn't bother scolding her as she scrambled awkwardly to her feet to come over to them. If their positions had been reversed, she probably would have laughed too. She knelt down by Emory's side, digging into the bag she had dropped by his side and pulling out a dark grey and blue kimono. He pulled it over him, replacing the jacket that Edun must have placed over him when she hadn't been looking.

She scrambled awkwardly to her feet. "Have you got him?" Saga asked, her gaze moving from Emory's prone form to the figures beneath the tree.

"Of course," Tena said. "Why? What are you doing?"

"I need to go there," Saga said and started walking in the tree.

"Why?" Edun asked, following after her. He grabbed her arm, trying to stop her. "That harpy still has Navi... Somehow that dog of yours became Emory and we're in the Lower Realms of the Dead! Why are you wandering off?"

"Tremblay's got a better chance of saving Navi," Saga's feathered wings rustled and twitched. "These things are a damned hindrance. As for Emory, you go to a school where half the student body are animal shifters, and you don't understand where Emory came from, and Shadow went?"

Edun actually had the good sense to look embarrassed. "But why are you..."

"Because Sidawi's over there," she said. "And we stayed to find him." She looked back past Edun to where Tena was hovering over Emory. He still wasn't moving. "Go help her with Emory... Please..."

Edun frowned but nodded. "Fine. Just bring that-," he stopped talking wand stared over her shoulder at the space beneath the tree. "Who... Is..." he started to say, consternation overtaking his expression, followed by realisation finally turning into a single, choked out word. "Ziva?"

Saga looked over her shoulder at the sight. The fake Ziva was indeed with Sidawi, but she didn't want to tell Edun that. "No... course not..." she said. "Ziva's in the Upper Realms... In Valhalla..."

"Right..." Edun said, his voice thick with unspoken emotion and maybe even disbelief. "I..." he pointed awkwardly in the direction of Emory and Tena. "You sure you don't want help?"

Saga nodded. "Trem can bring you over after he rescues Navi," Saga said, her eyes searching the sky for them. She felt guilty about not being the one to go, but what could she do? And she had to protect Navi and Edun from what Sidawi had done... It would only hurt them both. "Please, make sure Emory is alright... I'll bring Sid back and we'll get out of here..."

Edun nodded slowly. He reached out, his fingers trailing the feathers of her wings. "I knew I hadn't imagined them..." he murmured. Saga shifted awkwardly, not sure what to say. After a moment Edun cleared his throat and walked away, his head down.

Saga watched him crouch beside Tena and Emory, then searched the sky for Navi and Tremblay. She couldn't see them, and fear gripped at her heart. Should she go after them?

Or should she go for Sidawi?

She wished she knew the answer. It felt like no matter what she chose at the moment, the answer would be wrong. She was already abandoning Navi and now Emory...

She should follow Tremblay and help get Navi back. Yes, that's what she would do. She squeezed her eyes shut tight as she concentrated hard on the wings fixed to her back. She clenched her body tight, but try as she might, she couldn't get the blasted things to move.

"Come on, come on, come on!" she begged. How was she supposed to get anything done with those things? She gave up trying and decided to go with what she knew. She would run... Maybe she would catch up, maybe she wouldn't, but at least she would be doing something other than standing there doing nothing like an idiot.

A shadow moving behind the big tree caught her attention. A figure hunched over, cradling their arm against their body. "Vali!" she gasped.

The figure was approaching Sidawi, and they were talking. She took off running for them. There was the river between them though. Maybe she could make it across. Tremblay would get Navi back while Edun and Tena watched out for Emory. Everything would be fine. She could go after Vali and Sidawi.

She ran.

The distance to the river Acheron seemed to disappear and as she ran, those dammed, blasted wings seemed to spread out without her consent. The air blew beneath them, spreading them out further and further until she could have been an albatross taking flight and her feet lifted up, allowing her to glide effortlessly across the river, the tips of her toes skimming the surface of the river until her feet started to touch the ground on the other side. She jogged several steps until she felt her balance return and the wings contract in, close to her body.

"Saga?"

She turned to Sidawi. "Sid!"

"What are you doing here?" he asked.

"You sucked a bunch of us into Hades with your music," she said, crossing her arms over her body.

"What?" he said. "No. That was just..." The fake Ziva came to stand beside him. She wrapped an arm around his waist and leaned her head on his shoulder. "I got her back," he said.

"That's not Ziva," Saga said stepping towards them. Sidawi and the fake Ziva stepped backwards a step. "Sid, you have to know that."

"Of course, I am," the girl said.

"She doesn't even sound like her!" Saga exclaimed. "You claim you knew her better than anyone one. Take a good look at her and tell me with confidence that that thing is Ziva. The Ziva we all loved," Saga pointed across the Acheron to where Edun was and where Navi should be. "Because her brother and sister are just over there, and Annis is waiting back in Nýr Ásgardr. You tell me with confidence that that is Ziva, that you feel it to the depths of your heart, and we'll bring her back to Asgard with us, huh? What do you say?" Sidawi said nothing, just tightened his grip on the dark elf. "I'll tell you why you're not sure, why you doubt that this thing is really Ziva... Because you were there that night and you saw her. You saw me..."

Sidawi shook his head. "No..."

"Ziva isn't in the Lower Realms of the Dead, Sid," Saga said. She stepped forward another step.

The dark elf girl looked up at Sidawi, her big eyes wide and adoring as she looked at him. "Sidawi, my love," she said. "I'm right here... We're right here..."

"Listen to her!" Saga cried, "She doesn't even sound like a Dökkálfar!"

"Saga, you don't understand!" Sidawi said, tightening his grip on the fake Ziva. "You've never been in love."

"But I have had people die on me. I have lost those I would so desperately want to get back," Saga said. "Sid... This isn't the way..."

"You're right," another voice said, and Vali stepped from behind the elm tree. "You have lost..." He said thoughtfully. A smirk appeared on his face, twisting his lips into a grotesque vision of joy. Saga shivered at the sight. "What is your greatest wish? The thing you dreamt of night after night in your little, hollow, human life?"

She stared at Vali, not saying a word, but her thoughts were racing a million miles a second as she thought of the dreams... The dreams of a mother and a father who loved her. A life where she had been loved and wanted and normal.

"Ah," the man said, his handless arm, cradled against his chest. "I see... Allow me."

The tree above them rustled, droplets of water falling from the leaves to land in a pool... then a bubble... then a shape before her. The amorphous blob of water became humanoid, before it started to become fixed with the definition of a beautiful woman with long golden curls that fell down her back. She wore a pretty floral sun dress, the type you could find at any classy store on Midgard and when Saga looked into her eyes, it was as though she was looking at herself in the mirror.

"Mummy..." She breathed out, everything around them dying away.

"My darling girl," Brigitta said. "My greatest joy," she opened her arms to Saga. It took her not a second to decide, she dropped the spirit sword even as the spirits within it cried out to her. She ran into her mother's arms and as they closed around her, she felt peace. It was a sense she had not felt much of and there, wrapped in her mother's embrace for the first time in memory, she felt safe.

"Mummy..."

There was an echoed laugh and then nothing, but her mother brushing hair away from Saga's face and she barely noticed anything else that was happening. "Let me get a look at you my girl," Brigitta said. Her voice was sweet, like honey. It was everything Saga had ever imagined.

"How are you here?"

"I've always been here my girl, always."

Saga rested her head on Brigitta's shoulder and closed her eyes. Nothing could worry her now. "Is daddy coming?" Saga asked in a small voice.

"Of course, he is my girl," she said. "Of course, he is."

TREE OF THE ONEIROI

The picnic blanket was laid out on the bank of the river in the shade of an enormous elm tree. Nearby a young couple were flirting with each other as they fed each other titbits of food from their picnic lunch. The girl was beautiful with dark chocolatey skin and her hair artfully dyed in golden shades of blond and amber and it kind of looked as though she glowed. The boy seemed to be in complete contrast to the girl, with his fair skin and hair so blond it was almost white. He could have fronted a boy band!

Brigitta opened the large wicker basket and started to pull out all of Saga's favourite foods. Sandwiches with Vegemite, pasta salad, crackers and dip, a chocolate mousse for dessert. Out came even more food. Lotus chips, a pie and a bowl of pacay. Saga's eyes widened in delight as she sat down crossed legged across from her mother.

"Are there meat balls skewers?" Saga asked, peering eagerly into the basket.

"Of course, there is, my girl," Brigitta said, extracting a plate from within the apparently, never ending depths of the basket. "Tell me about school this week. What did you get up to?"

Saga talked excitedly about the inter school sports and making it to the state finals in track. She talked about how her best friend decided that messing around in science class had resulted in a fallen Bunsen burner and a scorched science bench.

A young man, a few years older than Saga approached, walking his big black dog. The dog ran ahead of him as he threw a ball and the dog bounded it after it, leaping into the air to catch it, then running back excitedly to drop the ball at his feet. The young man picked the ball up and tossed it again, the dog ran and jumped. It missed the ball and the dog turned in the air, diving into the river with an enormous splash that drenched the couple on their romantic picnic. There was laughter as the dog emerged from the river right beside them and proceeded to shake out his coat all over them.

Saga turned excitedly back to her mother, "Mum!" She cried, "can we get a dog?"

Brigitta watched the animal bound back across the grass to the young man and deposit the ball at his feet. The young man ruffled the dog's fur, whispered something to it, then threw the ball. The dog seemed to stand up and twist on the spot, before running as fast as he could across the grass.

A man sat down beside Brigitta, "what've I missed?" He asked.

"Oh, just your daughter asking for a dog!"

"A dog?" Her father asked.

"Yeah!" Saga said, watching the animal's every move. "Can I go ask to play with him?" She begged.

"Go on!" Brigitta said. "Have fun."

Saga jumped up from the picnic rug and ran over to the young man, just as the dog returned with his ball, dropping it, not at the young man's feet, but at her own.

"He likes you," the young man said.

"Can I throw it for him?" She asked eagerly.

The young man nodded. "Go ahead!" Saga quickly bent down and retrieved the slobbery ball. She eyed the dog, who was watching her every move with excited anticipation, his tail wagging as he shifted and skittered, waiting for the ball to be thrown.

Saga tossed the ball, and it went high into the air, the dog ran after it, leaping up into the air to try and catch it. He came running back to Saga and sat before her, the ball still in his mouth.

"What's his name?" Saga asked, looking up at the young man. He was, maybe eighteen years old, only a few years older than she was. He was good looking too with shaggy black hair that seemed to flip in front of his eyes constantly and eyes that were such a light, bright shade of brown that they were almost amber... Or when the sun glinted off of them, red.

"This is Shadow," he said. "Shadow, drop it!" He ordered, and the ball was dropped at Sagas feet.

Saga picked it up and threw it again. "I'm trying to convince my parents to let me get a dog," she said.

"Your parents?" The young man said, and Saga pointed over to the picnic blanket where they were seated, picking away at their lunch. "Oh..."

"What's that supposed to mean?" She asked, suddenly unsure about this admittedly, good looking young man. The dog bounded back up to them and dropped the ball at her feet. When she didn't pick it up, he nudged her legs with his head.

"Saga," the young man said.

"How do you know my name?" She asked, cutting him off.

"Saga," he said forcefully, "this world, this life... It's not real."

Saga backed away from him, one step, two steps, but the dog was suddenly behind her, preventing her from moving away any further.

"What do you want from me?" She asked, panic creeping into her voice.

"We need to take you back, we're still in Hades, Saga!" The dog barked excitedly at his master, trying to get his attention.

Saga shook her head. "I don't know what you're talking about," she said, trying now to sidestep the strange man.

Was this what they meant by stranger danger?

The dog was circling them both, preventing her from getting out of his potential reach. He had long arms but had yet to try and touch her.

"Saga," he begged.

"Tell... Tell your dog to let me go!" She said, a tremble in her voice.

"I can't do that," he said, stepping in closer to her.

"Let me go. I'll scream!"

"No, you won't," he said confidently. "The Saga Joy Carolle I know, doesn't scream! She fights! She fights for herself. She fights for her friends." Then he pointed at the picnic rug with the young couple on it. "Sidawi and Ziva."

"Who..." she started to say, but when she looked at the couple again, she didn't see the beautiful chocolate skinned girl with her hair dyed in shades of gold and amber. Instead, she saw a girl with skin as dark as onyx with hair as white as snow. The young man was still pale and blond and beautiful with his delicate elfin features... Except not... Now he had the distinctive pointed ears of the elf and she thought that he actually looked a lot of like Legolas from the Lord of The Rings movies.

"Ziva..." She breathed out, memories of the girl worming their way through the haze and fuzz of the reality she found herself in. She looked up at the young man and gasped in surprise when he saw that his eyes were in fact red orbs, and he had wings. One feathered wing of white and one leathery black, bat-like wing. "Tremblay..." Behind her, the dog barked and when Saga turned around, she realised that it wasn't a dog, but a wolf. "Shadow..."

Shadow nuzzled against her leg, and she reached down to scratch his ears, while looking back at the picnic blanket where her mother and father sat. Tears pricked at her eyes and she blinked rapidly to try and stop their descent over her cheeks. Instead, it only seemed to hasten them, and she raised her hand to her mouth to try and hold back a sob. "But..." she choked out.

"I'm sorry," Tremblay said, wrapping his arm around her shoulder and drawing her in close to him. He hugged her close and pressed a gentle, lingering kiss into her hair as the sunlight that had filtered through the leaves of the giant elm tree seemed to fade away into the murky darkness of Hades.

Saga brushed angrily at the tears that ran down her face and saw the things that had been her parents. "What are they?" she asked.

"Oneiroi," Tremblay said, "A manifestation of false dreams."

"Oh..." She said, staring at the two amorphous things pretending to picnic. "And Ziva?"

They glanced over to where Sidawi and Ziva were. "You said yourself that you took Ziva to Valhalla," Tremblay said. "What do you think?"

"She's one of those things too? One of those... Oneiroi?"

Tremblay nodded. "Yes. She's his false dream."

"I saw her... At the hydra," Saga said.

Tremblay hummed in consternation. "It is very strong then if it can wander so far from the tree."

"Tena thought that Sid was trying to open the gates of the underworld in order to bring her back..." Saga said.

"That's not how it works," Tremblay said, "and you've seen that. The collection of the dead was not for his use-."

Saga cut him off. "Vali was here. Where is he?" She whipped around, this way and that, trying to find the one-handed man.

Tremblay looked down at Shadow, " I didn't see anyone, did you?" Shadow's wise eyes stared back at him, before he shook his head, no. "Just you, Sidawi and those things..."

"You don't see the illusions?" Saga asked.

Tremblay shook his head. "I'm already dead, Saga. There aren't many false dreams which can affect me."

"Oh..."

"You've got to break the spell, Saga," Tremblay said. "You're the only one here who can."

Saga didn't want to do that. Within the spell... Within the spell you were happy. Within the spell you were safe, and your greatest wishes and dreams came true. Sidawi could live until the end of time within the spell and inside it he could love Ziva and his family would not disown him for it. He could love Ziva and not be ridiculed and exiled by his community. Why tear him away, back out here in the real world where everything hurt so damned much?

"No."

"What?" Tremblay asked. The look on his face saying that he wasn't quite sure what he was hearing.

"I said no."

"Saga-."

"No," Saga said interrupting him. "If you want him out so bad, you get him out."

"Saga! I can't..."

She choked back tears and clutched at her chest, the pain she was feeling making it hard to breathe. "Do... Do..." she swallowed hard and pointed towards the amorphous beings that had been her parents were. "Do you know... Do you know what you took me away from?" she choked out. "Do you?"

"Saga..." he tried to speak, but she didn't let him. Shadow rubbed up against her leg, but when she moved away from his comforting touch, he looked up at her with hurt eyes.

"I had everything I ever wanted. I had a family who loved me. I had my mum and my dad. They cared about what I did during my day and they... they... loved me... ME! Me! No one has ever loved me, but they did! And you took me away that, from them!" she cried, tears streaming down her cheeks by now. "If he is feeling even half as loved as I felt... I won't do that to him! I can't!"

Shadow climbed up her side, his paws trying to hold on to her as he stared up at her, trying to convey a message with his eyes alone. His tail wagged slowly, like he wanted to show his adoration for her, but knowing that happiness was not the right emotion. And he would know that, wouldn't he? Emory always seemed to know.

We love you.

The voice was confident in its words, but Saga looked around, the voice had been muffled and strange. Tremblay's lips hadn't moved, so it hadn't been him who had spoken. Where had the voice come from?

She stared down at the wolf, still trying to climb up her, but Saga couldn't look at him either.

"I won't do that to him," she stated again, stepping away from Shadow, leaving him to drop to the ground and stare after her forlornly.

"Saga," Tremblay started again and this time, he held up his hand to stop her from speaking. "The Oneiroi will kill him. It's called the Tree of False Dreams for a reason! That might look and sound and even feel like Ziva, but even you know it's wrong. That's why you lied to Edun and Navi about it. That's why you wouldn't let Edun come with you. That thing is not Ziva. Not for them, not for you and most certainly not for that lovesick boy over there. It will kill him just as those visions of your parents would have killed you and we were not going to let that happen," he paused and took a breath, something she had never really seen him do before. "If you care at all about Sidawi Harmeet, you will pull him out of his dream, or you will watch him die."

The cruel reality of Tremblay's words stung. She looked over to where Sidawi still sat with Ziva... Well, the Ziva-thing, and saw him smile. She hadn't seen him smile in all the time she had really known him. She had caught those looks of pure happiness in those few brief moments when she had spotted him with Ziva, but since her death? He had been taking each day as though there were a trial that had to be endured. Could she be the one to send him back to that? Did she really have a choice?

Saga stared at Tremblay defiantly. "I hate this," she said, before turning away from him and walking towards Sidawi. Shadow followed her, but like the house ghost, she didn't want him by her side either. "Stay," she ordered, and he looked completely crestfallen by her instruction. With a whimper of distress, Shadow lay down, his head between his enormous paws.

Trembley frowned and pursed his lips as though he was going to say something else to her, but instead he went and crouched beside Shadow. "It's alright Wolf Boy, she doesn't mean it."

Saga approached the picnic rug where it looked like Sid and Ziva were about to engage in a full on make-out session. When had that started? Saga cringed and cleared her throat.

There was no response.

She did it again, louder.

"Excuse me," she said when they didn't look ready to come up for air any time soon. "Sid?"

Sidawi pushed away from Ziva and looked up at Saga, an emptiness in his eyes and a pallid skin tone that she hadn't t noticed before. He had just been making out with his girlfriend... Where was the flush of young love? Where was the tomato like appearance of having been caught? Where were the swollen lips and harsh breathing? This wasn't right...

Sidawi stared up at her. "What is it?" he asked, his voice dull and lifeless.

"I... I need your help Sid," she said, wanting to try and draw him away from the fake Ziva without causing either of them any alarm. She eyed the fake Ziva cautiously. She could still the face of the girl she had once known and if she understood Tremblay correctly, she would until Sidawi's reality beneath the tree was broken.

"Now Saga?" he asked, his speech slow and drawn out.

Saga nodded. "Yeah... It's kind of important," seeing that he was surely going to tell her to get lost, she rushed on. "It's about Navi!" Hopefully, his sweet spot for Ziva's youngest sister would spark something within the shell of a young man she had known.

Sidawi sighed dramatically, but pushed himself up from the blanket, pausing to lean back down and brush a kiss against fake Ziva's lips. "I'll be right back," he said softly.

"Stay," she said a low, whiney voice, affecting a sad little pout on her lips as she trailed her fingers down his arm.

"It's your sister," he said, kissing her once more and sitting up.

"I'm sure she's fine," fake Ziva said and Saga cringed at the way she talked.

It must have struck a chord in Sidawi too, because he flinched. She wasn't sure if it was her lack of care, when Ziva had been all about the wellbeing of her siblings or if it was how she referred to herself. The realisation, moment of clarity or whatever it was seemed to pass almost instantaneously and then his eyes glazed over once again.

"Sidawi," fake Ziva wheedled as he dared to step off the blanket. Sidawi turned back to her, a smile upon his lips as he looked back at her. He started back towards her, taking her outstretched hand in his own and kissing her knuckles.

"Sid, it's really important," Saga begged, stepping closer. "Navi needs you."

She got close enough to take his elbow in her hand and tag on him. "Come one, this way," she insisted, tugging on him, trying to draw him away from the thing that was slowly killing him. Sid wouldn't or maybe he couldn't, leave her. The fake Ziva tugged on his other arm, leaving the elf boy torn between the two of them, unable to fight for himself in a tug of war for his life.

"Saga!" She looked back over her shoulder to where Tremblay was standing, Shadow still moping at his side, "You need to pull him out of it... Or knock him out."

Shadow perked up at that last bit, his head popping right up and staring at her, alertness in his bright, vibrant eyes. He was waiting for something he could do, something that would make this all better. Something glinted in the light, and he leapt up, bounding towards it, but Saga paid him no mind. Whoever knew what he was up to.

Except he came running up to her, leaping over tufts of grass, to drop at her feet the blade made of the spirits of the eastern warriors that the old woman had given her. Saga reached down and picked it up, only to almost drop it again as the spirits within the blade started to scream and yell at her.

"Sorry..." she murmured to the blade and that seemed to quieten some of them down. There was at least one who was screaming bloody murder, demanding to be released from the blade and allowed to resume his afterlife until a more suitable host was found. Oops... She would have to remind herself not to drop the temperamental spirit blade again. Shadow barked at her, then at the fake Ziva, going so far as to growl at the thing.

"Away," fake Ziva cried, swatting at Shadow. Like all of them, the real Ziva had adored Shadow, believing just as Astrid had, that if Saga and Navi were in Shadow's care, that they would be fine. She tugged once again on Sidawi's arm, trying to draw him away from Saga and Shadow.

He shoved Saga back and she stumbled backwards, desperately trying to find her balance back as she fell one, two, three, four steps backwards before falling into the grass, which while it appeared to be the lush beautiful green grass of the riverbank, was actually the hard, solid ground and roots of the base of the tree which stood between the flaming River Phlegethon and the Acheron. The heat coming off the flaming river was intense, perhaps even hotter than the burning inferno of Dorbe Manor and she felt as though she might boil alive from her proximity to the flames.

"Saga!" Tremblay's panicked cries were echoed by Shadow's incessant barking. He started to run to her, but Tremblay lunged, grabbing the large animal around the haunches and wrestling him to the ground before he could risk running any closer to the river.

Sagas fingers felt as though they might melt, and an acrid smell permeated the air. Burning. Something was burning. She turned her neck slowly and glanced over her shoulder. Right behind her, maybe a finger's breadth away, was the wall of fire, burning atop the river of blood.

The burning... Was her hair, the end of her ponytail, which had swept into the flames as she had fallen. In terror Saga tried to push herself to her feet, but the heat from the river was all consuming and as she tried to balance, she wobbled, her arms flailing closer to the roiling river of flaming blood. The heat seemed to sap her strength in a way she'd never imagined, and she allowed herself to fall back to the ground, collapsing hard on one knee. She crawled forward, away from the river. She breathed hard, finding that the air was cooler further away from the river. Tremblay was beside her, falling to his knees and taking the flaming ends of her hair in his hands and patting out the fire.

"Are you alright!" He asked.

Saga stared back at the river, wide eyed and in shock. She tried to speak, opened her mouth to answer him, but no sound came out. She was well and truly aware of just how close she had come to being burned alive.

Again.

"Come on," he said, helping her to her feet. As she gave him her hand, she realised the skin of her fingertips was blistered and red from the heat of the flames.

Great... Just great... More fire related scars.

Tremblay helped her to her feet and Shadow rubbed his body against her, as though he needed to be close to her.

"Saga, he's fighting you. You need to fight back now. You can't be nice now."

"Right..." Saga said, readjusting her grip on the hilt of the spirit blade. The coolness of it, seemed to soothe her burned fingers and she relished the feeling. "Kill evil Ziva."

Saga stalked across the field to Sidawi and Ziva. Without words or warnings, she raised the sword over the couple. They were once again making out and Saga cringed. As they rolled so that Sidawi was atop the hideous thing that seemed to be finding it hard to maintain Ziva's shape, she hit him on the back of the head with the hilt of her sword with every ounce of strength she had.

The elf collapsed atop the fake Ziva. It screamed in frustration. She shoved Sidawi off her and he rolled lifeless, to the ground beside the fake Ziva. She leapt up in that way that Saga had thought only possible in the movies. And while the real Ziva had been skilled with a staff, she had never been that agile to Saga's knowledge. Throwing knives had been her thing. Ziva could throw a knife more accurately than anyone Saga had ever known. Except this wasn't Ziva.

The illusion of the dark elf girl fell away as Sidawi slipped into unconsciousness and the amorphous blob of whatever it was charged towards Saga. She sidestepped the creature, the spirits in the sword telling her how to move the curved blade, which was different from the straight edged swords she was used to. She sliced a tendril of the being off and it fell to the floor with a wet, squelching sound but instead of lying there, still and dead, it squirmed and writhed.

"Ewww!" Saga breathed out. When Saga looked back up at the thing, she wasn't confronted by the former Ziva thing but by the figure of her mother. Her golden curls falling over her shoulders. Saga stopped short, unable to raise the spirit blade against her.

"False dreams, Saga!" Tremblay called out. "False dreams!"

She looked back at him and nodded. She could do this. She could...

Her feet were swept out from under her, and she fell to the ground hard, the wind knocked out of her. She rolled over, coughing, trying to breathe to find Sidawi staring at her, hatred burning in his eyes.

"Sid!" she gasped out.

"You can't have her," he moaned, sitting up and reaching for the sword. Saga snatched it away from him.

"Sid, that's not Ziva. You have to know that that thing isn't her!" She reached for him, but he rolled away as the thing took on this strange appearance, half Ziva, half Saga's mother, juxtaposed atop one another, lunged for her, arms extending out as though she was made of silly putty.

Saga rolled again and sliced with the sword. The goop being was sliced from where their belly button would have been, right through the head. The two parts flew apart, swaying in the breeze like those air blower guys she used to see at car dealerships.

Sidawi cried out in frustration. "Ziva!" Then threw himself on Saga, trying to wrestle the sword from her grip. "I'll protect you, Ziva!" He cried, releasing Saga's sword only long enough to punch her in the face.

Saga reeled in pain and thrashed, trying to dislodge the lanky elf from her.

"She's. Not. Ziva!" Saga ground out, managing to roll them over so that she was on top of Sidawi.

She didn't have enough space to use the sword, even just the hilt, so she followed his lead and punched him in the face, cringing at the pain it caused her fingers. Still, for good measure, she did it again, because he'd gotten up after only one the last time. He slumped back against the ground, not moving and Saga sighed in relief, slumping in exhaustion and sliding off of him to sit on the ground.

Shadow started barking incessantly but before Saga could move or look at him, she was wrenched backwards by the creature.

She kicked and flailed, trying to get a grip on something, but the thing was so strong now that it had lost the physical appearance of the lithe dark elf girl. The thing was hauling her across the ground and as the heat of the river Phlegethon came closer, Saga struggled harder. She kicked and finally, tried to dig the sword into the ground like an anchor. The spirits within it wailed about their dignity and their honour, but Saga just needed them to keep her alive in any way that worked.

The sword dug into the ground just as she had anticipated. The creature managed to pull her back. Saga held onto the sword tight as it gave way, digging deep gauges into the land before finally becoming stuck once more. The creature of false dreams, the Oneiroi, howled in displeasure as it hauled on Saga, trying to dislodge her from her new anchor. The sword held fast to the ground but if she didn't do something soon, her hands would let go and she would be at the creature's mercy once more. Saga kicked out behind her and felt her foot push into the globby substance that made up the Oneiroi and the feeling only solidified her idea of silly putty.

She was stuck. How in the name of... who knew what, was she going to get out of this one?

She realised she had to ask, because where were they? "Tremblay?" She called. "Shadow?"

She looked around, trying to find the ghost and the wolf only to find that they were obscured by the two creatures that had once been her parents.

She was on her own then.

Music, high and sweet permeated the air. The Oneiroi stopped its attempts to wrench her away from the sword. The notes of the song seeking to disorient the thing. Saga took the opportunity to let go of the sword and ram her head backwards into what she hoped was the creature's head. It let her go and stumbled backwards. Saga pulled the sword out of the ground, whirled on her feet, the sword whipping around with her to slice through the middle of the creature. The top half of its body slid down and to ground with a wet squelch before continuing to slide right into the flaming river of blood. There was a howling, wailing scream of despair right before the legs of the thing collapsed to the ground and rolled in after its top half.

Saga stared after the pieces for a moment, but they were gone as soon as they hit the flames, melting away into nothingness before her eyes. She turned and ran back for Tremblay and Shadow, but they seemed to be free from the creatures.

"What happened?" She gasped.

"Melted away as soon as yours hit the river," Tremblay said, running a hand through his hair. "That was..."

"Insane," Saga finished for him. "Come one, let's grab Sid and get out of here."

THE CITADEL OF BONE

When they crossed the river, Tremblay flying each of them over, one by one, there was no one waiting for them.

"Where are Navi and the others?" Saga asked when Tremblay landed for the last time, carrying Shadow.

Tremblay's feet touched the ground and the wolf jumped from his arms, shaking himself off after the indignity of being flown across the river. "I..." Tremblay started, his eyes scanning first the space where he had left them and then the horizon. "I don't know."

Sidawi was still unconscious and would most definitely hold them back. She had wanted Edun to help with him, she guessed that now she would have to help carry the elf. Emory would be of no use in his wolf form but at least he would be able to fight.

Shadow scurried across the ground, his nose down and loud, sniffing noises emanating from him. He stopped, sat down and barked.

"What is it?" She asked.

This way, the voice in her head said. She had only heard it once before, back under the tree of the Oneiroi when Tremblay had been pulling her out of the delusion.

She stared down at the wolf. "Was that you?" She asked him.

The wolf cocked his head to the side, barked and scratched at the ground.

Tremblay came over and crouched down to inspect what Shadow was indicating. "Footprints," he said. He ran his own fingers over the dirt ground. "Someone else was here. More than one someone. Animals of some kind too."

"So not the harpies?" Saga asked.

"Unlikely," Tremblay said standing back up. "Those look like cat paws or maybe dog... I don't know for certain. Around here it could be hell hounds, chimeras, anything..."

"Hell hounds?" Saga asked. "Like Hades's three headed Cerberus?"

Tremblay nodded, "and chimeras like our house crest, though in reality they can be made of any combination of animal."

"Oh goodie... More monstrous things to try and eat us," Saga muttered.

Shadow whined and pawed at the ground.

"Looks like Wolf Boy can track them for us. Lead on," Tremblay said.

Saga hefted Sidawi up and Tremblay came and took the boy's other side. "Why is he so heavy?" Saga asked with a grunt of exhaustion.

"Dead weight," Tremblay said.

"But there's nothing to him!" She complained.

The path they followed seemed to get easier to follow, as though more and more beings had converged upon this location and when they came to a large road that led into a grand city, they understood why everyone was headed in this direction.

"Oh..." Tremblay said.

"Oh what?" Saga asked.

"The seat of Hades power in this realm and the main population base in Hades."

"An actual city" Saga echoed. "An honest to God city, like what? Life just goes on when you die?"

"They do get hunted down and killed," Tremblay said with a smirk.

"And they didn't wind up in the deepest, darkest reaches if hell because?" Saga asked. Hades, aside from burning rivers of blood that would boil your soul out of existence and creatures like that fifty headed hydra was not an unpleasant place to be.

The city, inhabited by the dead, seemed so alive. Guards surveyed the perimeter, merchants hawked their wares, children played in the street. All around them was life. Except these people were all dead... Or were they? Saga had heard use of the term 'second life.' Was this what it meant? A whole new chance of getting your life right?

"It's not the same as life in the other realms," Tremblay said. "Here you never age. Die as an old man, live your second life as an old man. Die as a girl barely on the cusp of womanhood and you shall forever be that young maiden. Life goes on here, but for some..."

"So, Ziva and Sindre... They'll always be seventeen?"

"It's two hundred years after my death and I am barely a week older than my eighteenth year.

Saga looked up at him. "What happened?" She asked.

"That is a story for another day," the ghost declared. "Come on, let's find the others and get the hell out of here!"

"Sounds like a plan," Saga said, then together, with Sidawi held between them and Shadow by their side, they entered the city of the dead.

A church bell started to ring in the distance, followed by another. Soon, every bell in the town was ringing and there were guards running about, looking for something.

"Intruders," a ragged old woman cried. "There are living beings in the city!"

"More of them?" Another old woman asked. "Why are the living coming here? They already get all the other realms. Let us die in peace already!"

"Alarms for living people?" Saga asked, "Really?"

"It's not me and it's not you... Living or not, you're a Valkyrie, immune to such bans just as the Angels of Death are. It has to be them," Tremblay decided, motioning to Sidawi and Shadow.

"What do we do?" Saga asked, "Hide?"

Tremblay shook his head. "No... We are being summoned now."

That did not sound good. In fact, it sounded decidedly bad. "Summoned?" Saga asked in a shaky voice.

"Have you ever met a god, Saga?' Tremblay asked.

"Does Vali count?"

Tremblay shrugged, "I guess so, but I mean a real God, one of the greats, not their children."

"What? Like Thor or Odin?" She asked.

"A bit hard, seeing as how they're both dead," Tremblay said stoically. "But yes, like them." Saga shook her head." Well... just try to be respectful... Hades does not tolerate fools."

His last words were said as they were surrounded by city guards, who Saga was taken aback to discover looked like skeletons.

"The Lord of the Realm wishes to see you," one of them said in a gravelly, empty voice.

Saga gulped as they were led towards a citadel at the centre of the sprawling city that appeared to be made entirely of bones.

"That is so..." she didn't finish the thought when she caught Tremblay's warning look.

They passed through a gate, arched by what might have been the ribs of an enormous beast of some kind, the gates a solid plate of bone. They weren't given an opportunity to inspect the features further as they were hurried along, through a courtyard where skeletal soldiers trained, and skeletal washer women seemed to go about their work.

Saga shivered when one of the soldiers looked at her, a gleam in his hollow eye from the sun reflecting off something in there.

The doors were massive, made of the bones of what might have been a giant or some other large creature.

They were led through corridors made of bone. Skulls lined the walls at the levels of chair and picture rails, their empty eyes staring out at them as they passed.

Saga walked, Sidawi's arm draped over her shoulder and Shadow leaning against her leg, as though he needed to stay in constant contact with her.

At a set of grand doors their guards stopped, turned to face them, then without a word, opened the doors to the room beyond.

The sound of giggling laughter met Saga's ears, and she stared up at Tremblay in surprise. The surprise showed in his eyes too and tentatively they stepped forward.

At the end of red and black runner a giant throne of bones seemed to emerge from the floor and upon it sat a pale faced man with blue flames for hair.

A guard jabbed the butt of his spear into Saga's back, and she stumbled forward, almost losing her grip on Sidawi.

"Come in, come in," the man upon the throne of bones said. "Fear not little Valkyrie, you are welcome in my home. Take the sleeping one from them and tend to him," the man directed, and two skeletal guards attempted to take Sidawi from them. "No," Saga said. "We've got him."

Hades, for Saga could only assume that the man upon the throne was the God of the Underworld himself, stared at her, fire flaring up in his eyes before he said, "he will be tended to and cared for, as your other friends have been." He waved his arm out to the side and Saga saw Navi and Tena, seated on the floor beside a large, three headed dog. One head was leaning into an ear scratch from Tena while another was bent over, licking at a small puppy, which also had three heads... And to her surprise, a snake's tail. Navi was cradling another puppy on her lap and giggling at its antics. Edun stood nearby, watching the girls with a scowl on his face as a third puppy jumped up and down his side, trying to crawl up his leg.

"Puppies?" Saga asked.

"Hell Hound puppies, Saga!" Navi exclaimed as she nuzzled her puppy. "Aren't they just the cutest?"

Saga just stared at her friend. "I... We... I..." She stopped and gathered her thoughts. "We thought you were in trouble."

"They are," the voice was so low she thought she had imagined it, but when she turned around to face the speaker, she was confronted with Hades, leaning in to get a closer look at her. "It's been a long time since I've seen a Valkyrie in these parts..." He ran his hand down her arm and Saga flinched away from his touch. "And with the living too."

"The kids are just in their way home, Lord Hades," Tremblay said.

Hades straightened and turned-on Tremblay. "I didn't ask you, Ghost," he flicked his hand towards Tremblay and the man was sent skidding across the black marble floor.

"Saga!" Tremblay called out, reaching out towards her.

Shadow barked and Hades turned an eye on him. "And as for you, little living one," he said, then suddenly Shadow was beside Navi and the others. He stared back across the expanse of the hall and barked. He started across the room, but one of the skeletal guards blocked his way. Shadow howled in distress.

"Why are you doing this?" Saga asked him over the sounds of Shadow's distress.

"I take great interest in anyone who brings the living here. The little necromancer over there doesn't have that kind of power, but you... You have the power to bring the living to Hades."

"I..." Saga looked around, but everyone had been taken away from her. Distracted by guards or puppies. "I'm not the one that brought us here," she said.

"Then why are you here?" Hades asked, cocking his head sideways as he inspected her.

"We were sucked into a vortex by... by... I don't know what... I doubt it was the instrument alone, but Vali was chanting some kind of magic," she paused, and Hades waved his hand at her impatiently, urging her to continue. "Vali brought all the dead, the unsettled and the returned and he also sucked in the Angels of Death, and I don't know what else. He wanted to use all of them, all of us as an army to kill the hydra that guards Tartarus."

"An interesting story," Hades mused, finger tapping on his chin. "And one I've heard before."

"What?" Saga asked. "From whom?"

Hades waved his hand nonchalantly, "Oh, one of Odin's pestilent offspring..."

"Vali?" Saga asked.

"Ah, yes," he said pointing at her. "That's the one. The little boy who thinks he can be king."

"What did he say?" Saga asked cautiously.

"The Maiden of Death was coming to cause chaos and just as he said, here you are."

"Did he also mention how he trapped my friend with an Oneiroi or how he was using him to gather up enough spirits to fight the hydra and open the gates so that he could take Odin's empty throne?" Saga asked pointing at where Sidawi was now sitting up, talking it seemed, to one of Hades' skeletal attendants. "Did he mention how he played on his loss and grief... That he caused by the way, to create this situation in the first place?"

Hades glanced to where Sidawi was. "A lover?" He asked.

Saga nodded. "During the ride of The Wild Hunt a few months back."

Hades walked away from Saga and proceeded to pace the length of his throne room. "What to do? What to do?" He murmured to himself. He turned to her, his hair flaring up. "Where were you when I came across your little friends?" He asked.

Saga watched him, trying to figure out what it was he wanted, but he was a god. How did anyone figure them out? "I was trying to get Sid to come with me..."

"So you go, you get your friend and you come back. I waited quite a while there."

"Vali... He..." Saga crossed her arms over herself, hugging herself tight. "He knew my deepest desire..."

"Ahhhh!" Hades exclaimed. "So, you too were drawn in by the spell of the Oneiroi. Well, little Valkyrie then I guess that you too must undergo the trial."

"Trial?" She asked. "What trial?" Saga looked around, panic flooding her. What trial?

"Bring the boy," Hades orders his attendants and two skeletal... Men? Women? Things? She didn't know what they were, but they lead Sidawi over to stand beside her.

"Saga," Sidawi said. "What... What is going on?"

Saga shook her head. "I really don't know..."

Hades turned away from them and with the wave of his hands, two, no three, blob like creatures started to emerge from the floor of the throne room. Shadow barked furiously and dashed across the room, avoiding hell hounds and skeletal guards alike until he collided with the one right in front of Saga, just as it began to take the shape of her mother, just as it had done beneath the Oneiroi elm.

The second one took the shape of Ziva and Sidawi reached her. From the back of the room, they heard Navi cry out, as she stood up, displacing hell hound puppies from her lap, causing them to roll to the floor.

"Ziva!" The girl cried, causing Edun to look up. He grabbed for Navi and said something that Saga couldn't hear, but the look on her friend's face told her that Edun could see the truth, that the thing standing there was not their sister and just a prop to be used. Navi clung to her brother, burying her face in his chest as her body shook with sobs.

"What is this? ""Why are you doing this?" Saga cried, but Hades was busy staring at the wolf wrestling with one of his beings and then all of a sudden, the wolf was gone. "Emory!" Saga screamed, pushing past the god to see the empty space where Shadow had just been. "What have you done to him? Where is he?"

"Quiet girl," Hades snapped.

Furiously, Saga tried to grab at him. "Where is he?" She cried out, her fingers digging into the lapel of his jacket.

A moment later, she was sailing through the air, pain emanating from her right side. She had no idea how she had got there. She hit was wall on the far side of the room with a crack as her head collided with the hard bone walls. She slid down the wall into a crumpled heap, dazed.

"I SAID QUIET," Hades roared, his fire hair flaring up like a funnel of flame from his head.

"Saga!" Tremblay called and through the double vision, she thought she saw him trying to come to her until he too vanished from the room with the flick of Hades hand.

"Trem..." she groaned out, her hand reaching towards where he had been standing.

"All of you," Hades said angrily, "be gone!" And just like that, Edun, Navi and Tena were gone. Saga cried out and tried to stand, but her head spun and she fell back against the wall. "You come into my realm with the living. You try to kill my hydra-."

"We were protecting it fro-."

"DO NOT INTERRUPT ME!" Hades bellowed, her hair flying around her in his breath, all the way across the room. Saga cringed against the wall and Hades continued. "You manipulate the entrances to the underworld, you inundate my world with countless of the unsettled dead, eastern spirits, angels and who only knows what else. You wreak havoc with the Oneiroi, and you stand before me, little Valkyrie, blaming all of this on one of the Norse gods, one of my brethren!"

Saga said nothing, not knowing what to say. Sidawi watched; his eyes wide with fear as Saga cowered before the lord of the underworld. They were the only ones left.

"It was me," he said, his voice low and Saga wondered if she had actually heard him speak, but when Hades didn't respond, he repeated himself, this time louder. "It was me. I manipulated the gates. I brought the dead here..." Hades turned towards the young elf, ready to unleash his rage upon him but Sidawi hurried on. "The man... He said that if I did what he said, I would see her again... That I could bring her back to me..." His voice choked up and Saga felt for him. She had known that he was struggling, and maybe she could have done more for him... But Navi had been struggling too, as had had Annis and Edun. She had no idea how Annis was doing with everything, in the times that she had seen the older girl, she had been reserved, as she always was, but it was as though she was trying her hardest to step in Ziva's shoes and look out, not only for her siblings, but also for the other students from Dorbe Manor. Edun... Saga didn't know how to describe him. He would have moments of... not weakness, but uncertainty and sensitivity and he would open up to her, like that day in the music shop. But Sid... Sid had been forced to go on as though nothing had happened. His parents had not known about his relationship and only very few of their mutual friends had known. He must have felt so alone as he had tried to navigate a world without the girl he loved in it. "I just wanted her back," Sidawi whispered. "I just wanted to see her face..."

Hades whirled around to where Saga was still sagging against the wall, taking care of her aching head. "And you? Why are you here?"

"We... We figured out what he was doing and figured out that it was wrong... We were just trying to protect him..." She said.

"And yet you became trapped beneath the Oneiroi elm too," Hades said. "There is a desire, a dream, burning deep within you. To escape from it, you must, as I said, face a trial if you are to leave the underworld."

Saga and Sidawi shared a look. What could this mean?

"Follow," he ordered, and Sidawi did. Saga pushed herself from the wall, only swaying slightly as she did so.

She fell into step beside Sidawi, and they followed Hades in silence as he led the way from the throne room out through a series of passages that seemed to lead deeper and deeper into the bone citadel.

Hades stopped before a small door to it almost looked as though it had been put there as an afterthought and nobody had wanted to take the time or effort to redo a larger space. The skulls that lined the walls stared at them expectantly and Saga jumped backwards, crashing into Sidawi when one of them seemed to wink at her. Another, three or so down the line, clacked its teeth as though it was hungry and started the line of them off and all up and down the corridor, teeth clattered in an endless cacophony of noise. Saga and Sidawi inched closer together in the middle of the hall, as far from the clattering skulls as they could get.

Hades reached out and whacked the one closest to him. It stopped and like when the clattering started, in the effect ran down the line of skulls and back up again on the other side until the hall was quiet once more, then Hades pushed open the door and went inside.

Sidawi looked at Ziva and waved his hand forward as if to say 'ladies first' but Saga stayed where she was, waving him forward instead.

"I insist," Sidawi hissed.

"Oh no," Saga said, "I do. You got us into this!"

"Saga, please!" He begged.

"Are you two coming?" Hades bellowed. "Or would you like to spend the rest of your lives down here with me?" That got them moving and they surged forwards, trying to enter the door at the same time and getting stuck. "Morons," Hades said plaintively, "I'm surrounded by morons."

Sidawi pushed Saga forwards, succeeding in getting her to enter the room first. Saga stumbled in, coming to an awkward stop before the lord of the underworld. Sidawi approached sedately behind her. He was really starting to work on her nerves, especially after everything they had done for him. She stared over her shoulder at him, trying to get across her displeasure by the look in her eyes. Sidawi though, steadfastly ignored her, keeping his eyes on the flame haired god.

Hades stared at them; his eyes slit like a cat's in displeasure. His hellhound, Cerberus wound his way around the god's legs, one head always staring at them, no matter which way the animal moved.

"You entered my world uninvited and still living," Hades started, his gaze settling on Sidawi. "You wanted to rewrite the laws of life and death for yourself." Sidawi opened his mouth to speak, but Hades best him to it. "You will not interrupt again, you insolent little elf. You not only brought with you the living, but interfered with the roles of the returned dead, forced in the unsettled dead... Although that might turn out to be a blessing... Brought angels and other spirits and you even managed to draw in Lady Izanami... I will never hear the end of how she had to protect the hydra, do you have any idea what you have done? I now owe the woman a favour!" He complained. "And believe you me, she will collect. She always does!" Then he added in a sullen mutter, "and it's never small!"

He turned on Saga then, "and you, little Valkyrie," he said, tapping his finger against his lips as he thought. "The living beings you brought down here... I assume with the necromancer's help, the lot of you caused significant strife across the realm. The damage to my hydra, the harpies and the Oneiroi."

"I apologize for the hydra," Saga said. "We only ever intended to protect it from Vali's attempts to kill it... But it... It ate Edun and Sidawi..." She said in a low voice.

Hades eyed Sidawi, who just nodded as he attempted to sidle behind Saga once again.

"It matters not, your actions, no matter how noble they were intended..."

"The road to hell is paved with good intentions..." Saga muttered under her breath.

"What? What was that?" Hades asked. "Oh," he gasped, realisation dawning on him. "I quite like that... The road to hell is paved with good intentions... I might use that!" He smiled and walked the room for a moment, Cerberus trailing his every step. He repeated himself, laughed and said, "yes, I might just use that." Then he turned, suddenly serious again and stopped before the two of them. "You will climb these stairs," at his words, a soft spotlight illuminated a staircase that seemed to spiral up the height of the room. They could see no roof to the room in the near total darkness, but the stairs seemed to go on forever, spiralling into the distance like the stairs at the centre of the world tree.

"Climb stairs?" Sidawi asked. "We just climb them to the top?"

Hades nodded. "Simple, yes?"

"Yeah," Sidawi said. He looked at Saga. "Simpler than expected right?"

"Right..." Saga said, not entirely sure that he was right. There had to be something else. Something that Hades hadn't told them yet.

Sidawi grabbed her arm and led her towards the stairs. "Let's get out of here." Saga tried to wrestle her arm out of Sidawi's grip, but his fingers felt like claws digging into her flesh and by the time she managed to escape his grasp, Sidawi was four steps up the staircase and her foot had landed on the first step.

"Oh," Hades called after them. "Whatever you do, don't look back."

Saga, who had not yet looked up the stairs watched in horror was the two Oneiroi emerged from the floor once more. "Why?" she asked, but deep in her get, she was pretty sure she already knew the answer.

"Because if you look back," Hades said, "You'll be stuck down here forever."

STEP BY STEP

"Chop, chop," Hades said, clapping his hands together. Cerberus howled... Well, one of his heads did. Another barked and the third yipped excitedly.

"What did he say?" Sidawi asked, his body turning.

Cursing, Saga climbed the steps until she was right behind him and held him in place. "Don't turn around." She was so angry at him for not thinking before dragging her onto those stairs. She had felt deep in her gut that there was something Hades hadn't told them... And of course, there had been. "Don't you ever think?" She hissed.

"I'm sorry!" He hissed back. "But how hard can this be?" He climbed two more stairs, intent on getting out of there.

"Sid." The voice carried up to them and Saga had to once again hold the elf steady as he struggled to look back.

"It's a trick. It's not her. It's one of the Oneiroi again," she insisted, pushing him up the stairs.

One.

Two.

Three.

Four.

"Saga. My story. My joy." Saga froze, her fingers digging into Sidawi's arms, more to stop herself from looking back, but she felt him flinch in pain. She didn't let go. Those words, torn from the letter left by her mother all those years ago... She could barely breathe.

"Saga?" Sidawi asked. "Who is that woman?"

She looked up at the back of his head. "No one... She's no one because it's not her," Saga said, then to herself, "it's not her, it's not her, it's not her..." She pushed Sidawi up several more stairs.

"Remember when we met?" Ziva's voice called out. "No... Not when we met," she decided, "you were so Ljósálfar then... No, when you damaged your family's arcana book, and you needed me to fix it for you."

Sidawi stiffened. "I remember..." He choked out.

"You can't magic better a magic book," Ziva said, and Sidawi flinched.

"How..." He couldn't find the breath to speak. "How does she know that?" He asked Saga.

"Because you know it," she said, "come on." She gave him a shove up the stairs.

She felt him trying to turn to face her and she held him fast. "Do not turn around!" Saga ordered, and he stopped, climbing the next five steps in silence.

"Where is she?" He asked.

"Where's who?" Saga asked, following him.

"Ziva... The real Ziva," he begged. "Where is she?"

"The Upper Planes of the Dead," Saga said. "What in the nine realms made you think that Ziva of all people would be down here?"

Sidawi hung his head. "It is ingrained in us that Dökkálfar are beneath us... That they are undeserving... I... I know better... I do... But when that man said that I could get her back..."

"You believed him," she said, and he nodded. "Wanting her back isn't wrong Sid. Navi and Annis and Edun miss her too. I'm sure all her friends do... I know I miss her... Why didn't you come to us?"

"You're first years," he scoffed.

"Your own friends like Tymberlee?" Saga shot back.

"No one knew!" He cried, although Saga was certain that her Prefect had known. "If my parents had found out about Ziva, they... They... They might have hurt her or disowned me, or I don't know, but you saw what my father was like with Navi!"

She had seen. The man truly felt superior to dark elves and had been unnecessarily cruel to Navi when they had worked at his restaurant. "So for all this years... No one knew that you and Ziva were..."

He shook his head. "I... She never even told her siblings..."

"I know..."

Everything around them was black and all they could see were the stairs before them. "I miss her..."

They continued on up in silence, the sound of Ziva's voice becoming softer as Sidawi's enthrallment with her lessened.

"My darling girl."

Saga stopped, her eyes closed, and her fingers curled into fists at her side. "Go away," she murmured, "you're not real."

"Saga," Sidawi said, his hand reaching back to her. She took it and he pulled her up to stand beside him on the same step. She allowed him to ground her in reality. Resolute, she looked up.

"Look," she said, pointing with her free hand. Above them, far in the distance they could see a light.

"Is it the end?" He asked.

"I think it must be," Saga said and together, they started to run up the stairs, the end literally in sight.

They spiralled round and round, the stairs seeming to disappear as they passed them. There didn't seem to be a way back down and that was just fine with Saga.

Music came from the light, and she recognised Edun's pan flute, the song he played was that one by Thyra Bodil about the Valkyrie and the battlefield that Mannish liked so much.

"Come on," she exclaimed. "They're waiting for us!"

Edun's music helped to cover the plaintive cries of her mother and she wasn't sure how she was ever going to thank him for that. They were nearing the top, the light looked more like a doorway now and it was so close that they could just about touch it.

"Little Valkyrie," a voice said. The breath against her ear had her clutching at Sidawi so as to not risk turning around. "Little Valkyrie," the voice repeated, drawing out the two words with an almost sing song quality.

"Go away," Sidawi said. "Come on Saga, just a few more steps and we're free."

"I will claim Odin's throne, even without the armies of Tartarus," the voice went on, "and when I do, you will serve me!"

"I will never serve you!" Saga cried out. "Never! You hear me! Never!"

Sidawi pulled her forward; it was only ten more steps until they were at the top and they could pass through the doorway into the light.

Vali crossed in front of Sidawi, circling around the elf, luring her gaze. Saga almost turned to follow him. Where was that weapon that the goddess had given her? Oh right... Hades had taken it back, releasing the spirits to their afterlives. How would she fight Vali?

"Not here!" Sidawi exclaimed. "Not now!"

"He killed her and then he used her to manipulate you!" Saga said, wrenching her arm from his grip. "Someone has to take care of him for once and for all."

"It doesn't have to be you!"

Edun's music reached a crescendo and Saga was ready to turn and fight Vali. It would protect her friends if he was gone and no longer vying for the throne of Asgard... Or would it just leave everything open to someone else? She had no idea but there was always someone somewhere, vying for more power.

Still, Vali was the one who had killed Ziva... killed all those people in town while trying to activate her. She couldn't let that go on could she? She looked at Sidawi and thought of the pain he was forced to hide from everyone around him because he was Ljósálfar and the girl he had loved was Dökkálfar and now that she was gone, he was left to grieve alone and in silence. That was how Vali had manipulated him.

She stepped down a step. "What are you doing?" Sidawi asked.

She didn't answer him, instead, she closed her eyes and fisted her hand like it was holding the hilt of a sword. She had no idea why she did it or what she expected, but the semester before when master Iacono had tried to kill her, she had been carrying one of Ziva's throwing knives courtesy of Navi and when it had come time to fight, the knife had fallen from her hand only to be replaced by the strange sword Astrid had given her during the street fight.

"My little Valkyrie to build me an army of the damned," Vali's voice taunted her.

Nothing happened.

"Once I have you, I will gather the head and the spear, and the throne will be mine "

Now what?

"You couldn't even lead an army of the dead to open Tartarus," Saga shot back.

How was she going to fight Vali without a weapon?

She needed to think. What options did she have? Not many. No weapon. No backup. Sidawi was an arcanist? Could she use that? Sid who had caused all this.

"I can bring you to your mother."

Saga's eyes flew open, and she stared ahead. Below, somewhere far at the bottom of the spiral staircase she could still hear the voice of the Oneiroi pretending to be her mother.

"Another Oneiroi like that one?" She asked, her voice soft and childlike.

"Saga?" Sidawi said, his hand reaching behind him to try and grab her. Long, delicate fingers wrapped around her elbow, and he tugged hard, trying to give her a shake. Worry tinged his vice, but she didn't hear that.

She shook him off. "You got your dream."

A mother. Her mother. Vali had insinuated before that he had known both her mother and her father. If anyone could take her to them, it would be him... Right? Astrid wouldn't... Or couldn't...

A finger tapped her on the shoulder, almost digging in between the bones painfully and it was only the fact that Sidawi tugged her forward once again that stopped her from looking around.

The voice of her mother called to her, telling her that she loved her. Telling her of how proud she was. How delighted she was to call Saga her own. Then, there was the final straw, the one that would inevitably break the camel's back.

"Let's go home, your father is waiting for us, little story."

Saga had to choke back a sob as she brimmed with excitement.

Home.

Mother.

Father.

Home...

She was about to turn around when suddenly she was pulled forward by... By... By what? What could want to pull her away from her mother? She struggled against the hold, her mother's voice calling to her. She pulled free of the force trying to haul her away from her mother and then she was pushed forward. She fell against the stairs, the risers digging into her painfully. She'd fallen upstairs before and always hated the experience. Her fingers crossed into the light and then there were arms pulling her out if the darkness of Hades.

The music. When had the music stopped?

Saga pushed herself into a sitting position and covered her eyes. It was bright... Everything was so bright... Where had all the light come from?

People were saying her name, voices she recognised. Navi and Edun. Tasso and Jemima. Emory, not Shadow. Emory was there and so was Tremblay. They were safe. They were here. How were they here? Where was here?

She scrambled to her knees and stared down the spiralling staircase that descended deep into the depths of darkness.

"Sid?" She croaked out, unable to really find her voice. "Where's Sid?" Tremblay pushed past her, stepping onto the stairs. She grabbed for him, panicked and her fingers clenched into the fabric of his clothes. He was still solid. How was he still solid? "Don't! Hades will keep you there if you look back!"

"I'm already dead," he reminded her and disappeared into the darkness.

"What happened?" Tasso cried. "How come Jem and I got left out again? "

Navi slapped his shoulder. "That's not the important thing here," she scolded, before kneeling down beside Saga. "Saga... What happened with Hades?"

Saga looked at her briefly before looking back into the darkness after Tremblay. How long had he been gone? Had it been too long? She didn't know. Sid was a Prefect... Where was his house ghost? She had seen the Ainsli house ghost... but never Seipdeh Yeatwens, the house ghost of the Ljósálfar student house.

Maybe she didn't enjoy the spectacle of the interschool tourney, but even so, the house ghosts who could, always used the opportunity to follow their Prefects around. It gave them a wider view of the living world and according to Tremblay, they rather enjoyed it. They took the gossip back to the Realms of the Dead and exchanged it like currency.

So why had Sidawi's house ghost not come to Yggdrasil City or been with them as they had faced the hydra?

"Saga?" Jemima asked, reaching out and putting her hand tentatively on her friend's shoulder.

"Do you see anything?" Saga asked, still staring into the darkness, looking for Tremblay and Sidawi. She cringed and tried to shake of the sounds that seemed to emanate from below and could have sworn that she heard her mother's voice calling for her and she leaned closer towards the stairs.

"Nothing," Jemima, following her actions and trying to look into the inky depths of the underworld.

Navi came to sit on her knees beside Saga. She peered over the edge, into the hole that lead back down into hell. "Why's it taking so long for Sid to come back?"

Saga shook her head. "I don't know." She bit her lip and looked up at the others. "Tremblay was solid though, right?"

"Yes," Tasso said. "Something about this room here being in the vale between the living and the dead. He said that it was because this place exists but doesn't... I don't know, it really didn't make sense."

"None of this has made sense," Edun said, standing over them. "Come on, help her up " he said extending his hand to Saga. Emory was beside him in an instant, his hand also extended out to Saga. She looked back towards the hole, trying for any sight of Sidawi for Tremblay, but there was nothing, just the endless cries of whatever or whoever was down there. She glanced up momentarily at Emory's offered hand before she took Edun's and he pulled her to her feet. Emory glared at them but said nothing as he crossed his arms over his chest and Saga thought that maybe he growled, but she wouldn't swear to that.

"I heard you playing," Saga said to Edun.

"I'm glad," he said softly, "I couldn't think of anything else to do... I wasn't even sure if you would hear me... But..."

"Thank you," she said. "It helped."

Tena came running in, a small squirming thing in her arms. "Are they back yet?" She asked, breathing hard as she tried to catch her breath. "Hey, come on, stop it" she cooed to the creature in her arms.

"Saga's here and Tremblay went after Sidawi," Tasso explained.

At the same time, Saga was staring at Tena and the creature in her arms, but never got a chance to question it when Tremblay emerged from the depths, Sidawi cradled in his arms. He looked fierce. His skin had darkened with red veins running across the contours of his face and arms, reminding Saga of Rendon. His black, bat-like wing had a tear in it and the white, feathered side was darkened with soot and char.

"Tremblay!" Saga gasped. "What happened?"

"Hades' pet was not willing to release their new toy," he said, wavering slightly. His wings quivered before he dropped to one knee, the weight of Sidawi too much.

"Trem!" Saga went to him and crouched down beside him.

"Oh... And Hades said that he wants what was taken from him," Tremblay said as he lay Sidawi out on the ground before him.

"That would probably be Tena's new toy," Edun said, glancing at the girl, cooing over the strange creature.

"What's this," Tena asked, looking up and cuddling it close to her chest. "Did someone mention Tena's name?"

"Hades wants his puppy back," Edun said.

"What?" Tena gasped, "Meddy?" He can't have her back!" she cradled the animal even tighter.

"Meddy?" Jemima asked.

"Like medusa," Tena said, holding out the three headed puppy with the mane of snakes and a tail that slithered with another snakehead on the end of the tail. "And he should have thought of that before he sent us away! This one's keeping her!" She stroked a finger down the back of one of the snakes and the others looked away, not really knowing what to do with her. Tremblay shook his head but decided that Hades and his dog were the least of his concerns. "Come on," he said, "let's get out of here. We need to get Sidawi to Matron Damir."

Emory and Tasso picked Sidawi up, supporting the older boy between them as his head fell forward.

They left the strange room that existed between the realms of the living and the dead and as they did so, Tremblay faded away until the only one who could see him once more was Saga. He stared down at his translucent hands and sighed. "It was nice being solid again," he said.

"Aren't you always solid when you're in the realms of the dead?" Saga asked.

"It's not the same," he said, but didn't elaborate. They re-entered Agesilaus to find organised chaos. Matron Damir and a group of other healing angels were running a first aid station from the chaos of the club. The stampede itself had apparently caused only minor injuries with the worst being a broken leg. The members of the band and the angels who had been brought into Hades and had been returned to this realm after the encounter with the hydra were gathered together in one corner, although the band members appeared to be tied up and under guard.

"You found them!" Matron Damir said, bustling over to them through the mess of broken tables and chairs and spilled food and drink. She caught sight of Sidawi and turned all healer-y on them at once. "What happened?" She demanded.

"The boy tried to fight Hades," Tremblay said from where he stood beside Saga, but Raphaella Damir didn't hear him.

"Tremblay says that he tried to fight Hades..." Saga said softly. She looked at him. "But I thought he fought Vali..."

"It started with him... Apparently, but I never saw any sign of him and I... I asked Hades and he swore that he had not allowed Vali onto that pathway to distract you. Only Oneiroi."

Saga frowned as she looked across the room to where the stage was. The tear in reality was gone now, but she bit her lip and then said. "So Vali wasn't there... It was an Oneiroi... An illusion..."

The others looked at her, waiting for her to finish her thought, but nothing came.

"What was that Saga?" Tasso asked.

She shook her head. "Nothing."

There were disbelieving looking along her friends, but as she tried to stand up once more, eager to get away and be allowed to think for a while, she swayed.

"Saga! Jemima exclaimed, coming over to her and supporting the girl. "Come on over here and have a seat. Please."

Saga tried to protest. She rubbed at her eyes slowly, her arms feeling heavy. Every part of her body felt heavy and like lead. The adrenaline must be wearing off she thought as she allowed Jemima to lead her over to a partially broken chair, the backrest hanging from it awkwardly. All the legs were intact though, so she sat and allowed Jemima to tend to her.

"How many fingers am I holding up?" The angel asked.

Saga blinked, "I want to say six... But I'm pretty sure you don't have six fingers on your right hand... So, it has to be only three..."

Jemima frowned. "Did you hit your head?" She asked.

Saga tried to nod, but the movement caused a thumping pain inside her skull, and she stopped, instead, she said. "Yeah... Hades threw me across the room... I hit the wall pretty hard... Can I just sleep Jem? Please... I just want to sleep..." Her eyes fluttered closed.

"No!" Jemima cried, "you can't sleep! No!" seeing that she was making no difference in Saga's state, she bellowed across the room for her aunt, "Aunt Raffi!"

~ * ~

Saga just wanted to be left alone. She had no idea how much time had passed since they had returned, but what she did know was that ever since Tremblay and Shadow had bombarded her picnic with her mother it had been a never-ending barrage of activity. Now that they were back in Yggdrasil City, nothing had changed and Saga wanted to scream, even as Raphaella Damir and Jemima checked all of them over for injuries.

"Emory hit his head," she said petulantly when no one would let her be by herself. Her words caused the boy to look at her with a frown. "He was out for a long time."

"But that was hours ago," he complained as he tried to avoid the portly angel.

"Come here boy," Raphaella said, forcing him to sit down on the cot beside Saga.

"Gee, thanks," he said miserably.

Saga didn't look at him. "You scared me," she said in a soft voice while focusing on the bandage around her wrist from where he had bitten her the night of the sleepwalking... Had that only been the day before yesterday? It seemed so unreal.

Emory's hand crept across the cot and took hers in his own, interlacing their fingers together. "I'm sorry," he said.

She shrugged, trying to seem nonchalant about the whole situation. She didn't care... No, that wasn't true. She did care, she just... The look on Tremblay's face when she had refused to say goodbye to him even as he had hugged her goodbye and disappeared back to the realms of the dead to recover. Would he be back at Jimpsee house? Or would he be following Tymberlee around?

She squeezed Emory's hand but didn't say anything. She didn't want to ruin another opportunity of friendship with him and had missed his company... But at that moment in time, she found it very hard to not blame him and Tremblay for pulling her out of that fantasy life with her mother and her father. She had been happy there, at that picnic with not a care in the world, but most importantly she had felt loved.

As Raphaella fussed about Emory, Saga slid her hand out if his and stood up.

"Saga?" Navi asked from where she sat, close to Edun. "Where are you going?"

"I..." Saga looked around. They were a sorry lot for their journey through the underworld. Sidawi was huddled alone on a cot in the corner, rocking back and forth. He too had been ripped out of his fantasy. He had fought for his fantasy, for his dream... She hadn't... She had let them rip her out of the perfect life that she had always dreamed of, and she hadn't fought for it. Instead, she had turned around and ripped Sidawi out of his. What kind of hypocrite did that make her?

She scrubbed angrily at her eyes, trying to stop the tears that were threatening from falling and stalked from the healing tent.

"Wait!" Jemima ordered, coming after her and trying to take her arm and hold her back.

"I'm sorry Jem," Saga said, brushing the young angel off. "I can't stay here."

"Don't leave us again," Jemima begged.

Saga's teeth chattered as she shook. "I won't," she promised, "I just need... I..." she looked up at her friend, imploring her to understand. "Please..."

Jemima nodded and released her arm. "See you in our tent?"

Saga nodded. "Yeah."

She could hear Tasso asking after her as she walked away and had to let it stay like that, because she just wanted to be alone. Maybe she could go for a run and clear her head.

She walked aimlessly through the camp, avoiding anyone that she thought she remotely knew and finally found a place to sit in the shadow of the arena as she watched the sword pairs fight until she fell asleep, her dream full of the perfect life she could have led beneath the Oneiroi Elm.

"There you are!" Rendon declared, storming up to her.

She stared up at him dumbly, not comprehending why he was looking for her. The brightness of the sun obscured him from her. "What is it?" she asked, her voice thick with sleep.

"Have you found her?" another voice asked and Saga was surprised to see Anh-Ly coming up behind the daemon boy.

"She's here," he stated over his shoulder, before turning his attention to Saga and trying to pick her up.

"What are you doing?" she exclaimed.

"Your Grunborg Sensei has been looking everywhere for you," Anh-Ly said. "And by now, the stadion is right after lunch."

Saga blinked in surprise. "But I already ran the stadion."

"The finals!" Rendon cried. "The finals, Story Girl."

Saga stared up at him, not comprehending his words. "But it's not the... What day is it?"

"Frjádagr," Anh-Ly said, her accent sounding strange on the old Norse word for Friday.

"The day of the finals!"

"But what about the staff fight?" Saga asked.

"Later tonight," Anh-Ly answered. "You and Navi will be there, yes?"

Saga nodded. Had they somehow managed to lose an entire day while in the underworld? "Yes... We'll be there..." She said, not entirely sure how she was going to get through the day. "When's the race?" She asked.

"The first event after lunch. Luckily though, they're not running simultaneous events because it's the finals and it's too difficult to arrange for those in more than one event. Lunch might even be late!" Rendon said. "Not that a late lunch is good... but girl, you look dreadful!"

"I'm fine," Saga insisted and allowed him to pull her up to her feet this time. "What are you guys even doing looking for me?"

"Grunborg Sensei looked ready to decimate something," Anh-Ly said. "You disappeared from the healing tent more than three hours ago!"

"Three hours? I just needed a moment... I never meant..."

Rendon draped an arm over her shoulder and directed her towards the Toserra Sorose camp. "Lots of things happened down in the underworld?" He asked cheerfully.

"Something like that."

She tried to catch sight of Anh-Ly, but the girl was trailing them, and Rendon's grip seemed to indicate that someone had told him of her tendency to avoid everyone and be alone after major events. But Saga wanted to ask the girl if she knew anything about the strange eastern spirit who had helped her in Hades. The woman had obviously been more than a spirit, but Saga was sure that she had seen her around the camps, if only she could remember who it was that she had been following.

"Aunt Raffi is mad with you," Jemima said as soon as she saw Saga

"What did I do?" Saga cried.

"You left before she could look over your injuries from the sleepwalking incident."

Saga frowned. "Ummm..." She scratched at her bandaged wrist. It was itchy, but it didn't hurt. Shadow's teeth had dug in deep, leaving gauges in her flesh and the more she thought about it, the more she realised that she couldn't remember the last time it had actually bothered her. She had wielded the spirit sword in Hades without any pain and her feet, that had been scratched up from the run up the spiral stairs at the centre of the world tree. They had also never bothered her... At least not after... after when?

She unwrapped the bandage on her wrist and Jemima leaned in for a better look. Instead of angry, red bite marks they saw clear, flawless skin. "Huh..." Jemima said. "How did that happen?"

Saga shrugged. "I don't know..." She thought, there had been the niggling of pain during their outing at the club and then the Hydra had battered her around... That had hurt... And yet she bore no bruises from that incident... Only the cuts and grazes she had received from Vali... and she was tired. She was so damned tired that she was sure that if she crawled into bed, she would sleep for a week. "I..." She shrugged again, the uncertainty showing on her face.

They walked into camp and Saga ducked behind Rendon when she saw Tymberlee and Deluca powering through the camp, stopping anyone they encountered.

"Are they looking for me?" Saga asked meekly.

"They're getting everyone who has a final today," Jemima said. "All the Prefects are running around."

"Saga!" Tymberlee said she spotted them. "Where have you been?"

Was she talking about now or for the last day or so?

"Why are you looking for me?" Saga sked.

"You weren't at the meeting," Tymberlee said.

"What meeting?"

"The one for finale contestants," Deluca said. "Mistress Grunborg was not happy!"

"So, I heard," Saga muttered. "Anything I need to know?"

"There were some pointed comments about fighting," Deluca said, rolling his eyes, "Seriously, you'd think from the way they were talking that the comments had been pointed towards the pentathlon team and in particular."

"Stop thinking it's all about you," Tymberlee said. "There's been tension between all of our students and in particular, Shamel Aiyeola because of their treatment of Navi and Edun."

"And the dark elves from Rinsunid Cantera," Saga said, "and the fact that they have slaves..."

"Right," Tymberlee said. "Keep up Deluca, we're busy fighting all of the world's wrongs! Go on Saga, go do whatever it is you do before a race to prepare. We'll be watching!"

Saga nodded, "thank you..." She said, not really sure who she was thanking or even why, but it seemed the right thing to say. With that, she wandered off away from them, aware of Tymberlee's eyes on her as she disappeared into their tent.

YOU WIN SOME,
YOU LOSE SOME

Saga stood in the corner of the staging area for the stadion final, avoiding
the other contestants. Back on Midgard this had been her standard behaviour,
to take time to herself and just breath. In Nýr Ásgardr, that had been harder.
She had been an oddity that everyone wanted to investigate and as time had
gone by, she found herself enjoying the talks with Javaid and Dayan. Rendon
had been a distraction in the lead up to the last race, but this time, people
seemed to be giving her a wide berth and she was grateful. There was one
other Toserra Sorose student. A fourth year weretiger named Kenzari Tomek
Armas, who seemed to give everyone a wide berth. She didn't boast against
the competitors from Rinsunid Cantera or Ehras Magna like the others did.
She didn't hang out with the other students from Toserra Sorose. In fact,
aside from her name, Saga didn't know anything about her, despite competing
in the same event. Other than the one fox spirit from The Two Worlds
School, everyone else came from either Rinsunid Cantera or Ehras Magna.
She was the only non-animal shifter in the group.

She did notice the girl, Margot Featherswallow from Ehras Magna who
had tied for first with her in their previous race eyeing her with contempt, but
Saga ignored her.

When the race was called, she had nothing on her mind but the race. She knew the track, the circular road that encircled the Tree City and all she had to worry about was herself. Win or lose, it only came down to one step in front of the other as fast as she could. They all had supernatural speed, strength and stamina at their disposal and no matter what happened, she would take it in her stride. It was only one race after all.

Yeah... She didn't really believe that...

Running was the one thing she was proud of. It was the thing that she had put every ounce of energy into when times got too tough. She could put on her runners and just pound the pavement until she was too tired to think, too tired to care... She could do that now. She had wanted to run and now she could... With a literal pack of wolves at her heels.

She stood up straight, resolved to run the best race possible for herself.

But it wasn't as simple as that. Nothing ever was. She ignored the looks when she prepared to run and when the horn blew, she launched herself forward and ran.

When she saw Navi on the side of the track, with Tena and Tani... She could have sworn that she saw Ziva standing there. A blond elf standing not far behind her could have been Sidawi and Saga felt the tears prick at her eyes.

Eyes front. Nothing mattered but the finish line.

Werewolves howled while weretigers and werebears roared and growled in excitement. Hyenas cackled and there were other animal sounds too from the shifters and spirits from the other schools. She heard names called out, her own, by her friends and they spurred her on. But the Ehras Magna student to her left was pulling ahead, while the Rinsunid Cantera student in her right seemed to be his only solid competition as she took the turn in the track coming in third.

And then she saw her.

At the end of the track, a tall, beautiful woman with long flowing golden ringlets of hair and face that drew Saga in.

"Mum..." She breathed out on an exhalation of breath. She drew in another, deeper breath and pumped her arms faster, willing her feet to carry her faster and faster to her mother.

She never even noticed as she passed the two Weres and the crowd from Toserra Sorose became raucous, their cheers and jubilation the only thing anyone could hear.

But none of that mattered to Saga because at the finish line, her mother was waiting.

~ * ~

She pulled through the fabric rope that had been erected over the finish line and made straight for the golden-haired woman, only to stop short, wobbling as her balance almost failed her in the near instantaneous stop.

It wasn't Brigitta standing there. It wasn't her mother.

It was Astrid and she was beaming with pride, but Saga didn't care. She could have sworn that she had seen her mother there... the woman from the Oneiroi tree... Except... that woman had looked like Astrid too... Because Saga had no idea what her mother looked like. How could she? She had never met the woman.

Saga choked back a sob as the world seemed to fall away around her. She stared at Astrid and felt such a stab of betrayal that her heart ached, and her legs became weak causing her to sway unsteadily.

Panic crossed Astrid's face as she reached out, grabbing Saga and holding her upright even as the world seemed to sway.

"Saga!" she exclaimed. "What's wrong?"

"N... No... Nothing..." She choked out as Astrid tried to guide her to a seat, but Saga tried to fight her touch, tried to get away. She had to get away from all these prying eyes before the tears really fell.

Around them there were murmurs and whispers.

"Miss Carolle?"

Saga looked up, her eyes wide with distress and saw Master Everard standing there. "Yes?" She gasped out. Why couldn't she breathe? She couldn't get any air in her lungs. No matter how many times she gasped, nothing seemed to go in.

Concern crossed the man's face as he shared a glance with Astrid. "I'll have Matron Damir sent for immediately," he said.

"No!" Saga begged. She didn't want the motherly healing angel. Not now. "I'm fine," she promised, but neither Tilson Everard nor Astrid Grunborg looked convinced.

"They're calling the race results," Everard said, holding out a hand to her. "Can you stand?"

Saga pushed herself into a standing position and except for a slight wobble, her legs held. "Who won?" She asked, looking at them both.

Both teachers stared back at her in disbelief.

"You don't know?" Astrid asked.

"You did," Tilson Everard said.

Saga had proceeded through the awards in a daze. She still, even as she was patted on the back and congratulated, could not fathom how she had managed to overtake the two Weres who had been ahead of her.

Tasso had tried his best to retell the story of the race, but when it got to the part of her turning that bend and catching sight of the finish line, he seemed to have no answer other than a miraculous burst of speed that had allowed her to not only keep up with the two older Weres but beat them by at least three stride lengths.

It made no sense to Saga, but all of the attention was overwhelming her, and she just wanted to shrink away, to not be the centre of everyone's attention.

She needed to get away, because while whatever daze she was in had been a weird kind of strength in the race, it would most definitely be a detriment come the paired staff fight and she did not want to let Navi down.

"Come on," a voice said, taking her hand and drawing her through the crowd. She was surprised to see Emory on the other end of the arm.

He led her away from everyone and for a moment, she thought that maybe he was leading her back to the Toserra Sorose camp, but he wasn't going there either, instead he was leading her into the woods where the hunt had taken place on the first day. He didn't stop dragging her along until they couldn't see the outline of the tent city anymore.

"What are you doing?" She asked in a low voice.

Emory led her over to a log and sat her down. "Giving you that peace and quiet you need," he said, "No one was going to give you a moments peace back there," then he backed away.

Saga swallowed hard, trying to hold back another wave of tears that were threatening to fall. What was wrong with her? She had to stop all this crying. "Stay..." she croaked out, her voice failing her.

Emory stopped walking, but said, "What was that?"

Saga sniffled and wiped her face, trying to make herself somewhat presentable. "Stay."

"Saga," he said softly, "You can barely look at me..."

"At Shadow," she corrected.

"I am Shadow!" Emory exclaimed, standing there.

"I know you are!" She cried, "But yet... You're not! Not to me! You and Shadow.... You're two different people to me..." Emory went to say something, but she stood back up, arms held out towards him. "I know that's stupid! But I didn't grow up in a world where people could turn into animals! So, to me... to me.... You're you and Shadow is Shadow..."

"Saga..." Emory started to say, but Saga waved him off.

"I know, I know," she said, sinking back down to the log, "I'm mad."

Emory laughed. "Not mad, just..." he shrugged, "just... You have a different view of things."

He came over and sat down beside her. Tentatively, he wrapped his arm around her shoulders. After a moment, Saga leaned her head against his shoulder and they sat there, simply enjoying one another's presence.

~ * ~

They got some funny looks when they walked into the dining tent a little later, but the odd feeling was instantly dissipated when the Werewolves started to howl. The Weretigers and bears began to roar, and the hyenas seemed to cackle and laugh along with them.

Saga settled in at a table, sitting beside Navi. "They're excitable today," she said softly.

"They've been like that with everyone who's placed in the top three today," Navi said, pushing her food around on her plate. "Navi is too nervous to eat..."

"Tell me about it..." Saga said, staring at her own, untouched plate. Was it nerves though? Or was it the fact that Sidawi was still back in the healing tent with Matron Raphaella, unresponsive?

"You two will do great!" Tasso insisted, shovelling food into his mouth. He glanced over at Navi's plate and pointed his fork at it. "You going to eat that?"

Navi rolled her eyes dramatically, then pushed her plate towards him. "Have it," she said miserably. She heaved a deep sigh and rested her chin in her hands.

"Here," Saga said, pushing her own plate towards the ravenous faerie. "Have this too."

"Really?" Tasso exclaimed, his eyes lighting up as he pulled the two plates to him. He eagerly dug in and ate happily.

The crowd was starting to gather as the competitors got themselves ready for the evening competitions. The sword fighting competition was winding up and it was looking good for Toserra Sorose. Arya Abassi was going at it with an amazing level of speed as she attacked her opponent, defending and parrying the attacks of her opponent from Ehras Magna.

Her partner seemed to be in a defensive pattern, never able to get an attack out against his bear of an opponent... Was he a Werebear? It was possible. He was definitely not lithe and lanky like Arya. It was still anyone's match.

"Staff competitors," The staff weapons master from The Two Worlds School said coming to them. "Your matches will now be drawn."

Saga took Navi's hand with her free hand, her other, grasped tightly around their staves. "Ready?" she asked.

The little dark elf nodded slowly, but her eyes were wide as she stared at the old man. His long white beard seemed to fall to the floor and Saga wondered what his classes would be like. "Yes... Navi is ready..."

It was surreal as the names of the schools were read out, pairing them against one another. Kahawaiola'a Ocean School was paired against one of the smaller schools that Saga had not had an opportunity to get to know. Saga caught sight of Hilina'i and her partner. Neither of them were looking very confident and Saga remembered hearing that the school they had been paired against eliminated their opponents in two moves. A team from Ehras Magna were paired against a team from Shamel Aiyeola and a second team from Aquino Beccara was paired against the second Toserra Sorose team who had also won their deciding match.

When they were called, Saga and Navi gripped each other harder, and Saga was sure that she felt Navi sag against her when they were paired against Sakata and Anh-ly from The Two Worlds School.

"We're so going to lose..." Navi groaned.

Saga squeezed her hand. "We're going to go out there. We're going to give it our best. We're going to make Astrid proud no matter if we win or lose because she will know that we tried our hardest."

Navi nodded. "Right... and we..." She swallowed hard.

"Will be the Jackie," Saga finished for her. Navi nodded eagerly and together they made their way to the waiting area.

"Be the Jackie. Be the Jackie," Navi muttered to herself.

When their turn came, they walked out onto the field. "For Sidawi," Navi said.

"For Ziva," Saga added.

Together, they bumped fists and nodded in agreement, then turned to face the two talented fighters from The Two Worlds School. Anh-Ly and Sakata looked serious and ready to fight. Their faces wore stern expressions and their long, flowing dark hair was tied back in tight ponytails. Sakata's cat-like ears protruded from her head, making her look all the more menacing. They both held the staves at their sides, in that posture that left them running up the length of their arms, and down the length of the legs. The staves were just out of sight, hidden amongst the wide sleeves of their kosodes and multiple folds of their hakamas. Unless of course you were looking for the weapons.

"Saga. Navi," Anh-Ly said.

"Anh-Ly. Sakata," Saga replied.

The four girls faced off against one another, the honour and pride of their schools at stake.

The fields had slowly been filling as the dinner hour ended across the camps and the other competitors came to watch the finals.

"I am glad to see Kaneko Sensei was able to repair your weapon," Anh-Ly said to Navi.

"Yes," she said, bowing awkwardly to the other girl. "Navi is very thankful to Master Kaneko for his work."

"Are you ready?" the event referee asked the four girls. Saga and Navi nodded towards him, as did Sakata and Anh-Ly. The referee nodded. "Bow in or staff tap?"

"Staff tap," Navi and Saga said at the exact same time as Anh-Ly and Sakata said that they would prefer to bow into the match.

The referee's hand delved into his pocket and came back out with a coin. He glanced between the two sets of girls, "heads or tails, ladies?"

"Tails," Anh-Ly said confidently, and the referee threw the coin up into the air. It went up, flipped several times in the air and caught the setting sun, blinding Saga for a moment. When she could see again, the referee had the coin caught in his hands and was tipping it over into the back of his right hand, his left still carefully covering the coin, preventing anyone from seeing it.

With great drama, he started to draw the covering hand away and the girls all tried to subtly lean in for the first look. Their eyes, surreptitiously looking up, and meeting before the coin was finally revealed.

"Tails," he announced.

Anh-Ly bowed her head in what appeared to be a humble acceptance. "Thank you," she said, before smiling at Saga and Navi, any hint of their growing friendship missing from her eyes as she continued to speak. "There is no shame losing here today."

Saga nodded in agreement. She knew what the other girl was doing. The psych-out was a tried-and-true tactic in any competition. "That's true," she said, smiling back. "There is no shame in losing today."

Anh-Ly's confident demeanour slipped for half a second, before she stepped back.

"Ladies, positions."

And like that, they were kneeling, five staff lengths away from each other. A gong sounded. Anh-Ly and Sakata bowed faster than Saga had anticipated.

As she and Navi tried to catch up, they sprung to their feet, staves in hand with barely enough time to block the incoming strikes from both girls. Navi grunted under the strength of Sakata's strike. She was forced backwards as the other girl raised her weapon and, in a blur, swung it over her head and back down towards the small dark elf.

A swipe to her ankles. Saga jumped, just barely feeling the fast-flowing air from the staff before it struck. Anh-Ly's staff swung harmless under Saga's feet as she landed safely on the other side, just as if she had been jumping rope in the school ground... No one seemed to jump rope in Nýr Ásgardr. It was such a simple activity... Good for training too. She would need to get a skipping rope. Except at this exact moment in time, Saga needed to keep her thoughts on the girl in front of her. She had yet to make a single strike, instead only barely able to evade strikes that had the potential to knock her out of the match completely.

Anh-Ly tried to distract her, pulling her staff up so quickly that Saga's eyes followed it. The cat girl stepped forward and started to bring the tip back down behind Saga's head. Realisation shot through Saga as she realised what the other girl was trying to do. The tip of the staff was high, forcing Saga to look into the setting sun. It started down behind her, whistling through the air. Against all lessons, she allowed her eyes to follow the tip. Her body twisted around, contorting awkwardly. Out of the corner of her eye, Anh-Ly smirked with confidence. The staff started its final move and just as it was about to connect with Saga's knees, she leapt.

Saga launched herself over the staff, tucking into a roll, her staff clutched tight against her body. She hit the ground several feet away from the stunned Anh-Ly. Saga's shoulder connected with the ground softly as momentum propelled her forward until she was standing once more. Breathing deeply, Saga turned to Anh-Ly, her staff positioned defensively before her.

The watchers were crying out in surprise and awe. She heard both their names called out, but Saga couldn't afford to allow any more distractions. She had come to win, and she was going to give it everything she had.

The position she found herself in, placed her closer to Sakata than Anh-Ly and with a nod to Navi, Saga went for a surprise attack at Sakata. The girl whirled around, whipping her staff up above her head like the blades of a helicopter to defend herself against Saga's attack. Sakata didn't stay still for long though. She had Saga at her front and Navi behind her. She stepped forward, out of range of Navi's incoming strike, bringing the staff down on a rounded curve towards the side of Saga's head. Forced to step backwards, saga met the strike with a mirror of Sakata's move. They paused, then by mutual agreement, they stepped apart, drawing their staves down to their hips. Navi just barely missed getting hit in the ankle by Sakata, leaping aside at the last second.

Where was Anh-Ly?

Saga took no chances. She couldn't waste time looking for the other girl and she decided to take a risk and try a move she had seen the two cat girls pull in their first match. Taking a wide step, Saga drew her staff away from her hip as though she was drawing a sword and with a wide, sweeping stroke, she swept her staff over her head. Sakata ducked as the end came too close to her and Anh-Ly let out a squeak of surprise as the end connected with her shoulder.

And that was where the good things ended. Surprise had Saga releasing her grip slightly and momentum sent her staff sailing across the expanse of the field as though she had thrown a spear.

"Saga!" Navi cried out.

Any-Ly didn't give her any time to recover. She struck like lightning and all Saga could do to survive was try to catch the staff before it hit her... Only that allowed Anh-Ly to continue the movement and propel Saga across the field in a wild, uncontrolled roll, far, far away from where her staff had landed.

"Navi!" Saga cried. Sakata and Anh-Ly were both descending upon her, and Saga pushed herself to her feet. She needed to circle around the three fighters to get back to her own weapon. She took a deep breath and ran.

She never made it across the field though. Suddenly, she was on her back, the dirt of the field billowing around her as she tried desperately to catch her breath. Anh-Ly stood above her, the tip of her staff millimetres away from Saga's throat. She had been so intent on her running, that she had never noticed the girl strike out at her.

A few feet away, Sakata stood over Navi, her staff similarly positioned.

The match was called in favour of The Two Worlds School and as soon as it was, Anh-Ly lowered her weapon, reached down and offered Saga a hand. Saga took it gratefully.

"Congratulations," Saga said, coughing slightly.

Anh-Ly beamed in delight. "See you on the field next year?"

Saga nodded. "Definitely!"

Saga took a moment to look around the field. Sakata and Anh-Ly were being congratulated by the referee and people were calling out their names. She felt Navi's arm wrap around her shoulders.

"We did good," she said, looking around in awe.

"We did better than good," Saga said, wrapping her own arm around the small girl's waist. "Come on, let's go find our friends."

They were met at the edge by Tasso, Jemima and Edun, along with other members of the Toserra Sorose team. There were pats on the back and well wishes, commiserations and congratulations for a fight well fought.

"They were tough competitors, and you held your own well," said a boy Saga vaguely recognised. He was on the Pentathlon team as their stick fighter and was competing in the solo staff fighting finals.

"We didn't win," Navi said.

"No, but you will learn and next year, you will be even better!" Astrid said clasping a strong hand on each of their shoulders. "And you did so magnificently well! Now, all that's left is the pentathlon tomorrow and then we're all off, homeward bound!"

At the mention of the pentathlon, Saga groaned. "Harry is better now, right?"

"Even if he was, which he isn't, he was banned from competing," the boy reminded her and Saga groaned again, her whole-body slumping as she realised that there was no way out of it.

GOLDEN GIRL

Saga groaned as morning light shone through the fabric of the tent. She only had to get through today and then they were going back to Nýr Ásgardr. Tymberlee and Caoimhe were already wide awake, discussing their potential options for the day. Navi and Jemima were sleeping like the dead and Saga felt her breath catch in her throat. She stared over at Navi, her eyes staying in the girl until she could discern the steady rise and fall of her chest. She breathed out in relief.

"Something wrong?" Tymberlee asked, her questioning gaze setting on saga.

She shook her head. "No... Nothing... Other than being put on the team when I said no... I was clear with Donetta and Deluca!"

Tymberlee laughed. "Those two always did have a hard time taking no for an answer."

"I don't see what the problem is," Caoimhe said. "You run. We win. Those Weres get a taste of dust in their mouths and go back home with their tails between their legs. Everything is good."

"That is so simplistic," Saga told her. "And a lot of pressure."

"You already won the stadion," Tymberlee reminded her. "They'll be quivering in their boots today."

Saga sent her Prefect a disdainful look that she hoped expressed her every emotion on the matter. She quickly got dressed, hoping to get out of the tent before anyone tried to stop her. She was just brushing her hair back into a ponytail when the flap flew open, and Donetta strode in.

"There's our golden girl," she cried.

Saga narrowed her eyes at the exuberant third year.

"What's all the noise?" A sleepy Navi asked, sitting up in her cot and rubbing her eyes.

"Oh... geez, sorry. I didn't mean to wake anyone!" Donetta exclaimed, her loud voice carrying in the confined space.

With a huff, Jemima threw her legs over the side of her own cot. "And there goes any chance for a lie in," she groaned. Navi copied her, grumpily reaching for her uniform as she stood up.

"Girls, go back to sleep," Tymberlee insisted.

They both shot looks at Donetta, before resuming getting dressed.

"I ugh... Think I may not be a favourite person around here. So sorry," Donetta said before turning her attention back to Saga as the others mumbled sarcastically that she was excused. "But I just needed to make sure that this one knew where and when to be!"

Saga rolled her eyes. "I am familiar with the stadion track Donetta."

"Good, good! They're running teams first and then solos."

"I know."

"Good, good!" Donetta said, awkwardly repeating herself as she started to rock and forth on her heels. "Well... I'll..." She pointed over her shoulder at the tent flap. "Just go and let you all get on with things." And with that, she turned and fled the tent, the occupants staring after her.

Saga huffed an aggravated sigh and finished her hair. She pulled on her boots and looked over at Jemima and Navi. "Want to come to the healing tent with me?"

Jemima's eyes went wide with concern. "Are you alright? Do you need something?" She exclaimed.

"I'm fine," Saga said soothingly. "I just... Wanted to see Sid before the match today..."

"Oh," Jemima breathed out. Relief causing the tension to leave her body. "Right."

Tymberlee's eyes narrowed. "How is he?" She asked.

Jemima bit her lip awkwardly. "The last I had heard from Aunt Raffi was that he was still catatonic. He seems to hear... But he doesn't respond."

"What if Tremblay didn't get to him on time?" Saga asked.

"What do you mean?" Navi asked.

Saga slumped back down to her cot and took a great interest in picking at her fingernails as she tried to avoid them. "Hades said if either of us looked back... We would be stuck... Down there... In the underworld... We were pushing each other forwards even as they tried to convince us to look back..."

"They?" Tymberlee asked.

"The Oneiroi... They made themselves out to be our greatest desires... I... I... I almost broke," she admitted in a low voice. "And Sid pushed me out before I could..." She cleared her throat before the tears that were threatening to spill down her cheeks came. "I uh... I have to go. I'll be at track later."

She got up hurriedly and tried to make it to the tent flap, but Navi raced to her side, grabbing her arm and holding her in place. "Wait, Navi wants to come and see Sidawi too."

Saga nodded, but didn't say anything. She didn't trust her voice any longer. Navi rushed back to her cot, grabbed her bag and hurriedly pulled on her uniform. "Ready," she declared, hurriedly tying her long white hair in a messy half ponytail bun type thing. All those cool girls at school back in Melbourne would have been jealous of Navi's ease with the hairdo.

The little dark elf slipped her arm through Sagas and led her out of the tent.

"Are you ok?" Navi asked as they walked through the camp. The camp was already looking different from the day before. Weapons and gear were already being packed away and stored in semi neat piles of trunks and cases.

Saga pursed her lips, trying to think of what to say. "I... I don't know..."

"What happened in the race yesterday?" Navi asked. "You were doing good, but then all of a sudden you just pulled forward and..."

Saga heaved a deep breath. "Do... Do you know that I've never even seen a picture of my mother?" Navi grimaced, but said nothing, allowing her friend the chance to speak. "Yet... Under the tree... and later with Hades... There was this vision, this woman... Every fibre of my being knew that she was my mother... My father too, although his features were less clear."

"What do you mean?" Navi asked when Saga fell silent.

"At the race, I saw her again... She was there, at the finishing line, waiting for me... Except it was just Astrid... And looking back... Every time I saw... Her... I had given her Astrid's features... her hair, her eyes..."

"Oh Saga..." Navi breathed out, her arm tightening around Sagas and pulling her in close.

"I feel like such a fool..."

"Don't..."

Saga pulled herself free from Navi and turned a smile on her. Navi noted though, that the smile did not reach her eyes. "Come on, let's go see Sid and then get breakfast... Before Tasso eats it all."

Navi frowned at Saga's sudden and false mood change. "Right..." She said cautiously, walking beside her, almost having to scurry to keep up with Saga's long strides.

The Toserra Sorose healing tent was still full of people who had been caught up in the stampede at Agelaius. It wasn't as bad as Saga had first envisaged, with there being also a few injuries from events. Sword fighting, were battles and jousting seeming to make up the worst of it.

Matron Damir was bustling around the tent, already hard at work. Her silvery wings seemed to droop though, a few feathers floating to the ground. The woman must have been exhausted. Saga wondered if she had returned to her tent that night, guessing that Gabriella's would have been too far away for the exhausted angel.

"What are you doing here?" She asked, then she peered behind them. "Where's Jemima?" She asked.

"On her way," Navi promised.

"We just came to see Sidawi." Saga added.

The angel seemed to say in relief that they didn't want anything from her. "Good then you two can do me a favour and bring him his breakfast."

"Of course," Saga said.

"Over there," Raphaella said pointing towards a table where angels and helpers were making up plates of food to bring to the patients. A few ambulatory students were getting their own plates and sitting back on their beds or at a few small tables that were set up for dining. "Make him up a plate and he's through there in the private room."

"Has he spoken yet?" Navi asked.

Matron Damir shook her head. "No... And it's not just that, he doesn't follow instructions, he doesn't respond. He doesn't even look at you when you speak... Perhaps seeing friends will help."

They left the older angel to her work and made Sidawi a plate of food, then filled a metal cup with water. Navi carried the food carefully as Saga pulled the privacy flaps away from Sidawi's small space. He sat there, staring at the canvas wall.

"Hey Sid," Saga said, injecting a false tone of exuberance to her voice. "We brought you breakfast!"

He didn't even look at her.

"How about some water?" Navi said. "Nothing better than a nice, cold glass of water right after you wake up."

Still nothing. Saga and Navi looked at each other, worry creasing their faces.

Saga sat down beside Sidawi. "So the finals were yesterday... Navi and I got thrashed by the girls from The Two Worlds School. Did you meet Anh-Ly and Sakata?"

"I don't think he did..." Navi said, trying to hand him a tick slice of bread slathered in jam. "Here," she said. "You should eat."

Sidawi sat there, not a muscle moving or twitching. Navi looked panicked as she waved the piece of bread in front of him and got no response. Perhaps it was because they spent so much time with Tasso, but the idea of someone totally ignoring food, was foreign to them.

"Sidawi," Saga said firmly, "look at me." When he didn't respond, she reached out, her hand taking hold of his chin. She turned his head to look at her and gasped.

There was nothing there.

She was no great believer in the whole 'eyes are a window to the soul' thing but she had seen a lot of things, both on Midgard and since coming to this strange new world. Even Mimir who was nothing but a head on a pedestal had more 'something' there when you looked him in the eyes. Maybe it was life, she didn't know but touching him felt strange.

She felt cold, right down to her core. Touching him was like touching the dead. She pulled her hand away as though she had been burnt.

"What's wrong?" Navi asked, dropping the untouched bread back onto the plate.

Saga shook her head and tried to discreetly move away from the elf boy. "I... I don't know..."

"There's nothing there anymore," a voice said from the doorway. Dina Bess, their religious studies teacher and a former angel of death stepped inside. "That's what you're feeling. His body is alive, but there's no soul in there."

Saga looked from Dina, back to Sidawi, but she knew that the angel was right. "What does that mean for him?" She asked in a soft voice.

Dina frowned but came over to crouch before Sidawi. "It means that there are angels now scouring the depths of Hades looking for him."

Saga licked her lips slowly, her mouth dry with fear. "What... What if Hades himself has Sid?"

Dina stared at her in horror. "Then... Then the Seraphim had best be told," she said, as though following protocol would fix anything.

They left the healing tent feeling stunned. They had been unable to get Sidawi to eat. By accident, they had heard Dina and Raphaella talking about the possibility of putting Sidawi into a magically induced sleep that would keep his body preserved if they couldn't get him to eat, while the angels kept up their search and possibly their negotiation with Hades is it came to that.

Saga felt numb as she slid onto the bench in the mess tent beside Emory. She barely registered his presence until he put his hand on her arm, drawing her back into the present.

"What happened?" He asked.

She shook her head. "Tell you later," she said, looking around and noticing that Jemima wasn't there. "Where's Jem?"

"Gone to the healing tent to help out," Tasso said, filling his mouth with thick chunk of bread, topped with meats and cheeses.

"Good... Matron Damir was dropping feathers she's that tired," Navi said.

"Is that a thing?" Saga asked.

"Angels dropping feathers? Yeah, when they're sick or facing exhaustion," Tasso said. "We all have our quirks," he added with a smirk.

She was about to respond when she spotted Deluca coming straight for her. "Any chance you can help me avoid him?" She asked her friends as she ducked her head and tried to look interested in her food.

"Saga, my reserve. There you are!" He exclaimed.

Saga groaned. "Kill me..."

"But you like running," Navi said. "All you did all winter was complain how it was too cold to go out running."

"But he wants me to do more," Saga groaned.

"Is that so bad?" Tasso asked. "You're mad good with a staff and pretty good with a sword."

Saga glared at him. "And it has an aerial component. I will not do it!"

"But Pingu would fly for you, Navi is sure!"

"Your wings are beautiful," Emory added in a low voice that no one else seemed to hear. His eyes seemed to lock with hers as they just stared at each other for a moment longer than was strictly necessary.

She looked at him with wide eyes, surprised by his comment. "I..." She swallowed hard and finally managed to rip her eyes away from his.

Deluca was standing over Tasso and Navi, hands on his hips. "You coming, or what?"

Saga sighed. "Coming."

"Good luck!" Navi said. "We will come and watch!" She promised.

The officiator seemed weary and drained, a week of wrangling students, staff and spectators taking their toll, along with the strife at Agelaius. "Participant one will run the circuit, before running into the arena where they will tag in the staff fighter. No tag in, no start." They all nodded. "At which point contestant two will fight their way past five staff fighters trying to block their way. Not only must they clear the arena with the best time. Points are given for technique, both offensive and defensive. At which point you will tag in your rider before their jumps course. At the end of the course, they must tag in the sword fighter before they can move. The sword fighter will complete a course of dummies and combatants. The archer cannot take flight until the sword course has been completed and they are tagged in. Is this understood?" They all nodded again. "Are there any questions?" When there was no response, the woman nodded. "Fine. You have ten minutes to talk within your teams and get into position."

Saga was dragged aside by Donetta, who was apparently not taking any chances, ensuring that she didn't do a runner.

"I'm coming, I'm coming," Saga groused.

"A reminder after last year's debacle," Donetta announced to the Toserra Sorose team, "You must make contact with the person ahead of you. They use magic to tell. If the next person hasn't been tagged in, they will be deducted points. It's happened before. Saga, it's your first time here..."

"I've run relay before where we must pass a baton to the next person in line. I'm good," Saga insisted.

Elfina frowned briefly but nodded. "Ok... I need to get Redcrest ready. You two better get your mounts ready too", Elfina, their archer Yovani Anupam their dressage member and Maysun Zuniga, their sword fighter.

Saga made her way to the starting line for the stadion portion of the event. She stretched and the others watched her as she did so. She could hear the mumblings about her odd running habits and how she had managed to win. At least here, no one was accusing her of having magic shoes like they did back at Toserra Sorose during her first couple of races. She supposed that maybe the uniform shoes were a good call, but she wouldn't admit that to Astrid. "Competitors to your marks," a crier announced and the called was echoed out across each of the event areas. Saga walked over to her starting mark, looking around for Harian. The Weretiger was standing at the edge of the track, scowling at her. She scowled right back at him.

Down the line of starters, Saga could hear the usual murmurs about her. Some of the students she was up against, she had already beaten during the stadion events, and they looked ready to take her down, especially Margot Featherswallow from Ehras Magna who she had first tied with before beating her outright at the finale event.

Saga grimaced as the girl situated herself in the spot immediately to her left. There was something about the way the girl was looking at her that she didn't like. It was making Saga uneasy. The girl's eyes seemed to swirl with a strange wildness that Saga had never seen before.

"Ready!" The announcer cried out and Saga looked away from the Ehras Magna girl. She had a race to concentrate on.

A howl from the Werewolf official signalled the start of the event and Saga pushed off from her usual starting position.

Except her foot caught on something. She didn't have time to look back though, because she needed to get to Donetta, their staff fighting competitor.

From the side, Harian was bellowing in outrage. "Foul!" He exclaimed. "Foul!"

Saga pushed herself forward, now needing to catch up with the other competitors. Something was wrong. Her shoe felt loose. It wasn't the kind of loose from untied laces either. Nor was it the kind of loose you got when you forgot to zip your boots all the way up and they hung awkwardly around your foot. The Were girl from Ehras Magna ran past, her hands covered in dark fur as her fingers clawed at the air before her. Sharp nails extended from the ends of her fingers and Saga realised what it was her foot had caught on. That girl's control over her Were form must be spectacular to be able to only change her hands. Saga put aside her awe for a moment though as she kicked out, sending the boot hurtling through the air. She didn't bother to find out where it had gone and never noticed it collide with the head of an elegant elf in the uniform of Shamel Aiyeola.

Harian must have seen the were girl's actions, because he was still crying foul even if no one would listen to him. For Saga, it was an awkward experience of running with one foot secured in her remaining boot and the other clad in nothing but her sock. This all would have been fine back in her old world, where competition tracks were specially made, but here, this road, it was riddled with rocks and roots. Thankfully, in preparation for the events, debris such as horse dung, broken wagon wheels and various dropped food items had been cleaned from the road.

Saga put every ounce of training and coaching she had ever been given into overcoming the discomfort of running with only one shoe on. Sock crumpled up? Deal with it. Stone in your shoe? Push through it. Cramp? Overcome it. Shoelaces undone? Don't trip, just run.

She ran past a humanoid who Saga thought might have been a Selkie from the webbed fingers she caught sight of and an elf from Shamel Aiyeola. Then there were the glittering wings of a faerie from Aquino Beccara. A couple from the schools that she hadn't had an opportunity to meet anyone from. Ahead of her there was a fox tail... The Two Worlds School, she thought. Then there was the fully covered figure wearing what looked to be an executioner's mask as they ran. Had Rinsunid Cantera put forward a vampire instead of a Were? Then there was 'her,' the girl who had cheated. Saga needed to beat her. Nothing else mattered but passing that lousy mutt of a werewolf. If she needed to cheat to win, the girl had no honour.

Saga straightened her back and pumped her arms. Her sock was riding down her leg, clumping up beneath her foot. She needed to get rid of it, but taking the time to scrape it off would only slow her down. She didn't care if she didn't make it first, but that Werewolf could not make it before her. The finish line... Well, the entry to the arena for the stick fighting match was right ahead.

It was awkward, running with only one shoe and Saga knew that she was going to feel the aftereffects of her efforts here. That wolf was going to pay!

Saga ran. She pumped her arms, straightened her back even more. She clapped Donetta on the shoulder as she had been instructed. Magic emanated from them, illuminating a bright light that indicated a successful pass and Saga pushed the girl forward.

"Go! Whatever happens, don't let Ehras Magna win. Pass it along!"

The older girl nodded as she took off into the arena for her melee.

Saga leaned against the door and lifted her foot up to have a look. She stripped the sock off her foot and grimaced as the fabric pulled away like a band-aid stuck fast.

"You should go to Matron Damir," a voice said, and Saga whirled around, forgetting that she was still only on one foot. She swayed and reached out for something to grab hold of, her hands clawing at empty air as she fell too far away from the doorframe she had been leaning against.

And there was nothing there. She had swayed too far way and was angled all wrong to be able to reach it. She was falling until she found herself cradled in the arms of the person who had spoken. She looked up into the obsidian face of Edun. "Edun?" She asked, dumbfounded.

He set her upright and looked down at her feet. "Where is your other shoe?"

"Margot Featherswallow cut it off at the start of the race," Saga seethed.

"Ah..." Edun murmured. "That explains your weird run and Harry's incessant whinging at the start... Where did the shoe go?"

Saga shrugged. "I kicked it off and kept racing."

"With only one shoe on?"

"Yeah..."

Edun shook his head in dismay. Saga started to hobble into the nearby seats, but Edun gripped her arm tighter. "Come on, let's get you to Matron Damir now."

"No, I want to watch the others," Saga insisted. Wrestling her arm free and sitting down.

"I'll get Jemima then," Edun insisted, but Saga tugged on his arm, dragging him down to sit beside her.

"Later," she said firmly. "You and I need to talk."

"About what?" Edun asked, confusion clouding his face.

Saga stared out at the match Donetta was two bouts ahead of Featherswallow's and the Selkie from Kahawaiola'a Ocean School had fallen drastically behind, struggling to overcome the first staff opponent. The elf from Shamel Aiyeola was pushing through, and he was settled between Donetta and the Ehras Magna competitor. His staff skills were amazing to watch and the opponents who were set against him were sent flying across the field with quick ease. He was quickly catching up to Donetta.

"About you being in Sid's band."

"Band?" He asked, confused. "What's a band?"

"Music group," Saga clarified. "What were you doing on stage with him?"

"This one was keeping an eye on him for you," Edun said defensively. Saga turned to look at him but said nothing. Edun squirmed slightly, running his hand through his hair and realigning his shirt.

"Fine," Saga said. "Lie to me if you want."

"It's not lying!" Edun exclaimed. "Sid..." He looked around awkwardly, but everyone around them was watching as the competitors were tagging in the horse riders for the equestrian component. "What he was doing... Our sister..." He hung his head. "This one was angry... Angry that he came up with this plan and we didn't..."

Saga reached out, took his hand in her own. "It wasn't her Edun... I saw her... It... Because it wasn't her. It couldn't be her."

"Then what was it?"

"A figment created by that tree and those creatures, a dream. Sid saw Ziva, but just listening to her speak. It wasn't her. Not the Ziva I knew."

"What did you see?" He asked, tracing the back of her hand with his thumb.

Saga shook her head. "It doesn't matter... Sid was tricked into opening that rift between the realms of the living and the realms of the dead. His loss..." Edun seemed to rear back, ready to say something but Saga cut him off before he could. "No one lost more than you and Navi and Annis... But you had each other. People expected you to grieve, even wanted to help you do so... But only very few people knew about Sidawi and Ziva, and I think their relationship was a lot stronger than even the few friends that did know knew. When Sid goes home, either to Yeatwens or his parents, he has to put up with all the vitriol that there is against dark elves... Do you think if he told his parents that his heart broke that night, that they would care? What about his elf friends? Or would they declare him better off? It is... A really lonely thing to grieve when no one knows you're grieving."

Edun looked down at their joined hands. "So... Did we do wrong by him? "

"Did you know about them?"

Edun shook his head. "No..."

"When Navi and I would see him, he always appeared so happy, but people were often nearby. It's easy to make people believe that you're alright, especially when they don't want to see otherwise... Take it from an expert."

"Edun just wanted to..."

"See her." He nodded. "I know... We have these holidays back where I'm from... Mother's Day and Father's Day. Well, there are others like birthdays and Christmas that hurt too... But Mother's Day and Father's Day... They advertise them for weeks or months in advance. Things to do, gift ideas... At school they even give you time to make presents or cards... It's a kick in the gut every time those ads start and when you tell the teacher, but I have no one to make something for... They accuse you of slacking off and order you to just do something anyway... Holidays suck the most. The times when families should be together."

Edun nodded. "This one knows... It was Edun's birth remembering over the holidays..."

"Birth remembering..." Saga echoed slowly. "Birthday?"

That's what you might call it, yes..."

"Why didn't you say anything? Why didn't Navi or Annis?"

He shrugged. "It wasn't important..."

Saga nudged him with her shoulder. "Yes, it was. Ziva wouldn't have wanted you to forget it. We should do something!"

"It's months late!" He argued.

"So? Take it from some whose birthday always falls on the biggest holiday of the year-."

"That must be amazing!" Edun exclaimed, cutting her off. "A big party for your birthday all the time!"

Saga shook her head. "Actually, it's the worst. It just gives people another reason to forget about you. Anyway, as I was saying, take every other opportunity to celebrate that you can!" She tried to make it sound nonchalant but wasn't entirely sure she had succeeded when she caught Edun's concerned features looking back at her. "What about Annis? When was her birthday?"

"Annis' birth remembering was earlier in the year, before... Before Ziva..."

"And Ziva's?"

"Also earlier in the year... Well... Before school the year starts in First Month," Edun explained. "When's yours?"

"End of December just before the new year..."

They looked up as a cheer emanated from the crowd before Edun could ask when December was. She knew that they used different names here and amongst the different races, several different names, but she could hardly keep them straight, so she stuck to her own. The first archers had taken flight. Elfina, the top archer from Toserra Sorose was mounted upon a hippogriff, it's large wings seemingly blocking out the sun as target after target, both stationary and moving were knocked from the sky. An angel from Aquino Beccara took flight, her wings lifting her effortlessly into the sky.

"The last part," Edun said, his eyes fixed on the competitors high above them.

"I don't know how they do it!" Saga said. "You won't catch me up there!"

"But you have wings!" Edun argued. "You could go all the way in the pentathlon. You run, your staff fighting is exceptional and-."

Saga pointed up at the sky where Elfina Varley was shooting what looked to be her last target. As she started to descend, Edun was on his feet, pointing in excitement. "Look!" He exclaimed and around them, people were mimicking his actions, and their talk was excited. "We've won the time! We have the fastest time!"

Elfina's hippogriff landed amidst a puff of sand, followed closely by the angel from Aquino Beccara and horse of midnight black hair with flames for the tail and mane ridden by what Saga guessed to be a vampire due to the executioner style hood the rider wore.

"Yes!" Edun exclaimed, jumping up and pumping his first into the air. "Ehras Magna won't even rank!" He grabbed Saga up into a hug, squeezing her tight.

Gingerly she wrapped her arms around him, hugging him back until they both seemed to realise the position they were in and attempted to jump away.

"They still need to tally the technical and accuracy scores..." Saga said in a low voice.

Edun cleared his throat, then ran his hands down his clothes smoothing away imaginary creases. "Right... Yes..."

Saga backed away from him, not sure what had happened or when Edun had stopped being so standoffish around her and had begun... She didn't know how to describe it, but he seemed to enjoy being with her and even go to great lengths to seek her out.

"The team... I should," she pointed awkwardly towards where the teams were gathering, waiting for the final verdicts. Then she hobbled off, the cuts and scrapes on the bottom of her foot finally being felt.

GOING UP

Toserra Sorose came in second. Despite winning based on time technical and accuracy scores in the later rounds resulted in the end scores being adjusted. Ehras Magna had been disqualified, the actions of Margot Featherswallow having been seen by more people than just Harry Mau.

Jemima had fussed over Saga's foot but acquiesced when she refused to go to the healing tent, instead wanting to go to lunch with the group before coming back to watch the solo pentathlon runs.

They returned to the field to watch Deluca and Donetta do all five events and while they were poor runners compared to the Weres from Ehras Magna, the Weres had little success with the equestrian segment, losing points and time there before switching to a wyvern for the final aerial archery round. Nothing though could compare to the bird boy from the Two Worlds School. His run was slow, but his skill with the staff, his mastery over his mount and his skill with a sword saw him in the clear lead which was only exemplified when big black wings grew from his back, and he took to the sky for the final task.

"Tengu, right?" Saga asked.

Tasso shrugged. "No idea what he is."

"He's amazing!" Navi said dreamily watching as the boy shot out his final moving target and started to descend to the ground.

Tasso looked at her, wounded pride on his face as his mouth opened and closed uselessly while he tried to find the words he wanted to say. "I suppose..." He finally muttered.

"There's Deluca!" Saga cried, pointing out the pentathlon team captain. He was still high above the crowd, mounted upon the same hippogriff Elfina had ridden during the team event.

"His time isn't good today..." Tymberlee said, sitting down in the tow just behind them. "Hayashi Minato has already landed."

"Not to worry," Leah said, sitting down beside her. "We fix this one's archery and riding skills and in a couple of years, we'll sweep all the events for a win!" She shook Saga's shoulder vehemently.

"No!" Saga exclaimed.

"She doesn't do heights!" Navi, Tasso, Jemima and Emory chorused together.

"Exactly!" Saga said triumphantly, glad that someone was finally getting it.

"Even if she has a Pegasus!" Tymberlee said thoughtfully.

"He doesn't fly!" Saga exclaimed in dismay.

"Have you seen Sagas wings, Tymberlee?" Navi asked.

"Wings? Saga has wings?" The Prefect asked in awe, her gaze shifting to the young woman. "No... I didn't know that. How did I not know that? Wings? Seriously?"

Saga ignored them as the others started from go into great detail, describing her wings. They were not something she liked.

Emory nudged her. "You ok?" He asked in a low voice.

"So... Was this the last event?" Jemima asked.

Tymberlee nodded. "Yes. Tonight, there is a farewell dinner celebration and tomorrow we finish taking apart our camps. If you all make sure that your own trunks are packed before you go to sleep tonight, it will reduce the chances of you losing anything."

Saga shrugged. "I don't know," she said honestly, looking into his eyes. She bit her lip, hesitated, then asked, "are we alright?"

"Us?" He asked. "Why wouldn't we be?"

Saga was taken aback by that. "Last term... You... I...." She looked back to the field to see Deluca shoot his final target. "You barely..." She shook her head. "You know what, never mind."

Emory shoulder bumped her. "We're alright," he said softly.

The common area of the camp had been transformed with faerie lights, school banners and what seemed like an entire field of flowers. The comfortable logs and stools that they had sat on around the campfires had been replaced with elegantly laid out long tables, arranged in a diamond shape around the fire pit.

"Wow!" Navi exclaimed looking around. "This one hasn't seen anything so pretty since the Mistress hosted her Rose Gala... And Navi wasn't allowed to serve at the gala..." She skipped forward, arms wide as she spun around. She giggled delightedly. "It's like being a princess!"

"If princesses wore school uniforms," Edun muttered, stalking towards the Toserra Sorose tables, hands in his pockets.

"Don't be so mean," Saga said, whacking his shoulder playfully as he passed her.

A faerie from Aquino Becarra came by, sweeping Navi up in his arms as he danced by, taking her with him. Navi giggled wildly and the boy beamed with delight. "One of the formidable staff queens herself."

Tasso stalked over when they paused in their swirling dance for a breath and tapped the boy on his shoulder, a scowl on his face. "Mind if I cut in?" The faerie blinked at Tasso and seemed to shrink back, ceding the ground to Tasso, who stepped in, taking Navi in his arms. "Shall we dance?"

"Why did you do that?" Navi asked, allowing him to resume the dance pattern that the other faerie boy had started.

Saga shook her head. "Tas is so jealous. Should have seen how she was almost drooling over the pentathlon competitor from Two Worlds. Tas was not impressed."

"Hayashi Minato? The Tengu?" Edun asked, and Saga nodded. Edun scoffed. "He's such a show off. Know where you're sitting?"

Saga shook her head. "Hopefully with the others. It's not assigned seating, is it? Please tell me it's not assigned seating. The last thing I want is to be stuck sitting with the gods only know who for the entire night!"

"Woah! Slow down!" Edun exclaimed. "Let's go bag a section before you're all forced to break up."

They passed a group of Weres arguing with a contingent from Ehras Magna, singing the Toserra School song louder than they could howl the Ehras Magna fight song. They caught sight of Saga and a werewolf, started bellowing at the top of his lungs.

"Proud to uphold our name!"

His comrades all lifted their glasses of what looked to be jelly melon cider, "Toserra Sorose our school." One waved his banner around excitedly, as though it was a school pennant, "We wave our banners true."

The werewolves howled in delight and around them, more Sorosions, including Saga and Edun joined in. "Always striving for the best, in everything we do!"

"We beat you guys at stadion!" an older boy exclaimed, reaching out and grabbing Saga. He pulled her over to stand between the groups, as though she was being put on display.

A surly werebear from Ehras Magna leaned in, looking Saga over. "Alpha Ryerson is having that investigated."

Saga battered her eyelids up at him innocently. "Want to race me? Right here? Right now?"

There were hoots and hollers of delight and a steady chant of, "Race! Race! Race!" growing from the members of both school contingents. Saga and the werebear stared at each other, silently egging the other on as around them their cohorts chanted delightedly, all expecting a repeat performance of the day before.

"Good evening, everyone!" Tillson Everard had appeared on the makeshift stage, a pretty woman at his side from Aquino Becarra.

"Damn!" a boy from Rinsunid Cantera cursed. "They're starting already. I was looking forward to the rematch."

Saga grinned. "Later tonight?" she asked the werebear and he scowled at her. Perhaps he was used to his impressive size intimidating those smaller than him. After witnessing Harriet Frazee, the werebear in her Animal Husbandry class get nearly mauled by her project animal, werebears didn't scare her. Letting out a low growl, the werebear turned on his heel and stalked away. The Ehras Magna group looked around, uncertain of what to do, but the decision was made for them as Tillson Everard continued talking and other staff from all the schools made their way through the crowd of students, trying to disperse them to their tables.

"What a fantastic week this has been!" There were cheers and rounds of applause, howls of glee and boos of commiseration as the Tourney judge from Toserra Sorose continued to speak. Students continued to make their way to their seats and as they did so, the angel beside Everard took over. She spoke of the comradery amongst the students, the rivalries between the schools, the feats of glory achieved in each event and finally, the tragedy that had happened at the Agesilaus. Looking around, there were students still marked with the injuries of that dreadful night. Though none, as much so as Sidawi.

As they began to read out names, calling up students who had performed well over the week, outshining all the others in their chosen events, Saga slipped down in her seat as she caught furtive glances being thrown her way. The speeches moved quickly from there, announcing winners from one event after another. Werebattle, archery, sword fighting and what were the other events? She stopped listening, her thoughts swirling in her head as she tried to avoid thinking about the Agesilaus and Hell and Hades and everything that had happened. Sidawi. Navi and the harpies. The Hydra. Vali. The Oneiroi and her dreams. She swallowed hard and picked up the glass of water on the table before her to try and cover her face, hide her trembling lips as the image of the Oneiroi as her mother plagued her mind. Her mother. Astrid. Gods, what a fool she was. She had no idea what her mother looked like, and she felt stupid for what had happened at the race.

She felt stupid about everything that had happened and people knew that she had something to do with what had happened. People knew that somehow; she was at fault. She really hated it when attention seemed to be attracted to her. Beside her, Navi grabbed her hand, squeezing tightly and Saga squeezed back. Saga didn't risk looking over at her friend though. She might not be able to hold herself together if she did.

Her mind kept going back to the Hydra, to Sidawi's behaviour before it had all gone down to that moment on the staircase when he'd realised, she'd been about to break, to turn back and fly into her mother's arms. Guilt seized at her.

"Saga," Navi hissed.

He'd turned. He'd turned and he'd hauled her up past him, pushing her out into the waiting arms of her friends and it was all her fault that he hadn't made it back. She should have been stronger. She shouldn't have let him do that. Not for her. Not when it was already her fault that he'd lost Ziva and that all this had happened in the first place.

"Saga!" Jemima elbowed her from her other side.

"Huh?" Everyone was staring at her. On the stage, Tillson Everard was watching her, concern etching his face just as it had after the race. Could he really tell from all the way across the clearing that that her mind was elsewhere? "What?"

"They're about to call the stadion," Emory whispered, leaning across the table so that he could be heard.

"That was some of the finest running we have ever seen at the inter-school tourney. The Stadion must be a heated event at Toserra Sorose with this young lady leading the way. I understand from Master Everard, that as of yet, she is undefeated," the angel host from Aquino Beccara said.

"That is right," Master Everard said taking over and beaming towards the tables of Toserra Sorose students. "This young lady has made the stadion the standout event in Nýr Ásgardr, you've never seen the arena so full first thing in the morning.

Navi tenderly squeezed Saga's hand again, eyeing her worriedly. "Are you alright?"

Saga nodded, but didn't say anything, not trusting her voice to convey the same message. Why were they having a party after everything that had happened? Why had they run their final races and fought their final challenges when Sid and so many others were still being tended to in the healing houses?

"They've just called her your name," Jemima whispered.

Saga blinked, looking around distractedly. Oh gods, not again. She stood, her chair catching on a stone and tumbling to the ground with a resounding clatter that everyone heard. Slowly, she made her way through the tables and chairs, full of her fellow students and she could feel every eye upon her. Carefully, conscious of the racket her chair had made, she made her way to the small stage where the presenters stood. She wiped her sweaty palms on her skirt. When had they gotten so sweaty?

Cautiously, Saga concentrated on the two stairs made of crates that lead up to the stage. Master Everard held a medallion in one hand and Saga approached him. Behind him and the angel host from Aquino Becarra, stood the other event winners, including Sakata and Ahn-Ly who had beat her and Navi during the staff pairs competition. How had she missed that announcement? She had wanted to cheer them on for their well-deserved win.

She shook hands with both hosts and Master Everard lowered the medallion over her neck. "Well, done," he said. "you're a credit to Toserra Sorose," he murmured, so that only she could hear him.

She smiled weakly. "Thank you."

Standing up there, as the last few names were called, including Hayashi Minato for the full stadion run, was a nightmare. Her legs felt weak and as she stared out at all the expectant eyes, she kept imagining what it would be like to have her mother or her father there, a dream she thought she'd given up long ago. Spotting Astrid in the crowd didn't help at all.

When the last name was called, the crowd cheered and they were released back to their seats and dinner was served, before the night gave way to dancing, friendly rivalries and only one brawl between rivals.

~ * ~

After a night of revelry with new friends, the morning saw Astrid directing the dismantling of the Toserra Sorose camp. Trunks, bags and weapons cases were stacked. Animals prepared for their journey back to Nýr Ásgardr and students tried to duck out of chores for the chance of one last visit with new friends from the other schools.

"There's nothing for this one to do there," Tena said easily, as she sat on a stack of boxes. "Tani told Tena to stay out of the way. Can't have the teachers noticing Tena and all that."

"How did you manage to sneak onto the transport, anyway?" Saga asked. She closed the trunk of training weapons and locked it, before marking it on a sheet of parchment.

"Oh, that's easy!" she said and wrinkled her nose. "In Tani's pocket."

"I thought the airships had detectors for hidden Weres," Navi added. "To stop exactly that, from happening."

Tena shook her head. "We Wererats have been sneaking past those for years."

Saga scoffed. "So what use is it? It's not like you're going to miss a bear instead of a person."

"Except people think it works on rats. We just don't tell them otherwise, " Tena said with a mischievous smirk. "What Nýr Ásgardr like?"

Saga and Navi looked at each other and shrugged. "It's nice," Saga said.

"But?" The dark elf girl asked.

"But nothing," Navi said. "It's a school town, much like Dark Fields."

Tena leaned in, peering around them. Saga glanced over her shoulder and spotted Edun walking past. She grinned knowingly. "You thinking about a change of scenery?"

The girl shrugged. "Don't know yet. Maybe..."

"There's a lot of Ljósálfar in Nýr Ásgardr," Navi said in a small voice.

Tena wrinkled her nose in distaste. "Oh..." she said, disappointed. "Tena never met one before this week. Are they all that bad?"

They shared another look, thinking the same thing. Sid had been different. If given half a chance, he might have been able to start a revolution regarding Dökkálfar-Ljósálfar relations. Especially if he'd had Ziva at his side. That would never happen now. Sid was a shell of his former self.

"Some better, some worse," Navi said softly.

"And some absolute bastards," Saga spat, thinking about the elves that had shoved Navi aside at the Rolly Polly Kitty and ultimately got the two of them banned from the eatery.

"If people are accepting in Dark fields, maybe you might want to stay there... People also aren't so kind about Traveler folk, you won't have an easy time of it," Navi said. "There are cruel folk who think just because you have dark skin, they can declare you, their property." Navi was thinking about them too.

"Tena is no one's property!" The girl declared.

"You just need to remember that when someone's hauling you out of a cafe declaring you nothing," Navi said. "But enough of that. Why would you want to leave Dark Fields? You've got a good thing going there."

"Tena did," Tena said, jumping down from her perch. "But this one's teacher trying to kill Tena sort of soured things..." She shrugged. "See you around," she called, then disappeared into the crowd,

"She's a weird one," Jemima said standing behind them.

"You can say that again," Saga said without thinking.

"She's a weird one." Navi put her hand to her mouth, trying to stifle a giggle as Saga smirked. "What?" Jemima cried.

"Nothing," Navi giggled.

Saga wrapped an arm around each of their shoulders and directed them back towards the tent that had been staying in. "Come on. Let's go home."

Jemima nodded. "Tymberlee is looking for you both."

~ * ~

Students were everywhere, going up and down the rainbow discs that travelled the interior of the tree city.

Tymberlee directed her tentmates towards the waiting area, trying to keep everyone together as they were jostled by students from other schools and the numerous visitors trying to meet and congratulate the competitors.

Saga was looking for a way out. There was no way in any of the realms of hell that she was stepping foot on one of those discs and allowing it to propel her upwards. She glanced over the heads of a group of overly cheery leprechauns from Aquino Beccara and spotted her escape. Just past the leprechauns were a group of robust, lithe Werebears, a mixed group from Rinsunid Cantera and Ehras Magna. If she could dart past them, nobody would spot her until it was too late.

"There you are," Edun said, wrapping an arm around Navi's shoulders and them drawing Saga in on his other side.

"What do you want Edun?" Saga asked, trying not to grit her teeth in frustration. If Edun didn't let her go, she would miss her window to freedom. She glanced furtively towards the waiting area. It was almost their turn to get on.

"Our disc was full," he said easily.

Our. Saga craned her neck to try and see who he was talking about and groaned. Emory sidled up beside her, but just before he could imitate Edun's move and trap her between the two of them, she ducked under Edun's arm, barely escaping Emory. "I just remembered something," she said feebly.

"What?" Jemima asked, the only one of them who had managed to remain free. Saga swallowed. What excuse could she give? Almost everyone was looking at her now. Tymberlee was still distracted, trying to make sure they found a disc big enough for the group, but if she didn't break free from the group now, Tymberlee would haul her onto the disc herself.

"Uhhm..." she said, trying to come up with something. "I'm not sure I packed everything. I think I left something behind..."

Jemima canted her head to the side and stared at Saga. "You are the most thorough packer I have ever seen. Even more so than I am. You have everything."

"Really," Saga pleaded. "There's this bad feeling niggling at me, and I have to-."

Edun's arm suddenly disappeared from around her shoulders, and she breathed a sigh of relief. She took a step backwards. Emory's arm slid through her left arm. Edun's slid thorough her right.

"What are you doing?" She asked.

"Tymberlee is it here?" Emory called out.

"We're up," the faerie Prefect said, standing aside and allowing the two boys to carry Saga onto the platform.

"Guys!" She cried. "Put me down!"

"You'll miss the disc," Edun said cheerfully.

"I'll take the stairs!" Saga argued. "Just... let me go! Look... Please..."

"The stairs?" Navi asked, stepping onto the platform and hauling both her trunk and Saga's on behind her. "That's a week's climb!"

Saga blinked in surprise. "It is?" She asked.

"It is," Tymberlee confirmed, glancing at the two boys holding her. "Keep her still," she instructed, and they both nodded.

"This isn't fair!" Saga cried, trying to kick Edun in the shin.

"Calm down," Emory instructed her, drawing his arm tighter around hers and pulling her closer to him. Edun shifted, sidling closer to her.

"We've got you," Edun said softly.

Navi poked at Edun's shoulder with a long, elegant finger. "What are you doing?"

He shrugged, trying to avoid her poking finger but winked playfully. "Keeping Saga on the disc for Tymberlee," he said.

Navi frowned, crossed her arms over her chest and looked knowingly at Jemima.

"Wait for me!!!" A voice called. The disc was starting its ascent though.

"Tasso!" Navi shouted, waving for him.

Tasso flapped his gossamer wings, and his feet left the floor. He flew across the remaining distance until he landed beside Navi. "I caught you!" he said.

"I thought your disc was full," Saga spat, trying to wrestle herself out of Edun and Emory's grips.

"What disc? Our group went their own ways," Tasso said, looking at them all in confusion. Emory and Edun shot the faerie glares of contempt, that didn't compare to the glare Saga shot the two boys holding her.

The disc flew upwards and halfway up, they finally let go, aware that there was nothing she could do anymore. She had been navigated to the middle of the disc and couldn't even jump off at one of the catwalks that transacted the tree's interior.

"I hate you both," Saga spat at them, but Emory and Edun just grinned. They had won, they had gotten Saga onto the rainbow disc and there was nothing she could do about it.

"Bye!" A duet of girls called out and they spotted Anh-Ly and Sakata waving at them from one of the catwalks. "We'll train together again, yes?"

"Absolutely!" Navi called out and despite her frustration at the situation, Saga agreed, calling out her confirmation to the girls. She looked forward to being able to train with them again one day. Their skill with the staff was astounding and Saga wanted to learn more.

"Navi can't wait to train with them and their master," Navi said eagerly.

"Same," Saga said. "Do you think we'll ever get the chance?"

"It's possible," Edun said, "there's a student exchange during one of the holiday breaks some years. If it's with their school, easily."

Saga and Navi looked at each other, "Cool!" They both cried!

"That would be so amazing!" Navi added.

"And now you've done it," Tasso said. "They're going to be on and on about this until it ever happens!"

Edun laughed heartily, "Then we will listen, nod indulgently and go on ignoring them!" He ruffled both their hair and simultaneously, the two girls swatted at his hands, then patted their hair down.

"Edun!" Navi groaned in frustration, causing Edun to just ruffle her hair again.

~ * ~

In the weeks that followed their return to Nýr Ásgardr, classes resumed and the energy at the last tourney of the year had a jubilant feeling. It was all for fun. The one event wouldn't... couldn't change the standings now. And after the inter-school tourney, the whole school already knew who the best competitors were.

During that time, Jimpsee house had held a birthday party for all three Jensyn siblings. The house had been full of people from three-year levels. Four even after Tymberlee had invited several friends of Ziva's to join them. Everyone was there except Sidawi, who was most likely up in his room at his parents' house under the care of the nurse they had hired. His parents had not wanted to hear the story of what had happened. Instead, they had raged about the injustice done to their only son. His younger sister, a second-year girl who Saga didn't know, but Edun had insisted was a wretched girl to be around, had not been seen around school either and it was rumoured that she had been sent, at great expense to Shamel Aiyeola for the rest of the school year. The party had lasted long into the night with most of the guests taking up residence on any couch or available floor.

Edun and Annis had stayed the night in the big room on the third level, talking long into the night with Navi. Tasso had also been convinced to stay the night and was brought in on the ongoing hackey sack tournament that ad started back in Yggdrasil City before the beginning of the semester.

One morning in what would have been early December, Saga noticed that stalls and festive banners were going up around town. A track for some kind of run was being laid out and everyone seemed to be getting excited.

"What's going on?" Saga asked as they made their way through town. The signs promised all kinds of exciting foods and activities. "This isn't for graduation, is it?"

"No, graduation only happens at the school, usually in the theatre. This is way more awesome than graduation!" Tasso enthused. He had come over early that morning, eaten breakfast with them and was now on his way to class. Saga thought maybe he was feeling a little left out as the only one of them not living at Jimpsee house. Maybe Tremblay could fix that in the new school year... "It's Krampasnacht this week!"

Saga frowned. "Krampas... That's like evil Santa, right?"

Jemima and Navi looked from one another, then to Tasso and lastly to Emory, who was trudging along behind them.

"Who's Santa?" Jemima finally asked, and Saga sighed dramatically. "What?" The confused angel exclaimed.

"Nothing!" Saga said. "Just... A big deal where I'm from..."

"Go on, tell us!" Navi said. "And then we'll tell you about Krampasnacht!"

Saga did want to know about Krampasnacht, so she relented. "Well, on Christmas, Santa, who has been working all year long with his elves, delivers presents to every child around the world." She left out the reality of the situation, which was that she and many of the kids she had grown up with had rarely received Christmas presents. Jemima frowned and opened her mouth, ready to speak out, when Emory stopped her.

"And how does he do that?"

"From his sleigh, led by his flying reindeer. The lead one, Rudolph, has a glowing red nose that lights the way."

"That's the most ridiculous thing I've ever heard," Emory declared. "Reindeer do not fly."

"And they don't have red noses either," Jemima added.

"It's just a story," Saga said defensively.

"Even a story should be logical," Jemima said.

"Oh sure," Saga said. "Like faeries and angels and shapeshifters and elves and magic and literally going to hell. You mean like that?"

They looked at each other. "Ok..." Tasso said slowly. "I think I get your point..."

"Oh good, I'm glad someone does," Saga said. The others laughed. She still had so much to learn about this world and they about hers. She lagged behind them as they tried to figure out how a flying red nosed reindeer could exist, let alone lead a sleigh full of presents around the world. "He has eight other reindeer aside from Rudolph. There's Dasher and Dancer. Prancer and Vixen. Then... Comet and Cupid and Donner... and... oh, what's the last one's name? Blitzen! It's Blitzen!"

"So there now nine flying reindeer?" Jemima asked. "How does this work?"

"Do they all have red noses?" Navi asked.

"No, only Rudolph has a red nose, so he can lead the way, but the other reindeer are mean to him because of it."

"There are mean reindeer?" Emory asked. "Saga, listen to yourself. This story is getting more ridiculous by the minute!"

"Well, too bad!" She exclaimed. "There are songs and stories about Rudolph!"

They linked arms together, matching their way down the street towards college castle. Saga asked about Krampasnacht, and they asked about Christmas. Then, as they neared the centre of the town, Saga stopped, taking in the full effect of the Krampasnacht decorations. They were so different than Christmas decorations. Where she was used to bright, sparking tinsel, wreaths of green and cute decorations of elves, reindeer and Santa Claus, or native Aussie animals like kangaroos and koala wearing Santa hats, the decor going up around Nýr Ásgardr seemed to correlate more to Halloween... And really spooky one at that. There was no tinsel or glitter and nothing really sparkled. The colours were darker, more ominous. Instead, bright boxes, bags and rolls of paper to fill will with presents, the stalls and shops sold boots. Not like the boot maker though, they only sold singles.

"What are the boots for?" Saga asked, backing away from one shop keeper who turned around suddenly. He was wearing a garish daemon mask that sent her reeling backwards.

"You leave it outside your bedroom door and the next day, you find a present," Navi said, inspecting one boot that was made of what looked to be mismatched pieces of leather, almost as though they'd been off cuts from larger pieces.

"Or coal or a rod..." Tasso added.

"That's only if you've been bad," Jemima intervened, looking at a boot made of pale, almost white leather. "I've never had coal or a rod."

Tasso rolled his eyes. "Well... Neither have I!" he insisted, "Except for that one time Tonya got up before me and stole my gift and replaced it with coal... It would have been lardy cake too."

"Yum!" Navi breathed out. "Navi loves lardy cake."

Saga stared, dumbstruck at her friends as they inspected boots. "What's lardy cake?"

"It might just be better than Lucuma pie!" Jemima said wistfully.

"Not possible!" Navi exclaimed.

Emory stared at the selection of boots. "Do you have one?"

"Can't I just use my school boots?" Saga asked.

Emory shrugged. "You could... But if you get gooped or coaled..." He grimaced. "It's not a good idea to use a shoe you actually use."

"Hence the solitary boot stall," Saga murmured, eyeing the selection.

"Hence the solitary boot stall."

As Saga looked through the boots, trying to choose hers, a realisation occurred to her, as she took in the daemon masks and skeleton heads and goblins that hung from stalls and lamp posts. It was like some kind of weird, ghoulish Halloween-Christmas mush-up and she already loved it. "Christmas isn't all that big here, is it?" She asked, looking up at her friends.

"Not unless you're an angel," Jemima confirmed, paying for the white boot she'd been looking at.

"And then it's really just a bunch a boring church services," Tasso added., holding two boots, one in each hand. He would hold one up before his eyes, then lower it and inspect the other. "Which one?"

Jemima elbowed him in the ribs. "It is not!" She exclaimed. "Neither! You're getting coal!"

A smile slowly grew across Saga's face. "What is it?" Emory asked, drawing the attention of the others back to Saga.

She looked at them all with a joy she hadn't felt at this time of year for as long as she could remember. "I don't have to celebrate my birthday on the biggest holiday of the year anymore."

ABOUT THE AUTHOR

Annie Mars was born and raised in Melbourne, Victoria. From a young age, she was a voracious reader, loving anything from epic fantasy to crime thrillers and hard sci-fi. She's always had animals around her and currently enjoys the company of two cats, the grumpy Sammy and the eternally energetic Pawla.

For fun, she practices Aikido, a Japanese martial art, which sometimes makes its way into her writing.

Saga of The Tournament of Souls is the sequel to Saga of the Wild Hunt and the second in the Toserra Sorose Academy series. Annie's other works include The Kahzer Chronicles for Mythrill Fiction.

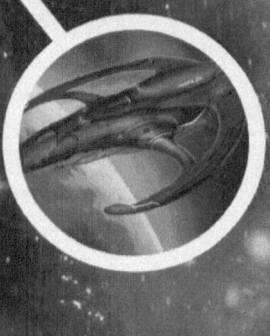

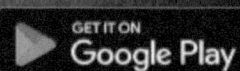

www.ingramcontent.com/pod-product-compliance
Lightning Source LLC
Chambersburg PA
CBHW030526120726
47904CB00005B/1639